CW01551859

**Advance Prai**

"I read this so fast I got blisters turning pages. *The Red Shoes* is so astonishingly good, original, beautiful and amazing…it's like a sumptuous meal with all flavors—salty, bitter, sweet, hot. I love the Gothic feeling of impending doom and the counterbalancing elements of light. Wynne's writing is free of compromise, fear…Wynne writes such brilliant back and forth dialogue, and I am astounded at the way he writes about sex—how deep it can go, the different ways it can satisfy. He has the rare ability to write on a plane floating just above life, or below it. And his voice doesn't sound like anyone else's. I think *The Red Shoes* is a great work of art."

—Kate Christensen, winner of the PEN/Faulkner Best American Work of Fiction Award for *The Great Man*

"The narrator is as fully realized and endearing a character as I've ever known. The first person worked so well here. The novel is cohesive, charming, sad and a true achievement. It's really very grand."

—Ben Schrank, author of *Love Is a Canoe*

"I loved the mysteriousness of everything and everybody in *The Red Shoes* and the way its preoccupations with loss, danger and safety would loom in and out of view in the surreal fog of drugs, sex and dark humor. I found it quite haunting and didn't want it to end."

—Stephen D. Adams
author of *The Homosexual as Hero*

"This walk on the wild side of human nature can be startling, outrageous, frightening, and sometimes even funny, but Wynne's smooth, commanding style keeps the shocks in these stories from becoming mannered or numbing."

—*Booklist*

"The other world John Wynne describes in these stories is terrifying. And it is breathlessly, horribly recognizable as ours. This is an incredibly powerful book."

—Rebecca Brown, Lambda Literary Award-winning author of *The Gifts of the Body*

"With so much tepid and sentimental fiction coming out, John Wynne's stories in *The Other World* are like a plunge in cold water. With a near-Brechtian intensity of focus and an infallible ear for dialogue, Wynne casts a laser eye on the things we say, so different from what we mean. A book to handle with asbestos gloves, but well worth the walk through fire."

—Paul Monette, National Book Award-Winner for *Becoming a Man*

**Praise for *The Sighting***

"There is nothing else quite like *The Sighting*, for no other writer has experimented with gay experience in the context of our adolescence in straight America in such a direct, sensual and imaginative manner."

—Gordon Montador, *Body Politic*

Also by John Stewart Wynne

*The Sighting*
*Crime Wave*
*The Other World*
*The Listener's Guide to Audio Books*
*The Needles Highway*

# The Red SHOES

a Novel

John Stewart Wynne

Magnus Books
An Imprint of Riverdale Avenue Books
5676 Riverdale Avenue, Suite 101
Riverdale, NY 10471

This is a work of fiction. Names, characters, places, and incidents either are the product of the author's imagination or are used fictitiously. Any resemblance to actual persons, living or dead, events, or locales is entirely coincidental.

Printed in the United States of America

First Edition

Cover by: Linda Kosarin, The Art Department
Cover photo © Robert Flynt, 1993
Interior Layout by www.formatting4U.com

Print ISBN: 978-1-936833-42-9
Digital ISBN: 978-1-936833-66-5

www.riverdaleavebooks.com

For Dennis

"I do not know what price I will have to pay for breaking what we alchemists call *Silentium*."

—Dario Argento, *Inferno*

"I do not know what price I will have to pay for breaking what we alchemists call *Silentium*."

—Dario Argento, *Inferno*

# PROLOGUE

Every day has its misgivings.

Man lives by faith, they say, but personally I think man wants to render faith unnecessary. If I slipped off a tightrope I'd for damn sure rather know there's a safety net down there than not. One that I could clearly see. But lately there seems to be a dearth of nets—maybe there's some manufacturing problem—because there aren't a hell of a lot of them around. Sooner or later I have to return to that thing man lives by.

The Episcopal Seminary stands in Chelsea as a bit of Old England, stern yet spiritual, judgmental yet welcoming, very green in the summer and soft, and I like it best then. I've lived across the street from this astonishing edifice for the last three years. In fact the red bricks of the Seminary wall and the rising chapel, sturdy as the tops of the two plane trees that touch it, are framed dead center by my French windows, thrown open even through the autumn. Quite a view, my friends have told me, describing it most often as "inspiring." But today…well, I've just walked back from the Seminary and, gazing out that window, I feel as distant as the radium blue sky. Let me tell you…

It was hot on the garden path. Several Seminary students passed me, smiling carefully, their footsteps silent, clinging to areas of shade like discreet ghosts. Everywhere flower beds had burst, spilled over onto the concrete walk. The wiry stems of the coneflowers were already bearing yellow daisies and the deep rose flush on the outer petals of the saucer magnolias amazed me. Overhead a blue jay screamed. And white clouds, thick and heavy, blew over the garrets of the neighborhood brownstones. But the sun was the main thing. Maybe because I've been through what I would call hell, the sun, as it bore right through my clothes, regenerated me, like a jolt from God.

I sat down on the gray stone bench facing the Chapel of the Good Shepherd. Above its entrance was a bas-relief of Jesus tending the lambs with his crooked staff and on the steps below these words were engraved: *Blessed are they that enter in through the gates into the City.*

Two full-paned glass doors led into the chapel. Through this glass, reflecting leaf-filled trees, I could just make out the recessed altar, dimly, and even shapes on the stained-glass windows, fitting together like pieces of a mystical puzzle that meant only what you wanted it to. And in that puzzle I saw his face as I always saw it. Frank's face, calmly regarding the person opposite him—me—and wanting somehow, in an amused and impossible way, to speak. I listened to the leaves, in ample bunches, moving back and forth.

It took me awhile to notice the man on the stone bench adjacent to mine, engrossed in his *Wall Street Journal*, oblivious to the world at large. His thick hair was dark but had a couple of strands running through it that had already turned white, though he couldn't have been over forty. He was tall and angular and the casual sports clothes he wore seemed at odds with the air of

2

privilege, even arrogance, he otherwise projected. Somebody else must have picked out those clothes for him.

It's been said that by simply watching a man walk into a room and sit down in a chair you know all there is to know about him. There's some truth to that. Just by observing this man I could see he was full of a tense, repressed energy. Once he looked up at me, hastily, through heavy-rimmed glasses, then returned to his *Journal* like a driver intently perusing a road map, determined to find the quickest route. To money, I supposed. I could see he was eyeballing stock quotations. Weird, the two of us coming to the Seminary for such different purposes.

Mine was to pray.

Once inside the chapel, I knelt on one of the pews nearest the altar, my jeans sticking to the faded brown leather which had heated up, even through stained glass. I was like a fly in a honey pot—feeling good and sticky—and just where I wanted to be.

This communication with God was always the highpoint of my week...God, take my burdens from me. Give my spirit a jump start back into the stratosphere where it belongs instead of under the soles of my shoes. Release me from the terrible mysteries of this world that are unsolvable—like Frank's death. And protect Frank, whose body I can see now in a circle of light, but whose soul I couldn't begin to objectify, though I know it is roaming somewhere in the life beyond. Nearer you.

When you lose the person you love most in life, you are changed forever. You stand on a precipice estranged from yourself. Half of you lies dashed on the rocks below while the other half doesn't even know the cliff has an unexpected drop-off. You have no idea who you have become. The new face in the mirror provides no clues. But I'll tell you this much. A man who can't find his splinters always hurts.

My communications always ended the same way, with me hearing sounds, muffled, incredibly far away, birdsong, the splash of water, laughter without care, then abrupt silence.

I left the chapel, moving past the man still sitting there reading his paper. I don't know why I looked at him but when I did he lifted the paper off his lap to show me his hard fat dick sticking straight up out of his fly.

You know the rush you get when you're shocked unexpectedly? Everything explodes in a nanosecond. You jerk to a halt, your heart beats fast, your ears feel hot, and your lips part, but before you can speak they close like a crocus—prematurely. All those explosions happened in me then settled like so much dust in the pit of my stomach.

First making sure no one was watching, as if I were somehow responsible for his behavior, I searched his eyes for some explanation. But they were vacant, green and glassy, though prominent behind his lenses, fixed directly on me as he masturbated his big engorged dick. Challenging me. But to do what?

I heard laughter from behind the chapel, probably coming from some of the Seminary students. As their laughter became louder, I realized they must be heading in our direction. So did he—but he made no move to cover himself. When I looked into his eyes again, they had changed. The vacant stare had been replaced by an unmistakable malevolence.

Abruptly I turned away and strode out of the Seminary garden, hands thrust deep in my pockets, thinking fuck you and trying hard to concentrate on the hundreds of flowers in my way, but unable to find the equilibrium to do it.

So you see, I'm standing here at my window, gazing at the chapel, but seeing it with new eyes, with the dullness of someone who's been raped. He'd waited. A stalker. When I was at my most vulnerable, lost in prayer, he'd struck.

Of course it wasn't about sex, everybody was a little savvier about that nowadays. It was about aggression and behind this bold act of exhibitionism was incredible anger, so close behind that it was transparent. This was one troubled motherfucker who needed to punish and to hurt. The question was why should I be so shaken up? It had nothing to do with me. I was probably his mother or his father. I'd just happened to stumble blissfully into the world he was getting back at…Was he still there now, dick stuffed back into his pants, reading innocently, or had he moved to some new hunting ground? Hell, I wanted to forget the whole thing, get it out of my mind and enjoy what promised to be an unusually balmy summer evening. In fact, I lit some candles in anticipation, though evening was far off. A low breeze coming up off the Hudson made the room comfortable and fresh. I kept seeing that bloated dick in my mind. I wished I didn't but the image was a little too strong.

\*

By dusk, however, it was humid and still, the promise of that mild evening having suddenly dissipated along with the fleeting afternoon breeze. Now all that moved were the gnats buzzing up and down the remnants of the candles, burned nearly to the bottom of their wicks. The sky had turned a dull gray, tinged now and then with thin streaks of yellow. I turned on the air conditioner mounted in the bedroom window. It was strong enough to cool down the whole apartment.

During the next few hours I skimmed through a couple of newspapers, half-heartedly tried to finish a middle chapter of an already predictable mystery, paid some bills online, made a couple of phone calls to members of my bereavement group, mechanically jerked-off, separated clothes into piles for an eventual trip to the laundry, and felt generally depressed. I couldn't put my finger on exactly why, but I did wonder about it.

Maybe it was because of the lack of a love life. It had been a long time, a few years since I'd had sex, an encounter that began by someone picking me up on the street opposite Clement Clarke Moore Park. I couldn't remember his face, name, or what his apartment looked like, but I did remember the length of time I spent with him—a half an hour. This passage of time without sex had occurred in me—a man of only thirty-five with an active sex drive and imagination. But sex was one thing and love another, at least in my mind—and it had been a long time too, four years, since Frank had died, and I hadn't loved anyone since him. Sex. Love. The lack of both was like two deprivations from two deep and timeless wells.

Those who meant well were always encouraging me to find both, preferably in one package, right? But that didn't seem an easy task. I couldn't think of any immediate prospects. I knew a number of darkened public rooms in Chelsea, but they weren't bars or clubs, they were church basements—the dark, musty spaces, sometimes lit by a single bulb or fluorescent tube, where my fellow journeyers and I met in bereavement, not passion. And that was fine for now. I didn't want to go to the bars or clubs or cruise Internet chat rooms, casual pick-ups weren't on my mind, and as for a new love, I was too guilt-ridden to consider it, not when the old one wouldn't die. But friends persisted—they told me I was handsome, desirable, and emotionally available—and I believed them. But if this lack was the cause of my depression, I was too ambivalent to find out for sure. I didn't want to hunt the unknown.

It was late. I turned off the air conditioner and opened my bedroom window. It had cooled down outside and there was even a breeze that had come up. As I stood at the window, I caught sight of some of my neighbors in the back windows of their brownstones that butted up against our common garden. I have to say, Manhattan isn't exactly a fertile ground for shrinking violets—it's much too small and crowded. At one point or another everybody says to hell with it and lets their hair down on the lit stages of their own homes. A voyeur's paradise. Or is it? After all, the night is a great aider and abettor...a camouflager...my neighbors across the garden, giving into their nighttime dramas with silent theatrical gestures, resemble nothing more than tricksters, con artists and charlatans, insubstantial figures ready to disappear in a puff of smoke as the blinds are drawn. Frustrating anyone who wants to see a piece of their souls. The only real thing in this landscape are the sounds of boisterous, traded laughter, or fights breaking out, blocks away, or the tinny honking of horns, or occasionally the whistle of the Jersey train, as lonely and as full of portent as any midnight train in the rural South.

When I finally fell asleep, Frank came to me and comforted me, just like always. I opened my wings like a butterfly when he did and moved them gently. Then we both flew away.

\*

What had saved me, not surprisingly, was my involvement with others who had suffered, I won't say a similar loss, I'm too arrogant for that, but a loss nonetheless and usually a deep and perplexing one. We gave each other much needed counsel and became, for each other, reliable leaning posts. Always supporting what seemed nearly insupportable so that the very surreal unlikeliness of living on increased, albeit at a snail's pace. As time passed in this way, sources of light did return to my life in varying degrees, sometimes faintly, like a night-light barely blinking, sometimes surreptitiously, like a small rectangular white band seeping under a door, and sometimes even spectacularly, like a starburst ending a nightmare that had stalled in unremitting blackness.

Times shared with members of my bereavement group kind of shocked me into a renewed vigor, dissipating my haze of self-pity. Together we white-knuckled the bar of the roller coaster—our only means of transportation through the process of grieving. Sometimes we even dared let go of that bar, lifted our hands up over our heads, screamed, whooped, cursed, and had lots of collective fun.

It was only when I got back home and shut the door that I understood so much had been taken from me when Frank died, and that I'd much rather have been engaged in all those activities, not with these new friends, but with Frank instead. That's my definition of love—when you want unquestionably the pleasure of a specific person's company—and no one else will do.

The superintendent of my building has a sixteen-year-old son who's a goofball named Tony. Most days after school he and his buddies can be found hanging out in our lobby. They're a loud, hyper, obnoxious bunch, either making lewd or derogatory comments about the tenants as they come and go or placing random calls on their cell phones and belching or farting when somebody answers.

But when I walked into the lobby this afternoon, Tony was alone, lackadaisically sweeping up the floor with a dog-eared broom, bravado gone, obviously embarrassed to be helping out his dad with this menial task.

As I pressed the elevator button I was surprised when he sidled up and started sweeping right next to me, staring dully at the floor. I've usually caught him eyeing me as if I were some very rare thing who ended up on his terra-firma like an exotic pollen.

Imagine my surprise when he said, "Hey."

I looked at him. He leaned on his broom with a confused expression on his face, brows twisted in a thinker's frown.

"How's it going?" I asked.

"You used to have a boyfriend who died, right?"

I was taken aback by his question but found myself nodding yes. But when he glibly asked, "AIDS?" I was about to tell him to mind his own fucking business when the word fell out of me like a key accidentally falls from a lock, "Alcoholism." I felt like I wanted to stab him in the gut and watch him bleed to death, that's how raw I was, then when he raised his eyebrows and asked, "But he was young, right?" as if he just didn't get it, I answered, "On this plane, yes," got into the elevator and quickly pressed the CLOSE DOOR button.

Frank had died before I even moved here. But word always travels. I guess somebody in the building who

9

*knew* had shared the information with the super who had shared it with his son. Whatever. It wasn't really a secret anyway.

Tony is a dumb, insensitive asshole, that's for sure, but he is also curious. He doesn't live in the subliminal discomfort that I do. To him, questions have answers.

God, if I only had a life I was happy with. Maybe I am an exotic pollen. In the scheme of things, that would not only be acceptable, but intriguing.

\*

Allison, Reg, and I shunned the planned events for Gay Pride Day, considering it an intemperate celebration of inconsequential fluff. And as for the parade itself, forget it—gone were the days when it was a beacon of protest or activism. It had reinvented itself into a cheap display of gyrating go-go boys bumping and grinding to the whips of commercial sponsors, their path cleared wide and free by grim-faced Dykes on Bikes taking their cues from the Hell's Angels at Altamont. Or maybe it was just a case of been there, done that, we hadn't changed with the times, were a few years older, were too critical. The parade wasn't ours anymore. Anyway we'd decided to celebrate the day our own way, just the three of us, by having a picnic on one of the Chelsea piers, enjoying the placidness of Hudson River life, taking in the views of the heavily-bunched green trees on the Jersey Palisades, and catching up on the week that was.

Allison lay with her head in Reg's lap, naming the clouds that blew by for various people in her life, past and present, willing most of them to change shapes, or blow on out to sea, but pressing a few to stand still so she could engage them in a dialogue of unfinished business.

Allison once said that for the last ten years she could put only one occupation at the top of her résumé—survivor. Her mother had walked out on the family when she was eight, effectively disappearing into the web of city life where she had become a bag lady. No one knew what had happened to her until she was found dead in an alley almost seven years to the day she had impulsively left home. Fighting back the pain had been all that Allison's life had been about. She hadn't had a chance—yet—to move beyond the passive sphere of grief, and sometimes to me it seemed unlikely she ever would. Yet in a way standing still for her may have been like hurtling forward at a shocking pace for anybody else. Her inaction was a triumph of the spirit.

Reg on the other hand was clawing his way out of despair like a proud mountain lion, caged, but determined to burst through the bars at any cost, so incensed was he by the injustice of his circumstances. His twin brother, Ted, had committed suicide after being accused of performing a pedophilic act on one of his students—a nine-year-old boy who was so emotionally unstable his story was in doubt from the beginning. Considering the lack of any physical evidence connecting Ted to the boy, or any corroborating witnesses, it looked as if he had more than a tinker's chance in hell to come out right side up. Yet even as things were progressing more and more favorably for him, he opted to pour rat poison down his throat. Reg couldn't understand why. But as he progressed in his grieving process he realized it didn't matter. Slowly he began to live for himself again and jolted us all, with the unquestioning stamina of a drill sergeant, out of our pointless bellowings of "Why me?"

"Why not you?" he would sometimes respond sharply.

As for me, I lay somewhere between Reg's excited rectitude and Allison's melancholic immobility.

She lay on Reg's lap, her eyes closed now, her long golden hair spread across his shorts and down his bare legs. Unsurprisingly she had had a string of unsuccessful affairs with men— unsuccessful because her needs were too great to ever be satisfied, but she never seemed to tire of trying to end her curse of romantic doom, while Reg was like a fire and brimstone preacher, letting us all know how imperfect his potential mates were but how he absolutely knew he was going to attract someone of character and constancy. It was just a matter of time. When he pressed me for agreement I had no thoughts on the matter, which usually pissed him off, but didn't affect his confidence.

It wasn't exactly like the three of us were in some bucolic Monet painting—six months past the turn of the millennium on the noisy, decrepit Manhattan river front—but it was as close to that as we were going to get.

"Have you filled out your application for the Court Assistant exam?" Reg asked casually, assuming the role of big brother. He was in his early fifties, after all, but he seemed so dynamic and full of energy I always just thought of him as my own age. Allison, who was my age, appeared younger, because of her fragility and almost childlike trust.

"No, I have a couple of weeks before the filing deadline."

"I'm listening to whatever you boys are talking about so be careful what you say," said Allison, half-asleep, but decidedly alert.

"No need to be talking in front of you," Reg ran his finger along her brow. "You only talk to clouds."

"Yes," she replied poetically, "and they roam the

world revealing everybody's most hidden thoughts and desires to anyone who'll only look up to decipher them."

What nonsense, I thought. And how boring in a sense. It seemed the three of us were always talking about what meetings were coming up, what problems we were trying to overcome while lapsing into a kind of elf-speak to provide a gentle backdrop for all the doom and gloom we were shadow dancing with. It isn't that I didn't love Reg and Allison—I did—and I respected them—passionately—but sometimes they seemed so intent on setting our paths in such heavy stone—rigid paths that allowed for no chance twists or turns.

"Well, you'd better not forget to mail that application in," Reg continued. "You've been drifting a little lately and as we all know floundering around is not in any of our best interests."

"You're right, Reg. I promise to see to it this week." Frank had left me a good amount of insurance, and I'd been living on this money for the last few years, having abandoned my job as a copywriter at an ad agency because I couldn't concentrate on my work. The State of New York had dangled an attractive alternative to both copywriting and floundering around—a secure, steady job as a civil servant.

"Don't put it off," Reg warned. "Next month we're going to have an increased meeting schedule and you and I are already committed to speaking to some new groups. Remember?"

"Of course. I'm looking forward to it. As usual." And I was.

We sat quietly for awhile, greedily drinking the sunlight like hungry plants, and as usual the sun on my body filled me with a sense of ease. Meanwhile the gaudy gay parade was no doubt in full throttle, oblivious to the three of us, our bodies entwined on a splintered pier sticking out over a river that was choppy for summer and that smelled of fish and refuse, relieved only occasionally by wafts of wayward fresh sea air.

I fell asleep, for who knows how long, lulled by the insistent swell of the water against the rotting piers. When I opened my eyes the world seemed gray, a collage of barely indistinguishable black and white shadows. I blinked a few times in increasing astonishment. Because not only were the buildings, the river, and the sky washed-out, but so was Reg's face, a darkening crater, and Allison's long hair was drained of any luster.

After what was probably only seconds the color began to seep back into the world.

I have to say, this was a first for me but I put it down to the normal adjustment of opening my eyes into brilliant sunlight after they'd been resting in semi-darkness. Still, almost defensively, I told Allison I admired the color of her golden hair.

"That's thoughtful of you to say," she said, unaware of my relief that her hair hadn't stayed that sickly mouse gray.

\*

As we headed back from the pier towards my building, we passed some of the spillover from the gay parade, high-spirited sexually-charged guys, showing off and raucously shouting at the world, at least for one day. I could sense Reg becoming more and more exasperated with these displays of what I assumed he would have labeled wanton frivolity. When a cute young blond, wobbly on his feet, stopped to pee in a flowerbed, Reg winced.

Allison laughed but I couldn't tell what she thought of it all—I wondered if as a straight woman she was somehow inwardly disgusted but putting on a liberal front for her friends or if she recognized the embattled souls as being of her own ilk and was blind to the rest of it. Someday maybe I'll ask her.

We turned the corner onto my block.

Stumbling down the middle of the street, oblivious to the cars trying to inch their way around him, was a celebrant with stunning good looks stuffed into spangled light gray spandex shorts, which showed everything, front and back. His bare, smooth, milky chiseled chest glistened, and shocks of straight black hair fell fashionably from his handsome face. He was a knockout—God knows. No question about it. To complete the picture, he threw us a real killer smile as he passed by, the effect of which was somewhat marred by the unattractive fact that he was high as a kite, and weaving, as if each step he was taking was an effort.

It was then I noticed he was wearing a pair of distinctive candy apple red shoes that glistened in the sunlight.

"Now that," said Reg somberly as he put his arm around my shoulder, "is vanity unleashed. And vanity is never ever attractive."

"I don't know, Reg. He has a certain *joie de vivre.* He's sort of having fun celebrating his beauty."

"No. Vanity turns in on you. It eats you from inside. There's no real beauty in him."

Upstairs I listened to my voicemail while Reg made lemonade and Allison curled up on a couch in the corner and flipped through a magazine. I had messages from several group friends who, like Reg, seemed spooked that it was Gay Pride Day too. I excused myself to return the calls and offer some support, but those earlier callers weren't at home now. Hopefully they had gone off with friends to a meeting or at least were engaged in activities that worked for them. Or maybe, just maybe, they were sitting right by their phones, not answering, apprehensive.

I had come to realize the phone was a lifeline to sanity. And uniquely for those grieving, it was discomforting not to be able to reach that friendly voice on the other end—it subtly brought back the original trauma of loss, when no one was there. I'd try them again after the fireworks.

Allison, Reg, and I took the elevator up to my roof which has an uninterrupted view of Chelsea. Over the top of the Seminary we could see figures gathered on the roofs of their brownstones waiting like we were for the fireworks to begin. And because it was dark and you couldn't see the lower sections of their buildings, they seemed to be almost levitating among the tree tops and numerous church spires that added some ceremony to an otherwise undramatic cityscape.

Allison drew close to me. "Did you hear that thunder?"

That's right. I remembered now. We were supposed to get some thunderstorms tonight. At first I thought that low rumble had been early fireworks going off, but I knew better when I noticed a streak of lightning far in the western sky.

"Let's hope it doesn't affect the show," Reg muttered.

It didn't. The storm came later, after the display had ended.

The fireworks were shot from barges on the Hudson. Which meant they were close by. In fact they exploded overhead, spectacularly. In anticipation of each shimmering burst, Reg and I put our arms around Allison's shoulders and squeezed tightly.

It's odd how you can stand linked to two friends and yet exist in an opposite world, one they couldn't find if they tried and one they wouldn't recognize if they did. I wonder what they would have thought if they had read my mind as, for whatever reason, the fireworks became in my imagination huge explosions of cum, thick cascades of sperm, color mad ejaculates that seemed to pour down from the sky out of some mystical horn of plenty. And in response to this bombardment, seemingly aimed directly at me, I yearned to lean my head back, open my mouth and hungrily swallow every drop that showered down.

My feelings were so intense that I gasped and fell slightly forward. Reg pulled me back in line and steadied me, never taking his eyes off the new golden explosion that dissipated in the night sky like a glowing flower—and when I looked back up in the sky, I happily saw that same glowing flower too, nothing more. Yet when the finale was in full force I had the urge to tell Allison and Reg about my whimsical association—after all it's not a stretch to place an erupting cock in the company of Roman candles, sparklers, firecrackers, etc.—but I stopped myself…underneath it all I was embarrassed, not by making the association, but by experiencing it in the way I did, so palpably and forcefully. I didn't feel like communicating that. So I just kept quiet and let the neighborhood around me quiet down as well.

\*

I sat on the floor, phone in hand, but I didn't return

those calls. Reg and Allison had left in polite haste to beat the approaching storm, but I doubt they did, they couldn't have made it home yet, and already slicing drops of rain were spattering against my French windows, obscuring my view to the outside. And the wind blew branches against the glass, strong rhythmic clicks, that interfered with normal street sounds. Blind and deaf. Too blind to be able to read those phone numbers in my address book and too deaf to hear those outcries. In the middle of dialing a number, I paused, slowly put the phone down next to me on the floor, and gazed at it as if it were something unfamiliar that didn't really belong there.

I crossed to the windows, threw them open and breathed in the stormy night air, gusts of rain coming at me fast, jagged lightning illuminating my long hands where large purple veins, rivers of blood, throbbed compulsively, full of life.

Of course we're drawn to water, we are water, and I'm a Pisces, one of those earth-bound mermen condemned to roam on sand, dirt, and rocks in a bleak search for the kingdom of the waves. I guess then it's no accident that I love the rain, that I spent the day on a Hudson River pier, and that I was being pulled toward water once again tonight.

I grabbed my raincoat and oversized black umbrella from the copper canister by the door and headed out.

I decided to set off towards the river again, ready to enjoy the spectacle of the water all choppy and rising in white-tipped cascades, and at least get as far as the galleries, whose windows would showcase paintings, lit up against the black night, colors blurring, with art lovers, mere shadowy figures, huddled inside or spilling out onto the sidewalks, waiting with a heightened sense of camaraderie, in doorways, for the rain to let up.

I walked west. But it was almost impossible to see anything up ahead as I had my eyes cast down so I wouldn't step off the curb into a torrent that would rise up past my ankles. Hearing the constant loud battering of the rain on the top of my umbrella made me tense. I had to hold the umbrella straight out vertically when I turned corners to keep it from being ripped out of my hands. While thunder roared.

I have to admit I had set out with some of the adventuresome spirit and moral superiority of a nineteenth-century romantic. Now I was a drenched unhappy numbskull. What a mistake. What had I been thinking? And how long had I been walking? I had no real sense of how far I had gone.

Yet I knew I had made it to the galleries. But their lights were off, they had sensibly closed, and no art lovers waited, flattened up against the sides of buildings. Except for an occasional car passing by, spewing water up on the curb, it was dead. I lost heart. And I didn't feel like going all the way to the river anymore. I just wanted to go home. But where was I now?

When a flash of lightning revealed the lay of the land, I found I had turned onto one of the cobblestone side streets of the deserted Meatpacking District. Corrugated roofs of the buildings on opposite sides of the street, sagging precipitously, half in collapse, seemed to be straining to meet each other. The gutters were choked with waste since the drains were clogged, masquerading now as fountains, bubbling up on street corners like new forms of life. Someone, I couldn't make out who, crawled out of a nearby cardboard box, which was soggy and disintegrating, and loped off around the corner. Once vacated, the box turned into pulp, quickly, its remaining shreds washed into the gutter.

Suddenly a stretch limo rounded the corner and moved up the street towards me, its headlights glowing in the deluge and water beating off its sleek black roof like hot bullets. But instead of passing me, it stopped—unexpectedly—in front of where I stood on the curb. It was eerie. Like a tank grinding to a halt on a war-torn city street. It was almost as if whoever was inside had stopped to watch me, as through a one-way mirror—I say a one-way mirror because there was no way I could see through the tinted windows, and the rain rolling down the dark glass provided a double shield of secrecy.

I don't much like secrets, mine or anybody else's, and I'm not great at keeping my own. My life is pretty much an open book. Not everything is disclosed, but not much is hidden.

Of course, all that was about to change now. At this moment—when the back door of the limo was almost casually thrown open and the veil was lifted, so to speak. The same veil that was about to descend on me, cloaking me from the world I had staked a claim in, and even distorting the passage of time.

But I had no way of knowing it then. I could only gawk at the spectacle in front of me, that had nothing to do with me after all, or not much. They obviously wanted to give me some kind of thrill, only it's hard to get a thrill when you're on the outside looking in. Like I was. Though they wanted to fix that. They wanted to include me, deep voices, choking with laughter, enticing me over and I took the bait, stepped right up, and gazed through the smoky haze lit subtly, like an underexposed photograph, by the pastel lights affixed to the ceiling and sides of the limo's interior.

I could make out the forms of four young men, I'd

say in their mid-twenties, with spiked hair, in tuxedos, passing a glass pipe back and forth among themselves, leaning indolently back on the leather seats, facing each other in pairs, ghost night riders whose faces were blurred by thick smoke. And on the floor between them, the naked boy, his upended ass pointed right at me, the neck of a champagne bottle stuck up his hole. Squirming and groaning, he tried to keep himself steady on his hands and knees so he wouldn't collapse on the carpet of red roses that had been strewn underneath him, thorns and all.

"Drink it, baby, drink it," coaxed a voice from a face I couldn't see, as the voice's hand reached down and maneuvered the champagne bottle a little further inside the boy's hole. Then the hand pulled back, empty, and beckoned to me, the voice exhorting, "You try it. Come on— give it a shove. He's loving it."

It was then I saw the red shoes, twisting violently at the end of his naked body as they dug into the floor, trying to provide leverage to keep him from landing in the middle of the pile of thorns. The scene...the game...the bottle as an instrument of rape...it was cruel enough, the thorns sticking out from the vibrant rose petals, crueler still. And there was a lot of druggy laughter as they passed the pipe around, egging each other on in a dizzy stab at male bonding. Still no faces were visible. Only pale clouds of yellow, baby blue and pink smoke hovered where their faces belonged, and drifted down the fronts of their tuxedos to settle like tinted fog over their crotches.

Of course it was him. From this afternoon. I could picture him not marching, but wobbling down my street. I guess it was only the natural progression of things that now I was staring at his pink anus lips as they sucked as accommodatingly as possible on the champagne bottle's rim.

One of the voices shouted impatiently at me, "What's wrong with you, asshole? This is a once in a lifetime opportunity. Fuck him!"

I just stood there, wondering what to do, umbrella hanging over my head, soaked through and through. Suddenly I felt it. That powerful sexual surge that tingles from the top of the head to the soles of the feet in one lost moment that ignores any reason or resolve. I leaned forward. My fingers closed around the bottle until I had a good grip. Surprised, I felt him push back on it, encouraging me. His legs splayed as far apart as they could and he stopped struggling. I hesitated.

Saved by the bell. Remember those school days when the teacher called on you and you didn't have the answer and you started to break into a sweat—and then the bell rang. Well, a taxi was pulling up behind the limo and now the driver started honking his horn, working instant wonders, like the bell, and set him free, the naked boy who didn't have the answer either.

They threw him out. They'd had enough. He didn't end up sprawled on the street though. Four pairs of hands lifted him out, gingerly, and set him on his feet, on those shoes, after they'd ordered him to "Pop it out!" and he had, fairly easily, pushing down on his sphincter muscles, until one of their hands was holding the bottle upright, the foam gushing out, a glass cock that had no plans to stop its orgasm, while the boy's pink ass lips quivered back into place, and they figured he was OK enough to get rid of.

As I helped him onto the curb, the limo's door banged shut and as it moved on, the taxi close up against it, someone rolled down the window and sent the bottle flying in our direction where it smashed against the grate of a butcher's shop, shards barely missing us, while a dissipated voice cursed, "Hey, bitch! You greedy whore, you drank all our champagne!"

Then we were alone, huddled up against the butcher's shop, side by side in the continuing storm, sheltered by an awning whose four corners spewed water at our feet like a waterfall after a flood. He leaned back against the wet bricks, naked except for the red shoes. His eyes were shut, arms folded across his chest. He was shivering. Lightning electrified the air around him. He started gasping for deep breaths, then he slowly turned his head towards me, his handsome porcelain face framed by his longish shiny black windblown hair. He was trying to speak, his lips were trying to form words, but nothing came out. His mouth hung open in limbo. His eyes were full of fear.

"What?" I asked. "What is it?"

"That man!"

It was one of the most desperate cries I'd ever heard, what I would characterize as a cry from the heart, and one that was to haunt me for a long time.

He closed his eyes again and leaned back against the wall.

"That man!" he had cried. Which man? I hadn't seen their faces, only forms in shadowed spaces, pastel lights as comforting as those around an aging actor's mirrored dressing table, and spiked hair and silky pleated tuxedo pants, fog concealing crotches, rain and voices, but did they know him well, was one of them his lover, "That man!"?

Funny. I hadn't been shocked by the debauchery in the back of the limo, after all that was a staple not only of pornography but of reality in all the sophisticated capitals of the world where the privileged and jaded had hours to spare for such excesses, but I was chilled by the intensity of his guttural cry and the bleak look in his eyes of a soul near ruin.

# PART ONE

If life is a mystery, the most mysterious part of it is ourselves, in particular the enigma of why we move against our own well-being, sabotage reason, or sanity if you prefer, to travel to a dark place, far from our hearts. I have a clue, though, based on my own experience. It begins with a sense of deprivation, which, made manifest, becomes all-consuming, a big gluey ball of rot you can always see somehow out of the corner of your eye.

I went through a period in my life, I guess when I was about ten, when I was dirt poor. My dad had lost his job and couldn't find a new one, not for at least a year. My brother was ten years older than me and had left town to start his own life. Whatever that life was didn't include sending any money back home. As the cliché goes, we made do, Mom, Dad and I, sitting quietly and gloomily in our clapboard Victorian on Kansas City's south side, just watching the four walls gradually darken with grime, or the furniture, in a domino effect, kind of collapse. And I was hungry then. Our goal was to keep the house, at any cost, even if it meant no food.

In the school cafeteria I would eye the leftover slices of bread after lunch and become obsessed with how to grab them, with no one seeing, and hide them in my coat pockets. Once the lady who served food from behind the counter caught my gaze, which was riveted on the remaining slices and she understood. Quickly she grabbed them up, mumbling something about how she had to refrigerate them for tomorrow, in case the morning delivery was late, so that I wouldn't get something for nothing. I watched her pat her hairnet in place as she softly shut the refrigerator door. Later in the afternoon I joined in the hearty laughter and jokes of my classmates as they devoured their favorite snacks. I stared— especially at the bags of potato chips, carelessly opened and left unfinished, which they took their time munching—but I had trained my eyes to affect a distant look while pretending to be taking in something neutral like the floor. And, oh God, the sound of that quick fizz as a Coke bottle top was being snapped opened. All I could concentrate on were these so-called treats, apparent things of naught, that others had at their beck and call. If I had come clean and asked to share some, forget it, I would have been seen with different eyes as someone very low and undesirable to have around. So I went hungry and kept quiet about it.

Now when my dad did land a job it didn't take long for me to snap out of my fixation about food. In fact, as soon as I saw it spread out there on the dining room table, it went out of my mind. Completely. I didn't give it a second thought. The difference was in the way I felt... not just content, but deliriously happy.

When Frank died I felt deprived in the same way. But that kind of deprivation is more subtle, sometimes you're aware of it, sometimes you aren't, though unconsciously you must be wanting to get rid of it all the time. I think that's why one day I put on the red shoes. When something takes too long to heal, it's time for a different bandage. Only I couldn't have spelled it out this way, not last summer, and as July deepened, its white skies holding exquisite heat, all I knew was that I was tired of carrying my mopey ass around town, giving and getting assembly-line sympathy, and for what, when what I needed most was some excitement, some fun, a massive injection of life's nectar. And it was surely out there. I'd seen signs of it.

As I sat on the stone bench in the early morning light outside the Chapel of the Good Shepherd I knew I couldn't exist in that gray light anymore, the gray light I had opened my eyes to on the Hudson River pier on Gay Pride Day—the gray light that had frightened me. No more.

Through the chapel door I saw the muted colors of the stained glass, muted because the light was still pale, but the colors were beginning to blend, beginning to form designs and patterns, and I had the sense that there was ornamentation in life, pleasant sensations, pins and needles that made the heart soar rather than sink in the mud. My anesthesia was wearing off.

I glanced at the empty stone bench adjacent to mine. A ray or two of morning light glimmered on the concrete; once a green leaf blew across it, and once a wren with a stick in its mouth settled on its edge for a moment or two. I stared at the bench for a long time.

I knew by the time I got to the 42nd Street Pier that I wasn't going. Allison, Reg and other group friends were waiting in line and had saved a place for me. I got out of the taxi just as everybody was starting to board the boat we had chartered to circle lazily around Manhattan. Reg noticed me and waved desperately. I decided to ask the taxi driver to wait and took only a few tentative steps forward.

"I'm not coming!" I called out.

"Why not?" Reg yelled back, exasperated.

Defensively I held onto the taxi door. "Because," I lied, "I have to get my application in for that Court Assistant job. I didn't realize this is my last day to apply."

"But this is a tradition!" Reg shouted.

That was true. It was our bereavement group's annual summer boat ride. But I didn't care.

"I haven't even filled it out yet," I responded. "It has to be postmarked today."

Reg started to move onto the boat backwards, still facing me. It was comical in a way, I expected him to somehow fall into the water, like in a movie gag. "I'll help you fill it out when we get back."

Allison had the sense to stand still and let the others move around her. "I made Thai chicken salad just for you." Her voice was so small and distant that I think that's what she said, though I wouldn't put my money on it.

"I've got to get it in the mail by this afternoon. It can't wait. Sorry. Enjoy!" And I hopped back in the taxi telling the driver, "Slipstream. Washington and West Twelfth." As the taxi pulled out of the lot, I didn't look back. Maybe I was afraid I'd turn to salt. More likely I wanted to look towards the future that literally laid in front of the taxi's windshield—the West Side Highway as we headed south—a road that was moving me along some passageway to freedom.

"Open sesame!" I cried aloud in joy.

"What's that?" the driver mumbled.

"Did I say something?" I laughed and he grunted, unamused.

Slipstream is a fashion studio in the West Village that does double duty selling clothing. It's usually full of models and photographers doing shoots until all hours, but this morning it was pretty dead, which was fine by me, as I only wanted to check out the clothes. It was Allison who had told me that their shop stocked the latest Eurotrash items, sexy, expensive stuff. Because I had a thin, tapered body, nicely proportioned, I knew I could wear these clothes to my advantage, with flair, even though I was only used to pulling on jeans and K-Mart sweatshirts.

The shop was empty except for a taciturn boy behind the counter who looked all of fifteen and jaded, like he'd been through one life, and please, don't bother him, unless you could offer him a leg up on a second one. He did manage to tell me in a lifeless voice to try on whatever made my socks go up and down, though he never looked at me when he spoke, only down at the glass counter he presided over. Me, I was in quite a different state of consciousness, weirdly energized, though we both were occupied in the same way, looking at ourselves for over an hour, me in the full-length mirror they had set up in the middle of the store as its centerpiece—an arresting and outrageous one framed by gold gilt that curved in and out histrionically at the top and bottom, like one you'd see in a fun house—and him into that dull glass counter top.

In the end I felt I'd emptied the store, like some fashion vulture, but of course I hadn't made a dent. Everything fit in three boxes. As the boy de-tagged the items and folded them neatly, he would linger over each one, letting some air escape from his mouth in a bemused way, his way of laughing. Sometimes he'd incline his head ever so slightly, perplexed, as if he'd never seen such an article of clothing before or that it just wasn't right for me and he wondered what the hell I was buying it for.

But I was excited by my booty and afterwards spent a lot of time in front of the more commonplace mirror in my bedroom trying on several items I'd bought, in different combinations. I left my French windows thrown open onto the common garden I shared with neighbors across the way. If any of them looked in my window, that was OK because they couldn't really see anything in the afternoon except my dusty shadow moving and posing in the mote-filled rays of sunlight. It was ninety degrees. I felt sensual and half-stupid from the heat.

Pieces of clothing moved over my naked body—two plain shirts, one indigo blue, the other a deep, deep brick red, a pair of unstructured black pants, slim-fitted, with no cuffs or loop for a belt, so that from the front and back I looked like a gigolo, a black unpleated jacket slung over my shoulder, giving me a modern, minimalist look. I put on some leather slip-on shoes with big soles and a leather buckle on the side. I decided to forego any socks. This was the outfit I wore when I went out later—with the indigo rather than the deep, deep brick red shirt. I did try on a pair of black Levis made of stretch-tight microfibers in case they were a better choice, but I decided to go with the straight black pants with no embellishments. The Levis could wait till next time.

Two of the boxes I didn't even get into—I'd save them for a rainy day.

I'd have to say, when all was said and done, I did look tasty. Well put together. There was my hair, though...blond and full, presumably hair a man would enjoy running his hands through...only it seemed a little long and unruly and out of style.

"Style?" scoffed my regular barber, an old guy, a Turk, who'd had a shop in the Village for years next to

Ray's Pizza on West 11th Street off 6th Avenue. "It's about a good clean cut. Something you can live with and the ladies will like." He was lost in the '50s, hit songs from those times filling the air, guys with crew cuts and pin-up babes staring down at you from faded cutouts that had been plastered on his wall since Sputnik was circling the globe. No need to change the pictures or the haircuts. Luckily for me. Because he gave me what was really a longish crew cut, only before he could cut much of the front off, I had him spike it and I had just what I wanted. I couldn't wait to check out the whole nine yards—the hair, the clothes, the affect —in each passing window. Reg and Allison would be getting off that boat now, exactly the same way they had boarded it, shuffling home in the heat, maybe deciding to give me a call. But I wouldn't be there.

I ate dinner at a cheap Mexican restaurant on West 4th Street. There was an available table in the window and I wanted to put myself on display, the new me, otherwise I would have gone somewhere else, as I don't even like Mexican food, it's way too spicy for me. I washed my chicken enchiladas down with six or seven glasses of ice water and kept going to the head to take a piss. Between pisses I watched the sun go down behind the movie house across the street. A guy or two passing by outside did throw a cruisy look my way.

When I left it was dark out and humid and the sidewalks were crowded. You couldn't help bumping into people as you made your way. I started to feel let down from the day's adrenalin rush, tired. Something was missing. As I moved further into the night I felt uneasily alone.

In the Village, sex emporiums aren't as common or even as titillating as they used to be but there are a couple left, including that real evergreen, The Pink Pussycat Boutique. Impulsively, instead of passing it by, I stepped down into it, whistling, hands thrust in my pockets, eyes raised upwards, fastened on the musty, cantaloupe moon that hung down low.

I guess I expected the place to be full of nightcrawlers salivating like a wild pack of sexed-up dogs, but there were only a few customers here and there, a few horny guys, alone, checking out the glass cases of dildos, rubber-sleeved pussies, fleshlights, vibrators, cock rings and pumps. A busty woman and her date were hee-hawing at the frilly maid's uniform pinned to the wall by two sleek whips, and a long-haired girl of about fifteen was gazing sharply at the displays of scented oils, gels, and lubricants. I would have cut out right away if I hadn't suddenly noticed the tall, good-looking man I could see watching my every move in the mirror.

He must have stood 6'2" at least, probably more, had salt-and-pepper hair, a fine aquiline Roman nose and very masculine features. He wore a freshly starched light blue cotton shirt, a pair of khaki shorts, sandals. He was holding a pair of tinted shades in his hands. I felt an intense sexual buzz coming from him right away. And it left me hot as hell and wanting him.

I needed to keep him turned on, interested. But how? I inched closer to where he was standing and peered casually into a glass case full of sexy underwear. He sidled right up next to me. We didn't look directly at each other but his fingers, gnarled and thick, began drumming on the glass top directly above a hot pink G-string covered with silver sparkles. Feeling flushed and slutty, I bought that G-string, not looking up at him or the saleswoman, just keeping my eyes on the thin black plastic bag that held my new purchase. Then with an

"Oh, sorry," I brushed against him slightly and left the store.

I knew he would follow me. I'd have bet the crown jewels on it. And sure enough when I reached an alleyway I leaned back against the brick wall, ostensibly to look inside my bag, and his arm was suddenly up against the wall, blocking my view of the street. It was a pretty bold move, letting me know I could forget about anything other than dealing with him.

"I'd like to see you in that G-string." His voice had a heavy New York accent. From one of the boroughs.

I laughed. "I imagine that could be arranged."

He let me see a half-smile, a real wolf. Then he fished a pack of cigarettes out of his shorts.

"Want one?" he asked as he lit up.

"No, thanks."

"Got a nice cunt?" he asked as he took a deep drag and slowly blew it out.

Hey, I could give it right back to the son of a bitch. "It's tight. Pretty juicy. It's got a pair of pretty puffy lips on it." After a beat, he threw me that half-smile again, to show he'd liked what he'd heard. I continued, "How about your cock?"

"It's more than a mouthful," he said dismissively, as if I had no right to ask what he was bringing to the table.

After that exchange I thought the best thing to do was to backtrack. "What's your name?"

"Silvio," he answered, but didn't bother to ask mine. I felt like saying something dumb, like, wow, nice Irish name, but I didn't. Instead I pulled the G-string out of the bag and started fingering it slowly.

"So when do you want to get together?" He put his fingers on the G-string too and started rubbing the material. It sure was hot pink and sparkled even in the

35

dark. Our fingers touched.

"Maybe next weekend," I said slowly.

"Saturday night?"

"That could work."

"You got a place?"

"In Chelsea."

"Live alone?"

"Yes. And you?"

"Yeah. I live in Bensonhurst. I have a free place too."

Wasn't that an artery of deepest Brooklyn? I pictured myself wandering on dark, tree-lined streets in Bensonhurst, dogs barking angrily as I crept by each house, a slip of paper clutched in my sweaty palm, with his address on it...

"No. Let's do it at my place."

Do it. Two simple active words that formed a general umbrella under which something was going to go on. What that was I wasn't sure, but I had a good bet he did. He was planning to get his rocks off just the way he liked to get them off, forget any suggestions I might throw into the hat. I slid the G-string from his fingers and stuffed it back in the bag. The night was getting more oppressive. I could see he had started to perspire, beads of sweat were forming on his cheeks.

"You work around here?" I asked, just to have something to say.

"Yep."

"What do you do?"

"I'm a cop."

I tensed involuntarily. "Well," was all I could say. I could see it gave him a kick to watch me coming to terms with it.

"Retired from the force this year. I'm forty-six. Still

do some consulting work for my unit."

"You look pretty rested—"

"Like I've just finished some consulting in West Palm? I have. I like the beach. And my dad lives down there."

"That's great," I said, going into flirt mode. "I thought retired cops sat around in bars, bloated, full of complaints. I never pictured them as vital, young, and as good-looking as you."

He suddenly leaned in close, right in my face. "I'm gonna fuck you. Hard." I was speechless. "I'm gonna ride you like a bitch." He moved back, satisfied, a smug look on his face, as he pulled a card from his wallet and a pen from his shorts. "What's your number?"

I gave it to him.

"Your name?"

I thought for a second, then, "Tim," I lied.

"I'll call you on Friday," he said. "Then we'll set something up for Saturday night."

"Sounds good."

"We'll see you then," he said and was on his way, friendly, confident, and real cool. As I walked home I knew this guy was hot for it, he'd definitely call, even though we had moved away from each other like pieces on a chess board, stiffly, no seductive exits necessary. But would I see him? Would I even want to after a week had passed? To tell the truth, probably not. Even though I'd been hot for it all day and night, time has a way of leveling everything off. But I decided not to draw a line in the sand, just go on about my life as usual, and let next Saturday night be next Saturday night, whatever it was, whatever it brought.

\*

It always amuses me when movie crews invade my neighborhood like gods descending among mere livers of life to indulge in some elevated, almost divine calling. Everyone works hard and fast, of course, in double time, in contrast to the energyless slobs coming home from a hard day on the job, just wanting to get inside their apartments and put their feet up, but finding their way blocked by officious interns—one hand held rudely out in front of their faces, the other grasping a cell phone with a sweaty palm and the solemnity of Job.

"An invasion of occupying forces, that's what they are," Reg, who obviously agrees with my point of view, once intoned. "I mean, come on. They just take over, man. Lunch tables up, laden with all kinds of food that no one really eats—it's way uncool—instead they'll go later arm in arm to some trendy restaurant, but they'll keep a homeless person away from that table come hell or high water. And vans full of obscene amenities hogging every inch of curb space, doors left open so we can crane our necks to catch a glimpse of the actors being danced attendance on as if they were some kind of modern day Marie Antoinettes. And all the cables and lights strung up everywhere like Christmas in July— think of the high costs of running those generators! As if all this will somehow inspire magic. Their motto: *veni, vidi, vici*. The fruits of their labors: almost always crap."

Then we had broken into long laughter, buoyed by our righteous indignation.

Feeling the way I do about it, I was in no mood when, walking up 10th Avenue, after a meeting, I saw the back of the Seminary, the most Gothic-looking section, ablaze with light, the part that is more than occasionally used as some setting for a horror movie, usually a tired retread of the child born of the devil, who grows up there, with green glowing eyes, alone in his room at night, but with a cherubic expression and a cheery hello for everybody during the day. It's only a matter of time before the little monster begins his reign of terror, right? Well, it was going on eleven o'clock but they were all still at it. Dozens of crew members huddled together in strategic clusters, each in charge of a different task. I crossed to the opposite side of the street so I wouldn't have to deal with it. But I couldn't help glancing over at the more than usual commotion going on. Flames, fake of course, and looking it, were bellowing out of the top windows of the Seminary and they had some kind of sound effects machine cranked up that was giving off otherworldly moans and groans. A fire truck was waiting patiently up the street, even though there was no fire, but just in case, I presume, something did catch on fire from all the bullshit. As I passed the firemen, I could see they were all having a good time, enjoying a kind of busman's holiday, lounging back against the engine, arms folded, making jokes about the goings-on. I was less enthusiastic. The Seminary was a place that served as my spiritual retreat, that provided respite from my worries, that hinted at a peace to come. It was being put to a cheap use now, as far as I was concerned. But hell, I didn't own it. I had to get over the fact that other people would find different uses for it. And let it go. Nonetheless the first thing I wanted to do when I got upstairs was to call Reg and complain.

"You'll never guess," I said, as I threw open my French windows and looked down the block.

"What?" Reg asked.

I cradled the phone on my neck and stared at the flames licking into the sky. Now, from further away, and from behind, they did look real, as if a conflagration had actually started in that rear part of the Seminary. And I could hear those pumped-up otherworldly moans as well, and from a distance they seemed to have crystallized in the air and had an authenticity about them. I suddenly didn't feel like talking about it. I moved away from the window.

"Nothing."

"Guess what I'm up to?" Reg acted as if my answer was perfectly satisfactory. "I'm online, working on my profile again…and scanning a few other guys' possibilities…evaluating their stats and their hopes and their dreams—"

"And availability."

"That too," he laughed. "But they're all available, of course, or they wouldn't be on it. I mean, this is a civilized way to meet somebody. You find out about them from the get-go. You meet for coffee. You talk. Gone are the days of standing at a crowded bar hoping for a one-night stand. Gay men are evolving. They're not letting the fucking straight homophobes keep them closeted and on their knees in the back of some bar. We're ever evolving and progressing. And I'm telling you there are really some interesting profiles here. Full of admirable characteristics as far as I'm concerned. I really think you should be on here too. You know they say there are nearly fifty men on every block in Chelsea who've put their profiles on here. There's a change in the air and it's for the better."

\*

That night my dream began with his heavy black boots moving surreptitiously through the Seminary garden. Very slowly, but with a somehow menacing, unstoppable purpose. The sky was dark but a full moon cast a strong light on the chapel and on some of the ripe white, yellow and red flowers that were bent over the edges of the path, heavy on their stems. His black boots crushed them as he passed and their petals became liquid pools in the moonlight, bright stains on the concrete.

He wore the black hooded robe of a monk, appropriate enough for stalking the grounds of a Seminary, and his form cast no shadow on the ground. He paused on the path, as if alerted by the sound of someone approaching, and then sought the refuge of darkness, stepping back into the shadows of the chapel wall where the moonlight was as dim as the glow from a nearly spent candle. There he stood waiting, silently. No one else came along to bother either of us—not him, who was obviously there for some dark purpose, nor me, who could do nothing but observe him and, although I was only a few feet away from him, I remained unseen by him, kept invisible by the heavy cloak of my dream.

Once one of his boots moved into a patch of moonlight and I saw a worm crawl up onto it and unwind itself, stretch out to its full length, luxuriating, twisting itself in circles with an ugly pleasure, and it seemed an eternity until it slithered off back down into the dirt to disappear into its hole.

He had a key. That was the scariest part, since it was the very thing I didn't want him to have. When he felt the coast was clear, he moved away from the wall and took this key from the pocket of his robe to inspect it, though he remained faceless behind the deep recesses of the folds of his hood. Then he hurriedly passed me, disappearing into the Seminary.

I was following him. No, that's not quite right. I was

ahead of him. That was it. I was going up the stairs, into their rooms to warn them.

"He has a key," I kept whispering, and in my mind I saw it turning in a lock but what lock I didn't know, nor how far he was from us.

They slept peacefully in their rooms, the Seminary students. Two or three to a room, all on their beds, naked, in repose. But they were unusually positioned, languidly hanging their heads and arms off the beds, mouths wide open and eyes closed, some with their legs up against the wall, some with their feet hooked onto the window sills. Though they were naked, there was nothing lust-inducing about them. They were naked as they were born and as they would die, artless.

"Wake up, wake up, please," I kept entreating them, going from room to room. "I'll tell you everything I know. Don't you see?"

I knelt down by one student whose head hung off the side of the bed, his mouth in an open O, and I remember thinking, this is where life comes from, from this mouth, this is the source of life, but I kept saying over and over, "I'll tell you everything I know," as if from my very being could come words so startling and prophetic that they could induce a nimble grasp of the meaning of eternity.

And then the boots were next to me. I shivered and peered into the hollowed creases of his black hood, trying to see who he was, but it was no use. His face remained an empty hole. He took some lighter fluid from his robe pocket and emptied it into the student's mouth, filling it to the brim, like a pool that was on the verge of overflowing, but hadn't quite, and then he dropped a match into the liquid pool and as flames shot out of the mouth, high into the air, the student opened his eyes and in them I saw love, the eyes radiated with a yearning love I have never seen before or since.

I watched the boots move away, and followed them back down into the garden, the heels mowing down the heavy flowers once again, but this time they were blue flowers, and purple and black ones, so fat that they oozed out a gooey ink as he squashed them. I thought that ink would surely stain the bottoms of his boots, thus providing the clue to identify him.

Then it was dawn.

I stood at my living room window and gazed outside. The Seminary had burned to the ground, with just a few charred remains of the place left; it was like a country field, empty, laid to waste, with a pile of smoldering sticks and stones in the middle of it. Then I saw the robed, hooded figure move slowly across the field and stand next to the only remnant left that I could recognize, the broken down altar, surrounded by pieces of stained glass. The figure knelt there and pulled back his hood.

Amazed, I saw that the figure was me, holding a thin match up in the air. That dream me looked up and locked eyes with the real me, staring down at the barren field through my open French windows. But in a theatrical transfer, I suddenly and very strongly felt myself to be the robed figure on that charred field. And now the weaker me, the fake, closed my French windows and slowly drew the curtains, unable to look down at myself anymore.

I had many times knelt at that altar, had many times searched for images in that stained glass, searched for Frank or for God.

My communications had always ended the same way, and I was thankful that they ended the same way once again, now, as I prayed anew, with me hearing those sounds, muffled, incredibly far away, of birdsong, the splash of water, laughter without care, then abrupt silence.

*

Saturday rolled around.

I don't know what I expected from Silvio. It had been so long since I'd had sex I'd kind of forgotten what it was and how to do it. I don't think he had, though, and I cringed when I thought I might fall short of his expectations. Last night when he phoned to confirm I almost told him to forget it but I was too horned up not to go for it. No one's really ready for that first encounter anyway, the situation's just too loaded. I decided to picture a blank slate which after tonight would be filled with twisting loops and squiggles and a reality that didn't matter to anybody but him and me. And not much to us. If things didn't work out, the slate could be discarded dispassionately. Or were there always bruises? I didn't know but I figured I'd better accept one thing: you play, you pay.

I spent the afternoon filling out my Court Assistant application. The real deadline was on top of me; it had to be postmarked by Monday. After I finished it and took it to the corner mailbox, I ran into Bob McBride, my neighbor directly across the hall, walking his little Jack Russell. For whatever reason I told him what I was mailing.

Bob was a wiry, energetic man, always quick with a reply. Today he didn't disappoint.

"Funny you should mention that," he squinted at me. "Yesterday I got a letter from the U.S. Postal Service and I thought...no...wait a minute. It couldn't be. Then...well, yes, of course...what else could it be?"

He waited for my reaction. When I only blinked, he decided to end the drama.

"Well, it turns out the letter was asking me to come in for an interview for a carrier position I'd tested for. Now, do you know when I took that test? I mean, how many years ago?"

"Two," I guessed.

"Twelve."

In those twelve years he'd buried his wife, put his daughter through college, worked two dozen shoestring jobs, converted to Buddhism, and watched his hair turn gray. Yet he was thrilled to get the interview.

"My God," I said. "Will I have to wait twelve years?"

"Oh, no. I doubt it," he spoke with the authority of a man who knew how to navigate his way through the civil service maze. "Everybody wants into the Post Office. The waiting lists are endless. You, they'll call right away. Court Assistants are always leaving in droves. It's a burnout job."

As far as I could see, Bob had three things going for him. An indefatigable spirit, uncompromising honesty, and a rent-controlled apartment. The Jack Russell started to chew aggressively on my pant cuff.

"I got to go," I said.

"Big Deal, get down!"

Oh, yeah, I forgot, the dog's name was Big Deal.

As I yanked my cuff out of the dog's clenched teeth, Bob wished me good luck and told me to hang in there. What he didn't add was there's a sucker born every minute and they just put a baby blue tag on your wrist. As I dropped the application in the mail I wondered if I'd run for the hills, too, with all the other Court Assistants, after a couple of months of dealing with the crazies and the craziness. I doubted it. Maybe I was naive but I thought there was a way you could provide a service to anybody who needed it, even the most desperate of the desperate, and still hold onto your sanity.

Silvio was due at 8:30, an hour away.

It was only after I'd straightened the apartment, dressed the bed with deep purple sheets and conspicuously arranged my shimmering pink G-string on top of one of the pillows that I began to feel edgy. A little nervous in the stomach. I wondered what to wear over that G-string. I could consider my choices while I took a warm, relaxing bath.

Once I was stretched out in the tub, my head resting back on the gently curved tile, I gave myself up to the water, a true Pisces, letting it soothe my tautness, imagining I was floating down some supernatural river to its estuary, a wide open mouth. In that moist cave sleep held me lightly, early evening breezes tantalizing me, promising my body pleasures I never dared dream of.

I don't know how long Silvio had been downstairs ringing the buzzer. But by the time I opened my eyes I had an intuitive feeling it had been about five minutes. I hoisted myself out of the tub, dripping wet, and hurried to the intercom in the hall.

My water-soaked thumb pressed the button.

"Hello?" I said unhappily.

"It's Silvio," came the curt, masculine reply.

The digital clock on the intercom read 8:15. He was fifteen minutes early. Johnny Eager here. No time to put on something sexy or even towel myself dry. Reluctantly I buzzed him in.

When he knocked on my door, all I could do was

open it bare-ass naked, affecting a sensually defiant pose, as if this behavior was *de rigueur*—hey, this was how they did things here in Chelsea. If he was taken aback he didn't show it. Well, maybe for an instant I saw his body stiffen in surprise, but in a bold move that matched mine he broke into a big grin, moved in quick and panther-like, closed the door behind him and folded his arms. "Slut," was all he said but in that one word and in the way he said it I felt appreciated and condemned, liberated and ashamed, unsullied and lewd, all at the same time. I guess that's what the word meant. Everything.

He wore a red T-shirt and jeans that smelled warm and clean, as if he'd just pulled them out of a drier, and beige moccasins with no socks. He seemed half fancy man, salaciously contemptuous and very free, and half ardent lover, obsessed with claiming the object of his desire.

I stood there naked in confusion.

Silvio wasn't dumb. He was the kind of guy who could seize an opportunity the minute it came up, and he wasted no time in goose-stepping me into the bathroom. He fumbled around in my medicine cabinet as I stood there with my mouth open. He finally found my razor and shaving cream, backed me up against the sink, turned on the hot water and started to shave off my pubic hair. He also shaved my balls. He went about this task silently and methodically. When I was smooth as a baby's bottom, he gave a satisfied sigh. "Feel better now?"

"Yeah," I answered, actually enjoying the cool, light sensation around my genitals, even though I'd just been emasculated. We'd left the beaten path. The woods loomed dark and deep.

"We're finished," he said in a clipped tone. As if I should have realized it was time to get on to other things.

As he put the razor and cream back in the cabinet I saw in the mirror that I was blushing.

His intrusive behavior wasn't my fantasy come true, but come to think of it I didn't have any explicit fantasies. This was as good as any. It was what was here, what was real. I could easily embrace the yin-yang concept of dominance and submission, and when all was said and done find it an intriguing aphrodisiac.

There was another aphrodisiac. Grass. After we'd settled on the couch he took a joint out of his pack of cigarettes and we smoked it. It was either strong as hell or maybe I just wasn't used to smoking but soon I was leaving the inhibitions of the world behind in a patch of dust. Dust that formed in a thick cloud around my head and swirled inside me like sexy, ultraviolet starlight, sending warm, repetitive ripples from my head to my toes, creating an almost unbearable desire to rest my head on Silvio's lap and unzip his fly.

Instead I had the wherewithal to act as if I hadn't been affected at all. Granted I had been—and, I decided, for the better.

True, it hadn't been fun at first, to be naked, sitting stiffly next to him while he lit up, fully clothed, long legs stretched out in front of him, at ease, while I felt like an eel in a jar, embarrassed at the way he was eyeing my newly shaved crotch. But once the joint was finished I felt as if I'd leapt off a Greek vase and that it was the most natural and emancipating thing in the world to walk around in the buff in front of him. When I crossed the room to close the curtains, I felt his eyes glued to me in admiration.

He asked me to come over and sit at his feet while he smoked part of another joint. I think he was talking about some new trees he was planting in his back yard out in Bensonhurst, but I couldn't concentrate on his words for long because I was too preoccupied watching his big hands and marveling at the deep drags he was taking, seeming to trap the smoke inside him forever. But eventually smoke would pour out of his mouth in fat clouds.

He wanted a beer too or "brew" as he called it and when I brought it to him, leaning over him to set it on the table beside him, I realized I had become more comfortable, but it was only because I was high. That must be the nature of the beast. I found some soft jazz on the radio.

"I'll be back," I said confidently. "I'm going to put on that G-string."

"Got any porn?" he asked, lighting a cigarette.

"Well, no," I lied, knowing I had a few porn DVDs hidden in the back of my closet in some box or other. I just didn't want to root for them.

"Then put on the game, will you? We can lose the music."

He meant the baseball game on ESPN and his arrogant tone implied that a queer like me knew nothing about sports and that he, a real man, a macho cop, did. Well, he was right. After I'd turned off the radio and found the game, I couldn't tell who was playing who or who was winning what and I didn't care. I saw his eyes intentionally leave me as the center of attention and focus on the spectacle of male competition, relegating me to my rightful subordinate position.

It was all just a sexual game and obviously a turn-on for him to further delineate a top/bottom distinction between us, and as I had a major buzz going I went with it. Willingly. Or should I say, naturally? Because something about it did feel right. At least for tonight with him.

Stoned, I stumbled around my bedroom, lights off, glad that for a few minutes I didn't have to pretend to walk in a straight and steady line. I took a few deep breaths. Once I had put on the fabled G-string that had brought the sports-loving cop and me together, I checked myself out in the mirror. There was enough light streaming in my window from the brownstones opposite to let me see clearly. I looked like an alabaster ghost, beautiful in a way.

"Slut," he had said.

I opened the closet door. The red shoes rested in the deep recesses, isolated from the commonplace pairs lined up in front. Not knowing why but feeling a compelling urge to wear them, I reached for them with hands that trembled slightly.

Sex comes from such a lost, primitive place, we can never understand its meaning until we're in its throes, until we've released that second being within us, shut down, shadowed, who doesn't know how to think or speak but can only communicate in burning grandiose sensations, from the heart of a fireball. When I put on the red shoes, I called forth that other sequestered self beneath my own skin, as translucent as a lantern exposing all my desires, devoid of the rationality, temperateness and dignity needed to withstand the light of day. For this was something else. For it to work you had to destroy that careful construct, yourself.

I glided back into the living room and planted myself between him and the TV. Silvio forgot all about the baseball game. He let out an involuntary groan and I saw him stiffen in his pants.

"Turn around," he ordered in a hoarse voice. "And spread."

Sounding just like a cop. Ordering his suspect in G-string and red shoes to obediently bend over, stretch the legs wide, and prepare to commit fornication. I've heard that one of the most common sexual fantasies is to want to feel overpowered. That was me, warm and faint, feeling via Chaucer "fair as is the rose in May," and primed, with faith in my overripe person. He may have had the tool. But powerless, vulnerable, and excited to expose the most intimate part of my body, I realized I held the key to his libidinous desires. And so a heightened potency blasted through each of us.

"Show me your cunt."

I teasingly fingered the G-string, snapping it, moving it from side to side with the maddening unpredictability of leaves blowing in the wind, letting him glimpse my bud, not in flickering candlelight but in the cold glow of a 100-watt bulb. Looking up at him from between my legs, I could see his body harden, tense, a stud in limbo, talking himself out of exploding right there in his pants.

"You fucking bitch. You just bend over when any guy suggests it. Don't you? Some nights you probably have a line of guys outside your door. Waiting for their turn."

"Yeah, I do. And this is what they get to see." I spread even further, maneuvered the dazzling pink string away from my hole, and puckered for him, in and out, in and out.

"Shit," he moaned, hot as the living hell for it. "I bet if I tossed a quarter on the floor you'd snap it up quick with that slick twat, wouldn't you?"

"Yes," I decided to agree.

His voice got hoarser. "You get wet just thinking about that, don't you?"

"Very wet, sir." I made my voice smaller, weaker,

to turn him on.

"You whore." He jumped up and jammed a gnarled, meaty finger inside me, leisurely unzipping his fly and pulling out a veiny cock which he hung in front of my lips, pushing his hand down on my head so I couldn't lift it higher than his waist, while he wedged a second equally thick finger in next to the first. He worked both fingers to massage and spread me until I was wide open.

Then came a fresh command: "Polish my knob."

Lurching forward I tried to catch his cock in my mouth. But laughing, he stepped beyond my reach then squatted down eye-level with me and whispered softly and deliberately, "Why are you a fag?"

"Don't know."

"How come?" He wasn't satisfied with my response.

I tried again. "I…I…want to please…men…"

In my awkward position I was ready to crumple to the floor so I grabbed onto his legs for support. There…again…that freshly laundered fragrance of his jeans…He pushed my hands away roughly and grabbed my hair, holding me up by a few blond strands.

On the flat screen a hunky player was up at bat. He whacked the ball into the stands and there was a free for all, a real melee as fans jostled, kicked, and punched each other to get to the little white trophy. Silvio held my head back and shoved his cock down my throat, and I gagged on the fullness of it. But my eyes were still on the flat screen and even though I missed seeing who was lucky enough to end up with the prized ball, through watery eyes, I did get to see the hunk who'd hit the home run get jumped on and high-fived by his buddies. In fact, they lifted him up on their shoulders. Victorious.

"What's wrong?" Silvio crooned mockingly. "Don't

you like a rough top?"

It was just as well his cock was down my throat and I couldn't talk, otherwise an honest response may have popped out, "Not all that much." I mean it was work being used like the town pump. I was relieved when he finally stood back. I sank to my knees in front of him, my G-string down around one ankle, legs akimbo, red shoes expanding like wildfire on the pale carpet.

"You liked that?"

I caught my breath. "Yes...I did."

He casually finished his joint, standing sideways so I could view his hard-on, potent and in charge. I dreamily started to masturbate, watching him.

There was a substantial, round, wooden table by the window where I had filled out my application earlier that day. It still had papers, pens, and paper clips on it, but with a brush of the hand, Silvio sent them flying.

"Assume the position," he commanded. "Face down. One leg on the floor, one up over the table."

Still high, I did as instructed, half-climbing onto the table, somehow. Out of the corner of my eye I saw him tear open a condom with his teeth and slide it over his cock. "You won't be needing lube. Your ass is a natural can of Crisco." Before I had time to think about the article I'd read demonstrating how to slip a condom on your partner in a sensual and erotic way, he was drilling his swollen head in my hole. I cried out. He slapped my ass. Hard. "No, goddamnit, like this," he pushed my leg that was on the table further up so he would have a perfect entry.

It was agony at first, of course, but then the planets moved into alignment, the end of the lost road came into focus, the reasons for living started to make some kind of sense, and I knew beyond a doubt that behind my closed living room curtains a summer moon was looming over the Seminary wall.

We clicked.

Thrusting deep inside me, he bit my neck, moaning, losing it, coming with a terrible shiver.

And the hard wooden table became our bed as we both fell into an exhausted sleep.

*

Later we slept in my bed, a much more restful proposition. Silvio stripped for the first time and lay back on my purple sheets, hands behind his head.

"Nice pussy," he commented.

I lay naked beside him, running my hands through his hairy chest, and I smiled at him. That was probably not just the only compliment I'd receive from this taciturn cop but, in his books, the ultimate one. Whatever. It was nice to have a man in my bed.

Reg had tried to drill it into me that two guys should never have sex until after the third date. That was the appropriate length of time "to get to know each other" before deciding whether or not to take the plunge. To me that sounded like bourgeois double talk. And why was three such a magic number? If anything such a scheme would preclude two people from getting to know each other. You have three opportunities to build defenses, create expectations of what the relationship should be, become inhibited so that you are afraid not to live up to the other person's rapidly developing preconceptions of the good, not terribly sexual person that he imagines you to be. And vice-versa. After three dates you start hiding. Inside. But Silvio and I, we hadn't hidden. It's true, I didn't know his life story, his favorite song or what his favorite color was. But we had communicated with our basic selves, had lit two interior lanterns, and many things about each other had been revealed.

At least, through him, I knew more about myself.

"You liked all that stuff, huh?" he asked, sort of out of the blue.

"That stuff we were doing in the other room?"

"That stuff."

"Yeah, I guess I did."

He grinned, proud of himself for having performed his part well, then suddenly put his arms around me and gave me a deep kiss, retreating quickly, lying back again, hands behind his head, distant, having gone just far enough.

I felt I could be more adventuresome. When neighbors across the garden pulled their living room curtains apart, a shaft of light in the shape of an oblong box illuminated his soft cock. It was the only light in the room. I lay my head down on his crotch, mesmerized, and he didn't push me away. There was a peace inside me. Why? I heard him yawn. I felt him stretch. He smelled of sweat, dried cum, and the earth in late fall.

"By the way," he said. "That's quite a pair of shoes."

I was startled. I looked up at him curiously.

"A sexy pair of motherfuckers," he added.

I laughed uneasily. "There's a story there."

"Oh, yeah?" he asked, reaching for a cigarette. "Want one?"

"No, not right now." I'd never told anyone about how I ended up with those red shoes, the very same shoes the boy had worn that eerie night. They were lying now on their sides in the middle of my living room where I'd kicked them off before coming into bed, creating an unlikely new centerpiece. The centerpiece of my apartment. Why did I suddenly think that? I jumped out of bed and started pacing, hands clasped behind my back. If Silvio was intrigued by my sudden agitation he didn't show it, he just lay there smoking quietly, not pushing me to say more.

My uneasiness passed quickly though and I eased onto the rocking chair in front of the window, put my feet up on its edge and hugged my knees, rocking for awhile. Out of the corner of my eye I could see dusty specks in the night sky, which may have been stars.

Finally I said lightly, "It's kind of a mystery. But you're a cop. Maybe you can crack the case, tell me what it was all about."

"I'll give it a shot," he said with wary bravado, as if I'd just given him a present he was suspicious of and afraid to open but unwilling to admit it.

I didn't know how much his shot would be worth anyway. I doubted it could penetrate the short spell of insanity that had happened that night.

*He leaned back against the wet bricks, naked except for the red shoes.*

I brought back time as thoughtfully as I could, speaking slowly, more for myself than for him, as if in reliving that night I could locate the key to its enigma only through quiet contemplation, or find that one overlooked piece of the boy that would make him a real human being instead of the phantom he remained.

I told Silvio about the afternoon spent on the pier with Allison and Reg, the fireworks cascading over the roof, my impulsive desire to wander west towards the river in the storm with the enthusiasm of a kid stomping through delicious puddles, the wild, handsome boy getting bottle fucked on the floor of the limo, and the two of us ending up shivering together against the wall of the butcher's shop.

*Lightning electrified the air around him. His lips were trying to form words.*

"He was upset," I remembered. "When I asked him what was wrong, he cried out, 'that man!'"

"Who did he mean?" Silvio asked.

"He said it with such terror I didn't ask. I don't think I really wanted to know."

"Yeah, I could understand that. Why get involved?"

"But I did get involved. I felt I had to do something." I sighed. Silvio stubbed out his cigarette and waited for me to continue, resting his hands behind his head like before, distracting me with this sexy pose. I closed my eyes and went on, going back to that moment as if I were really there again, as if I would see the boy, wet and trembling before me, instead of Silvio if I opened my eyes again.

\*

Instinctively I reached out and grabbed the boy's hand and held it in a gesture of protection.

"Thank you," he said gratefully.

The water splashed from the bricks onto his pale chest. It ran down in thick rivulets over his cock, a fountain of human skin that poured its flow into the gutter. When a patch of lightning, more distant now, lit him up, he looked just plain stark against the night. He squeezed his hand tightly in mine.

"Are you injured?" I asked him. "You know—"

"I don't know." His voice was unusually deep and resonant for his age. "I mean, it doesn't hurt back there. Well, not really. Just a little."

"No more than you'd expect?" I grinned, relieved he wasn't too concerned. I guess I expected him to grin back at me but he went someplace else. To Panic Land. He pressed his face close to mine and begged, "Help me! I've got to get out of here!"

"Out of where?"

"This city. I've got to get out right away. Tonight."

"Well, unless you've got a pair of wings or a ticket for a midnight flight to Paris, that might be difficult to arrange."

"I want to go to Binghamton. On the bus." He stated this matter-of-factly, his panic suddenly dissipated. I searched his eyes to see if they were still full of fear but they were pretty blank, deadpan.

It's then I thought of a wave crashing on some desolate shore, the water pulling back, spent, only to gather its momentum to come crashing down again. His behavior was like that wave, his impassivity only a lull. But unlike the storm around us that was winding down and moving on, his own turmoil was going nowhere fast.

"Before you leave for Binghamton, don't you think you'd better put some clothes on first? The bus might get a little drafty."

He didn't laugh at my stab at humor. He said simply, "I don't have any clothes." All right. If you don't have any clothes nothing much is going to crack you up. Curious and curiouser.

"Can you help me get some?"

I didn't see how I could refuse such a basic request. "We'll go to my apartment. You can pick something out. We're pretty much the same size."

"That's really nice." He smiled at me.

For the first time I noticed how deep set his eyes were, they were limpid, quiet eyes, what they call "doe-eyes"; I think they were a dark, creamy blue but it was hard to tell in the gloom.

His whole body was starting to relax a little in the face of some kind of hope. But he was still shivering.

"We might be able to find a cab now that the rain's letting up. Or we could walk. I live close by. That is if you're up to it."

"I just need to get out of here," he half-whined, which I took to mean, forget the fucking cab, let's go. I gave him my raincoat and holding the umbrella over both of us, navigated him through the lonely streets of the Meatpacking District. He was adept at winding his way around the empty trucks, back ends stuck in their garages, front ends jutting out over the curbs. And I saw him avoid the puddles that had formed around the wheels with precise steps, as if he were on some landmined terrain. He was a man on a mission, intent on getting from point A to point B without any slipups or unnecessary distractions.

By the time the Seminary loomed up in front of us, freshly washed by the rain, the chapel tower shimmering with its own inner polish under dark flying clouds, a few brave souls were starting to emerge from their apartments, just as we were heading into mine, their hands outstretched suspiciously as if they had to feel the empty air with their own flesh before they dared take another step. I half expected to see Tony and his buddies sprawled in the lobby with nothing to do except act like the consummate assholes they were. But they weren't there to gape, no one was. It was late, past midnight. The only sign of life in the place came from the Jack Russell in Bob's apartment directly across from mine. When I put the key in the door I heard the dog growling. I wondered if I was doing the right thing.

I made the boy take a hot shower immediately while I put some coffee on to brew. I thought he'd want to luxuriate under the steamy faucet but he was back out with me in a minute or two.

"How was it?" I asked, wanting a shower myself.

"Oh, great."

But could I trust him unwatched in my apartment while I showered? Was it risky? Not that I thought he'd steal anything, there wasn't much to take except some cash stuffed in a sock in the bottom drawer of my bedroom bureau. Anything else—the TV, the CD player, the microwave—he'd have to practically strap them on his back to get them out of here. It was just the idea of this stranger with free reign, even for a few minutes, in my own space, unsupervised. It would feel like an invasion of privacy, a loss of control. And yet I desperately wanted a shower, I was soaking wet. He looked so refreshed standing in front of me toweling his hair dry.

I hit on an idea. I fished a fluffy white terrycloth robe out of my closet for him to wear, handed him a steaming cup of fresh coffee and said, "Come on. Talk to me while I shower." He sat down nervously on the toilet while I hopped in and turned the handle full blast. The water was blood-warm, rejuvenating, and cast an unexpected sunny spell on me. I wasn't surprised that he spoke tentatively, in an unfocused way, but from what he was able to get out, I learned he was a dancer from Binghamton, that he was eighteen and that his name was Jared. Through the shower curtain he looked like an astral spirit, a white shadow with no grounding.

Steadily the water trickled down into both corners of my mouth, soaking my tongue, filling my cheeks so full I had to spit it out all over the tiles. Or swallow it. Out of the corner of my eye I saw his shadow rise and pace in circles, sometimes floating close to me. When I pulled the curtain back he was standing at the sink pouring his coffee down the drain.

"It makes me jittery," he explained.

No shit. But it wasn't just the caffeine. Could it be he was a junkie in need of a fix? After all he'd been wasted the first time I saw him, stumbling down my block. But there were no signs of track marks on him. There had to be a different explanation.

I purposely stood behind him to towel myself dry so I could watch us both in the mirror. He was in distinct focus now, unclouded by either the gauzy curtain or my imagination, bundled up in my white robe, his black hair still glistening wet, a few loose strands falling into his eyes, eyes you couldn't help looking at. They were pretty shell-shocked. Which didn't surprise me. What did surprise me were my own eyes: they looked just like his. A wave of nausea rumbled through my stomach while I wondered why. Sure, I'd been jolted by the nastiness in the back of the limo. Other than that…Jared hadn't done anything to me. I wasn't afraid of him. If anything I pitied him and wanted to help him feel easy in his mind. To help achieve that end I plastered an insipid smile on my face. He saw how bogus it was. Embarrassed, he gazed down into the sink, leaving me smiling in the mirror at myself.

I turned away. "You must be hungry. How about something to eat?"

"I don't have time."

Exasperated I snapped, "Of course you have time. Do you think there's a bus leaving for Binghamton at this hour? You'll have to wait till seven or eight in the morning."

That cold reality made him retreat into the living room and no doubt was responsible for his stunned look, his inertia, his curling himself up on the middle of my rug like a silent Buddha.

I pulled on a pair of sweats and a T-shirt, and casually settled down on the couch, my body language suggesting our only option was to chill. Until the sun came up. "You mentioned you're a dancer."

"Was," he answered. "Was a dancer."

"Oh, at eighteen your career is over?"

"That's right. Any gift I had for dancing is gone."

"How do you know that?"

"I just do. It's one of my stats now. That's all. My name is Jared, I'm eighteen, I come from Binghamton, I came to Chelsea, things got fucked up, my gift for dancing is gone."

"You're pretty hard on yourself."

"Myself? I'm not myself." His voice started trembling. "I don't know who I am but I'm not myself."

I almost went to him, to put my arm around him, to comfort him, but I decided to leave him alone. And let him talk. Almost always you learn more by moving back, not going up too close. I lay back on the couch, lit a candle and closed my eyes, breathing in the thin smoke from the flame and listened…

\*

The bits and pieces of his story came to me all out of order, with odd emphases, i.e. what I thought might be important he disposed of in a hurried, dismissive manner, while clinging to details of some frivolous moment with loving attention. His corruption of his recent past had no doubt been created to avoid facing some trauma, which I tried to hunt down between the lines. It was hard to recognize his clues, though, which, I felt, were never quite on the up and up, like those of a fraudulent mystery writer who flagrantly withholds them all, even through the final chapter.

After I'd reassembled his haywire adventures into a nice linear structure, I realized Jared's tale, except for one jarring oddity, was nothing out of the realm of possibility or even probability.

He'd come to the big city to fulfill the only ambition he'd had since he'd been old enough to spin like a top—to dance. It meant everything to him. The first step was to find a hip, avant-garde company to join. He longed for the camaraderie of other free spirits in a world far removed from gray, conformist Binghamton. In his mind's eye, they'd all live together in communal bliss, performing, traveling, dreaming and yes, even sleeping together—present-time harlequins full of piss and vinegar. But it was not to be. It didn't even come close.

Jared's dad put him on the bus for Port Authority the day after New Year's. He thought he'd freeze his ass off waiting for his dad to give him the five thousand dollars before he climbed on board. It was a kind gesture, the family didn't have much. His dad was making a ceremony out of it, it was a special moment, and Jared didn't want to rush him. His breath came out fast and formed an icy cloud between them. His dad finally handed him the envelope and he was off. As the bus turned onto the cold highway, Jared thought about his dad lingering inside the terminal, hesitating before going home to his waiting wife and three daughters, all younger than Jared, totally unworldly. He pictured his family sitting together in their modest living room, a row of paper dolls unfolded, holding hands, one of the dolls torn off at the end, missing.

Jared had one gay friend in Binghamton, a librarian fifteen years his senior. He'd taken a recent vacation to Manhattan and turned Jared onto the place he'd stayed— a rundown hotel in Chelsea at the end of 23rd Street on the West Side Highway. It offered weekly and monthly rates. It also offered hourly rates. I knew the place. It offered anything to anybody who had a few bucks and fewer expectations. Just a seedy hole in the wall, its three-story facade a dreary amalgam of broken bricks and twisting fire escapes, tattered curtains blowing in the windows of rooms that looked empty but weren't.

Apparently Jared had been oblivious to the other guests; happy with a cheap monthly rate, he'd taken a back room that looked out onto the rubble of a construction site and he'd been too green to mind the whores, cons, addicts, and nuts he had to pass in the hall on the way to the common toilet. Nor had he minded the stone-faced proprietress, ageless, whom I'd seen every time I passed by, night or day, sitting in the open doorway on a folding chair bathed in an arc of pink light. For New York, spread out like a well-trod welcome mat, had called his name too. And he was eager to check it out.

It's hard for a young gay guy coming from the land of the overly curious not to feel heady at the prospect of anonymity. But even anonymity can be fleeting. It didn't take long for him to notice the blatant stares of horny men, subtle as hot potatoes. It turned him on to be the center of some glamour game as opposed to being shunned as a freak on the streets of Binghamton. He ate up every bit of attention thrown his way and soon forgot about the stage he'd always dreamed of because he was already on one, a stage that required no greater skill from a performer than being able to walk onto it. Every street was easy street if you were eighteen, still fresh-faced from the North Country and able to flirt back. Time was your best friend who only laughed at your indiscretions and looked the other way.

Jared had put off a few auditions so he could enjoy a few affairs. I hardly blamed him. He also wanted to look more chic, even foppish. He began hanging out in vintage clothing shops, especially in the East Village. One of his favorites was a shop on Avenue A north of Houston, which always had some funky, sexy item hanging on the racks. One day he saw a pair of red shoes in the window. He paused for a moment but passed them by. Around midnight he happened to pass the shop again. This time the shoes seemed irresistible. They sparkled in the dark, deep and hot, all on their own accord. The next day he bought them. He knew some day the right occasion would come up where he could show them off.

They say there's a whole world out there and Jared had been dying to find it. At first. But it soon became apparent it was too much for him, such a vast space, so he shut himself off into one inhospitable corner of it.

The days passed not as he'd hoped but as they pleased. What a nightmare. Waiting his turn with a group of other dancers, slowly realizing he was locked in some diabolical pattern of failure. During every audition, when it was his turn to be called forward he was unable to exhibit the graceful style that had made his artistry unique; in fact he couldn't even execute a series of simple steps. Dismayed, he was unable to make anything other than the most awkward, ugly movements. Sometimes he heard astonished laughter or gasps or kind words. It was all the same to him. Shocked and embarrassed, he fled. There was always some new man who understood. Who said it didn't matter. There was safety in numbers. The new men outnumbered the auditions twenty to one.

He was licked and he knew it. He gave into a short existence of poisoned oblivion until the money ran out and he was flat broke. In fact, he'd been thrown out of his room that very morning. He felt feeble, agitated. He wanted to go home.

He didn't like talking about the sex he'd had, and if an unsavory memory accidentally came up, he fluffed it off as if it had never really happened. But he had to admit to the debauchery in the back of the limo. I'd been there, seen it. So he bit the bullet. Yes, in farewell he'd strutted his stuff in the parade, a defiant gesture to the city, the same as giving it the finger, he explained, and he'd found a place at last where he could wear those red shoes. He'd gotten as high as he could, thanks to some twinks marching alongside him who'd been so knocked out by his good looks they'd been glad to share whatever goodies they had.

That night he lurched toward the river. Hadn't somebody mentioned fireworks? And so four young men in a limo, out on the prowl, had spotted him spread out on one of the piers, depressed and stoned out of his mind. The end.

But not quite. I didn't buy it. He'd fucked up and had to leave town. I could understand his bitterness and disappointment. But why the fear?

"You didn't talk much about the hotel," I said. "How did you spend your time there?"

"I can't remember much. Some things maybe…"

Perspiration started running down his forehead. It was still dark out, thin inky branches blowing in a wet post-storm breeze against my French windows, one or two insinuating themselves through the open panes, right into the room.

It was a transient hotel. New faces came and went, most of them troubled. Jared hadn't known much about trouble so he didn't recognize it in anyone else. The transients were just human matter he occasionally bumped into in the middle of the hall. He never thought about them unless one of their interests clashed with his. Like the night of the stomach cramps. Coming out of nowhere not long after midnight. He had to make his way down the hall in complete darkness, feeling his way against the wall, cursing the broken bulb overhead. When he flipped the bathroom switch nothing happened. He lit a match. The bulb above the sink had been removed. Continually striking matches, he wiped off the toilet seat, bolted the door behind him, dropped his pants and sat down. It was a false alarm; he felt he had to go but couldn't. He slouched on the toilet in the dark. Before long, an incredible golden beam of light appeared under the crack in the door wavering back and forth. It must have been the beam from a flashlight. Probably one of the transients wanting to use the toilet.

"I'll be just a minute," Jared called out.

There was no reply.

But the beam didn't go away. Instead it got stronger and seeped further under the door, almost reaching Jared's feet. The person on the other side had to be crouched on his knees in order to direct that beam so precisely. *Jesus Christ,* Jared thought, *I'm just trying to take a fucking crap and this motherfucker is busting my nuts over it.* He knew who it was. That wino in the room next to his. He'd heard bottles rolling across the floor at all hours of the night.

Suddenly the beam pulled back and disappeared, but

Jared smelled something acrid and heard something sizzle. Could the wino have set his fucking room on fire?

Furious he jumped off the seat, pulled his pants back up, unbolted the door, and threw it open.

The hall was dark. When Jared lit a match he saw it was empty.

Striking matches all the way, he stormed down to the wino's room. The door was ajar. Jared knocked and when no one answered he pushed his way in, sending a bottle crashing against the floor. But other than that there was no disturbance. No smoke, no fire. The light of the last match framed the wino's head in a halo, illuminating his bloated red face, jittery even in deep sleep, his hands gripping the pillow in a vise. Jared turned away, wincing.

Somehow he groped his way back to the bathroom in the pitch dark. He felt for the toilet seat, dropped his pants again, eased himself down, relieved, and kicked the door shut.

He had been waiting for Jared behind the door. Hiding. Now he started to light up. First his feet began to crackle and sputter like freshly lit sparklers. Then the electricity burst through his entire body, fusing each limb together with fire, jump-starting that half-dead fleshless bone between his legs into a functional incendiary penis, scattering rich glowing gold veins through his vibrant death's head, static crackling inside the blackened burned beads that passed for eyes, a putrid sensuality settling onto that wide, ridiculing mouth as the white teeth parted, spitting sparks all over Jared's body.

He raised his seismic arms and jerked forward, a living, moving electric field. Jared screamed. The thing clasped one frenzied hand over Jared's mouth and pinned his shoulders down with the other, keeping him sprawled across the toilet, quiet...

The Electric Man came to him at will. Jared never knew when to expect him. He came day and night, rain or shine. The visits increased as the weeks went by.

Sometimes Jared would know he was near from the smell of burning wires or the sound of an electrical discharge. Other times he could see him coming.

One night Jared peered out his window and spotted him making his way spasmodically, at peak voltage, across the scattered debris of the deserted construction site. Another time the Electric Man was waiting quite patiently on the fire escape, sending off weak emitter signals, searching for Jared with his dazed eyes. At the end he could just come right through the walls, leaving burn marks on the plaster. With a sinking feeling, Jared knew there were no locks or bolts to use against him. And it was pointless to hide. The Electric Man would seek him out, hunt him down, never leave him in peace. Whenever the Electric Man appeared, Jared had no choice but to lean back against the wall in resignation and let the Electric Man seethe and convulse his way towards him. Jared closed his eyes tight.

I shook him awake.

Yawning, he opened his eyes, blinking at me in confusion, wondering why I was rousing him from the most pleasant of dreams. In other words he had no memory of what he'd just told me. He was as fresh and as immature as the dawn that softly curled around us.

I was a little frazzled though. I realized I wasn't dealing with a child who had nightmares but with a grown man who was suffering from delusions. And he hadn't been asleep when he'd been telling me his story, he'd only nodded off after the point where the Electric Man had him pinned against the wall. I could see why he wanted to get out of here. I wanted to help him if I could.

I called Port Authority. There was a bus leaving for Binghamton in an hour and a half. I offered to take him to the station in a cab. He agreed. He was willing to eat a couple of pieces of toast and drink some orange juice. While he breakfasted I suggested he get hold of a therapist when he got back to Binghamton, somebody who could help him sort things out. I was gentle, I didn't say psychiatrist. I also had him leave me a contact number of that librarian friend of his who'd turned him onto Manhattan and that hotel in the first place—just in case I felt the need to check up on him. In the bedroom we found him some suitable clothes and tennis shoes, and I relieved my sock tucked away in the bottom of my bureau drawer of a couple of hundred dollars. Which I gave to him. Incredibly his eyes started to tear up as he thanked me profusely. I couldn't take that and walked away from him, relaxing in my rocking chair by the window, telling him to go get dressed and to make it fast. We had limited time. I heard some sniffles as he left the room.

Outdoors, bees were buzzing in the common garden, thrilled to be among the full droopy roses during one of the ripest weeks in summer.

A chunk of time passed and there was no sign of Jared. The moment came when I had to knock on the bathroom door, to hurry him up. "Dressed yet, Jared?"

All I heard was a tiny moan.

Alarmed I pushed the door open. He was squatting by the toilet, a trickle of blood dripping out of his ass onto some sheets of toilet paper he'd arranged carefully on the floor beneath him. My white terrycloth robe was lying beside him, and I could see a bright new bloodstain soaking through the material. We stared at each other, our mouths open.

I finally licked my rapidly drying lips and said, "We'd better get you to a doctor."

"No," he insisted. "It's not serious."

"You might have a piece of glass—"

"No, I don't. It's only because I tried to move my bowels. It tore the skin, that's all. There's a little cut. It's nothing serious. I can have it looked at in Binghamton if it doesn't heal. But look, the bleeding's stopped. I'm fine." Then he added, "I've got to get out of here, no matter what."

I could only agree. I thought he would be better off. To be honest I wanted him to go too so I could have my life back, even though it had only disappeared for one night.

As Jared dressed I put on a pair of gloves and ignoring his protests to let him clean up the mess, I flushed the tissues down the toilet and wrapped the robe in a plastic bag and carried it to the trash chute at the end of the hall.

As fate would have it, Bob McBride was just leaving his apartment to take Big Deal out for his morning constitutional. "What you got there?" he asked exuberantly.

"Nothing much, just the usual clutter," I responded cheerily to keep him far from the truth.

*

Silvio lit another cigarette. I hadn't looked over at him for quite awhile. I was glad he was there.

I climbed back into bed with him, leaving the rocking chair to creak a few times on its own. Laying my head in the crook of his arm, I ran my fingers thoughtfully along his chest.

71

"Before we left for the bus station," I said, "he insisted on repaying me, on giving me something in return. For my help. All he could come up with were the red shoes. So that's how I ended up with them…I wore them tonight for the first time."

"Ever hear from the guy?"

"Never."

"Think about him?"

"No. He needs help, though. He's got some weird psychological disorder. What do you think?"

He paused for a moment. "I think you should suck my dick."

That's right, deflect your own inability to come up with an explanation by devaluing my whole experience and by reasserting your dominance over me. What better way to literally keep me silent than by shoving your dick down my throat?

But apparently I had it wrong.

He explained. "That bit about the kid being fucked with the bottle in the back of the limo. You have to admit that's a turn-on. I get hard just thinking about it."

"And the rest of his story?"

"I was drifting in and out. The grass you know."

He saw my long face.

"I was listening," he insisted. "I caught most of it."

I doubted that. He'd gotten the gist of it, that's all. Maybe there wasn't any more to get. My annoyance started to drift away. I mean why shouldn't Silvio get stiff over the fuck in the back of the limo? He was a red-blooded All-American male. What did I expect? Anyway he sure liked those shoes.

"Come on, baby, suck me like a good bitch."

As tired as I was, I tried.

Afterwards I'd have to say he fucked me like a real

bastard—he'd gotten his second wind. He held my legs in the air, wide-open, and slammed his cock inside me. Not much finesse here. But after I got used to it, I went with it, just gave in. And then suddenly I really got into a rhythm with him and felt a little of the delirium of last night when he'd fucked me on the living room table. I didn't want him to stop and was disappointed when he came so soon. The power of sex. I was starting to understand it gets you on its trip even when you don't want to go. And usually makes you glad you went.

Groaning he pulled the rubber off his cock. It was full of cum.

"Shit," he said carrying it at arm's length into the bathroom and dropping it into the toilet. He didn't take time to flush, but hurried back to bed, flopping onto his stomach and turning his head to the wall.

"Before you turn out all your lights, what's your last name?" I asked lightly. "Leave me with something to ruminate over."

"Brancato."

*Silvio Brancato.* "That's a beautiful name," I whispered to my sleep-filled partner and I meant it. Of course Silvio Brancato thought my name was Tim but he wouldn't give a damn if he found out it wasn't. I turned over on my side away from him. We both slept as the sun rose.

Silvio woke like clockwork at nine a.m. He jumped out of bed and hit the shower without a word. Of course I woke up when he woke up and just hoped I'd be able to crash after he left. Then I remembered. I was supposed to meet Reg and Allison at the Metropolitan Museum in an hour and a half for the Blake exhibit. I didn't have a clear head, I still felt tired from the grass and I hadn't had enough sleep; also I didn't see how I could make the transition from the excitement of last night into a more mundane afternoon. Last night might not only color the coming moments but swallow them whole. But I'd have to deal with it. It was too late to reach either of them to cancel with any kind of plausible excuse.

Silvio left in pretty much of a rush with the same words he'd used when we parted on the Village streets a week ago, "We'll see you later." He had lingered a moment though when he pulled up his underpants, making sure I was watching while he gave his cock a few shakes before putting it away. All in all I thought our time together had gone really well.

\*

*Satan Watching the Endearments of Adam and Eve.* It is night. Adam and Eve lie naked in their bower filled with pink corals, bluebells, and laurel. Bulbous peonies droop over their bodies. Adam gazes into Eve's eyes with a profound joy, one borne of comfort, passion and a new awakening. Eve has sensed paradise for the first time. She has coupled with Adam and no longer feels the fear of separation. But in the dark sky above floats the angel Satan, propelled by magnificent gossamer wings. Incestuously coiled around him is a fearful serpent with a crimson head. Satan hovers over Adam and Eve in their bower, provoked by the innocence of their embraces, and stares down at Eve who gazes past Adam to meet the angel's eyes, which are like two brilliant red stars. His beautiful lips are parted with lust and his muscular torso is coldly seductive. Lowering her eyes, Eve blushes. Then as Satan drifts away, she lethargically plucks a bluebell and drops it absentmindedly into Adam's outstretched palm.

All of them are naked, but not only that, they are gloriously naked. Adam and Satan are built like brick shithouses and Eve is Junoesque. I wanted to slip into Blake's luminous, mystical watercolor and insinuate myself into their midst, become a quiet fourth figure, unnoticed, unwanted, well content to smell their ripe flesh and watch them cradling each other in ever-changing configurations.

"What do you think?" Reg asked.

I shrugged. Interpreting Blake's illustrations for Milton's *Paradise Lost* was a kind of personal journey, wasn't it? Everybody saw the same imagery but experienced its meaning differently. Anyway, I didn't have any words for him, they had all raced through my head and floated to parts unknown like Satan in the night sky. Not so Allison. Fortunately she saved the day by remarking on Blake's compelling vision, his delicate use of color, his affinity for Milton. She even commented on his life. Unacknowledged and impoverished, he lived alone in the world of his imagination but was able to leave us gifts in his *Paradise Lost* illustrations far beyond any that his worldly counterparts could offer.

"I'm pretty impressed," I said. "More than that— I'm blown away...I'm also tired as hell." I gave them an enigmatic half-smile that made them wonder. I hadn't told them about Silvio yet, though I was dying to.

When something exciting happens to you, you want to tell the first person who'll listen all about it. Your best friend. A perfect stranger. You aren't picky. You just need to let it all out...The problem was I thought Reg and Allison just wouldn't get it. I knew them. They'd think I'd been used and that I should be ashamed of my lowdown behavior. Only I wasn't ashamed, and I'd used Silvio as much as he'd used me. It was a two-way street.

Still…Maybe I'd better find that perfect stranger. One who'd listen blankly while I shouted Silvio's name out loud and admitted I wanted more. Fuck. What was going on here? I still must be high. Why else couldn't I shake off the thrills of last night? I wasn't great company for Reg and Allison. I definitely should have crashed after Silvio left and let them fend for themselves. Since I was only half with them, they'd have been better off.

Surprisingly, Allison put her arm around my waist and whispered, "You seem so happy. Light as air. What's going on?"

Then I was right. I'd junked a lot of baggage that had kept me pinned to the ground and now I was free-floating, able to pursue life.

"I'm having an affair," I whispered back. Since I wouldn't have felt any better if I'd said more accurately, 'I fucked my brains out last night,' I let the cleaner version stand. "But don't tell Reg yet."

"Oh, no, not until you give me the go-ahead."

"No thirty questions?"

"Not even one. Just go at your own pace."

I kissed her on the cheek.

Reg, meanwhile, had himself surrounded by members of a German soccer team, strapping, athletic males bombarding him in sharp pitiless English with questions that covered the waterfront: How do these museum headphones work? What is there to do in Times Square? Can we play soccer on the Great Lawn? How do you get a green card?… Of course, flustered though he was, Reg was in his element since he loved to play the teacher and to give advice. I chuckled and returned to Blake.

*Adam and Eve Sleeping.* Two female winged angels with long golden hair float on the night sky lit only by a half moon and a solitary star and pause above Adam and Eve sleeping on their flower-filled bower. Adam's sleep is deep; he's exhausted following a night of sexual oblivion with Eve. But Eve's sleep is restless. By her ear is a putrid toad with a slimy green protruding tongue. The angels are alarmed as they recognize that the toad is Satan, come down to earth in one of his thousand disguises. The toad is croaking insistently in her ear and she appears to be half-listening as she dreams, a gentle smile forming on her face as if she were hearing celestial music. The angels regard Adam with pity as he lies in repose, unaware of the coming darkening of his own faith. Then, afraid of Satan, they begin to glide away towards the solitary star in the dark night while willing themselves to forget what they have just witnessed.

Again I wanted to enter that watercolor and lie between them, Adam and Eve, become entwined with them, listening to the croaking of the toad Satan and the lightly flapping wings of the departing angels.

"Getting hungry?" Allison asked, sliding her arm around me once again.

"Well, I am." Reg had extricated himself from the entire German soccer team and was ready for the picnic we'd planned to cap off our Blake visit.

"What did you bring?" I asked.

"You'll see," Allison laughed. "First I have to go get the basket at the coat check upstairs. You guys can stay here. I'll meet you at Turtle Pond in about ten minutes."

Thank God Allison was so good to us since she worked as a caterer and had access to all kinds of leftover goodies from really upscale events. She called herself the ultimate corporate raider. Since the firm that employed her loved her to death, because she was so pleasant on the job, so unobtrusive a presence, they insisted she be the one to make off with any of the spoils that remained. So she always came to her gigs prepared. With that ingratiating smile and two large empty shopping bags.

Reg and I took advantage of the short time remaining by becoming engrossed in, guess what, more Blake. *The Temptation and Fall of Eve.* Standing side by side we contemplated Eve's downfall, her rejection of Adam in favor of the serpent whose thick scales coil around her body in a vise, its flaming head staring cunningly at her while she makes her fateful, irreversible decision. Adam turns away from both her and the tree of life which still bears succulent fruit but whose roots are now jagged knives that tear down into the earth. Hands outstretched, Adam begs the heavens for help, but nothing is sent to comfort him except lightning bolts in a pitch black sky in the middle of the day. Eve bites into a piece of succulent golden fruit. I noticed that Reg and I weren't viewing Eve alone. A third had joined us—one of the German soccer players—a straggler who held back from the rest of his teammates as they left the gallery in a tightly-knit group. Tall and lean with long blond curls, he had a rapt expression on his face, a heightened look in his blue eyes and a curious smile on his face that seemed out of place. Flanked by Reg on one side and the German on the other, I felt penned in, unable to concentrate. The guy was a little rude. He could have waited till Reg and I had stepped back before pressing in so close. Trying my best to ignore him, I turned my attention back to Eve who seemed to me, after tasting the fruit, to have become consumed by some unanticipated fear. Desperately she tries to find Adam but he had already been swallowed up by the dark sky. She is all alone in the pleasure garden. In hell. The German looked around surreptitiously then pulled something out of his shorts, brought it to his nose and fumbled for a second before taking a quick sniff. A moment later he tensed up, then sighed, and his curious smile widened, became a grin. He never took his eyes away from Eve. As he moved his hand back to his shorts I saw it held a tiny clear vial of powder. Reg saw it too. We made eye contact and moved away.

"Coke," Reg said when we were out of earshot. "That jerk's snorting coke."

"Is that it?" I asked. "What—to intensify his experience? That's redundant. Blake gives you everything you need."

"And then some," Reg agreed. I wondered if he meant Blake was a little too much, too intense. I didn't think so. I loved the power of those watercolors, the way they had pulled me into them and held me there. Except for the last one. Something had made me walk away from it prematurely.

Turtle Pond, formerly Belvedere Lake, was not too far into the park, close to the back of the Met. We'd chosen that spot because it was a humid afternoon, miserable actually, and we didn't want to go too far afield. We just wanted to stake our claim on the nearest patch of shade and be done with it. And we knew we'd find it there. We spread out on a smooth sloping rock that lay in the shadow of two crisscrossing elms and looked down onto the pond. A few turtles sunned along its edges.

Allison's latest corporate raid had been a winner. She covered the rock with an impeccable white linen cloth. We ate slices of roast beef, fettuccini, crusty peasant bread, endive salad, and raspberries, all washed down with sparkling water kept chilled in a cooler. And Allison had managed to hijack some crystal glasses and real silverware. Only it was too hot to talk. Our senses were dulled. The heavy repast only dulled them further.

Reg wrote furiously in a notebook. Peeking, I saw he was jotting down thoughts about Blake's concave, symmetrical designs. Stuff that bored me. Allison winked at me once or twice in a maternal way, assuring me our secret was being kept. About Silvio. Kept from Daddy, I thought, because preposterously I pictured myself as their child, Reg stern and practical and Allison wise and kind, and me stopped from turning into an adult because I was still full of wonder. I was putting myself down, I realized, and stopped these thoughts cold. I had different sensibilities, that was all. And different strengths.

With a start I remembered Frank and I had sat on this same rock, under these same crisscrossing elms, on the evening of the summer solstice six or seven years ago, only it had been cool then and we had tried to count evening stars appearing like ghosts in a white sky. Frank kept looking at his watch, insisting we stay put until it was dark so he could tell me the exact length of the longest day of the year. Only it had been so pleasant we'd fallen asleep and missed the turning, waking up much later together in the dark. Laughing, we'd walked home together and vowed we'd try again next year.

The Swedish Cottage, set back from the pond in a briar thicket, was known for its Sunday afternoon puppet shows. A performance had just ended and kids were streaming out, many of them pausing at the pond to take a look at the turtles. I don't know why kids are fascinated by animals and reptiles and dinosaurs. They never did much for me. But most are and this noisy, excitable bunch was no exception. They wasted no time in flopping down in the dirt and used a long stick to try to reach one of the turtles paddling in the middle of the pond.

Passing them on the path and hardly affording them a glance was a girl of about ten or eleven with an almost painfully erect bearing. I don't know if you could call her pretty but she had a presence. She wore a vanilla silk chiffon sun dress that went to the knees and a pair of thin sandals. Her abundant light brown hair was swept up in a chignon, held in place by a bone comb. She moved to the opposite end of the pond, away from the common rabble, where she too eyed one of the turtles who was swimming aimlessly in circles as quick as his little fat legs could propel him. She stared at the turtle, not with fascination, repulsion, or delight, like the other kids, but with a glacial air that separated without question the creature's lowliness from her eminent state. I thought she might be anorexic. A young ballerina. But she exhibited neither the insecurities nor the trembling passions I associated with ballerinas. Their raw drive and emotions seemed beneath her. She was a queen, not an artist.

"Sidonie!" a woman called her from nearby. The voice was low and rich and was unmistakably Southern. The girl turned and joined her parents waiting for her on the path, the mother just as elegant and mannered as her daughter, the father tall, dark haired with glasses, erudite and composed. They took her by the hand and started off along the path.

"Wait a minute," I said. "I've seen them before."

"That family with the little girl?" Allison asked.

"Yeah. Haven't you?"

"No," Allison said.

Reg added his two cents. "They are completely unfamiliar."

"Oh, come on. Think. This is going to drive me nuts. I know I've seen them somewhere before. You have too. In Chelsea, probably."

"I doubt that woman slings hash at the local Greek diner or rents DVDs at Alan's Alley. Places you are likely to frequent," Reg observed tartly. "They're part of the upper crust who most likely have a chauffeured Mercedes-Benz waiting for them outside the entrance to the Met."

"Reg, they could have a townhouse in Chelsea," Allison argued. "It's in the realm of possibility."

"No, not a townhouse," I said slowly but no further enlightenment came. I couldn't place them in any context.

I didn't have an easy time of it when I got back home. All I felt was the emptiness around me. How could I top the night before? It was crazy to want to do the same thing over again right away but I did. I was still horny. I considered calling Silvio. Just to see what he was up to. Well, to see if he was in the mood to get into more role-playing games. I even picked up the phone and started to dial his number. Then I put the receiver back down. I'd prefer he call me. To show his interest. I wanted to be the pursued and not the pursuer. Well, if I didn't have him here right now I had the remnants of our night together and I didn't clean them up or throw them out but kept them proudly on display throughout the rest of the night as if they were the treasured mementos of some twenty year relationship. Silvio's empty beer can on the table next to the couch. My G-string and red shoes on the middle of the living room carpet. An empty condom wrapper on the floor near the window. The bed sheets stained and rumpled. In fact, I slept on them. But I didn't fall asleep immediately. I tossed and turned.

Just as I was sinking into sleep, the electric light came on as it sometimes does when the mind isn't resisting remembering. It wasn't them I'd seen before. It was him. The father who'd walked hand in hand with Sidonie. The masturbator from the Seminary. There wasn't any doubt in my mind that they were one and the same man.

*

The truth is I'd thought of him once or twice, in disgust.

The memory could raise itself like an ether in some watery part of my brain and come to the top but then it would subside. And occupied as I was with my own recovery, going to meetings to give and get support during the long process of grieving, waiting to hear from the State Court system about the upcoming exam, Silvio, and the humdrum to-ings and fro-ings that connect the days, I'd nearly forgotten the incident completely. Until I saw him that second time, a picture of respectability, oh so proper, strolling with his genteel wife and stately daughter under a canopy of thick-leaved trees in Central Park. Seeing this new side of him did make me wonder about his story. What could such a man be like who lived this double life with relative ease?

Many afternoons in late September found me on the Seminary grounds, either to pray or read or just enjoy the change of foliage as autumn began. His bench facing the glass chapel doors was usually empty except for a few yellowing leaves that had slipped down off the darkening overhanging maple.

It's hard to imagine but sometimes you eventually do come face to face with what you've managed to conjure up, for better or worse. On a Friday, about a month after I'd seen him in the park, I went grocery shopping. I was carrying three heavy bags back from the store, clutching them under my arms while struggling to insert the key in the lobby door, watched by Tony, apparently on a break, leaning against the brick wall, casually smoking a cigarette and anxious not to help. I finally got the key to turn the lock and I staggered inside, so preoccupied I hardly noticed him sitting on the banquette in the middle of my lobby punching in numbers on his cell phone. But when I passed close to him I realized I was face to face with him again. The masturbator. What wild coincidence could have brought him directly into my building? Things like this just didn't happen.

I turned my face away, stepping quickly toward the elevator, mortified more than angry at this unexpected confrontation, just wanting to get upstairs and into my apartment as soon as possible.

But he had come up behind me. "Excuse me."

"Yes?" I stared straight ahead.

"You live here, don't you?"

Reluctantly I admitted, "I do. Why?"

"Maybe you can help me." He smiled graciously. "If you don't mind, that is?"

His voice was low and gentle. And soothing. Had I made a mistake? I looked closely. No. Absolutely not. It was him. Tall, a couple of inches over six feet and angular, with hunched shoulders. It was the same man who'd been sitting on the bench outside the chapel that day, there was no mistaking it. And I realized my first impression of his age had been close to the mark— even with his shock of dark hair streaked with just one or two white strands, and even with his heavy-rimmed glasses, he couldn't have been much past forty. His expression was one of a stranger in distress from some bygone era.

It asked me plaintively: How can you not come to aid of a man of such refinement?

It was clear he didn't recognize me. Holding onto my bags nervously I asked somewhat skeptically, "How can I help you?"

"I was wondering if you know a tenant by the name of Sam Martinson who lives on the fifteenth floor."

"No, I can't say that I do."

"Oh, dear. I was afraid of that. There wasn't a label with the name Martinson next to any of the buzzers outside. That's why I wanted to check the directory in the lobby. Oh, you see, a very nice lady let me through the door. I rather think she thought I lived here. Of course I don't. We had a nice chat about the restoration going on at the Seminary…"

His words petered out and I could see he was running back the hours, trying to place me. "No luck, I'm afraid," he continued more slowly and carefully, his mind laboring, "his name wasn't on the directory inside either."

"Maybe you have the wrong address."

"No," he said. "That's quite impossible." He paused a moment and then I could see the gig was up. It had been the mention of the Seminary that made him finally realize the connection between us and he frowned slightly, his lips parting in a silent gasp. Hurriedly he put on a friendly mask, keeping up the pretense that we were complete strangers, and wasn't the weather beautiful this time of year?

Only I didn't play along. I put my hand up to stop him rattling on. "Why?" I asked in a quiet voice.

"I know…the Seminary," he said despondently. Then added in a heartfelt way, "What can you think of me?"

"Right now, nothing."

"Fair enough," he replied. "I'd like a chance to explain. No, to apologize—and explain." I was silent. "Please, I owe it to you. Won't you even listen to me."

"I don't know," I said confused.

"Let's go upstairs, not stand here with everybody listening in."

"To my apartment?"

He looked injured. "I think you can see for yourself I'm not a dangerous person, just a human being." He added, smiling, "Much like yourself, I suppose."

"It doesn't make sense to take you upstairs," I said, yet responding to the clear argument he was making for his case. I waffled. "There's no one by the name of Sam Martinson living here, is there?"

"There is."

"Well, there's no fifteenth floor. We only have twelve."

If he was irritated by my reply he only flinched and tried not to show it. "There's no fifteenth floor then," he said. "But there's your floor."

"Yes, the lucky seventh," I said.

He laughed. "Well, then…"

"I don't know," I replied as the elevator doors opened and I stepped inside and he followed me. It was now or never—whether or not to order him out. It turned out to be never.

In the ride up in the elevator I scolded myself. This was totally inappropriate, absolutely unacceptable, but who was looking, anyway? A part of me was intrigued by what he'd have to say. That was the same part of me that had liberated myself to explore the unknown, even the forbidden. And this move was surely forbidden by anyone's measure.

As for him, he leaned passively against the side of

the elevator, hands in his pockets, seemingly unconcerned about anything and exhibiting a cool reserve.

As I unlocked the door and brought him inside, I damned myself for what I was doing. "Look," I turned to him quickly and said earnestly, "I think I've made a mistake. You'd better leave."

But he seized the opportunity to calm me down, to tell me everything would be all right, that he wanted to make amends for his egregious behavior. It's not that I didn't believe him, I had no idea what to think, but I was surprised to see how hard he was working at ingratiating himself to me. To be light, conversational, my new best friend.

He extended his hand warmly. How could I not at least shake it?

"I'm Crewe James," he announced confidently, starting to stroll around the living room, stuffing his hands back in his pockets, taking everything in with a pronounced vigor as if he approved of all that lay before him. Suddenly, in a childlike way, he exclaimed, "Oh, this is wonderful! You love books too!"

It was true, I did, and there were more than a few of them strewn around on tables and kitchen countertops, some favorite mysteries by Ruth Rendell, Fredric Brown, Margaret Millar, as well as a couple of bookshelves full of literary classics in the corner.

"What do you prefer?" he persisted. "Fiction or nonfiction?"

"Fiction, mostly. A lot of French literature in particular."

"Really? I read a lot of non-fiction. Politics, economics, history."Why did I detect that he felt reading fiction was a lesser endeavor? He hadn't said so. But did

I care what he thought? He was going about his business here, making himself at home, and I was standing back letting him, as he gently pried and probed, fascinated by his technique of trying to insinuate himself in my life. It was so obvious and cheeky that it was riveting. We seemed to be playing at some intrigue without direction or rules.

I didn't introduce myself and he didn't ask my name; I assumed he wasn't interested. But when he started questioning me about this and that—Where was I from? How long had I lived here? Did I like this building?—he called me by name, "John Laith." Was he a psychic who had zeroed in on my name off the directory in the lobby? No. Without being obvious, he had no doubt seen my name on the rent bill lying on top of the small desk in the entryway.

He hadn't gotten around to explaining the reason for his behavior at the Seminary. He was more interested in engaging me in small talk, taking a bemused and artless delight in anything he learned about me. And I let him—I didn't press him yet for the explanation he had promised. Like a mind reader seizing the initiative because something had told him I'd permit a further step toward camaraderie, he requested something cold to drink, just like an expected guest might have done. "A beer, maybe. I don't like troubling you."

"No trouble, only I don't have any beer. I've run out." I thought of Silvio who'd finished the last one. "I don't drink alcohol myself."

"Oh, no? Well, cold water would do."

I had ice water in the fridge. I poured us a couple of glasses. Taking his glass in hand, he sauntered over to the sofa and sat down with a "May I?"

"You already have."

He laughed. "You're right. In that case, why don't you join me?"

"You've certainly put on the charm. Why?"

He seemed perplexed. "I'm just being myself, friendly. If you call it putting on the charm, then why not? I don't see any harm in it."

"But who are you really and why did you do what you did?"

"I've told you who I am. Crewe James, a man who made a terrible mistake and is apologizing to you now. As to why, I'm sorry, I don't have all the answers. I did it suddenly, inexplicably, without any thought. How do I know? I'd never done anything like that before. I must have been feeling a lot of stress…I must have been triggered somehow…well, never mind…but you, won't you at least accept my apology…and if not, why not?"

"If you put it like that, what can I say. I do accept it but I still want you to know it freaked me out. I was frazzled by the whole incident."

"Of course." He looked up at me and smiled as if he understood perfectly. "That would go without saying, I should think."

He took another sip of water and gazed around my living room with an easy appreciation and sense of relief, now that that was off his chest. "I must say this is a nice spot. I like your view of the Seminary."

The sun had started its descent, throwing its golden hues against the building's rust red bricks. Somewhere close by a bird squawked angrily. We both laughed. "My goodness, wonder what that's all about?" he asked.

I looked down, embarrassed to have been laughing with him.

"Of course, I have a nice view. Very nice. Of all of Central Park. I own a penthouse apartment on Central

Park West with a large wraparound terrace. Incredible Park views and of the east side of Manhattan as well. I guess that's one of the benefits of being in the real estate business. I own several apartment buildings. You see? Several important buildings, actually," he added self-importantly under his breath, as if he were speaking to himself alone.

I think I was supposed to feel a little cowed, but I wasn't sure what I felt.

He sighed and was quiet for a moment then leaned his head back. His fingers rested on his leg. Sort of off in the clouds, he began to tap his fingers.

Then, "John Laith," he said, suddenly standing up. "John Laith…"

He sauntered to the open French windows, breathing in some air. "I do like you, you know," he murmured, gazing towards the chapel.

"You don't know me."

"You're a pretty quick study. And I know when there's a bit of chemistry in the air."

There was. But how? I'm not sure why I was attracted to this kind of rather average looking man with elaborately studied manners who used turns of phrases from what seemed like some earlier era. Maybe that in itself was why; here was someone intelligent, worldly, with whom I didn't feel quite the stranger in a strange land like I did with Silvio. There was talking and listening going on. And curiosity from both sides.

"Isn't there?" he asked. "We're attracted to each other, am I right?"

I knew what he meant by "attracted" by his tone of voice.

And it was true. I soon found myself pulled up against him, returning a passionate kiss and feeling him rubbing my hand over his bulge. At first it was disconcerting to realize I'd seen what he had down in his pants already but with the next kiss it didn't seem to matter, nothing did. We stood bathed in golden light, entwined.

I don't know how long it was before he drew a small silver pipe from the pocket of his corduroy jacket and asked me, "Do you mind?"

"Hmm…" So he liked to smoke too, like Silvio. And of course, who was I kidding, I'd found I liked it too. But this wasn't like being with Silvio. Here I was shy. There was no need for vulgar words or provocative poses or running into the bedroom to put on the red shoes and a G-string. In fact I was in a quandary about how I would feel with my clothes off in front of him, nervous, like a schoolboy getting naked in front of someone for the first time.

"Let me use the kitchen table," he said. "That'll be a bit easier."

After settling down at the table, he pulled a cell phone out of his shirt pocket with his left hand and dialed a number, while with his right he extricated a Ziploc bag from his jacket pocket, opened it and took out a clump of very redolent, fresh grass. He spoke quietly into the phone while he crumpled a liberal amount of the grass and mashed it down into the head of the pipe with his thumb.

Even though I was nearby, it was impossible to hear his conversation, his voice was so low and, anyway, his focus seemed to be on the pipe. He clicked the cell phone shut and motioned me over. I sat stiffly next to him on a high backed chair as he used a lighter to fire the grass, slowly, turning the green leaves scarlet, and sucked in deeply. He held in the smoke while he told me, "That was my wife. I told her I'm being delayed by an important meeting and"— here he blew out a cloud of smoke then finished—"not to wait dinner. By the way this is expensive grass, very high quality." He passed the pipe to me.

I let out a cry—the pipe was hot.

"Be careful," he admonished. "Just the thumb and finger around the middle band…"

I followed his direction and he used his lighter to burn the grass while I sucked in.

I got a good hit, swallowed, then blew out the smoke which lingered in the air over his wedding ring. "It's OK that I'm married, isn't it? That's not a problem for you?"

"No," I answered, already knowing, having seen his wife and daughter as well, though he didn't know that. But I was up in the clouds and could hardly have formed words much less known if the answer I'd given was truthful as I couldn't think straight.

He took a second hit, removing his heavy glasses and laying them on the table, his green eyes which had been so piercing that day in the Seminary garden very watery now, and through the huge cloud he blew out, turning gray before almost disappearing. Through the haze he slid the pipe into my mouth as my hands were shaking and lit it for me adding, "Well, you may be one of the ones that get off on being with a married man."

I nodded yes to his statement, though it wasn't true, blowing out a big puff of smoke as he said, I thought, almost sarcastically, "Well, here's your chance then because you've got the real thing." I hardly was listening.

Our smoke co-mingled in the air like a stubborn frost holding out against the coming warmth. But come it did. A pure saturation of creaminess that held me and stole from me all mindful things, leaving in return an exquisite nothingness on which I was free to form my own tableau out of the most insane pleasures.

It was a crash dive into paradise with a glorious landing.

*

I don't know how long we'd been in the bedroom, it was all a blur. But it was deep into the night now and Crewe and I, naked together in bed, continued to share an intense, deep sexual intimacy I could never have imagined was possible. It had gone on forever, it seemed, and yet I didn't want it to stop.

The sound of jazz found its way through my open window, probably blowing in from a party across the court, or it could simply have been coming out of my mind or body. It didn't matter.

From the angle where we lay in bed I could watch myself in the mirror, glowing white and warm and prickly. And I could watch him too, an enthusiastic lover. I went down on his thick cock to the base, swallowing infinity. And afterwards I watched in the looking glass as yet again Crewe took hold of my ankles, lifted up my legs and spread them apart. And penetrated me. Though those clinical words hardly described the magic I experienced all around me.

When his cock was inside my body, it wasn't just a cock engaged in the act of penetration, it felt like a gun of pure euphoria, a weapon, yes, but one meant only to calm all my fears in a rootless world. An instrument of both reassurance and forgetfulness. My pleasure kept increasing, which amazed me, as I wasn't used to having much of it, living for a long time now on such a drab, bloodless plateau where such terrible and lonely things happen to all of us.

We stayed locked in the throes of passion. For long sweet hours. Until that moment came when we each poured forth in a fusillade of orgasms. There couldn't have been only one. Afterwards our breathing began to return to its normal rhythm, became steady again, punctuated only occasionally by groans.

He rolled off me, panting. For a long time, we lay quietly, Crewe on his back, his arm flung across his face, me staring at him with a kind of awe. It seemed a long time before Crewe finally spoke and when he did he said dully and with some despair, "I feel dead inside."

As high as I was I knew he didn't mean that he was tired out from fucking. He meant something else and I cringed hearing it, realizing it was meant for me to hear.

*

I couldn't believe it was already midnight when Crewe started getting dressed. Had we been going at it for that long? We had. The grass had fueled the sex, that was it. It was the strongest shit I'd ever smoked. But it was all in a night's work for Crewe—maybe he smoked so often he'd built up a steady tolerance for it. I hadn't. It was all I could do to locate a bathrobe and slump down at the kitchen table, and it took all the strength I had to compulsively trace circles around the rim of an empty coffee cup.

But Crewe was cool personified, speaking and functioning normally, meticulously buttoning his shirt, declaring how easy it would be to find a cab this time of night. I couldn't imagine even attempting what he was about to do: find all his clothes and get fully dressed, make parting talk with someone he'd had long, fervent sexual intimacy with, then stumble outside to hunt down a cab, chat up the driver about nothing of consequence, pay the correct fare without dropping the change all over the floor, ride the elevator up to his waiting wife to explain the import of a business meeting that not only kept you from a prearranged dinner but lasted into the dead of night.

Crewe slipped on a pair of dark glasses. Ah. There was the Achilles' heel. A midnight departure behind a pair of purple shades meant his eyes were bugged out, dilated, an absolute giveaway.

He knelt at my feet and said earnestly, "I need this again. We can't let this be the last time. It's only the beginning."

"I know...I know..."

"I'll phone you tomorrow. What's your number?"

As I gave it to him he deftly programmed it into his cell phone.

"I'll leave my cell phone number for you," he scribbled something on my phone bill. "Of course I can't give you the number of my landline as my wife could pick up."

His wife. Would she be asleep when he got home and roll over on her side, hardly aware of him as he slid into bed next to her? Or would she be awake, having put Sidonie to bed, making him a late night cup of tea, lemon and honey on the side, ready to share the events of their day, true or not? Would she be pacing angrily through that Central Park West apartment, glancing at the park, but too upset to see its charms, smashing her small fist on a table or shattering a crystal figurine on the floor, anxious to deconstruct any excuse or explanation Crewe dared to offer? Or would she be stretching voluptuously on coral satin sheets, in the nude, opening her arms to him, needing to take him inside her?

"Do you have a boyfriend?" He touched my knee gently.

"Well...not right now..."

"Good," he said, relieved. "What good news."

I had no idea how to respond.

He lifted himself up. "I'll be off now, John Laith."

As I saw him out I made a feeble attempt at a joke, "Just as well Sam Martinson lived on the fifteenth floor, after all."

He liked this and broke into laughter. When he composed himself he said, "Very good. Very good." But there was something brittle and just a little unkind about his laughter, as if the joke was funny but on me.

Maybe the grass was starting to make me paranoid. Though I'd had an incredible night in many ways, I still wanted him to go, to get on that elevator, impenetrable shades and all, to begin his crawl back to his real life. But how could that be more real than this.

I stood at my bedroom window for a long time. The jazz had stopped —if it had really been playing. A corn-colored yellow moon was limping across the wide deep arc of the night. I suddenly felt so satisfied, totally in tune with myself, whole. And yes, happy.

Sleep came easily that night but, oddly, so did waking and just as the night began to merge with the coming light. All was dimness. I opened my eyes, staring up, suddenly wide awake. Slowly floating down from the ceiling was a piece of white fluff, like a piece of cotton candy or a giant dandelion seed...or a cobweb in the dawn. As it got closer to my face I was amazed to see that this...piece of fluff...glistened with an ethereal beauty like spun silver and was embedded with tiny multi-colored stars that twinkled as it rotated lightly in front of me. I'd never seen anything like it. But, well, the garden did grow some weird flora and as for the sparkles, a trick of the light? Had it blown in through my open window? Probably, for soon it slowly floated outside and got lost in the rising of a soft pink sun.

\*

Though I didn't realize it at the time I was beginning to push Frank away, the love of my life. Of course he was dead. But he was alive inside me. I was carrying two people in one body, in one soul, and the weight of that was crushing. I wondered if there would be any more visits to the chapel to search for his face peering at me through the stained glass, that impossible mosaic of mystical confusion, or of spreading my wings like a butterfly waiting for him to join me in flight.

"All this dwelling on the past," Reg remarked, somehow in tune with my thoughts, after we left our evening bereavement group where I'd dared not mention the night before with Crewe, and slipped into a corner Starbucks, ordering a couple of Venti Breves Mistos and sipping at the disappearing froth as we checked out the crowds moving along in the gathering dark. "You've really put in your grieving time, not to be crass, God knows. I know we can never say when it's time to let go, each person is different, and only you know where you are in your own recovery, so forgive me if it's presumptuous to say it, but I think we're both starting to move on, just a bit."

"Reg, you have the ability to shine a light directly on me when I haven't asked you to yet."

"What's that, sarcasm?"

"Half-sarcasm."

"Did you know that word comes from the Greek meaning 'to tear flesh.' Thanks, anyway, but I'd like to remain intact. Though that's quite a struggle. For all of us."

"How so?"

"Look," Reg explained. "You're not the one tearing my flesh, don't get me wrong. Society heaps its sarcasm and disdain on us every chance it gets. Tries to tear off the last shreds of individuality and dignity we have to cling to."

Reg was just getting wound up, I realized, and I knew I was in for one of his lectures or, as he would have preferred, serial observations.

"I mean, just look at what we're shown on TV. The commercials, those great tools of corporate greed, they let us know exactly where we stand. They're the present day Barnum and Bailey hucksters trying to manipulate us into buying tickets to their freak show. They're trying to scare us to death! Just consider all those purple pills tumbling towards you on the screen. You didn't start popping them early enough so it's too late for you to lower your cholesterol or blood pressure—you're ready for that first heart attack or at least diabetes. Whoops, you smoked— here comes cancer! Your teeth aren't white enough, your hair isn't silky enough, you're not pumped up enough. You're not finding that edge. You're just not cool, dude. And the worst, yes worst, you didn't save enough for your retirement with the most elite investment firm— though you were repeatedly warned by those that did, the ones relaxing on their deck chairs staring smugly at the ten different shades of turquoise surrounding some Bahamian reef. In short you lived the unexamined life."

"Maybe we—I—have lived the unexamined life. I

don't even know."

"Of course you've lived the examined life. You've lived your own life, that's all, not theirs. You deign to be yourself."

His last punctuating line was enough to bring us both to a kind of enforced silence as we worked on finishing our Mistos. Then we walked outside to the corner of 23rd and 8th where I found my friend wasn't quite finished. "Talk about being inspected and analyzed to death. Look up above you right now for God's sake. Do we really need that? A spy machine just like the others hanging over every corner of our neighborhood."

Like one of the creatures from *War of the Worlds,* a thin oblong camera on a cement bean pole hovered down over us, photographing us with its lifelike mechanized eye, trying to blend in with the street lights.

"Invasion of privacy, that's what it is. Who needs to have access to me twenty-four/ seven? To see where I'm headed, how I'm dressed, who I'm with."

"They're just the latest addition to the landscape, hunting down potential terrorists I suppose, documenting hit and runs or slip and falls or drug deals going down. Or gay bashings, come to think of it. What is it? You think somebody at the FBI or CIA has a special thing for you—that you're their pin-up boy or something?"

Reg threw up his hands. "You just don't get it."

"Reg, you know something?"

"What?"

"I don't know about this moving on stuff."

"Listen, John. Move on you will. You don't have a choice. It's called the process of life."

We hugged, said "Ciao," and I walked home through the hustle and bustle, the breeze tousling my hair, happening to notice several others of those science-fiction cameras peeking down at me from strategic spots. I wondered if any human beings were watching me now through these cameras, and if so, who they were and what they thought of me. Could they tell if I'd been living an examined or unexamined life? Or was there no one watching, just some dead emotionless eye fixed in space, knowing nothing at all.

\*

It was midnight when I got home. I lit a couple of bright scarlet candles in the living room, their shadows on the wall flickering like visitors, silent but energetic, watching me sit in front of my computer and open the envelope I'd found pushed under my door with a sticky note from Bob McBride on the outside: "Put in my box by mistake. Cheers." It happened to be the announcement of the upcoming Court exam two Saturdays from now at 3 p.m. at Art and Design High School at 57th Street and 2nd Avenue. Bring two sharpened pencils. No latecomers admitted. You will be fingerprinted. If you've had an arrest for firearm possession you must let us know though this will not in itself be considered enough for disqualification. Anything else, I wondered. Yes, Reg, what would you think about this state-sponsored brand of spying? Well, I'd show up for the test anyway.

My only e-mail was from Allison: "Hi, just wanted to let you know I'm pregnant. Don't know who the father is—could be one of two men—but not to worry, this time I'm thinking of having the baby and keeping it! How would you feel about being an uncle? And it's all hush-hush for now, OK? Don't e-mail or phone me back just yet. I couldn't stand it if you disagreed. XXX's AL"

What feelings I had about becoming an uncle would

surely be dwarfed by the feelings she must be having of becoming a mother. Was it a miracle, seeing her own mother had died a bag lady in an alley, or was it a disaster, seeing her own mother had died a bag lady in an alley? Frankly her announcement was so casual it seemed delusional—as if she'd made up her mind to go shopping to pick out a doll she could rock and put to bed.

Two men—like Allison—I was involved with two men. To me that meant I was desirable, was wanted. To reassure myself I only had to listen to my phone messages. I was glad they'd both left messages, but it was Crewe I'd really wanted to hear from. But always Johnny on my spot Silvio was on first with a simple, "Hi. Would you like to get together this weekend? Let us know." Then Crewe. "This is the second time I'm trying you tonight but the first message I'm leaving. The first time I tried my wife was in the bath. Now," he lowered his voice dramatically, "I've slipped into the study while she's asleep." Then in tones he thought seductive—"You see, I just can't wait to see you. You don't know. Please leave a message on my cell that I can stop by tomorrow at two. That's when my wife goes shopping." Like the consummate business professional he was, he left his phone number in crisp tones to make a good impression, and like the consummate satyr he was, he made sure I had the number if somehow I'd misplaced it. This way there was no reason not to get back to him. I left him a casual cell message saying that would be fine, I'd see him tomorrow. Actually, it would be time better spent if I tried to answer the multiple choice questions in my exam prep book for the upcoming test but there'd be plenty of time for that later.

Even with the excited flush of anticipating him tomorrow I felt uneasy. Where were my morals in all of this? Where were his? And where were hers? Didn't the wife always know underneath....

I'd get back to Silvio tomorrow to set up something for the weekend. By that time, it shouldn't be too difficult to slip into the required mood. I blew out the candles, at the same time hearing Bob McBride's little Jack Terrier in the apartment opposite begin to whimper and whine and paw at the door. He kept it up like a lament. Was somebody in the hall who didn't belong there, maybe a tenant who'd gotten out on the wrong floor? I peered out the fish-eyed peephole but the distorted wraparound view of the corridor showed nothing. Suddenly the dog's baleful steady wail turned into a dangerous low guttural growl; I could picture his lips pulled back, teeth bared defensively. Could McBride have fallen, injured himself, or even died in his sleep? Relieved I heard McBride's voice, "What's wrong boy, come away from that door."

Moonlight, dim and murky, led my way into the bedroom. But once inside I froze. Next to the open window, behind the floor-length curtain something moved, the curtain rustled, I could make out the bulge of a tall man's form, the thin material accentuating his musculature and body curves and the imprint of a face behind the curtain like a mummy in a shroud. I could have panicked and fled. Or called 911 or pounded on Bob McBride's door for help. But instinctively I knew I hadn't interrupted a robbery, there was no fire escape to climb through the bedroom window and no sign of forced entry into the apartment. And would a man have stood stock still behind that curtain while I'd settled in— or even if he had, would he be planning to spend the night like that? Nothing made sense. My fear turned to foolhardiness and I took hold of the curtain by the creases around his bulging forehead and ripped it back. But there was no one there. Just an empty space. Jesus. Confused, I wondered if Crewe's tough as shit grass— liberally laced with THC—had given me lingering hallucinations. I didn't really know how long those effects were supposed to last but did know at this point I hadn't completely recovered from them. Yet would that have led me to imagine…well…what?

As I turned away, letting go of the curtain, I noticed something on the floor behind its shadowy recesses. I dropped to my knees. There I saw not one but two of the sparkling cottony spheres shot through with minuscule red, blue, and gold blinking lights, just like the webbed ball that had drifted down from my ceiling last night and floated out the window. For the first time I noticed how stunningly beautiful these cobwebbed clumps were. The base of the fluff was the purest, cleanest white I'd ever seen. I thought of twilight on a fresh blanket of snow on our backyard hill when I was a boy, gliding fast down the incline on my bum because the family couldn't save enough pennies, nickels, dollars for a sled, but not caring, not on your life, just thrilled to enjoy the feel of the ice through my clothes, the bitter cold on my legs and back as I slid all the way to the bottom, looking up into the sky and seeing the neighbor's Christmas lights blink on in the trees—an enchantment—and I never wanted to leave that magic. That's what these spheres seemed like— resplendent, shining omens. I carefully wrapped them in a towel which I lay inside my top bureau drawer so I could show Reg, get his opinion about what he thought these spheres could be and why they had drifted into my apartment. But the next morning when I opened the drawer and folded back the towel to have a second look there was nothing inside, not even dust.

From the start his idea seemed tragically flawed at worst and a farce at best. I just didn't get it. It seemed so unnecessary and ego-stroking. He had come at two exactly, I was to discover over time he was never late, and he'd brought his own beer with him this afternoon as he would from now on. It was after we'd shared more of those gut-wrenching libidinous pleasures together for several hours and he was dressing to leave that he turned to me as I was curled up on the couch, all warm, sluggish, and pleasantly vegetative and suggested the three of us meet and go out together. Crewe, me, and his wife.

"She'd like you," he intoned. "You're intelligent and cultivated."

So let me be intelligent and cultivated on my own.

"We three could be companions of sort."

"How's that?"

"Oh, not in a *ménage à trois* sense of course. But I could tell her you're a new member of my book discussion group who just happens to know more about fiction than the rest of the other fellows. It's kind of an old boys club, we meet in a private room at the National Arts Club on Gramercy Park. It's a charming, very relaxed club."

"I think I've walked by it. It's on the south corner of the park, isn't it?"

"Yes, you do know it. Well, you could certainly pass as someone the group would welcome in, especially if you showed some interest in the possible purchase of an apartment. Clemma would buy that, I'm reasonably certain."

"But how could such a bluff not help but further

confuse a confused issue?"

"There'd be no impact on our relationship—the one between you and me. Clemma would gain a companion and I could spend more time with you in her company. And of course," he added quietly under his breath, "you'd be the soul of discretion; that is as long as you'd like to keep partaking in our little garden of earthly delights."

It sounded somewhere between a threat and a plea.

"Do you want another hit off the pipe?" he asked, sucking one in for himself as he tightened his Scottish plaid scarf over his suede jacket.

"No thanks," I waved my arm dismissively. "I've had enough. By the way, I can't picture strolling arm in arm down the street, you and me on either side of your wife."

"I didn't mean that...exactly. For instance we have a box at the Metropolitan Opera that seats four. We use it mainly for business purposes, entertaining prospective buyers. I must say the seats are superb. Clemma's so close to the stage when she throws bouquets, the artists always pick them up then bow or curtsey to our box. That's the kind of threesome I'm talking about, a unique evening at the opera with gravitas, so to speak."

My mind rambled but my words came out simply and clear, "It's too odd, Crewe, I'd be uncomfortable."

"You think it over." His face darkened a bit, having hoped for my quick acquiescence and not having gotten it. "You're of a literary persuasion if I've understood you correctly. And obviously have good taste in fiction. You read upscale mysteries and the great classics of French literature as you have advised me. I can see for myself the different series on your shelves, selected volumes of de Balzac's *La Comédie Humaine*, *Madame Bovary* by

Flaubert, Zola's *L'Assommoir*, books I paged through at University, to obtain a working knowledge of their implications and placement in history so I could appear erudite and culturally proficient enough to win someone over to buy an expensive apartment from me. But I never read them for sheer pleasure like you did. But since you are so enamored of creative writing I have an assignment for you. I don't want you to hurry through it, I want you to take your time, put all your flair and original thinking into it. I want you to write several essays about my cock, detailing all of the different things it means to you, all the different ways it makes you feel, honestly described, in fine detail, needless to say, so that I can read and enjoy your little essays when I come over next time. What do you think, that would be a fun assignment, wouldn't it? Of course while you're mulling over my original proposition."

I smiled wanly to humor him, furious at his gall and unbridled ego and determined not to honor his request and waste any time on such a foolish project; however, I wasn't sure why, I was uneasy at the idea of crossing him directly. When he returned, I'd just somehow have forgotten to have written it, that's all, geez, sorry.

"What's that noise?" Crewe asked, knowing full well it was the sound of a door shutting in the apartment above and footsteps crossing the floor.

"It's the girl upstairs coming home from work."

"Doesn't that bother you? Fortunately we don't have anybody above us."

"No, she doesn't bother me. It's somehow predictable and reassuring."

He laughed. "I can just picture her coming in from a day at the office, kicking off her shoes, ready to draw herself a nice, relaxing bath. Oh, I'm sure on the way home she stopped at a deli and bought herself a few flowers or some of those plum-colored feathery dried sprigs they wrap and staple in that god-awful paper. She's probably trying to arrange them right now in some vase or other, just to bring a little cheer to the place, you know, to make the place as nice and homey as possible with the resources she has."

I was at a loss for words. It wouldn't be the last time.

Crewe was at the door. "I must say this was as wonderful as our first encounter. Well, to be accurate, I should say this was as wonderful as our second encounter. Wouldn't you say so?"

"Yes..."

"You've really saved me some wear and tear, knowing I have something I can count on when the need comes up...And my need comes up very often. As for you, you don't have to worry about me disappearing. I'll satisfy you in the same way you satisfy me. I've done a pretty good job of that so far, I would imagine."

"Yes," I admitted, wanting to lie but not able to.

"Well, thank you again for a splendid time." He was ever polite as he left.

Yes, yes, you satisfied me, and the time was splendid but there's something wrong here and it's not the sex. But why think about what was wrong when you could be thinking about what was right?

*

I met Tim R. on the Brooklyn Heights Promenade on Saturday afternoon. He lived in an apartment at Clark and Columbia. On the phone he said he'd be on the first bench to the left as you entered the Promenade from

Clark Street, that he was a carrot top and would be in a navy blue windbreaker. He was easy to spot and I shook his hand as I eased down next to him, introducing myself as John L.; his voice had been shaky on the phone, I'd given him a fifty-fifty chance of showing up, but with those odds I'd been happy to make the trip.

His therapist had recommended our gay friendly bereavement group and I was to act as his welcomer, the one meant to nudge him towards meetings. Without meetings you went nowhere.

The air was fresh and breezy, the sky cloudless, opaque. We studied the Manhattan skyline which stood out in sharp focus, in contrast to his unfocused mind. He had the same eyes I remembered having once—open but registering nothing because of a blinding loneliness.

His lover had died three weeks ago from AIDS. They'd been together seven years, four years short of the time Frank and I had been soul mates.

"It's funny," he said pulling the windbreaker around him, eyeing me cautiously. "Opening up to a complete stranger like you…but my therapist, he's worried about me…" He stopped cold.

I helped him along. "Worried you might do something stupid?"

He nodded. "There's always the possibility."

"But of course you won't," I reassured him, shivering anyway. "You're young. You have your whole life ahead of you." Though my words were so simple that they rang hollow, they were true nonetheless. "What you need is time to change and see new possibilities, allow yourself the intimacy of grieving and give yourself total permission to take as long as it takes."

He stayed quiet.

I tried to engage him. "How old are you?"

"Twenty-nine." He smiled obliquely.

"That's a lucky age. It's a natural end and a natural beginning. There are plenty of members in our group your age. And others older and younger of course. I just want you to know I'll personally take you to your first meeting. One of the best ones is at the Center. Have you been there?"

"Many times," he said. "That would bring back a lot of memories. Will and I used to go to the Saturday night square dances there."

"Oh, yes? That was your partner's name, Will?"

"Yes," he answered. "And still is. We came here together from Montpelier. To start a life in the big city, but we didn't realize…at least I didn't realize Will was taking too many risks…he wasn't looking out for himself…I probably should have guessed…"

I nodded, understanding, looking away from him towards the building blocks of Manhattan to let him know I got the picture and he didn't need to say anymore about it. Yet I did wonder if Tim R. had been infected by his partner and hoped to God not.

He said bitterly, "I think I'd have better luck by picking somebody up off the Promenade right here and starting a new relationship with him, rather than getting involved in some group mind-trip thing."

"No," I turned to him and said emphatically, "No way. It would be too soon. You wouldn't have had enough time to have let go of Will and…and…"

"What?" he asked, curiosity showing up for the first time in his voice.

"Well," I parroted the group line I thought I believed, "have the distance that only time can give and the maturity to choose a new partner who's healthy for you."

He turned his head toward me. "Have you found a new partner?"

I broke into a slow sweat. "Well, no, not yet."

Suddenly he was my interrogator.

"Why not, you told me on the phone you've been in this group for years."

"I have, but it takes time."

"How long was your lover sick with AIDS?"

"It wasn't AIDS."

"What?" Tim R. jumped off the bench confrontationally.

"I thought your therapist explained—our group is made up of men and women, straight and gay. It's for anybody who's suffered a loss…But of course I can put you in touch with an AIDS specific bereavement group," I rebounded. "That's what you need, I should have thought it through, in fact that's what I would have personally recommended…only your therapist felt—"

"What do you know about anything?" he shouted. I was aware of onlookers sizing both of us up.

I was still sweating. I said quietly, "I know that death is death."

"No it isn't, sweetheart. Not that kind of death. When somebody dies a hundred times, one death more ghastly than the next. And when somebody goes blind at the end and comes across the room to hold you and can't because he doesn't even know where you're standing. You're a fake!"

He stormed off, back around the corner of the Promenade onto Clark Street, leaving me sitting there on the bench shaking, keenly aware of other people's gazes, my eyes welling with tears, trying to stare nonchalantly at the pigeon pecking around my shoes to deflect attention. Alcoholism isn't a picnic. Frank had died too in a hundred ghastly ways or even more and though he hadn't been blind physically he hadn't seen God's healing grace in time.

*

And now who was I? Fake or real, I was a wreck. At home I made three phone calls in rapid succession. The first was to Crewe, who expressed disappointment I hadn't called him earlier as his wife had gone out shopping and he would have had the time and opportunity to slip over; I briefly mentioned I'd been talking to someone whose lover had died of AIDS, to which Crewe responded, "God was good to me, he made me a top." And then he insisted I come over for brunch tomorrow since it would be nearly seventy degrees, a real patch of Indian summer, and we could have a bang-up brunch on the wraparound terrace and I could meet his wife and daughter. Rattled, I scribbled down his address and said I'd be there at one. The next call was to Reg who fortunately wasn't home. I left a message that I needed a break from our group, that I couldn't speak at any new meetings or sponsor any new members for awhile, please try and understand, it wouldn't be forever, I needed space. And terrified at the prospect of spending the night alone, I made my third call to Silvio asking him to drop by. Relieved, I found he was all too happy at the prospect.

Somebody, I forget who, told me you need to have an extra man saved up "for a rainy day." At the time I thought he was an idiot, now I realized he was a prophet.

It's said that many men are totally fetishistic. They're satisfied by knowing they're going to have the same sex over and over. In fact, introducing a new scenario or attitude is threatening to them. Silvio was one of that type. Although he'd dispensed with shaving my crotch, everything else was a repeat performance by order of his majesty the cop. It was fine with me to put on the red shoes and play the slut. It was a pretty easy role, though he was rougher than I liked. I made do. Actually I more than made do. I got him comfortable enough to let his guard down a little and relax with me. I even got him laughing over nothing during those moments when he didn't think he had to play the macho stud to impress me. Not that we didn't do our usual thing, we did, we got stoned and fucked and sucked ourselves silly. That seemed to be the point of it all. To get your mind off everything else, to not even have to think. His verbiage was the only thing that changed in any way, he tweaked it a bit adding: "Does the doorman know what a bitch you are, admitting strange men to your apartment for no other reason than to have a good time?" and a bit of a stretch, but more creatively: "Bill would have loved you at the White House."

*

It didn't occur to me to see if Crewe thought it was a good idea to ask Allison to the brunch until Sunday morning. When I asked him over the cell phone he said, "You mean as your beard? Why not? Just remind her about our book discussion group—that's our connection."

"OK."

Allison was wanted less by me as a beard than for her company and for moral support. Luckily she agreed to go. I told her we were going to have brunch with the family we'd watched near Turtle Pond after the Blake exhibit. She didn't ask how I was involved with them now, just accepted my lame explanation of a book group connection. But she was intuitive and knew there was more to the story. She brought the host and hostess an expensive Blake illustrated tarot card deck she'd bought at the museum the day of the exhibit, a gift that presciently cemented the connection between the Blake watercolors that had overwhelmed me then and our visit to the Jameses.

I'll be damned if there wasn't a special elevator at the lobby level in their apartment building on the corner of 86th and Central Park West, and that after being announced by the concierge, we boarded for a direct ascent to their penthouse terrace. Instead of into a hallway, the elevator doors opened directly onto the large, fabled wraparound terrace, some twenty-six stories up, and Allison and I walked out into the piercing blueness of an unexpected closer-to-the-clouds October sky. A handsome woman, tanned and fit, her dark hair twisted up into a purposefully casual bun, dressed comfortably in a light sweater and plaid pleated skirt, was at one of the terrace corners, pruning chrysanthemums, which spilled out of the jaw-dropping mouth of one of the many gargoyles that decorated the cornices. She turned towards us with a sunny wave. We approached her timidly. Somewhere church bells chimed one o'clock.

"I'm Clemma." She took off her work gloves and extended her hand. "How nice Crewe's friends have joined us for brunch." She had that Southern drawl that I remembered hearing when she'd called to her daughter at Turtle Pond. We began to introduce ourselves but she stopped us, "Oh, no need for introductions. Crewe already told me your names. John and Allison, is that right?"

We nodded.

"What a beautiful spot," I said agreeably.

"We're very fortunate," she replied gratefully, putting one hand against her chest. "We've been here fifteen years now, are always saying we're going to find some place bigger but just keep adding on right here…It's not a huge, showplace apartment. Sometimes it's difficult to entertain here. But it's home." She grinned. "We care more about giving it our personal touch. There's something about making it your own," and here she sounded really Southern, "and once you've done that, sharing the sweetness of it."

There was a pause and Allison handed her the gift of the Blake tarot pack wrapped in blue tissue and brown twine, saying "Hopefully this will be a small addition to your home. It's from both of us," though it wasn't. Clemma expressed delight and carefully unwrapped it at a snail's pace, with great concentration, just how I imagined a lady of the manor would open a gift. But once unwrapped she held the pack in her hand and studied it, expressionlessly, then dropped it on one of the deck chairs as if some kook on MacDougal Street had accosted her and asked if she wanted her fortune read. Nonetheless she moved close to Allison and gave her a faux peck on the cheek, meaning her lips never actually touched Allison, only nipped at the air.

Coming onto the terrace was a middle-aged man-in-waiting in a bright red jacket with gold buttons up to the neck, carrying a tray with three bowls and a basket of rolls set in a linen napkin. He was balding and had shiny skin and seemed shy. He glanced at us fleetingly, put the basket on the table which already had three place-settings and waited for the instructions that were forthcoming, "That's all we need, Douglas, expect for three glasses of iced water." Then she turned to us. "I hope you like cantaloupe soup."

What to say? The three of us sat at the table. We gazed over the golden treetops of Central Park and beyond to where the apartments on the East Side and Central Park South formed a circular chain, and instead of impressing me, reminded me how overcrowded Manhattan was.

"Crewe and Sidonie aren't back from their walk in the park. It's their Sunday morning tradition. But it gives us a little time for a *tête-à-tête*."

The bastard, I thought, leaving me to fend for myself with his wife, not knowing her story and—presumably—her not knowing mine.

I knew right then that nothing was ever going to be straightforward with Crewe, like it or lump it. Something was always going to mean something else that meant something else. "So, Mr. Laith," Clemma took a leisurely sip of the clear yellowish liquid that filled only half the bowl, "my husband tells me you may be interested in purchasing one of our apartments."

"Why, yes." I nibbled on one of the rolls that didn't seem particularly fresh.

Allison kept a poker face, dipping her spoon in her bowl, then taking it out and setting it on the table.

"Well, I'm glad he was able to show you something you liked. It's always struck me a bit odd that my husband doesn't always use a broker to show individual apartments. His business is the buying and selling of the properties themselves. But sometimes, I guess, he'll go the extra mile himself for someone he considers an acquaintance, not a stranger. Which apartment is it?"

"I'm considering several—at the moment. Your husband still hasn't gone over all of the details with me."

"Oh, no? That's surprising. I rather thought he had.

But I was away last month at our villa in St. Barts and I guess I haven't kept up on my husband's latest dealings. I mean, I'm not in the middle of his discussions with his colleagues at their office up by Columbia. But I'm sure he's still got a few irons in the fire."

I steered the conversation in a new, safer direction. "Well you see, Mrs. James—"

"Oh, please…Clemma…"

"I've been more involved in his book discussion group at the National Arts Club, at least up to this point."

"Oh," something dawned on her. "You're the one. Who likes fiction. Whatever are you doing in their boring club? You and I should start our own book discussion group. Crewe and I are as different as two peas in a pod—that's the South coming out in me. On his bedstand are the most lugubrious volumes of the Napoleonic wars, Greek philosophy, and folded reproductions of the original designs of Madison Square Garden and several biographies of its architect Stanford White, while on my nightstand is the latest fiction recommended by the *New York Times*, or memoirs disguised as fiction, it doesn't really matter to me. It's a wonder Crewe and I ever meet in the middle."

Douglas set down the ice water in front of us and I gulped at it greedily.

"I can't really eat much at one setting anymore," Clemma said, "but if you want more soup just ask. I also have to watch my husband to be sure he doesn't put on weight."

I couldn't see myself commenting about Crewe's weight and I'm sure Allison couldn't either, having only seen him once at a distance. At this juncture neither of us could think of anything to say.

Clemma seemed at a loss herself and finally turned

wearily to Allison and asked condescendingly, "And what's new with you, my dear?"

"I'm pregnant."

Clemma shot a quick look at me, sizing me up as a dark horse, then back to Allison: "I see. By the way you blurted that out I surmise that your pregnancy was unintended and you're a bit confused."

"If you mean was it an accident, yes, it was."

"Those kinds of accidents are mostly preventable. I haven't reached menopause yet so I have to be very careful. One child is enough, thank you very much. Crewe is very cooperative and always makes sure he's adequately protected."

Was that said for my benefit? To let me know that unlike some married couples at this stage of their lives they were still sexual with one another—in case I had ideas to the contrary and had designs on her husband. No. I doubt her comment was meant for me. I just imagine she was giving Allison some motherly advice too late. But then again why was this woman of such fine well-bred Southern upbringing talking about sexual relations at all? As the thought left me jarred and wondering, the elevator doors opened and Crewe and Sidonie joined us.

Crewe was bubbling with conversation about all the fun they'd had in the park, he and Sidonie having had a contest as to who would be the first to name all the species of trees correctly, bird-watching, leaf-tossing, trying to discover new untrodden paths. Crewe punctuated his commonplace anecdotes with low giddy laughter while Sidonie was more reserved, a little taller, and if possible thinner, than I'd remembered her when she was staring glacially at the turtle in the middle of the pond. Her light brown hair fell down on her shoulders and she wore a paisley dress, and somehow, incongruously to me at least, held a big white balloon in her left hand, something I would have expected a girl a little younger to be holding.

"And who named the most trees correctly?" I attempted to interject myself into all the fun.

"I did." Sidonie was quick to take credit where credit was due.

"That's only because I let you," Crewe said.

"That's not true and you know it," Sidonie said with an edge, instead of laughing it off.

Crewe shrugged and answered, "Think whatever you like." He leaned over and kissed Clemma on her cheek and shook hands with Allison and me. "Sidonie, kiss your mother," he said and the girl almost reluctantly kissed Clemma on the other side of her cheek.

"Did you have a good brunch?" Crewe asked robustly. "Sidonie and I were hungry so we had a bite at a restaurant. She wanted her favorite chocolate chip pancakes and, seeing she's thin as a wraith, I let her indulge."

Rude as hell for all these high-class manners. Allison and I would have liked to have wolfed them down as well, instead of stirring the squeezed nectar of an out-of-season melon around and around in a bowl.

"The brunch was exquisite," I beamed, going over the top, hoping it would sink in that what they had given me—us—was totally inadequate. But they were clueless.

"What did Daddy have to eat?" Clemma asked her daughter.

"Two croissants with butter and jam."

"Crewe!" Clemma exclaimed. "Your cholesterol. What are you thinking!"

"Tattletale." Crewe turned to Sidonie. "You know

what happens to tattletales, don't you?"

"No."

"Why they get tattled on themselves at the first opportunity." He studied Clemma and me, leaving Allison in the cold. "And you two got to know each other…" When there was a notable silence from both of us he added, "I hope just a little. Clemma's very modest, I'm sure she didn't mention she comes from one of the old-moneyed manufacturing families in Charleston."

"Crewe, don't start," she said. "It's the height of boorishness to rub someone's family hierarchy in other people's faces." But she was thrilled.

"It's really because of Clemma I've been so successful. Well, that's not exact. We each brought something to each other. She brought her family name and the money that came with it when we were engaged at college, when I was at Harvard and she was at Vassar, and I brought the brains. I cultivated many of her connections so when we were married and moved to New York her friends trusted me to do their real estate deals for them."

"Which he's quite adept at. Making money. Investing it is a different story." Clemma beamed at Crewe indulgently. "Though he's always looking at stock quotations, he doesn't understand them a bit and wouldn't know how to invest money for anyone, much less ourselves. So he brings in the money and my side of the family invests it for us."

"Yes," Crewe agreed. "We've had quite a successful coupling in that way. And me coming from the middle class, from a nondescript little suburb of Philadelphia. But determined to succeed, you see?" He paused. "How do you think someone gets a scholarship to Harvard with no connections?" he asked no one in particular in a barely concealed tone of bitterness.

But Clemma was ready. "By being brilliant, darling."

That brought the conversation to a halt. The only sound besides the hushed traffic twenty-five floors below was the squeak of the balloon as Sidonie retied it to her wrist.

"That's Sidonie's Sunday balloon," Crewe said, smiling. "I don't know why but every Sunday since she was about seven she's asked me to buy her a balloon during our walk in the park. It's gone on for years now." He hugged her to him. "And she always chooses a white one. Then all she does when she gets up on the terrace is let it fly off in the air. You're quite a sophisticated girl, you know, I'm surprised at your age it still holds such delights for you." Sidonie said nothing, continuing to move the string around and around her wrist. "But of course Daddy's happy it still brings you such pleasure."

Allison said, "I'd like to use the bathroom please."

Clemma was quick off the mark. "Of course, my dear, just go in the doorway and it's right inside the first door to the left." Allison took her leave and disappeared inside. I was surprised they hadn't offered us a tour of their penthouse. Maybe that was déclassé, a no-no, a tacky idea, an intrusion somehow—or something to be saved later for a dinner party. I mean, it wasn't a museum and they weren't putting the place on the market. Why should I, someone without gravitas, a word Crewe had used in our recent conversation, expect a guided tour?

Clemma stood up. "No use calling Douglas. I told him to brush down your suits. I'll take the breakfast dishes in myself to wash up. By the way," she added casually, "are you going up to your office this afternoon?"

Crewe threw me a quick glance. I shook my head no as imperceptibly as I could manage.

"Not this afternoon," he said, resigned. "I thought we could talk about St. Barts. I want to go over the tax papers and I want to hear your idea on renovations and adding that pier."

"Good idea," she said, putting the bowls, napkins, glasses and silverware on the tray Douglas had left on a side table and whisking them indoors.

"I'll be in to help in a minute," Crewe called after her as he ogled me, brushing my leg with his under the table. "By the way, how are your attempts at describing my cock coming along?" I looked around in dismay to see if Sidonie was standing there listening, but she had drifted off to the edge of one of the balustrades, by one of the gargoyles. "Silly boy, give me enough credit to know where my daughter is before speaking to you in that way. Well?"

"The essays…They're coming along."

He stared at me intently. "Why didn't you want me to come over this afternoon? You were given a perfect opportunity."

"Not under these circumstances."

"What circumstances?"

"Please."

"Don't you miss my big cock?"

"Of course I do."

Allison was back. She slumped down in a chair next to me and stared for a moment at the two of us. Writhing just a little, Crewe left to help his wife with all three of the dishes.

Sidonie stood by herself next to the gargoyle. I told Allison I was going to go have a talk with her.

"Hello. Mind if I join you?" I sidled up next to her.

"I'd rather you didn't."

"Well, that's not a very nice thing to say."

"I'm not always a nice person."

"Oh. Why not?"

She looked at me, annoyed, as though not only was I prying but talking down to her as well.

I tried again. "Do you have any nice friends your own age?"

The silent treatment.

"Do you like school?"

"Since you're obviously not going to do as I asked and leave me alone I might as well answer your rather basic questions. I don't have any friends my own age and I don't want any either. As for school, I like it very much since it's very easy for me to attend."

"Oh, yes? How so?"

"I'm home schooled at the kitchen table by my mother and my father who are extremely intelligent people. Better teachers than any I could ever have anywhere else. Now, have I satisfied your curiosity? Or is there something else?"

I gazed at her for a moment before responding. "Actually there is. I'm sure your parents are giving you an excellent education. You're very bright like they are. But what's your goal? What do you plan to do with this education?"

"You mean," she asked, talking down to me now, "what do I plan to be when I grow up?"

I nodded.

"A judge."

I don't know why I was caught off balance by her answer but I was. I felt awkward. "None of this is really any of my business. I'm sorry," I mumbled.

She squinted at me. Then her lips half curved and

she gave a silent laugh, shaking her head at me with a kind of pity. Then she said, "You already heard my dad talking about what I do with my Sunday balloons. So that's no secret to you now. Do you want to watch what I do?"

"If you'd like me to."

"It doesn't matter much to me one way or the other." Straightening her spine, she made her bearing more erect and regal than I thought could have been possible for a girl her age; she tilted her face to the sky, whispered something I couldn't hear and let go of the balloon. She stayed quiet, keeping her eyes shut. I watched the white balloon drift up into the azure for what seemed a long time. Suddenly the wind got up, whipping her brown hair around her cheeks and tightly closed eyes, and pushing down on the balloon, making it bob back and forth, up and down, lashed by the air. It was finally batted down by the crosswinds and when she eventually opened her eyes she saw that it was stuck in a treetop directly across the street. She shrugged, looked at me almost disappointedly and walked inside where I heard a door shut—to her bedroom?—behind her.

I rejoined Allison at the table but realized she was napping, her legs stretched out in front of her. I could hear distant voices inside the penthouse, I supposed Crewe's and Clemma's. Weren't they going to come back and check on their so-called guests? I don't know if I was overreacting, but frankly, it felt galling to be so ignored and I wanted to leave now anyway, so I decided to slip inside and let them know.

I walked through the door, silently making my way down a long corridor with extremely high marble arches, peering into open doorways as I passed them by.

I saw first what was obviously Crewe's study, the

walls covered with framed sketches of apartment buildings, presumably ones he owned. There was a white leather sofa against one wall next to which was an antique pinewood desk. A computer sat on top of it.

I looked into the room directly opposite the hall from Crewe's study and found myself staring into their bedroom which Clemma had already mentioned. There was a big brass bed in the middle and yes, there were the two nightstands stacked on either side with books. The blinds were pulled open and through the window I saw they had a spectacular view of Central Park, of Belvedere Castle with its medieval turrets and a little further to the south I could even see Turtle Pond, the round body of water along whose edges I'd first seen Sidonie contemplating the turtles. The bedroom walls were covered with rich red and gold Chinese wallpaper depicting mandarins, courtesans modestly hiding their faces behind gilt fans as they crossed lacquered bridges, and willow trees languidly bending over rivers on which small fishing boats with colored lanterns floated. Matching sheets and pillowcases of white silk with muted designs of reeds and bamboo flutes seemed to undulate with the changing patterns of light and shadow caused by the floating autumn clouds moving across the sun streaming in from Central Park. It was hard to believe, but to my untrained eye this exotic design scheme worked. There was an odd elegance to the room.

Further down the hall I passed a small mirrored dining room full of silver antiques set on heavy mahogany chests. Across from it was a small guest bedroom with wicker furniture, the walls a canary yellow and the decor chosen with a hint of the Caribbean in mind. Next to that was a luxuriously appointed bathroom with ivory panels and a bathtub with fluted edges shaped like a coral shell, sunstruck beneath an open skylight which framed the dazzling blue October sky.

I passed another room whose door was shut, it must be Sidonie's, and opposite, across the hall, a small windowless formal parlor with straight-backed velvet chairs and portraits of dried up old souls, men and women staring out, startled, fearing that something of themselves might be revealed and wearing black hats and bonnets with low brims for concealment, their bones protruding.

Then I was peering into what appeared to be a spacious living room, a number of glass doors leading out onto the terrace. The bright space was full of comfortable sofas with rugs and magazines strewn about in front of an imposing marble fireplace, exotic Egyptian scrolls hanging on the rough sand colored walls.

The voices were coming from the kitchen at the very end of the hall.

As I approached, I could make out glass cabinets filled with crystal and china, jutting out at ingenious angles fitted into a backdrop of blond wood. The kitchen was the largest room in the penthouse, containing a massive stove with a dozen burners, beside which stood a sturdy wooden table with stiff backed chairs. Florentine tiles on the wall depicted peacocks parading their splendid gold and green plumage. Through five or six large ornate gabled windows there were views of the luxury buildings that wound their way up the north side of Central Park West. Crewe and Clemma were talking— no, they were arguing and didn't seem to notice I had come up to the entryway.

"No," Clemma was saying to him, "not again. The police called the last time, remember, and it was my great misfortune to pick up the phone when they did. I'm the one that had to answer 'yes' when they asked me if a Mr. Crewe James lived at this residence. Listen to me, I won't be put through such an embarrassment again. Ever. And can you imagine if your buyers had—" Here she stopped breathless, noticing me standing in the doorway. They each turned their backs on me, quietly, to compose themselves as I mentioned Allison and I had to be on our way.

There was much fussing at the terrace elevator about how nice our visit had been; even a recalcitrant Sidonie was shepherded from her room to bid us good-bye.

Allison couldn't resist. "Don't you have an elevator that opens into your hallway? In case of bad weather or something? Or is this it?"

Clemma barely kept her cool. She thought the niceties and good-byes were over. "Of course there is. An indoor elevator that opens close to our penthouse door. But that's for our use."

"Oh, I was just curious," Allison said, waving good-bye as the elevator doors closed. We started our descent. Allison pressed something into my hands. "I was pretending to be asleep," she said. "I was waiting for the right opportunity. Couldn't let them keep it." It was the Blake tarot card deck and it felt right to have it in my possession—where it belonged.

\*

"You know what would make things even more fun this afternoon," Crewe asked me as he sipped his beer on my sofa the day after the brunch. "I mean, I do have time, it's only a little after two and I don't have to be home till nine for dinner."

"What?"

"To add a little white powder to the mix. You know, we have some green stuff, why not add some white stuff too?"

"What do you mean, what kind of white stuff?" I asked warily because of his sudden enthusiasm which had not been there when he'd walked in the door and found I hadn't written any essay—at least not yet, I lied to him sweetly—for his entertainment.

"A little blow, you know, coke."

I'd never tried any, I wasn't sure.

"It makes the sex incredible," he added, certain that would snare me, which it did. I'd seen plenty of movies where people snorted powder through a straw off some kind of jagged mirror, but I didn't exactly run with a fast crowd who was into this kind of thing. I expected him to pull a piece of broken mirror out of his jacket pocket now. Instead he said, "I know how you can get some."

"Me?"

"There's a woman, her name's Teresa, she lives in a studio down on 16th Street between 8th and 9th. You just have to ring her and she'll deliver—very discreet, you know—she sometimes straps a doll onto her front like a papoose, looking real innocent and motherly when she makes her deliveries."

"You've got to be crazy. It's illegal. I'd never let a drug dealer come here—to my apartment. What would the super think? Or the neighbors?"

"Of a woman with a baby? Well, suit yourself, but you're missing out."

"Why don't you get it, then, if it's no big deal?"

"I have more to lose, don't I?"

"Not really. A bust is a bust and jail wouldn't be a holiday for anybody."

"How do you think I get my grass, which is the best

money can buy? From an acquaintance of mine who happens to be in my book discussion group. A well known banker as it happens, but he rarely partakes these days. But you do, and I don't mind sharing it with you. Why don't you do something for me in return?"

"Because it smells."

"I see." Crewe studied his fingernails quietly. "Actually, maybe I should go into the office today—we have a few buyers who really are looking to close the deal on some buildings."

"Fine." I didn't take the bait but I didn't want him to go. "I should be studying for my exam."

"What exam?"

"For a state job. The test is on Saturday."

"You don't want a job. Why would you?" he asked, disturbed. "You don't have one now, I assumed you were living on a trust of some kind, that you didn't need to work."

"Not exactly. I'm not broke but what I have won't last forever." Suddenly I didn't want Crewe to know anything about my finances, or Frank's insurance money or even anything about Frank himself. He'd asked me if I had a current boyfriend and seemed content with the answer that I gave him—no. Now I knew why. It would interfere with his coming over here and getting his rocks off because I wouldn't always be available, in the same way my having a job would make his sex life more difficult, having to dance more carefully around Clemma's schedule to fit me in.

"If you're worried that a job would keep us apart, it wouldn't," I assured him. "I'd see to that."

"But we'd have less time."

"Look, I'm going to take the test, that's it. It could be weeks, months, a year before the list comes out and I get called for an interview and become a possible hire. My next door neighbor waited twelve years to get his interview. That's how the government works. I could be old and gray before anything changes." I felt I was apologizing, trying to make things better for him, a millionaire who I'm sure had grabbed his own opportunities.

But he sulked anyway. Finally, "I'm sorry but I do have to go because I need to check things at the office."

I was furious. So it was a game of the carrot and the stick. Fuck him.

"By the way," I asked. "I hope you didn't think I was eavesdropping yesterday but I couldn't help overhearing when I came into the kitchen to say good-bye."

"Oh, the police thing." He brushed the subject off like the lint from his jacket. "A crazy kid I was seeing at one time told the police I was bothering him, kept calling him after he'd asked me to stop, none of it was true of course, he was overreacting and the police were very sympathetic, took my side. Of course, I never called him again so there wouldn't be any further misunderstandings." Then he added with some anger, "But as you can imagine it was awkward."

For the two of them. Then she knew about his proclivities and from what I'd heard that afternoon didn't much like them. Maybe he'd lied his way out of it to her, insisting he'd been set up by somebody, a business rival.

"What could you have thought?" he suddenly asked sunnily. "Oh, well, good-bye for now. I'll call you soon." And he left. Making sure he was going to be the one to call me. After I'd been punished enough? And as the afternoon dipped into evening I realized it was a punishment, being deprived of his passion.

But I should have known it would have been just as bad for him. He phoned the next morning acting as if all were well with the world and asked to come by at two. "After all we have two days worth of unfinished business to squeeze into one!" He'd found a good thing, hadn't he, so why let an unimportant tiff interfere?

He never mentioned the essays again, he'd given up on them, figured he'd lost that round but knowing there surely would be others he could put in his column.

We got high with his grass, passing his little pipe back and forth to each other.

"Good thing I went into our offices," he acknowledged. "As it turns out I made a sale with a Swede for a townhouse on 67th and 2nd I never thought I'd get rid of. The taxes on it are through the roof. But I'm sure he'll sell the individual apartments somehow and get rid of the place within a year for a profit anyway. But everything's more difficult now in this slow market—" here he paused from talking to himself in that unique way of his that made me feel I'd been hearing something quite by chance, something, of course, I wasn't competent enough to grasp, and he gazed up at me with an unsubtle eye for the part I was able to understand all too well—"so I won't be required to spend all that much time at the office anyway. And here, it's my turn today..." He reached into his pocket and pulled out a vial of powder. The small gold glass vial had a little spoon attached to it. He unscrewed the lid and asked for a plate, which I brought to him. He held the vial over the plate and filled the spoon with powder, some of the dust spilling over onto the plate which he put his finger into and touched to his tongue, and afterwards tilted his head back and snorted. "Ahh..." was all he said. Then he emptied a liberal dose of powder from the vial onto the spoon and instructed me to tilt my head back and snort it. After I did I felt the warmest glow rush through my body, like heat lightning that brought along with it a steady, pulsating horniness. "Oh," he laughed, "you like it well enough when I bring it." I couldn't wait for him to take his pants off. We both got naked and moved into my bedroom. He brought along the grass and the powder, which he called it, never referring to it as cocaine. I guess that was his preference and the only reason he'd had to distastefully blurt the words blow and coke out to me yesterday was because I was so dense.

We smoked and snorted all afternoon as we had sublime sex, in a honeycomb full of dark and light shadows; I responded to this stimuli on a new and higher plane than I'd ever experienced. Every sexual feeling was over-sensitized, sharpened, then somehow refined.

After we'd exploded in tremendous orgasms, hours later, and lay there panting, recovering, but still on the glorious but finite threshold of tingling sensations, Crewe threw his arms behind his head and turned to me and said, "My wife's trying to poison me."

"What do you mean?" I struggled, impossibly, to sober up and take in what I'd just heard in a meaningful way. But I was too high.

"Clemma, she's slowly trying to poison me. I have to watch her all the time. At home. Even when we're out at a coffee bar I have to be careful. Or at the opera during intermission when she brings me a glass of champagne."

I wasn't really hearing this, was I? Of course I was, but was I supposed to pry further for more facts, feel sympathy or danger for him, even believe him? When no sane response presented itself to me I lay there quietly, willing myself to forget his accusation, willing it to go away. He helped me along by getting out of bed and starting to dress. "My goodness," he said. "I didn't realize it was getting dark, I'll have to jump into a taxi, Sidonie's waiting for me to give her a lesson before dinner. Latin and Greek derivatives I think it is today." Coked up and stoned, he was going to sit with his daughter at the kitchen table and play professor? Well, God bless him; maybe he was just the person who could manage it after all.

"As I said, it was my treat this time," he said as he screwed the lid on the not quite empty vial and put it back in his jacket pocket, "but fair is fair, next time is your turn. This isn't cheap stuff after all. I'll provide the grass and we can share the cost of the powder from now on—or if you'd like, that could be your contribution. And, anyway, I'm not always able to get hold of my connection."

I lay in bed after he left, still hopped up, unable to sleep; I tried to go over the multiple choice questions in my sample exam booklet but couldn't concentrate. My phone, which used to ring all the time, didn't anymore, at least not much. Certainly the usual people, members of my bereavement group, had mostly stopped calling; now it was usually either Crewe or Silvio on the other end of the line. When I'd told Reg I needed a break he'd left a message that at first I was relieved to hear, now I wasn't so sure; instead of going into one of his typical rants, this time about the dangers of isolation, he'd just said he understood and to call him when I was ready to come back. To come back. To where? To what? The unrelieved boredom and misery of grieving! Like it or not, I'd been thrown a lifeline from some sluggish, swirling river of forgetfulness, to grasp at moments of sweet oblivion like a drowning man, where every unpleasantness was supposed to be replaced with pleasure and escape. Now that I held that lifeline, that thin perfumed cord in my hand, I wouldn't let it go.

\*

Naturally I liked the combo of the grass and the coke. Crewe knew what he was doing all right. Just give me a little taste of that and I'd want it every time we had sex. And go to unexpected lengths to obtain it—when only a few days before it was totally out of the question that I would have had anything to do with copping any sort of illegal drugs. What a difference an afternoon makes. I didn't like the idea but Crewe insisted he was making the buy as easy as possible; he'd take me through it step by step.

It was Friday afternoon, a cheerful sunny day in late October when the bricks of the Seminary were shining like gold bullion and the sound of children's laughter coming from the nearby school playground filled the air. I was standing at my window looking at people I didn't know engaged in the most mundane activities, strolling, talking, peacefully making their way, mothers or nannies pushing baby carriages, and messengers on bicycles ripping along. Nothing out of the ordinary, except that Crewe was sitting on the sofa flipping through a magazine instead of starting to strip and taking out his little silver pipe, getting ready for the only event that linked our days together. He may have been thinking along the same lines because he made an allusion to our usual pattern: "You know, one reason I look forward to coming here is the lack of any game playing or wasting time with talk or trivialities. You're always ready to get down to business. No wasted time. You make things very comfortable and easy for me in that way and I appreciate it." He closed the magazine and dolefully and, I could tell, truthfully, added, "You don't know how I wished when I was about fourteen or fifteen that I'd had someone to go to like you. If there'd only been some older man in the neighborhood I could have visited on my way home from school who wanted me every day and who I could have stayed with—doing it, you know, like we do—till dinner time…and sometimes on weekends too. But I didn't…and I can never go back and make it right…"

"But we have today," I added inanely, feeling I should comment somehow.

He looked at me. "Yes, oh, yes, we have today and it's a new day for us, isn't it?"

Put the essays in my column, the copping of the coke in his. My stomach churned and I looked away from him out the window again. A homeless woman pushed a heavy cart of rags and old newspapers down the street and I thought of Allison. I didn't want to do what I was going to do but since I was going to anyway, I just wanted it over with.

Crewe tried to make it easy. "Though I'm financially conservative, I'm socially liberal, there's nothing wrong with any of this, my goodness. We're free agents I should think. I'm holding your hand and doing you a favor. You'll thank me when you feel at ease enough to get it on your own. I've set it all up for you— all you have to do is follow through. What's the difficulty?"

I'd withdrawn a hundred bucks from the ATM that morning and Crewe had grudgingly handed me a hundred and now I was to give both bills to this Teresa and she was supposed to hand me an eight-ball of coke which Crewe told me should look like pieces of white rock. "It's pretty good stuff, so my contact says, and for heaven's sake, I'll walk you over there and wait for you, hang around the shops on 9th Avenue till you come out. What could be simpler? I made the call to her from my cell, she's expecting you to knock and she knows you by the name of Paul. You just do a quick exchange with her then you and I can do our thing."

But as we walked down along 9th Avenue, I was looking up for those pod-like cameras. I didn't see any but what the hell did I know, maybe they hid cameras in plain street lights these days. And the shaking affect I presented was of someone looking for an opportunity to commit a crime, the scruff of my jacket pulled high, cap pulled down and jaw slouching. I even wore gloves, though it wasn't cold, so I wouldn't leave my fingerprints on anything. I left Crewe on the corner, my fingers digging in my pocket, making sure the two one hundred dollar bills were there and feeling like some Miami kingpin without any protection.

Her apartment building was between 8th and 9th Avenues, on the south side of 16th Street, midway down the block. It was just a regular 1950s five-storied nondescript pea green building with a glass door and camera on the lobby ceiling turning back and forth and pointing down at me. The outside door to the vestibule had been jimmied by a dirty scrap of cardboard and a little bird told me it was Teresa's method of admitting her clients. I'm sure anyone doing anything illicit for the first time—say a man visiting a hooker, which in my mind I pretended to be—is a wreck. You don't know who the hell is going to open the door, a beautiful babe, a syphilitic hag, or a cop. I rang her buzzer—4B—the buzzer with no name. Why wasn't I surprised when no one buzzed me in. Fortunately an elderly lady carrying her bags back from the drugstore came up and opened the inside door to the inconspicuous lobby and let me pass inside with a motherly "How are you today?" and then turned to the right on the ground floor and put her key in her door while, since there was no elevator, I bounded up four flights of stairs, whistling, anxious for her to know I lived there too after all and wasn't a mugger following her or anything.

I reached 4B at the end of the hall on the fourth floor. No doorbell. I knocked. I could hear the peephole from the apartment across the way open and shut, and involuntarily I pulled the cuff of my jacket up, a suspicious move. Open the door, bitch, was all I could think, don't leave me standing here like the guy who's just been shot, the one the gang leaves behind after an armored car robbery. Just ready to be picked up—and what easy pickin's!

Finally I heard a slow shuffle from inside and her peephole opening. Then without a word the door opened just enough to admit me sideways and shut again behind me, and I heard a bolt slam into place as I found myself in a dark hallway, cluttered with all kinds of shit I could barely see. I stumbled along behind her shadowy figure through her railroad flat to end up in a small room taken up mostly by a bed and a stove where something foul was bubbling in a pot.

"Sit down," she said invitingly, indicating the edge of the bed. She, from what I could see of her in the dim glow of a single pink bulb under a cheap tattered lampshade, was a woman in her mid-thirties in a red Chinese silk robe, opened at the neck to reveal her white cleavage, very thin-waisted, with a heavily made up semi-emaciated face that reminded me of a wren's, and a carefully coiffed head of blonde hair.

"Paul, isn't it?" she asked.

I nodded.

"Teresa," she extended her hand. "You live in the neighborhood?"

I didn't want this woman to know a thing about me, that's for sure. "Sometimes."

She laughed coquettishly and musically. She looked like a wren but laughed like a nightingale. "Sometimes, what does that mean?"

"I'm house-sitting right now. Look, if you don't mind, I'm kind of in a hurry." I started to take the bills out but she stopped me by putting her hand on my hand that was still inside my pocket. Instinctively I moved away.

"Don't worry, you're not my type, I like them a little more rugged. I was only telling you not to be so quick on the trigger. The stuff isn't here yet. The man who's making the delivery is late. And believe me, I'm as anxious as you. I'm dying to cook up some crack." She nodded to some dirty pans on the stove, then proffered me a filthy looking glass tube. "Want a hit of resin while we wait? I managed to scrape some together."

"No, no I couldn't. I'm not feeling very well, you know. I'm just making this pick-up for a friend."

She laughed gaily. "That's what they all say, darling. Please try to come up with something a little original. Who referred you to me anyway?" she asked as if she were a high-class madam with a book—the kind of book every client fears.

I drew a blank.

"Come now, you don't even know?"

The hell of it was I didn't. Crewe hadn't said, damn him, strolling outside the cutesy little shops on 9th Avenue.

"Of course I know," I said. "How do you think I ended up here?"

"I'm certainly beginning to wonder," Teresa said. "You seem awfully nervous, dear." Then she put the crack pipe in her mouth, bent over to get a lighter, and when she did, her Chinese robe fell open and I noticed a penis hanging between her legs. After she lit up and took a hit and blew out the smoke, I watched as it settled onto what was now quite obviously an elaborate wig that I'm sure had never been washed. She coughed. I could see that whoever this she-he phantasm was who answered to the name Teresa was slowly dying. "What do you do for a living?" she asked interestedly.

"I help design sets for Broadway shows," I lied, desperately grabbing at something oh-so-New Yorkish.

"No!" she screamed. "Look at my walls."

I'd never seen walls with more layers of grease and grime—it must have been layers of crack smoke mixed with normal dirt and dust that had accumulated over the years and been carelessly preserved because washing the shit off just didn't matter anymore. On these walls were hung crude drawings of fashion models in outlandishly ultra-feminine get-ups. Frilly nightgown stuff. "I did those," Teresa stated proudly. "I used to be a costume designer. I worked the dinner theater circuit, mostly in Florida."

"Very nice indeed."

"Do you have any contacts in the theater here? That you could show some of my designs to? I really would be grateful for any help. I need to get a new start. Back into the business. I seem to be going nowhere."

"Well—I don't know. Let me think it over."

"Sam. Sam Martinson," her bell had finally rung. "That's who sent you here! You tell him for me it's about time he paid me another visit. The bastard, I haven't seen him for weeks. What is it, he's suddenly gone straight or something?" She lifted the pipe to try to get another hit of what she called resin when there was a pounding on the door. "Oh, it's him already. It didn't take him long to get here from the East Side. Quick, follow me." I followed her, stumbling over cans of paint, piles of satiny underwear, old floor fans, down the darkened hallway into a bathroom where she shut me in saying, "Don't say anything, don't even move. If he knew you were here we'd be in a real pickle."

I heard footsteps of someone negotiating the thin dark hallway much better than I had, someone who knew the terrain well. I stood as still as a figure carved in ice. So Teresa was the middle-man or middle-woman, whatever. He sold her the coke and then she added her overhead. I suddenly wondered if this guy whose voice I could hear softly in discussion with Teresa would need to use the bathroom. And what she would say to him if he did. If I wasn't afraid that this guy would catch me and what that might mean I'd say fuck this shit and run out on both of them. If they were two giant sleazeballs, what was I, staring down at madam's pubic hair in the toilet bowl?

But he soon left and I fled that bathroom quick as a rabbit and down into Teresa's parlor with my gloved hand outstretched clasping the two one hundred dollar bills. I saw disappointment in her face because I got to her more quickly than she had anticipated. She was holding two equal packets full of white rock, one in each hand. I realized that, addict that she was, she'd obviously put in an order for herself too and had meant to take some out of my packet and add it to hers. But she was too late. I got to her before she could do it. With a frown, and silently, she handed over my full packet.

"That wasn't so bad, was it?" Crewe asked as I joined him on the corner of 9th Avenue. "Though I must say you took longer than I expected."

"Well, you go next time. I'm sure you could wrap things up much more quickly than I did, and I'll do the window shopping instead."

"Oh, he's getting nasty. Or should I say hungry?"

I stopped and glared. Normally I wouldn't have, I'd have taken it from him. But not after what I'd just been through.

He cleared his throat and changed tactics. "Everything worked out then. You did get it…She didn't cheat you on the old family recipe, did she?"

"Can we discuss it when we get back to the house if you don't mind?"

"Oh, he's very touchy." The last word on it, I hoped, and he had to have it.

At home I felt dirty. I took a shower. Afterwards, as I toweled myself dry he told me to watch him pulverize the rock with the handle of an ice pick, to show me how it was done for future reference. I don't really know why he wanted me to watch since after he opened the packet and emptied the pulverized contents onto a plate and began to fine-chop it and draw individual lines with one of his credit cards, he made a show of keeping the front side of the card turned towards him so I couldn't see any of the numbers. He was so trusting. Like I was going to rip off a millionaire who could come after me like a Mack truck.

He cut two straws down and gave me one. "Here, snort a line," he encouraged me. "You've certainly earned it."

As we each snorted one and I felt it hit me I said,

"That was clever, giving the name Sam Martinson to Teresa, good old Sam, our phantom of the fifteenth floor."

He giggled the Crewe James conspiratorial giggle and agreed, "I thought you'd get a kick out of that."

In the bedroom we had incredible sex, what else, how could we not? But as we wound up towards a climax I was distracted, bothered by something I couldn't put my finger on. This Sam Martinson thing. My contact. It had been Crewe in her apartment then that she'd called a bastard for not showing up for so long. Hadn't it been? I couldn't help pushing away from Crewe and asking, "What, honestly, do you think of her, this Teresa?"

"Dunno, never laid eyes on her."

"But she said a Sam Martinson had been there and had referred me. She said he'd been there himself...But there is no Sam Martinson. There's no fifteenth floor. I thought she was talking about you."

"You're mistaken," Crewe said, exasperated. "There is a Sam Martinson. Now can we finish first?"

We finished having sex rather unhappily.

Before Crewe left he said, "Now, how do we divide the powder fairly."

"You tell me," I murmured, not caring.

"One of us divides the pile in two and the other chooses which pile he wants." When I didn't respond, he divided it painstakingly several times until the two piles appeared to be finally satisfactory to him. Then he told me to choose one. I pointed to a pile without much interest and he scooped his pile up vigorously into a larger vial than he'd brought along the first time. "This way no one can feel cheated."

"Since I was referred by Sam Martinson," I dared to say in an icy tone, "I'd like to know who he is."

"Oh, that day I thought he lived in your building," he said easily. "It turns out he lives in the building next door and I'd gotten the building numbers mixed up. You understand? He lives on the fifteenth floor of the building to your right."

Thanks for the explanation, rather for the slight clue, I thought, as I lay sleeplessly, tossing and turning in my bed that night. That means you met him after you met me and that he'd gotten goodies for you from Teresa during the time I've been seeing you. What else did it mean? Maybe Crewe was used to visiting my neighborhood more often than I realized. In fact, he'd been visiting my neighborhood before we'd been properly introduced. Sitting on that bench outside the Chapel of the Good Shepherd. And look what he'd been up to. With a wave of revulsion I revisited that moment but with a stronger wave of revulsion I revisited all the moments I'd had with him since. Where had I been in my own mind? What had I been thinking then if at all and what was I thinking now? For some reason I thought of the red shoes lying in the closet. Oh, no, that was too simple. I couldn't blame anything on a pair of shoes. Not his behavior and not mine. But then the revulsion began to dissipate when I thought instead of the release that being with him had given me, the wild pleasures of it all and at that very moment I noticed someone standing at the foot of my bed.

I thought at first it was a man, maybe Crewe had come back for something, but of course he didn't have a key to my apartment—no one did. And then I sat up straight in bed, mouth gaping open. In a glowing soft gossamer light stood a tall angel in long white robes and wings that reached from his shoulders to the ground. The edges of the wings were lined with that cottony fluff I'd found pieces of in my bedroom and interspersed into the fluff were twinkling golden, red, and sapphire lights. I'd estimate the angel stood about six foot four and had a high forehead and long white hair to his shoulders, though he wasn't old in age, and had a full beard. His lips were full and eyes wide. He stared at me—no, into me—and his expression was grave and stern. A broad and shining sword was held in place by a golden belt around his waist, the tip of the sword almost brushing the floor. He nodded his head in a disapproving manner, locking eyes with me. And his eyes had anger in them. I looked down, unable to face his approbation, it was too powerful. All I could say softly, as I trembled, afraid, was, "You've been here before, haven't you? Several times before." And before I looked up I could sense some kind of retreat on his part, some dissipation, and when I had the courage to lift my head I saw him pointing a finger towards me as the glowing light around him faded and he disappeared ever so slowly in a glaze that lingered slightly, even after his majestic figure was gone. I threw my face down on the pillow, my eyes not having believed what they had seen, but knowing in my gut what was the truth, that he was as real as I was.

*

Needless to say, concentrating on the exam the next afternoon was challenging. So many disconnected thoughts ran through my head as I attempted to circle the correct answers to multiple choice questions that had four choices each. Some were straightforward, like legal terminology—you either knew what *voir dire* or *pro se* meant or you didn't. I took my best stab at it but I guess I should have studied a bit harder because I wasn't sure. In the section where I thought I'd shine—rearranging paragraphs in their most logical order—I was in doubt. No matter how I arranged them they ended up having their own random logic, like life. Each paragraph could have been a beginning, a middle or an end depending on the way you wanted to construct the scenario. How New York State wanted me to construct it—there was the rub.

The test was given at the Art and Design High School and I'd waited in a long line that wrapped around the block with hundreds of other applicants. Each of the classrooms was full, including the room I was in. We sat on the kind of hard-backed wooden chairs I hadn't seen since grade school. No one there had a very happy expression. Most of the test-takers left early, discouraged, sheepish, and covertly slipping their half-finished booklets into the monitor's hands. What a moneymaker for the State. It cost seventy-five bucks a pop to get one of those pencils and booklets.

I stayed till the bitter end, until a bell rang and a voice on a loudspeaker booming throughout the school instructed everyone to close the booklets.

I had no idea how I fared but I did try. The embarrassing truth was, I knew I hadn't given it my all in the prep work stage. I'd been too busy the last few months. And the disconnected, disconcerting thoughts in my head swirling around and keeping me from full concentration were of course pieces of all the confusion I had somehow invited into my life and hadn't sorted through. Certain faces spun before me quickly, Crewe, Clemma, Sidonie, Allison, Reg, Silvio, but especially the faces of Adam and Eve from the Blake watercolors. They were the most present, the most haunting.

Of course I was exhausted from the way I'd spent the last week. And shell-shocked. How had it happened I hadn't been in the library each day, studying up? What a mistake, or more accurately put, an accident of the mind. I wanted to go back and start over. Then I remembered how the angel, yes, the angel, had pointed his finger towards me and I knew there was to be no new beginning. I was where I was on the path; a city had crumbled behind me leaving barbed wire, shards of glass, and concrete, preventing me from turning around and going back—the only way lay ahead through a strange and difficult terrain. But surely there was an ahead. Was that what the angel was trying to convey?

I was cautious. I took it easy—for me. I indulged in long November walks by myself, down by the piers, where wet leaves and river fog were sometimes all I saw. Or I spent time at cafes in the Village, like the Café Dante, where I lingered over my favorite coffee, Orange Fantasia—dark, rich coffee with a sediment of chocolate at the bottom of the cup and a twist of orange peel at the top—or I lounged at the Café Reggio, reveling in the worthless bric-a-brac decor and eavesdropping on the NYU students who thought so highly of themselves and were involved together in the most fantastic projects.

I wasn't kidding myself that this pleasant lull I was enjoying wasn't influenced by other events. To be honest, what would I be doing if Crewe were still in town? I had a feeling things would be different.

Though I saw him once or twice after the Sam Martinson moment, it was rushed because it was the time of year he was going back and forth to St. Barts, preparing the villa for the holidays. According to Crewe, he, Clemma, and Sidonie left for the island shortly before Thanksgiving and came back after New Year's Day. The few times I was with him, briefly, in mid-November I was annoyed, thinking he was seeing this other guy at the same time he was seeing me—until I realized I was doing the same—with Silvio—and cut him some slack. Though before he left, as he was telling me it would be murder for him to be away from me that long, I felt relieved—as if I'd been given the time to be able to draw back into myself and linger, to see who I'd been before I'd started colliding with the crazed intensity Crewe had brought to my doorstep. Unfortunately, I had to admit I did think about him while he was gone and that wasn't very comfortable. But the difference was I felt free to think about and do other things too. And I told Silvio I needed a rest, I didn't really see the reason for being involved with two men anymore. What was the point? I did read parts of novels now and then. But mostly I walked and walked, in the day, in the night, in a sometimes still warm breeze and in the cold. And the more I walked, the more I remembered myself.

One of the most pleasant days was Thanksgiving Day itself, odd because I was never one to overemphasize the holidays or go bananas over "occasions." But I had a little group over around two o'clock that included Bob McBride from next door, and yes, Big Deal too, curled up at his feet, Reg, and Allison, the caterer, who didn't cater today but helped Reg and me cook the turkey, asparagus, and squash and make the stuffing, nothing fancy. She brought a man along who contributed a store bought rhubarb pie. His name was Logan and he was lanky, pleasant, and doted on Allison, which pleased me. When I asked her if he was one of the two possible fathers she said she'd let me know later but she forgot. I hoped he was.

The five of us were in a jovial mood, happy to be together. McBride kept ribbing me about the court test, advising me to take twelve years traveling the world, then come back to New York and see if the State was ready to make me an offer I couldn't refuse. I didn't tell him I wasn't even sure if I'd get a passing score. Today it didn't seem to matter, there was too much of a simplicity to everything.

Reg was reassured to see me in such a good mood. He told me I looked in the pink of health.

We toasted each other with sparkling water. There had been no pressure on anyone to have made the perfect meal, to have made trendy conversation, to have chosen the most cutting-edge CDs to play, or to overplay the effervescence of the moment. And fortunately when Allison asked if anyone wanted a reading from the Blake tarot card deck, no one did. It was that kind of day.

When everyone had left and the sun began sinking I couldn't help but think of Frank. I cleaned up, enjoying the lingering scent of the remnants of the food and, as usual, lit some candles. The bells of the Seminary chimed. It was peaceful. After everything was put away I lay on my back on the floor. There had been no twilight, the sun had left and it was night. Memories of Frank came flooding back, and for some reason, one specifically of a summer's night shared long ago when we were fresh to the city and had proudly attended a gala for the Boston Symphony at Carnegie Hall, not a usual event for us by any stretch, we'd rented tuxes even, put on the dog, though we could barely afford to, and in love, in trust, after the concert had walked all the way back to the little studio we were renting off Washington Square Park.

I don't remember every moment of what happened that night, far from it, not even one word of our conversation, but now I strongly felt the ghostly emotions that cemented that night long ago to this one. In a fog I called to Frank, trying to transmit my thoughts to him...

A dying rose loops your lapel, the only blood on your black and white tux and with a Kleenex you could twist it off. Have you drifted in to take me again? It always seems you've brought a crystal ball, its fevered glass remembers us. The window is thrown open on the park. Dark trees, shadows under candles, dresses of summer! A moist lone room. Your hair is in my mouth. I remember...Night breezes pouring from your throat. Have you come again? My face is still and bent toward the ceiling where park lights become puppets, a charming green. Who are these lights? These shifting characters? Ah, you never were. There was only an old shoe within me, deep.

\*

It was during the time of the blizzard that there was a true sea change. It was only mid-December, usually too early for this kind of thing. One morning, not long after the sun rose wan and meandering, big soft flakes of snow began to fall heavily. I turned on the TV. The weatherman said to expect between ten to twelve inches of a steady pounding snow in the next twenty-four hours with increasing winds in the afternoon that would create "blizzard-like conditions." By noon when I looked outside there was an accumulation of three to four inches piled up against the Seminary wall already. Just as I thought "Thank God I don't have to go out anywhere in this," the phone rang. It was Crewe calling from St. Barts.

"Well, what a surprise," I said. "How are things?"

"Oh, fine, just fine. I miss you."

"Well, me too. But you wouldn't miss what I'm seeing outside my window."

"But I'm looking at the very same thing."

So it wasn't Crewe calling from St. Barts. He was calling from his penthouse in New York. It seemed that on the spur of the moment he'd had to return to the city to personally attend to closing some deals that couldn't wait till the new year and that after he finished them up, there would be no need to return to St. Barts, at least not this time around. Clemma and Sidonie were having a wonderful time down there on their own and could make it back to New York by themselves in early January.

"They certainly don't need my company to enjoy paradise...But I need yours." My throat got dry as I stared at the full-formed snowflakes raining down while I steeled myself for the proposal I knew was on its way. He wheedled, "Why don't you come over right now and stay as long as you'd like, through the storm. I'll build a fire in the fireplace, I've got plenty of wood. You should see how beautiful the snow looks over Central Park! And," he lowered his voice in longing, "we could spend hours and hours in bed together. All afternoon and all night. And all morning if you want."

His invitation did sound promising. He made it seem terribly luxuriant and gave a new meaning to the term winter wonderland as I pictured him lying naked in front of a fire, the snow and ice thick and heavy, stuck to or dripping down the glass doors that led to the terrace behind him.

"But I don't know if I could get up there in all of this."

"Nonsense, they just said on the radio the winds won't get bad till this afternoon. It would be tough to find a cab, I grant you, so just go over to 7th and get on the number 1. All the trains are running as of now."

"You've done your homework."

There was a slight pause. "Of course."

"But what about food and stuff?"

"I got back before any of this inclement weather started, thank God, and I managed to get to the market for some eggs, some cheese, toast, tea, that kind of thing, and I just ordered a couple of porno movies to watch— one straight and one gay—from the store around the corner and they're going to deliver them any time now. So you see life goes on even in a snowstorm."

"You certainly make it tempting."

"One little thing. I rang Teresa and she has some stuff. She's expecting you. You can pick it up on your way here."

My blood turned cold at the thought of stopping by that creature's habitat but boiled hot at the thought of having a nice wintertime party with Crewe.

"I have some here too, of course, left over from last time." I imagined he did have some there but doubted it was left over from last time. "And I just got the most incredible grass."

"How much is—the powder?" I almost said blow.

"The usual—two hundred," he replied. "So by my calculations you should be here within one to two hours. The weather will cause a bit of delay but not much. I'll ring downstairs to the concierge and let him know John Laith is going to be visiting me and he'll send you right up. If you have any trouble, phone my cell."

"OK," I said, not at all liking the drug copping part but figuring since he'd taken care of everything else it was fair enough.

"I'll see you very soon," he said "and I'm really looking forward to it."

"So am I."

Fortunately I always kept around five hundred bucks wrapped in my sock in the bottom drawer of my bedroom dresser so I didn't have to slosh over to the cash machine. I threw on a T-shirt, a pair of long underwear, a sweatshirt, sweater, heavy blue jeans, a double pair of woolen socks, some rubber boots, waterproof jacket, scarf, and knit cap and hoped for the best.

Unfortunate, I thought, that Crewe had to leave glorious St. Barts for this mess. But when I got outside I realized this was just about as beautiful as any place could be, vast gentle flakes settling onto barren treetops and onto dusty gray rooftops, turning them white and sparkling and pure, creating a spiritual transformation. Ninth Avenue was already closed to traffic; I clomped down the middle of it as people passed by me on skis.

This time I had a few more balls as I rang Teresa's buzzer, figuring, wrongly I'm sure, that cops would rather linger over coffee in some diner than venture out into this and bust somebody. Also now I knew what to expect from Teresa; she was as nasty as her dirty business was. I figured I could just slip inside her door, make a quick exchange, and be on my way. This time she even buzzed me in on my first ring.

But I shouldn't have underestimated the determination of someone who thought I might be able to help her. Today she opened her door quickly, and I slid in like an eel and slithered down the dark hall that had more junk for me to navigate than the last time. She insisted that I join her—for a moment at least—and once again offered me a seat on her bed, which this time was dressed with shell pink rumpled sheets spotted with obvious cum stains. I chose a spot between the stains and sat down carefully. She was wearing a black negligee, wig askew.

She put a pipe in her mouth, added a piece of rock and lit up. She coughed out the smoke like it was her dying breath, which one of these times it would be—I just hoped it wasn't now.

"Any news from the theater?" she queried. "Did you think of any way to help me? Things are a little desperate at the moment…"

I figured to get what I wanted and then get out quickly I had to play this fucking charade. Well, I announced, it just so happened I had talked to someone about her design abilities and— yes—at some point he might be interested in seeing some of her sketches.

"Oh, yes, who?" She took another hit and offered me one. I declined, citing "the snow, you know, I can't afford to fall." I made up a name for some bullshit producer who I told her was trying to find backing for a show; if he got it, then I would introduce them. "But now I have to go. I need to travel someplace before this storm gets any worse."

She stared at me for awhile, running her fingers along the hem of her negligee. I could read her expression and saw she didn't believe me—about anything—the eager producer, the fact that I had to be somewhere before the snow got worse, all of it.

She said blankly, "You're getting real good stuff this time." She handed me a packet of rock—about two thirds of the amount I got the last time but for the same price—obviously she'd already done her thing—and waxed, "Oh, I think I asked you this before, do you know any rough trade? Someone who might be looking for a nice roll in the hay with somebody like me?"

"Maybe," I said, unsure what to say.

"Maybe," she said, tittering. "The gentleman says 'maybe.'"

I thrust the two one hundred dollar bills into her hand. At least this time my wearing gloves was understandable. But she said "Huh-uh. Here." She pointed to her cleavage. Annoyed I stuffed the bills between her puny breasts. Christ, what you had to go through for a good time.

"By the way," she said, "Sam Martinson did come here the other day. I told him about you. Seems he never heard of you, Paul, whoever you are. Oh, I know he didn't make the call for you, someone else did, using his name for the referral. He'd like to find out about that too. He told me he feels like he's in the middle of a mystery. Maybe the three of us should have a little crack party here and the two of you could sort it all out."

When I didn't respond, she shrugged, fingering the bills between her breasts as she turned her back on me. "You can let yourself out."

With pleasure, lady.

I had to wait longer than usual for the subway, standing in dirty melting ice on the platform, snow spotting my blue jeans up to my knees. The ride up to the 86th Street station was crowded. It seemed everyone had somewhere to go before things got worse, I was only one of many. When I stepped out onto Broadway the giant flakes had thinned out into what seemed like thousands of smaller ones and the wind had already picked up. I made my way to Central Park West with a stinging sleet blowing in my face and scolding air currents pushing me back one step for every two I took forward. Crewe's building loomed above in the darkness of an early afternoon. By the time I reached the entrance I could see this was turning into a really bad storm, worse than I'd imagined.

A doorman pulled back the door for me and let me

pass through, along with a blast of sleet. Brushing myself off, I stepped up to the concierge sitting at the lobby desk and introduced myself. He picked up the house phone to advise Mr. James that Mr. Laith had arrived. I heard Crewe's voice on the other end. I could see the concierge was a pro, the old-fashioned type who'd worked his way to a plum position in a top building through sheer professionalism and know-how. He replaced the receiver on the hook and instead of commenting about the weather, or anything else, for God's sake, he gave me a look.

Trying to appear unintimidated, I confidently asked with the spirit of a legitimate guest, "Oh, by the way, where's the elevator?" He paused before he said brusquely, "The one at the end. It takes you straight up to the top."

As I approached the elevator I could feel his eyes on my back. I sensed it was obvious to him I was no friend or business associate of Mr. James but a whore come to visit while his wife was out of town.

Hell, maybe I was misreading him and he didn't think anything of the sort and this was just a sudden twinge of guilt on my part. Nonetheless I was relieved when the gilt doors of the elevator opened and I stepped inside, out of the way of his scrutiny. The interior of the large elevator was very classy with lemon panels of flowering trees cascading from the cornices to the baseboard. I pressed the button for the penthouse.

The doors opened into a long mirrored hall and I realized that around both corners the mirrored hallway continued with entrances to at least half a dozen penthouses with terraces that faced different views of the city. Crewe's faced the park. But which was his door? He must have anticipated my dilemma as down to my right was an already open door that probably led into his penthouse. Sure enough, as I approached it, I heard Crewe call for me to come in. Once inside I not only shut the door behind me but locked it for good measure.

"You can just take your wet clothes off right there," his disembodied voice floated my way. "I'm in the kitchen making tea. There's a towel for you on the table. You can go in the bathroom and freshen up after you've got all those wet things off."

After I'd "freshened up" in the bathroom, I put on my still dry sweatshirt and long johns and joined him in his cavernous kitchen where he was sitting at the round, heavy wooden table, sucking on his pipe, his eyes glassy and fixed on invisible thoughts. The room reeked of marijuana, even though one of his gabled kitchen windows was cracked and a draft was blowing in along with flakes of snow. He'd laid a heavy blanket under the window which was already wet. Through the window which faced north I could see thick patches of ice and snow swirling around the tall fabled twin gables of the Art Deco luxury building, the El Dorado.

"Well," he said as he handed me the pipe, "you got here after all. I wasn't sure if the weather was going to cooperate. But I did keep my fingers crossed."

I got stoned on that first hit, it was so strong. "It wasn't so bad in Chelsea but when I got up to your neck of the woods I realized I'd made it just in time."

"Neck of the woods. How quaint. Do you want some tea? I have some ready."

"Definitely."

As he approached the stove I could see he was wavering; I held my breath that the tea would make it into my cup and not down the front of him; fortunately he held steady and was able to pour some for me. "Can you smell the logs burning? I started the fire about a half hour ago." I didn't smell the logs burning but did feel a rippling warmth and heard a crackle and pop coming from the living room. When he handed me my cup, I saw how dissipated he looked, like he'd been smoking for days.

"Do you want lemon or honey?" he asked.

"Neither, I'm fine." The tea felt warm and was aromatic, restorative.

"Didn't you ever think it was unlikely I ended up in your building that day? I mean what odds would you give for that happening?"

Well, if he'd been looking for somebody he thought lived there…"I'd say it wasn't expected by me but wasn't out of the realm of possibility either—given the circumstances."

He laughed. "Not expected by you. I like it."

How to respond?

"We can start out anywhere," he said. "We can be as adventuresome as you want. We can wait to do it in front of the fire till it gets darker. Then there's my study, that's where the DVD player is…we could watch the porn they delivered. I gave it a once-over, it's so-so. But there's no rush. We could start out in bed if you like, I've piled it up with big pillows, you can make yourself at home. I've put some towels down on the sheet, have to be a little careful. But you decide."

"I'm agreeable to starting out in bed."

"You did get the powder?" I nodded. He brought out two plates with two straws and did his pulverization, cutting the lines, distributing the piles evenly onto two plates, both of which he carried with him as he guided me into the bedroom. "This way we can each do a line whenever we want one."

The bedroom was as I'd remembered—a brass bed with pillows and sheets patterned with reeds and bamboo flutes, towels spread across it, and a big comforter at the bottom, as white as the blizzard I'd come through, and the two end tables were each piled high with books. Through the window the gray sky seemed as immobile as a painting. The sound of the sleet beating against the window was the only thing that brought me into contact with the outside world. Crewe lowered the blind and turned on his bedside lamp, removing some books from each of the end tables, making way for the plates of coke he laid down in their places. Then he stripped naked. I took my long johns off but kept my sweatshirt on, still chilly.

Crewe ushered me up to his dresser, picked up what seemed to be a cufflink box and opened it. "I've collected these from all over the world." They weren't cufflinks inside though but cock rings. "And now you get to choose one for me to put on."

"Well, I don't know which ones feel the best to you. It's your decision."

There were at least a dozen, probably more. Metal and steel and plastic rings, leather snap-ons, plain or with studs, quite a variegated selection.

"Why don't I start off with this one?" he suggested. "It's the umbrella. Of course I picked that particular one up in London." Indeed it resembled an umbrella that had just been opened and was made of rubber. I guess it was the right choice considering the weather.

It was a conundrum—which side of the bed to lie on—his or hers?

"It doesn't matter," Crewe said, "just remember there's a plate of powder on each table. Don't spill."

I climbed in on her side. Why take over his? Still it

felt strange to be lying in her bed—well, their bed. Crewe settled in on his side and was now phoning Clemma in St. Barts. "Let me get this out of the way. Then we won't be interrupted."

Lying next to him I could hear her voice faintly on the other end as he held the cell phone away from his ear on purpose so I could be a party to their conversation.

"Clemma James," she answered briskly.

"Hi there," Crewe answered.

"Oh my God. We heard the weather reports from down here. Are you all snowed in?"

"Yes," he answered. "But I'm well stocked with all the items I'll need to last out the storm. Don't worry, everything's fine. Any business matters can really be taken care of from home."

"Well, I was a bit concerned."

"No need to be," he replied, looking pointedly at me in a smarmy way as he slipped on the umbrella ring and tugged on his cock, making it erect. "I have everything I need right here. Oh, and those new pillows you bought are wonderful—I had no idea they came in such a large size…" Here again he caught my eye, apparently making a double entendre as he masturbated. But why? Did he think he was turning me on by showing me he was a real swinger? Was he getting some kind of satisfaction by fooling her? Was he fooling her? Or was it just done for the benefit and pleasure of Crewe himself, reveling in his own duplicitous actions? It all seemed beyond me and made me uneasy. When I heard him ask her to hand the phone to Sidonie I was amazed. Was he going to masturbate and leer at me while he chatted with his daughter? Luckily, Clemma advised him Sidonie had gone on a picnic to a nearby cove with the family who lived next door, "you know, that Dutch politician who thinks so much of himself, but at least he has a daughter Sidonie's age, though of course she has no use for the girl, but she agreed to go anyway because she said she was tired of me!"

Crewe laughed and pulled me into him, kissing me. He put my hand down on his cock. He kept the cell phone between us so we both could continue to listen. "Well," he said, "I just rang to give you the latest weather report. Promise to call me if you need anything, all right? And I'll try to come down for Christmas if I can wrap everything up here in time." I remembered his mentioning to me that he was definitely not going back to St. Barts this time around. "Tell Sidonie to e-mail me and let me know how she's spending her days."

"Of course I will. Oh, I almost forgot to tell you, they started work on the pier today. Rather I should say a few locals brought a lot of wood in a truck and piled it up in our front yard. What an eyesore."

"Just ignore it. They'll finish it up soon enough. I had an e-mail from the contractor."

"All right then, bye for now, darling."

Crewe arranged one of the long double white pillows underneath me, making me comfortable. "Oh, Clemma, thanks again for the new pillows. You're ingenious. I've put them to good use already."

"I'm glad. All right, Crewe, enjoy them. I'm sure we'll talk tomorrow."

Crewe said good-bye, snapped the cell phone shut and did a line of coke.

I did a line too and immediately felt that golden rush. Unsettled, I knew I needed to be somewhere else in my mind, and cocaine and THC blurred reality and softened the edges, at least I hoped they would soften them enough for me to concentrate only on the eroticism of the moment so I wouldn't have to think about Crewe or Clemma or Sidonie and these cheap, unkind games I didn't want to be a part of. Crewe laughed and said derisively, "What she doesn't know won't hurt her...the best thing is she can't show up unexpectedly, can she, with every airport shut down for miles. No unpleasant scenes to deal with, thank the dear Lord." I could tell he was high as a kite, more stoned than I'd ever seen him.

Suddenly he pointed to the closet and for a minute I thought he was trying to convey that someone was in there. But he was just illustrating a point. "I had an acquaintance once who happened to have a very inquisitive wife. One day when he was on the job apparently she had nothing better to do than go through some old shoe boxes of his at the bottom of the closet and in one of them she discovered nude pictures of her husband in, shall we say, some extremely compromising positions with another man. Hell hath no fury as they say. It wasn't enough to divorce the man and take his apartment, she had to have copies of the photos made and sent off to his mother and his boss. So you can't be too careful, you see? It's comforting to know she has no way of walking in on us."

"That's for sure," I agreed, not relishing the thought of Clemma catching Crewe and me together on her newly purchased pillows. What are you supposed to do anyway if you're caught in a situation like that red handed? Grab your clothes and run? Try to reason things out? I didn't know, but I had to keep reminding myself that my relationship was with Crewe and Crewe alone. He was the one cheating on his wife, not me. His alliance with her was none of my business and I wanted to keep it that way. It made me feel better.

Crewe whispered to me, "It's so right. You don't

want anything else from me but this."

I don't know if the world would correctly call what we were doing "making love" because some ways of love are hidden from the mores of conventional thinking. But to me we were. At any rate there was no question we were engaged in a passionate affair, losing ourselves in the unconscious feelings we eagerly gave each other. It was exactly where I wanted to be. And it was where he wanted to be too.

Crewe and I worked sexual wonders together because we complemented each other perfectly. I felt I was rejoining some part of the world I'd lost, a world of abundance where I now felt totally present.

Of course it was the drugs that were both plunging us into this land of enchantment and holding us prisoner there. I knew that—but so be it if that's what it took to get us...where? We were in a tower of steel. And from this tower we could peer down at all of mankind without any shame.

We had plenty of coke in the bedroom but nothing else so we found ourselves making occasional trips to the kitchen to relax at the table, drink tea and, most importantly, to smoke more grass. I wondered if I looked as out of it as he did. I hoped not but I wasn't going to pass any mirrors just in case.

Funny what drugs do. Everybody reacts differently under the influence. They made him ramble on about nothing, energized him, released his inherent yang I suppose, while my Pisces self withdrew, as usual, into yin mode, became quiet, subdued, practically fetal. The tea felt good going down. I almost said "it warms the cockles of my heart" but didn't, not only because I was too stoned to make it come out right, I just didn't want to hear Crewe repeating it back to me in that obscure, contemptuous "isn't that clever" way he had.

"Time to do it in front of the fire!" Crewe announced. "Let's keep switching rooms, it makes it more fun!"

I suppose it did. He added a log to the fire and had everything already prepared, a fluffy white rug and multi-colored Persian pillows thrown around indifferently. Before lying down I paused at the glass doors to the terrace where it was freezing; in that living room the only really warm place was directly in front of the fire.

It must have been around eight o'clock by now and snow was piled up six feet high on the terrace. The sleet had lightened up and I could see the promised ice-capped trees of Central Park bending in a harsh wind, the snow blowing haphazardly around them.

Already hanging in the sky was a bright full moon, which appeared breathtaking at first—cold, lifeless, yet spectacular—but as I stood for a moment in its strong patch of light, I felt suddenly that it was actually alive, some round vessel of archaic wisdom determined to pry off my worldly mask. I turned away from its brilliance. Just as strains of Wagner's *Götterdämmerung* filled the room. Crewe had put on the von Karajan version with the explanation, "It's a great accompaniment to sex, you'll see." Yet ever the gracious host, "If you think it interferes with our enjoyment, I'll take it off." But its rapturous swelling motifs and voices floating up from Valhalla was just the thing to make me more passionate than ever. Crewe responded similarly. Everything was heightened by the combined spirits of the music, fire, and moonlight.

I rarely spoke during sex, but for one moment I let my thoughts out and expressed the passion I was feeling to Crewe.

He turned on his side facing me, his eyes glowing with cunning and hostility. He stared me down with a smile. And with relish and pleasure informed me, "There's no passion here. It's lust. There's a difference between them. This is pure lust and lust only—for both of us—nothing more."

Shocked and humiliated I told him I wanted some more tea, to which he responded, "Oh, yes, let's go to the kitchen and smoke some more then move into my study for awhile. We wanted to try different rooms anyway, don't forget."

I hadn't forgotten. I gulped, or rather choked down, another cup of tea, forcing my mind to go blank, trying to forget his words and that expression on his face.

I could still hear Wagner in the background as we entered his study, only now the strains of the music seemed softly bombastic, falsely romantic. Crewe made quite a show of opening his closet and wheeling out a tray with a DVD player on it and placing it in front of the white leather sofa, which we settled down on. There was one window in the back of the room with the blinds pulled down. He dimmed the lamp by the sofa.

He was right, the porn was so-so. I masturbated him to some scenes of women in flashy scarlet and black silk skirts crouching deftly onto different men leaning back on sofas, staring blankly, perfunctorily into space. At intervals the porn starlets played musical chairs and rotated from one cock to another. Maybe you had to be there. But I could tell that Crewe was hardly concentrating on the porn, he was thinking about something else, though once he lukewarmly praised the scene as being "hot." "We should try that position sometime, we never have," he offered his opinion and I automatically nodded my head in the affirmative while confusion raged in my mind. The gay porn was just as dreary, some bleached blonds in skimpy bathing suits fondling each other in some tropical resort, blowing each other in a communal outdoor shower, palm trees sparkling in the sun.

"Is this doing anything for you?" Crewe asked.

"No."

"I have an idea," he said. "Let's try that position, you know, I'll sit back on the sofa and you can ride me." He switched off the DVD player. That would be awkward enough I figured but I'd give it an unenthusiastic shot. He plopped himself down on the sofa with, "If you don't mind getting our plates of coke from the bedroom…oh, and a towel."

I fetched the plates and went to the bathroom to get a fresh towel. When I got back I saw he'd cleared a space under the lamp on the table. I gave him the towel, which he put under him then I laid the plates on the table while he turned the lamp switch on high. The bright glow didn't help get me in the mood to try to straddle him. I gingerly lifted one leg up on the sofa. My head turned toward the window. There was a gap of about ten inches where the shades had been pulled up during my short absence. I was surprised to find that his study faced another apartment building across 85th Street instead of onto the terrace, and I could watch figures moving back and forth in their rooms. I could clearly see one man standing at his window staring skywards, presumably to check the weather, but I saw that the way Crewe had planned it the man would be seeing more than that. I took my leg off the sofa, crossed the room and lowered the blinds. "I don't really feel like an audience."

He blushed. Caught. Then, "Oh, don't be such a prude. I doubt anyone was looking anyway."

"But you hoped otherwise. Obviously. It didn't occur to you to ask my opinion on the matter?"

He didn't say anything.

"What you did is deplorable. I don't like it. It's a turn-off. When I'm with someone I like it to be private."

I knew he was an exhibitionist. Yet to think of him wanting to be watched having sex by neighbors on his block whom he'd have to pass in the street or even outside of his own building was unfathomable to me, exhibitionist or not. And the way he hadn't taken my feelings into consideration—it was fine by him if strangers saw me having sex with him without my even knowing it. It was more than fine by him, it was preplanned, it was desired.

He pouted. "You know how to pour cold water on steam heat. That I'll give you. You should think outside the box. There's a world of possibilities out there, for heaven's sake. Don't you have any wild fantasies you haven't tried?"

"No."

"Well, you might want to ask yourself why not. Loosen up a little."

"In what way?"

"What about introducing some new sex play into our repertoire?"

"For instance?"

"For instance you could blow me in the back of a taxi or at my office...or we could try a three-way."

"I'll think it over." I remained calm, knowing it would never happen. The back of a taxi for Christ's sake; I could see the driver peering through the rear-view mirror, not quite as turned on as Crewe was. As for a three-way, I wasn't the sharing kind. Of course that would help depersonalize everything for him, degrade me, and somehow, through that, degrade himself. It was a web no spider could ever spin. Only a sick, intelligent man could attempt to weave two people into such a soulless filament.

"You'll think it over?" he repeated my words mockingly, the amount of drugs he'd consumed showing. "Don't strain yourself. There are others who would only be too willing to do it with me. In fact, they are doing it with me. What do you think I've been up to the past few days? I've been back home nearly a week. I haven't been idle. Oh, you're my favorite, don't get me wrong, you're the one I've been looking for. For a long time. And I finally found you. I was saving the best for last, that's all, letting others sample me in the meantime.

"I've had one or two others up here during the week. Why not? My profile on the Internet receives a ridiculous amount of interest. I can't help the attention it creates, can I? I make it simple for anyone to make an appointment to meet me. I let just about anybody do me at least once unless they're really old and ugly. I don't fuck them like you, but I do let them blow me.

"The first time I saw you at the Seminary while I was sitting on that bench—I was killing time before my appointment with a new Internet prospect. It was the same with Sam Martinson. I was really planning to meet up with him that afternoon I turned up in your lobby. But he lived next door. Luckily for me as it turned out—or we wouldn't be together tonight. Sam and I did manage to get together later. He was all right, nothing special, but he did prove to be a good contact for powder.

"You know, one of the benefits of setting my own hours is that I've had plenty of time to let a lot of men try me, and most of them lived in Chelsea, I have to say! Just before I met you, I went to this one guy's apartment a little up from you on 10th Avenue. He was a slightly older man living in what I'd politely call a closet, nowhere to sit down really and make yourself comfortable, communal bathroom down the hall, that kind of thing. I don't know how he survived, I suppose on welfare and food stamps. He was certainly grateful I stopped by for a few hours."

The sleet had started blowing hard again against the window.

"Come with me," I told Crewe and started down the hall. He followed me with some trepidation. I turned into the small elegant dining room. I flipped the light switch, which illuminated the crystal chandelier hanging low over the mahogany table. Pieces of polished silver shone to advantage. I opened a drawer of the buffet and removed a silver knife, fork, and spoon and laid them on the table.

"Why are you doing that?" he asked.

"You say you've had strangers come up here that you contacted over the Internet." I thought of the doorman sizing me up as a whore and now I knew why. "You didn't know them, they didn't know you. Weren't you taking a risk, being high and having valuable pieces of silver not locked away, as well as antiques in full view in every room? Weren't you afraid someone might steal something?"

His glassy eyes just stared and he made no move to answer.

"Or if one of them had wanted money or a piece of silver, was going through hard times, was desperate, would you have given him something, anything valuable, monetary wise."

"No."

"But you gave them all without question the most

intimate part of yourself. In fact, you threw it their way as if it was something you didn't value, unlike money or silver. Isn't that right?"

"Yes."

"Why?" I asked.

He paused, confused, like he'd never quite thought of it that way. "I don't know..." He glanced at me with a bit of respect for asking a good question then said, "Let's go smoke some more." Then he staggered off towards the kitchen where he boiled more tea. I followed slowly, passing the living room, casting a glance at the glass doors to the terrace where heavy flakes of snow and fine punishing sleet obscured my view of the night. Then into the kitchen where Crewe, forgetting about the tea, was stuffing a big clump of grass into his pipe. Snow was swirling in at the window and the protective blanket on the floor was soaking wet. "I mustn't forget to phone a potential client tomorrow about an apartment I own on upper Riverside Drive. I have to try to get his commitment to buy. His credit is perfection itself. And he has the money. I wouldn't have thought it but this storm is a godsend, at least I don't have to meet up with him in person."

"I don't know that you could."

"That is a matter of opinion. Here." He held the pipe out for me. I took a hit and coughed out the smoke while he inhaled, held it deep, then turned and slowly blew it through the window into the snow.

"Crewe," I said as I sat down at the table and folded my hands in front of me. "Don't you ever want to stop all that? The things you were telling me about. Start over fresh...you know..."

He stared at me rudely like I was ruining the party and let me sit there, my question unanswered, as he stepped into the hall and weaved his way towards his study. From where I sat I eventually heard the sounds of Crewe sniffing heavily and frequently. It just didn't sound safe. I made my way to the study to find him holding one of the plates to his face on which he had set up a major line of coke for himself, what I had remembered hearing in some movie was referred to as a California line. "That's too big," I told him. "Isn't it?" He did it anyway, then laughed quietly and disparagingly, asking rhetorically, "I wonder if they're home in their penthouse down the hall."

"Who?"

"My good neighbors. No, I'm their good neighbor. They think very highly of me, don't they? Well, why not, my reputation speaks for itself. That's why they asked me several times to babysit their daughter. It was a drag, of course, but how can a neighbor refuse? She was in a playpen, how much trouble could that be? Clemma had to look after Sidonie anyway, make sure she didn't wake up from her nap, keep her tucked safely under the covers, so I was the one who usually agreed to do it. Of course after I got inside their penthouse and her mother left, well, then I'd have to think of some way to entertain that dear child in her playpen...but there were fishes after all in their aquarium...which she liked...I tried to get her to watch the fishes...'Watch the big fish! Ooh, isn't it lovely?'" He held the plate of coke towards me. "Want one?"

Trembling, I put the straw on the plate and did a small line.

"You asked me, you asked me did I want to stop all this and start fresh..." His next words were tortured. "It's too late!"

He turned shakily and stumbled out of his study into

his bedroom where he advised me he was going to have a little rest period. He laid the plate on the table on his wife's side of the bed with surprising dexterity, then fell onto the mattress and crashed. I guess all the grass he'd smoked had somehow blunted the effect of the big line of coke he'd just done.

I was alone. In his house.

I wandered into the living room. The dying embers of the fire threw funny shadows on the wall and the warmth had ebbed away. The marble fireplace was cold to the touch. Snow was all I could see against the glass. How I wanted to leave Crewe passed out in bed and go home. I wanted to get out of his apartment so badly yet it was impossible. Not because of the weather; I would have braved this storm, crawled over mounds of ice-crusted snow like an alpaca to make my way to the subway since I figured I had no chance of finding a cab or getting car service. But the real obstacle was that I couldn't go anywhere in the condition I was in, not even if it had been warm weather. I was too fucked up on drugs to feel confident I could make it home safely. But I didn't feel safe here. I didn't feel safe anywhere. Especially from my own thoughts that flew at me like a flock of ravens, unforgiving and black.

I realized Crewe was a master, a perfectionist in the true art of undermining. By throwing out bits and pieces of thoughts or incidents that were intended to purposely disturb me, a person with feelings, he made sure he remained the focus, the center of my attention. He knew I would be trying to figure out what he meant by all the perplexing clues he had planted in my mind yet he would always be one step ahead of my inferior thought processes, assessing my responses with a troubling immediacy and seeing where he needed to take me next.

The squeaky wheel gets the oil, they say—and the obsession. Once Reg had advised me, "Never get involved with a married man. It's the perfect prescription for obsession because you can never have him." I obsessed about Crewe not because he was married but because of his frightening intelligence and shrewdness, which he put to use by making me doubt myself and by keeping me in the dark about who he really was and why he even wanted or needed this relationship with me.

And, by the way, why had I wanted a relationship with him? Alas, I had no idea.

That's what spelled obsession to me, the not knowing, that's what made me engage in exhaustive circular thinking and, most astonishingly, was beginning to leave me with a gradual lack of belief in my own value system. Somehow Crewe's belief system was attempting to take over mine like a cancer.

I walked aimlessly back into the hallway. It was after midnight. I guessed I should just shove Crewe over to one side of the bed and try to crash too. But I knew I was too strung out to sleep. And even if I could sleep it wouldn't be relaxing, lying beside Crewe in his and Clemma's bed.

The door to Sidonie's room was open. Maybe I could lie down on her bed for awhile. I switched on the overhead light to her room. It seemed atypical for a girl her age. It was austere. And nearly empty. There was a simple single bed with a black woolen blanket and thin pillow on it. Next to it was a small chipped table holding only a lamp and across the room against the wall, a small bureau. That was it. There was no white fluffy comforter or double-sized down pillows in here. Yet I didn't feel Sidonie's parents had purposely deprived her of any luxuries but that she herself had made a conscious decision to live as a kind of ascetic. Hers was like some meager room in a cloister, except there was no rosary on her bedside table and no crucifix hanging above her bed.

I flipped off the light and lay down. Everything glowed in a semi-darkness, the hall seemed enveloped in a haze of gauze, probably because of the combination of the light in the kitchen and the snow shining from behind the glass doors in the living room. Sidonie's mattress was hard and so was the wood frame that held it. I turned and twisted, uncomfortably. A dream I'd had last summer came back to me, the dream about an intruder loose in the Seminary garden, making his way inside, stalking the sleeping Seminary students. I remembered trying to rouse them with urgent warnings to "Wake up! I'll tell you everything I know...Please, wake up..." But what had I known? And why was there such an urgency? Well, that's the lunacy of dreams, I guess, they drift away before they can mean much.

Fuck, I couldn't sleep on this bed of nails. I felt cold and I was high. In a gracious Central Park West penthouse. Far from home. Through the dimness I could make out an old-fashioned china water basin on Sidonie's bureau—which somehow didn't surprise me— and something else too, a book. I approached the bureau where I saw the book was a large photo album on which the words ST. BARTS had been emblazoned across its front in gilt letters, presumably by Sidonie. I thought of paging through it but wasn't particularly interested and was further discouraged when, out of the corner of my eye, I saw inside the formal parlor directly across from her room the hanging portraits of those dried souls, their black brimmed hats and bonnets pulled down low, so you couldn't see their eyes wanting to watch what you did and see who you were.

I walked back down the hall into the living room. I heard creaking sounds in all of the corners, the kind you hear on boats in the dead of night out on the ocean, but of course it was just the floorboards settling. I listened to the moaning of the wind; in my mind the moaning seemed unexpectedly human. A cold seeped through me that had nothing to do with the ice and snow pummeling the glass doors. It was a different kind of cold—the destructive cold of an unquiet life force that had lost any beauty, energy and purpose. I'd read about houses of the damned— and believed in them—houses that were built wrong from the beginning, sometimes by unscrupulous or cruel architects, houses in which those unfortunate enough to reside were tormented by unbearable suffering, ill-will, jealousies, hopeless grief, madness and, always in the end, disaster. The House of Peacocks in Brussels, the Tanz Akademie in Freiberg, Germany, the Salamandre Maison in France, the Archive Building in New York, and the Chateau Marmont in West Hollywood were just a few I remembered. Evil dwelling places inhabited by lost souls or fiends. Could this be one too?

I realized I disliked Crewe James intensely. That was too kind. After what I'd learned tonight I realized I hated him. I couldn't pretend any more that I was involved with anyone other than a deviant who made me sick—no matter how much I longed to keep up the pretense that things were otherwise. I'd taken my head out of the stinging sand at last; his vague yet not vague insinuations I could no longer wish away. I'd heard and seen too much. I had given this man a kind of gentle love, the only kind I knew how to give, in the only way I knew how to give it, and he had sucked it up as his possession and made something else out of it, something dark and loveless to suit his own purposes. It was no longer recognizable to me and no longer meaningful in the same way. And I realized something else too. For the first time I was afraid of him, I didn't know why.

I stepped up to one of the glass doors, pressed my fists against it and peered out through the flakes and ice. I was shocked. Snow, some twelve inches deep, was heaped up to the top of the cornices and filled the gargoyles' mouths. Icy gusts moved the snow into fancifully shaped mounds from one end of the terrace to the other. The bright moon had left, leaving behind a paleness, a dim imprint in the dark, while it continued its way on its nightly journey.

First I noticed the familiar blinking lights of ruby red, blue, and sparkling gold. The lights that lined the outside edges of his wings. He was standing at the end of the terrace, still a tall imposing figure, his long legs anchored deep in a snowdrift, the angel, now looking like the hermit pictured in the tarot, a lantern in his hand, a concerned look on his face as he held the lantern high and moved it back and forth, staring towards the penthouse. Snow and ice had frozen his beard, and icicles had formed on his face like tears. The lantern itself had a thick coat of ice hanging from the base. For what seemed a long time the angel peered forward, anxiously. I pounded on the glass to let him know where I was standing, to make him see me leaning against the pane. That's when he started fading into the snowy mist, the blinking lights dimming, but with his lantern still lifted high. I tried to push open the glass door against the piles of snow but couldn't. I was only able to turn the door handle back and forth uselessly. As I labored he disappeared completely into whiteness.

"What are you doing?"

Startled, I quickly let go of the handle and pushed myself away from the glass. Crewe was standing in the doorway to the living room, his arms folded.

"Nothing," I answered guiltily.

"Come back into bed," he said and left the room. I could hear his footsteps moving down the hall.

I stood there quietly for a moment then followed him into the bedroom.

*

When I woke the only thing that registered was that it was day because an orange light was seeping through the blinds. For a brief moment I thought they were my blinds and I wanted to open them and look out into the garden. But when I rolled over, Crewe's green glassy dilated eyes were staring at me.

"How did you sleep?"

I couldn't answer right away. I was trying to gather my thoughts, all of them unpleasant as they vied with each other for attention, one after the other, the night with Crewe, the mystery of and my inability to communicate with the angel, the realization that the trip home in the snow would be cold, slow and miserable and, because of the new dread I felt for the man in bed next to me, how to behave with him? Should I tell him now how I felt about him, about us, just let it all out—or say nothing and start making my way through the snowdrifts to the subway, pretending nothing had changed—and deal with it later. Which was the wiser choice? Suddenly the only thing I knew for sure was I was going to have to fly by the seat of my pants as Crewe was already reaching for me, pulling me close to him, and this was no time for contemplation.

"Don't."

"Don't?" He looked at me in surprise.

"I'm tired. Really. I didn't get much sleep." Though I felt like I'd slept the sleep of the dead.

He took a look at the alarm clock. "Why it's four o'clock in the afternoon. You've had plenty of sleep."

"Is it that late? I can't believe it. I had a lot to do today."

He pulled me even closer into him and kissed me. "That's right. Had. But the day's over, isn't it? So we have a new mission now."

I thought when I woke the dim orange light had been the light of dawn. I shivered, realizing it was the dim orange light of evening.

"I have so many things I have to catch up on. I've got to get going."

He frowned, genuinely confused. "I thought we could try to find a cab and go to your place together and spend the night there, you know, and start all over again. After, of course, we have some tea and toast here, to bring ourselves up to par."

"Well, you know, I'm not really in the mood for all that…"

"You? Not in the mood?"

"I have a headache. Like from a hangover." Couldn't I just say it was over between us? Did I have to go with the tried and true excuse that I had a headache, always a lie? At least it was now. And he knew it.

"You know what would help with your headache, don't you? A line or two. Then you'd feel right as rain." He pulled the plate from beside the bed and held it for me. He even kindly lifted the straw for me until it was under my nose.

"Just a little sniff," he urged. "I promise you'll feel

all better."

I thought of making my way over the snow banks on yet a new high, after having leveled off enough to go home in a state of physical regeneration while trying to reclaim my own destiny. I pushed the plate away and got out of bed. He reluctantly laid it back on the bedside table, not even doing a line himself, and eyed me warily and silently as I struggled to put on my long johns and sweatshirt.

It was intolerable, his watching me. I gathered up all my clothes as the orange twilight further dimmed and walked down the hall into his bathroom and shut the door. I sighed deeply for what seemed forever, leaning against the door. Eventually I heard his footsteps pass by. That gave me the adrenalin to finish dressing, though it was an effort, heaping on all the layers that felt so cumbersome, the woolen socks alone the weight of rocks. The clothes were still damp, that was why, like they'd been taken out of a dryer before the spin cycle was over. I'd probably catch pneumonia going home. Or the sheer weight of everything, material and emotional, would bury me under an icy drift before I could reach my lobby door.

When I came out of the bathroom he was sitting at the kitchen table eating some toast and drinking some tea. I walked over to him to say good-bye.

"Oh, I've made you some toast," he said. "And tea. And put out some butter and a nice selection of jams." The hot toast smelled wonderful. And I was starving, I hadn't eaten anything since yesterday's breakfast. My resolve to rush out quickly melted. What harm would it be to spend five extra minutes to fortify myself before the long slog home?

"Oh, thanks," I said starting to sit down but he

stopped me with, "If you wouldn't mind, can you just bring me the paper first, it's right outside in the vestibule."

"Of course," I said. I brought him the paper and he thanked me, stretching his legs out comfortably. He was wearing a cozy full-length expensive robe and fine woolen slippers. He seemed to have the contentment and peace of a pampered Persian cat licking himself by the fire while I was the Iceman Cometh, huddled anxiously, waiting for the first destructive gales of a global warming meltdown. I buttered my toast nonetheless and piled it high with savory orange marmalade and let myself enjoy it. I sipped leisurely at the hot tea and added some cream to it. It was delicious. All the while Crewe was engrossed in the paper, like the first moment I'd seen him on the chapel bench. It was as if I wasn't there. It was unsettling, but fine by me. Better that than a useless conversation. In fact, I helped myself to more toast and tea—for two reasons— one, because I was hungry and two, because I didn't want to show him that his unresponsiveness bothered me. As I finished my last bite of toast I looked up to see Crewe terribly intrigued by some article, heavy glasses perched down on his nose. Well, I hoped I could just let myself out rather than endure a pleasant good-bye at the door or questions about when we were going to see each other next. I'd slip away. When I got up Crewe didn't take his eyes off the paper but said casually, "Aren't you forgetting something?"

"No, I don't think so…"

He pulled a set of keys out of his robe pocket and dangled them in the air. I looked closer. They looked like mine. He took his eyes from the paper and gazed at me nonchalantly. "You wouldn't be going far without these I wouldn't think. They dropped out of your pants as you carried your load of clothes to the bathroom. Lucky I found them, wouldn't you say?"

"Oh, yes. Well, thank you."

He handed them to me and turned back to his paper.

"Well, good-bye then," I said.

"You have a safe trip home now."

*

Apparently my judgment was poorer than I realized. My frantic escape from the balm of the cerebral, soothing world of recovery had been a fool's sprint. Away from the fear of faith. Where man stands alone. Or has to get down on his knees alone.

When I had welcomed faith and hope into my life, there had been something intoxicating about it, bringing with it the almost giddy promise of peace at the end of the road. I had performed service many times, reached out to strangers for help, strangers who had become friends, and I had extended myself too, to anyone who was grappling with faith, to anyone who was too damaged to hope again. This was how things worked. Through community, through a shared bond of crisis-solving and caring, without judgment, a renewal of the spirit was an anticipated gift. But over time, nothing had magically appeared to make my life better. I'd done my part, I thought, to begin to reap a few of the benefits of healing. But what I'd reaped so far had just seemed to keep me breathing on a life-support device, incapable of really living within the wisdom of acceptance. Yet on that night of the storm, huddled with Jared against that wet brick wall, dodging bolts of lightning, a new vitality had taken hold of me, the kind I thought would bring about healing as well, a different kind of healing, but a healing nonetheless. I'd taken matters into my own hands. But not wisely or capably. When turned loose, I'd demonstrated less coping skills and strengths than I'd had at any other time in my life.

I thought of the hours I'd spent with Jared, of his red shoes, of how he'd worn them, vainly, and how for him they'd become ruinous, a symbol of his turning away from his purpose in life…he would never be that dancer he always dreamed of being. Was I turning my back on my own purpose now too? To want so badly to heal. Jared had wanted to thank me for helping him. But he had next to nothing to offer me in return. He did have a pair of red shoes he no longer had any use for. They belonged to me now.

The snow was rapidly melting; it had turned warmer. Lakes of filthy slush filled the streets; the last clumps of snow fell off branches in front of my feet. Yet I was home, light years away from Crewe's penthouse and I hoped light years away from Crewe, someone who'd become more of a stranger to me than any passerby on the street.

The more time you spend with a man the less you know him. A human being most resembles his own residence, which he rarely thinks about—the universe, vast, complex, indecipherable, and perpetually changing. There is one exception to this confusion. The constancy of your soul mate.

The minute Frank and I walked separately into a drafty college auditorium during our first Thursday night "Introduction to Film" class at UCLA, just as Méliès's *Le Voyage dans la lune* was beginning to unspool, we glanced at each other and without saying a word knew we would be together forever. Though we sat a few seats away from each other it gave me pleasure to peer over at Frank and watch his reactions to the film, to hear his quiet laughter as a group of sexy chorus sailor girls heaved the spaceship into a canon and let it fly, turning around to salute the audience—and show off their legs. And to notice his curiosity as the moon loomed closer and closer during the rocket's celestial journey, and how after the landing was made with a splat the space pioneers just curled up in the folds of the lunar surface and could think of nothing more delectable to do than fall asleep. I was happy to find my reactions were the same as his. And I had the feeling that, like me, he was eagerly anticipating some meatier fare. The film promised in our syllabus next Thursday was to be chosen from among the works of Sjöström, Dreyer, or Murnau. I hoped it would be Sjöström's *The Phantom Coach* as I'd never seen it but had already seen Dreyer's *La Passion de Jeanne d'Arc* and Murnau's *Nosferatu* more than once. Frank laughed aloud when the moon men, actually acrobats from the Folies-Bergère, attacked the somnolent explorers—but his laughter wasn't the kind of sophisticated know-it-all laughter I was soon to experience from New York moviegoers, eager to be the first on their aisle to reveal to everybody else that something was passé and an impossible cliché. Frank's laughter was wry and empathetic. It wasn't showy, it wasn't about him. He was able to covet something for its own merits, to put it within the context of its inception and accept its time and place—yet still enjoy an easy chuckle. And when he made a point of seeking me out as the lights came on and everybody stood up, he leaned over and whispered to me, "Hope it's *The Phantom Coach* next week," and I answered without thinking, "If it isn't we could make a list of every revival house in

L.A. and write a letter requesting them to show it." Wow, with a crazed line like that, I had definitely gone out of my way to show him I wanted his friendship. But my overeager comment hadn't been necessary. It was love at first sight for both of us. I didn't have to go to the trouble of begging revival houses to show *The Phantom Coach* or drop my books on the pavement outside the auditorium and have him pick them up and offer to walk me back to my dorm to know that the cement that bound us together was already too strong to separate. That's God's one mercy, I guess, on His planet of lost logic. He gives you one chance to know the core of one other being as well as you know your own and though circumstances will bring trials and misunderstandings to visit you both, the cores never change—until, unnoticed, they become one.

My poor mother. Every year she tried to grow roses in a cracked oblong box that sat in the kitchen window. She filled it diligently with dirt like a freshly dug grave but nothing ever came to life. Except on two occasions. Once when I was about four I remember watching something stunted, colorless, and ugly trying to push its way up through that earth. But it couldn't—and I was just as glad. Yet two years later a pair of exquisite roses shot up, unexpectedly, in that same window box, a red rose and a cream rose, intertwined, oblivious to the briars. But I wasn't—and that was why I didn't want to reach out and try to touch the petals. I figured I'd somehow prick my fingers on the briars and they'd bleed, so it was hands off, but when I smelled their perfume I cried.

They grew majestically in our Kansas City suburb, a suburb that was unquestionably teetering on the brink of becoming a newly formed slum. There was litter and trash on the street now. Bars were opening and five-and-dimes closing. Change was in the air. Even a child could notice. The roses provided a proscenium to both the night's sordid neon and the day's drabness. In the square light of day overworked men and women, having left their homes before dawn, rushed back to their families at three or four o'clock, but after darkness fell they reappeared, some husbands, some wives, usually from different families, furtively and with shame pushing open the swinging doors to the bars to sit alongside stunned derelicts. Eventually my mother's solid victory, those roses, drooped and wilted and sunk back into their dank graves. But their moment in time—who could take that away from them?

On one of those nights when the roses were at their ripest, I reluctantly tuned my gaze away from them, slipped off the kitchen stool, and climbed the steep staircase to my bedroom. As I lay down to sleep, I closed my eyes tight and whispered aloud, "Somewhere there's a garden calling, *John, John, John...*"

\*

Crewe had to work fast. Though I hadn't said so and had tried to appear calm and non-confrontational, he knew I was on the run. I hated that he could read me so well but there was nothing I could do about it. And of course he knew why I was running. He'd made a rare mistake that night in his penthouse—he'd gone too far. Maybe it had been the drugs, maybe he'd been drunk with a sense of power over me, maybe he'd just been feeling his wild oats. But his cruelty, which he'd enjoyed revealing in a clever, calculated way like a slow and constant drip from a leaky faucet you barely notice, had reached a breaking point. And forget the faucet—the dam had burst. I still didn't know what game he was playing, but I knew a man like that didn't like to lose. He wanted a good return on his investment. So far I'd dodged his bullets as best I could. Now I just needed to keep out of the way of his gun. But guile, or what I assumed was guile, was his preferred weapon. Much better than a gun. Less messy. No blood to wipe up.

When he left a message on my voicemail that he was mystified why I wasn't returning his numerous phone calls, that it was inexplicable to him, he wondered if it wasn't about time to come check up on me, have a talk with the super to see if I'd been seen in the building, even phone my police precinct. He said he was afraid I'd met with some kind of unfortunate accident. I had. But not the kind he was thinking about. I'd run into him. The thought of how he spent his days frantically having anonymous sex with stranger after stranger revolted me. Yet he reveled in it. Maybe he was driven to do it against his will but the way he had bragged about his conquests led me to think he was doing exactly what he wanted and enjoying the hell out of it. How he was feeding the poor and lonely with his almost divine appearance at their doorsteps. A sexual saint bearing enough bounty for everyone. He was too intuitive to know I hadn't been struck by a cab or moved to Europe or had a new boyfriend. He knew I didn't want to see him anymore. Yet I wasn't able to actually make a phone call and tell him that. I was intuitive too and knew that would anger him, and where there was anger there were always consequences to face. What they might be I wasn't sure. So I did nothing, facing the fact, of course, that doing nothing can never turn off that dripping faucet or plug any holes in a dam. He was the aggressor who would make some kind of move. But how did I fit into his vision, why wasn't I just another trick he could have some kicks with, another notch on his belt he could tighten and then move on. Why was I different for him?

A desperate man takes desperate measures. Subliminally I was always worried about Bob McBride, seeing he was an older man and was now working full-time for the United States Postal Service, lugging heavy mailbags through the streets in all kinds of weather. Being McBride, he threw himself into his appointed rounds with unflagging dedication. But I knew eventually it would take its toll. Whenever I saw him in the hall his breathing was heavier than normal. When my doorbell rang on a frigid night the last thing I wanted to do was crawl out from under my comforter but when I grabbed my bedside clock and saw it was two in the morning I thought I'd better answer, thinking it could only be McBride, with some kind of health emergency.

I pulled open the door and Crewe silently stepped inside. Gone was his ridiculing expression, his superior air. He seemed at odds with himself. Though he carefully held a blank expression on his face I could see he was turned inward, hardly acknowledging me.

"I slipped that kid Tony, or whoever he said he was, a twenty to let me up," he said dully.

"Oh."

He wore a long thin black coat, a little light for the weather, that reached down to his ankles where it widened a little like a bell or a drooping peony. It seemed very fashionable, like a version of an upscale 19th century parson's frock. A black cashmere scarf was wrapped around his neck.

Passing by me he moved into the bedroom. My stomach heaved for a minute then I followed him in where I found him lying still on his back on my bed, eyes staring at the ceiling, contemplatively.

"Crewe," I stammered. "You woke me up. It's late."

His mouth tightened and he said nothing.

"You took me by surprise," I continued. "I can't just get in the mood suddenly—"

"I know," he interrupted. "You don't have to make excuses. It's all right. I came to talk, that's all."

Why should I have believed that? It flew in the face of everything I knew about him. Trust your gut. After a little back and forth he'd be nudging me toward his crotch.

"Sit down," he said.

The only place to sit was in my trusty rocking chair, which I pulled away from the window through which a cold whistling wind had somehow managed to penetrate. I moved the rocker to the middle of the room some-ways back from the bed and, wrapping myself in a blanket, curled up in it and continued to watch Crewe stare holes into the ceiling. Whatever he had to say was not going to be directed at me. He couldn't even seem to look my way. I became impatient wanting to know what he was up to now. But I was reminded how Jared had opened up to me, not by my coaxing him into it, but by my moving back and letting him have his space and comfort zone. It was hard though to imagine Crewe James allowing anyone, even if it was the last person on earth, to define his comfort zone for him, if he even had one.

"I'm an impulsive person," he spoke impassively into the air. "I leave a lot of details out, you know, while I'm living for the moment, that kind of thing. You need to know more about me. That's making you uneasy, isn't it? I've been thinking things over, the reason you're suddenly gun shy about me. You want to hear answers to your questions, don't you?"

What questions? I hadn't asked him any.

"I suppose I don't blame you for being curious about me. Not that I like it much, in fact I don't like it at all. But if it means that much to you...if it could influence your decision making processes...what choice have you given me?"

What was he going on about? He had advised me that I was curious about him and in a strange way maybe I was, like a child who wants to know the story behind the generous witch who proffered the poison apple to Snow White. Nothing could bring any benefit to my life by listening to anything this perverse man had to tell me, that much I was sure of, and I promised myself that whatever he had to say would have no influence over my decision to be well rid of him, but, as I had heard Jared out, I'd hear him too, but with more vigilance and suspicion.

At brunch on his terrace he'd mentioned he was from a suburb of Philadelphia and in his tone if not in words had revealed he held some bitterness about not being better connected to a more affluent, influential circle of acquaintances that could further, I assumed, his needed quest for power. That's where he'd made sure his wife had come in. He wasn't going to make the mistake of marrying for love instead of for profit. Fair enough. He could lay claim that this was the manly thing to do if he wanted to be able to make his way in the world on his own terms.

I listened to him talk in a monologue. About his childhood. Quite typically he'd never shown any interest in mine but, of course, he was the only one that mattered, wasn't he? For a worldly man who'd carved himself such a secure place in a hardened, competitive city where no one wants to give anyone anything of importance, where one has to find a way to take it or steal it, Crewe sounded as perplexed, lost, and confused as Jared, a boy who hadn't had the slightest idea how to make his way on the most rudimentary level, who had sought no riches, whose goals were modest, those of an artist in an experimental dance troupe, who, if he triumphed in his dream, would only be able to pay his bills and nothing more, and maybe, if he was lucky, get a mention in some avant-garde publication. Though their lives held up either end of a spectrum, they communicated their thoughts with the same insecurity.

An only child, Crewe had been lonely. His father was his best friend, his only friend, the one who read him stories at night, who tucked him into bed, who encouraged him to study hard, who recognized what an intelligent boy he was, who told him there was a good future ahead for him if he was only willing to seize the moment. His mother was often missing in action, a little bit "ditzy," not purposely distant, just lost in her own world which apparently was a cause of much concern for Crewe's father. Crewe got the message loud and clear that his father was disappointed with his wife. And because Crewe identified with his father, he too eventually found the same faults with his mother.

His father, Parker, was a white collar man who held a steady job as a mid-level manager at a Philadelphia insurance company. "Thank God for that job," would be his nightly litany to Crewe as his son brushed his teeth preparing for bed "or where would we be with your mother, the way she is?" *Your mother, the way she is.* Those were the last words that Crewe would ponder as he drifted off to sleep and as nightly he heard the front door downstairs quietly opening and closing, almost surreptitiously, and then the sound of a key turning the lock in the door from the porch outside. Only once did Crewe peer out his bedroom window and see his mother on the porch, agitated, but carefully locking the door and dropping the keys in her purse then nearly skipping with excitement towards the car. Where did she go every night? From the sounds of his father loudly sighing in the bedroom across the hall, he knew he wasn't supposed to ask.

There were scenes to endure, not knock-down, drag-out fight scenes, but scenes of inexplicable willfulness and the inability to compromise between Parker and his wife Martha. Crewe wondered if this was normal in families. Two parents at such loggerheads all the time, Parker trying to convince Martha of the "things you are supposed to do, the perfectly normal things" that an existence in a newly-created middle-class suburb demanded, the conventionalities that were expected, bringing the boss and his wife over for dinner, being neighborly with other families on the block, asking Martha's sisters and their children over for the holidays, for Crewe's sake if nothing else, so he could realize he had blood relatives too, like the children he went to school with. Parker's sister was married and lived in Oregon and had no children. They didn't travel. Parker felt it wasn't a healthy existence they led, not with Martha selfishly carrying on the way she did.

It was an esoteric argument for Crewe until one time he did go to a birthday party for a school friend at a neighbor's house and he saw for himself the care that particular mother lavished on her son and then he got it. His mother was different. From then on he grabbed onto his father as much as he could for attention and approval.

There was so much unspoken in that house in the

midst of other houses that looked like their own, standing on the same grass, cut the same way, like a piece of pie that was needed to fit together neatly with all the other pie pieces to make up a socially acceptable, very well kept up subdivision. Crewe knew not to discuss anything about his mother with his father—but any other subject, why, of course. But don't bring up the two locks on the basement door. Don't bring up the sound of the key turning in the front door lock when it was going on midnight and the sound of his mother coming in and struggling with something heavy in the downstairs hall and the sound of her taking the locks off the basement door and then dragging something heavy down the stairs. Don't ask. It's too horrible.

His mother left the house every night at seven o'clock, his bedtime, and returned somewhere between eleven and twelve that night, and he never wanted to disappoint his father by asking why, and he never asked his mother because he was afraid of the answer. During the day Martha never left the house. She slept late and Crewe sometimes waited patiently until she came downstairs to make breakfast, anticipating they would all have a nice meal together and sometimes they did, but more often than not Martha would disappear in the basement leaving Crewe to play marbles with his father, or have his father show him maps and pictures of the United States and Crewe would inquire as to what the largest cities in the country were and what went on there. Though it wasn't a conscious thought of his then, of course he was biding his time until he could leave his subdivision and the community that had hemmed him into a place of nonexistence. After an hour or two in the basement, Martha would come back upstairs, weirdly energized and in a good mood, and come over and tousle

Crewe's hair as he shot marbles across the floor and smile at him lovingly, but it didn't mean anything to him because he knew she wasn't thinking about him when she did it but of what was in the basement.

And God knows as he got older, around the time he was nine, his dreams turned to nightmares and he imagined a basement full of snakes or ugly, wicked gnomes or the Devil. Living in the same house under his bed.

More and more he asked his father to take him fishing on the weekends or hunting. Just to get away from the house and into the country. But Crewe never had the patience for fishing, it gave him too much time to realize how unhappy he was, waiting long stretches for some fish to finally nibble at the bait. He preferred hunting. Lying in wait for a hapless rabbit or deer to wander into a nearby brush. He never felt like pulling the trigger though. The stalking part was enough. But Parker did chock up one or two kills though he never showed any excitement over it. Crewe felt that his father was keen to carry out his wishes by taking him hunting and that he was just doing what he was supposed to do, shoot something, to please his son. It soon became obvious to Crewe that neither of them enjoyed it much. It was only an escape from his mother's afternoon forays into the basement.

Crewe mentioned one October afternoon when he and his father were walking down a trail after a fruitless afternoon of hunting for prey. It had turned cold and a light rain was falling, making a steady patter on the already fragile leaves and turning the dirt into a soft mud. They walked silently having nothing to say that hadn't already been said earlier in the afternoon. Suddenly Parker suggested to Crewe that he walk in front of him, not side by side. When hunters walked in pairs animals were scared off. Together they made too much noise. Maybe it wasn't too late to scare up a rabbit. Crewe walked in front of Parker looking from side to side into the brush. The rain came down a little harder. From behind Crewe heard the steady end of his father's rifle making sounds as the muzzle dragged on the ground with each step Parker took. They walked on but Crewe no longer heard the sound of the gun's muzzle as it swept the ground. Everything was silent except for the rain and in a moment of unexpected panic Crewe felt the back of his head terribly exposed. His stomach churned but he walked on, not turning around. When they reached the parking lot they got into the car quietly, just like always, and drove home.

Where Martha had fixed a hearty dinner of fried chicken, potato salad, green beans with diced almonds, a clump of iceberg lettuce with Roquefort dressing, hot dinner rolls, and a strawberry pie. Crewe's stomach was still nauseous but he tried at least one small taste of everything. Martha hardly noticed but Parker looked at him sadly.

Crewe left the table and curled up in his chair with a book about the robber barons of the late 18th and early 19th centuries. He devoured each of their adventures, men who through raw drive, unscrupulous behavior, and uncanny craftiness had amassed great fortunes, ending up completely superior to the masses that envied them and whom they held captive under their capitalist thumbs. One of them was Stanford White, the renowned architect who exemplified the excesses of the Gilded Age, a time when the disparity between rich and poor was legendary. Crewe especially dwelled on the section that explained how White had led a double life in his own masterpiece—Madison Square Garden—entertaining voluptuous showgirls, while his wife and family kept their gazes fixed elsewhere. But White had paid the ultimate price as punishment for his seductions. He'd been murdered by the husband of one of his previous mistresses—the poor husband so tormented by thoughts that White had defiled his wife that in his muddled mind she would forever be an impure creature who would never be able to forget the lure of sex she'd experienced with White. The line "the lure of sex" hit Crewe hard in his stomach.

He needed his mother. Especially now. Right now. That night when she left the house as always at seven o'clock and he heard her key turn in the outside lock, locking him out of her world, locking him into the house, he revolted. Feeling he had nothing to lose and everything to gain he crept quietly from his bed and tiptoed down the stairs, not even making one of the floorboards creak. He went out into the garage and opened his father's toolbox and took out a saw, then silently stole back into the hall and inched his way to the basement door where as noiselessly as he could he slowly and painstakingly sawed off the locks. He flipped on the light switch and took the stairs two at a time to end up at the bottom finding nothing more than hundreds of boxes stacked up against the walls with the contents of each box neatly labeled with crayons in his mother's handwriting. Crewe didn't have the patience to read each label; he unloaded the stacked boxes one by one onto the floor and tore open the box flaps and turned the boxes upside down to empty them. Spilling all around him was everything imaginable, a jumble sale beyond compare.

Dresses, shoes, purses, costume jewelry, toys, dolls, games, cosmetics, kitchenware, hundreds of towels, wash cloths, rugs, sponges, soaps, detergents, ties, boy's sweaters, men's pants, scarves, paperbacks, records, thousands of greeting cards, wrapping paper, ribbons, empty gift boxes, tins of food, cans of soda, bags of bird seed, pillowcases, lampshades, furniture covers, curtains, umbrellas, disinfectant sprays, air fresheners, dusters, none of these things used, usually with the sales tags still attached to them.

"Now you know," he heard his father's voice at the top of the stairs.

Parker drove him to one of the neighborhood shopping centers where the big Sears store was open until eleven every night. They spotted his mother's car parked outside. His father parked the car at a discreet distance so they could both be unseen observers. Parker and Crewe stayed there for a couple of hours, until the Sears store closed. Like clockwork, every half-hour or so, Martha emerged from the store's entrance, always accompanied by a shopping cart attendant who loaded up the empty spaces in the back of the car and in the trunk. Martha was full of mirth and shared a great camaraderie with each of them, young, old, black, white, Hispanic; she was jovial and convivial with these attendants as she never was with Crewe and his father. Crewe felt pangs of jealously he'd never experienced. And always they escorted her back, in a protective manner, always keeping one eye out for carjackers, muggers, or rapists, until she was safely once again inside the entrance to the store.

"Had enough?" Parker turned to Crewe.

Of course he'd had enough. Who wouldn't, after having discovered your own mother considered her real home a Sears store and who seemed to like the lowly shopping cart pushers more than she did you.

Never a word was said by anyone about the matter. Martha spent an entire weekend putting her gain back into the boxes. With Crewe and Parker she acted the same, totally unabashed and probably relieved not to have to bother to lock up the basement anymore. Her routine continued as usual, leaving the house every night at seven and returning after eleven, after the Sears store had closed. Crewe was a boy but knew his mother needed help. But wasn't his father supposed to take care of that, see to it in some way? Wasn't that a husband's job? Crewe just let his mother go. In fact he let his father go too, not in as obvious a way, but he refused to go fishing or hunting with him anymore when his father tried to talk him into it. He threw himself into his school work and stayed away from home as much as he could, studying at the library every afternoon and sometimes into the evening.

When he came home from school one afternoon, as he brought in the mail from the mailbox, he noticed a letter addressed to his parents from his principal. As he made his way towards the front door he decided to open it and see what the principal could possibly have to say. It was a congratulatory note advising the Parkers that Crewe had scored the highest IQ in the eastern part of the state for a boy his age and asking them to phone to discuss the good news. When Crewe reached his bedroom he shut the door and thought for awhile, holding the letter in his hand, then taped it to the back side of his bed board. He didn't tell Martha and he didn't tell Parker. It was enough for him alone to know about, and he realized its meaning, that it was somehow a way to get to the land of the robber barons, men who took charge and made circumstances work to their advantages.

Crewe noticed his father becoming more and more

depressed, he guessed that's what it was. Uncharacteristically Parker missed a number of days at work but it was during the wintertime and everybody had a touch of the flu. He didn't even get dressed but sat around in his robe in an easy chair staring at nothing. Or so Crewe would find him around about six each night, the time he usually got back from studying at the library, until his mother left the house at seven, now passing Crewe nonchalantly on the stairs as he went up to bed and she went out to enjoy life. As he cast a glance down at his father when he reached the top of the stairs, he saw his father's expression fixed on him, and it was always the same, one of bewilderment, as if he felt sorry for Crewe and wanted to rescue him from something, but he sat frozen, glued to his easy chair, never saying anything.

One cold night Parker came into Crewe's room and woke him up. From a sound sleep. He told Crewe he was at the end of his rope, that Crewe was the only one who could save the situation, the only voice his mother would listen to, even hear. Crewe rubbed the sleep from his eyes. His father told Crewe he wanted him to confront his mother at the Sears store in the middle of one of her sprees and beg her to come home, to pretend to cry and plead with her to give up the folly that was making fools of the only two men in her life and giving them a miserable existence. Only a son could reach a mother, a husband never could.

Crewe was speechless, sleepy and confused. Parker had warmed up the car; it was already nice and toasty. Crewe dressed lazily, pulling on some jeans and a sweater and a black bomber jacket and a baseball cap. But when Parker came to get him he was still wearing his robe. He wasn't ready. He told Crewe it was because he'd been riffling through Martha's bureau to find some of Crewe's baby pictures so Crewe could pull them out and show them to her as a last entreaty if he needed to. He told Crewe to go down and get in the back seat of the car while he got dressed, it was warmer in the back.

Crewe stumbled down into the garage. The car was idling. He climbed in the back seat and shut the door. It was sticky in there, heavy, like a cave. The windows were all closed, that was why. As he reached his hand over to roll one of them down, he glanced out the back window and noticed exhaust blowing around the edges of the garage door which had been taped shut. He turned the door handle so he could climb out of the car but fell back against the seat before he could manage it with his eyes wide open. He kind of saw his father standing there outside the car looking in but not moving, at least he thought it was his father but his vision was starting to blur. He fell forward onto the floor. Eventually he heard the car door being opened and felt the sensation of his body being pulled out and his father lifting him up while he slowly opened his eyes feeling like he had to throw up. When he opened his eyes he saw the shocked look on his father's face. Shocked because Parker realized Crewe was still alive. Letting out a scream he dropped the boy on the garage floor. The world died somehow at that moment but Crewe was still alive. All he could see was the muffler blowing out exhaust a few feet from his face. His father made no move to help him or lift him up. In fact, he thought he heard his father coaxing him to try to sleep, telling him if he just went to sleep everything would be all right. Then he felt his father's shoe in the middle of his back inching him toward the muffler. Exhaust was covering him like the breath of hell. He did sleep. Or he passed out. The next thing he remembered were tears falling off his father's face onto his own as his father laid him in bed, pouring water down his throat, telling him it was all a bad dream, it would never happen again, he would see to it, he would promise. Crewe would never be in any more danger, he'd even take Crewe to his own mother's grave over at Wilford Cemetery where Crewe could watch for himself as Parker swore over her tombstone that the wrath of God might strike him if his son ever had another troubling day in his life. He would slit his own throat before he would see harm come to his own son and so on.

When Crewe was twelve he could look out for himself and he did. He was the one who had taken a cue from his mother, she'd helped him after all by having inadvertently taught him about the usefulness of locks, and he removed the flimsy lock on his bedroom door, drilled a new hole and installed a much stronger one and fixed a bolt on the inside of the door as well. When he wasn't studying in the library he was masturbating in his bedroom. Those were his sole occupations, and he took to each naturally and enthusiastically.

When he got to Harvard he saw a therapist who after hearing about his childhood "gave him permission" to break off his relationship with his parents. How could he break off something he'd never had? But he went through the pretense of pretending it could be done by writing them each a letter telling them he didn't want to be part of their lives, now or in the future, just to get the therapist to like him and to trust him. He understood that it was time now for him to get a lot of people, the right people, to like him and to trust him.

That was how Crewe ended his unpleasant reverie…a little ominously…at least it was for me, knowing how well I knew the manipulator he acknowledged being as he brought his story to a close—

by the way, without ever looking towards me or recognizing my presence in any way. But as I looked at him lying back on my bed in that long black parson's coat in the pale winter glow of night he looked as white as a corpse.

*

Reg and I decided to meet for some hot chocolate the next afternoon just around the corner from my apartment on 9th Avenue at a trendy but cozy bistro, a Chelsea rarity, where on any given day you could find yourself sitting at a table between a movie star and an unknown aspiring artist, no attitude or curiosity coming from either. Today Reg and I were happy to get the table by the window next to the Christmas tree in the corner, already decorated, its multi-colored lights a welcome antidote to the gray gloomy sky. I hadn't seen Reg in awhile and I noticed he was eyeing me more than casually; today I wasn't only a listening post for his provocative patter, his outspoken views, which I always loved to lose myself in, but a friend whom he wanted to find in good shape. After all, I'd stopped being involved with my support group. That spoke volumes. The truth—that I wasn't in good shape, that I felt my mind was fucked over and that I was worn ragged by excess sex and drugs—I was determined to keep hidden from him because I felt I would return to my normal self in a few days anyway. And that being the case, why worry him? Or expose myself to his judgment?

I had been naive. It had never occurred to me until now that thousands and thousands of men in New York competed in a rat race of frantic sex and drugs to escape whatever demons were leering at them. I'd lived a contented, sheltered life with Frank, all the while having no conception that anyone else was living any differently. Or that there would come a time down the road when I'd be running from my life. But these men to whom sex and drugs were everything, where love just didn't seem to be a part of the scene, why, they seemed to be what was out there, everywhere, according to Crewe. And according to Jared. Just waiting to self-destruct. There was a metaphysical sinkhole in New York City that you could disappear into forever.

But there was a dichotomy here. I was associating, in purely therapeutic terms, "dysfunction" and "addiction" problems as unwanted, and as a source of escape for those who couldn't cope. The more sex, the more drugs, the less pain. But there are men—and women— who are at heart libertines, who do not live for escape but for pure pleasure and who have always had plenty of opportunities to indulge, all the way from the first Roman orgy to the next click on the Internet.

I stared at the Christmas tree and fell from the present moment into pre-revolutionary Paris and imagined Crewe standing by a magnificently decorated Christmas tree hung with fiery jewels, endless strings of pearls, and finely blown crystal ornaments, catching the light of the candle glow, and perched on top of this tree, a lusciously carved ivory angel, delicate, feminine, beautiful, her arms raised up into the air, her imploring eyes moving beyond the five-tiered chandelier to the marbled ceiling, suggesting she didn't want to be on display in this luxurious house, but home in heaven. Crewe glanced at his family, his three young cherubic children and his Botticelli wife beneath him on their knees, enthusiastically tearing open boxes wrapped in red silk. An old roué, Crewe wore an impossibly elaborate, expensive powdered wig on his head and plenty of rouge on his cheeks, and a trace of red lip gloss on his dried, cracking lips, his painted face indecent to behold. He'd just ordered up his carriage and his cane from his manservant and was preparing to bid the family adieu to revel in yet another anxiously anticipated night of elaborate decadence, lured by the promise of some not yet experienced thrill, though he had gone through thousands of nights in the very same way. It confused me. Was there something to what Crewe said after all about man's inherent lust? Many of the men who walked on the streets of this neighborhood, some of the very ones who were now strolling by our bistro window, might be among those whom Crewe and Jared had sought out, ones I assumed were just playing harmless sex games and could snap back into their own lives afterwards. But I knew now many couldn't, they were too damaged, they had no other lives to fall back on as they had allowed their fantasies to become their only realities. These men didn't have to be conjured up, they were here, they were for real and some of them were crazy.

"Christmas?" Reg threw out the word carelessly. Because he was afraid it might bring up sad memories but he still needed to know that I had a plan in place.

I smiled and shrugged.

"Not going out to L.A. this year?"

"I don't think I could get a ticket at this late date."

"You never know. Doesn't that friend of yours and Frank's still live in the bungalow?"

"I haven't heard otherwise but then I haven't been in touch with him."

Reg continued eagerly, "But it's a great place, right? In Stone Canyon. It has a country feel to it?"

I nodded. "It does in a way. Well, it used to when we lived there at least. Set into the hillside and really private, lots of brush surrounding it, and always a heady smell of jasmine in the air. And at the far edge of the lawn a spectacular view of the city down below."

The server brought our mugs of hot chocolate topped with an ample amount of whipped cream.

"What a wonderful place for a holiday getaway. With balmy weather to boot," Reg commented.

"Well, I'm planning to stay right here and party with you guys on Christmas and New Year's Eve too." I meant with him and Allison and some of our program friends.

"Good, good." But somehow he didn't sound like he meant it.

"That sounds a little distant."

"Have you ever thought what it would be like spending time out there? Or even living there again? The idea's even crossed my mind once or twice."

"It has? I thought you'd consider it too plastic."

"I don't think it would hurt you to have a change."

I stared at the whipped cream for awhile wondering what he meant.

"You're in a pensive mood today," I finally said.

The new somber Reg had made some kind of point and now the old curmudgeon returned, maybe to put me at ease after he'd managed to sow a small seed in my mind and had let me know he knew something was going on with me. "New York City. Its *raison d'être* has disappeared in this computer age. Along with its pride. It's the end here for the working man like it was for those men in the mill towns at the end of the Industrial Revolution. Mark my words, the worldwide information highway has cut a swath through the heart of this city like a tornado, completely destroying its thinning supply of cultural riches that used to be affordable to struggling artists and the middle-class alike." He paused, tapping his finger dramatically on the table top for emphasis, managing to turn a few heads at the same time. "I'm older than you, I've lived here longer. It used to be a pleasure to browse through specialty book or record shops, develop relationships with the owners who would search down what you wanted and when they found it be tickled pink because they shared your own enthusiasm. Well, those places are gone now. If any remnant of them exists I hope they're lurking somewhere on the Internet. Where everything is available to anyone now on this side of the moon. That's why everyone's real residence is their e-mail address. You don't think we really live in cities anymore do you? We live in cyberspace while we walk the streets of Pompeii."

"Funny," I said. "When I walk around here I haven't noticed any petrified remains of long forgotten artifacts."

"That's because a lot of them are gone," Reg said. "Search and destroy. That's their game. First up was leveling Times Square and building Disneyland over its restless remains. Edgar Allan Poe's house was on the list too, apparently a worthless reminder that a genius once walked about Washington Square. They tried to bulldoze Carnegie Hall, Radio City Music Hall, and Grand Central Terminal—and nearly did—but for the will of God and Jackie Kennedy, I don't know who to thank first."

"The beautiful lady of course," I ribbed him.

He snapped indignantly, "Yes…the ladies and the gentlemen. The wealthy. Unlike me, they can attend opera galas and fancy dress balls, but I'm afraid the fat lady sang her last aria to me years ago."

"Longer than that," I laughed. "She never sang one

to you. You don't even like opera and told me you'd never be caught dead going to one."

"That's not the point," he sniffed. "I would like to go to BAM, you know, and see some experimental stuff. But I can't afford to. I can hardly afford to step outside my door. I mean, whoever owns this city ain't got no respect for we the people anymore. Who does own it anyway? The Chinese who bought it from the Japanese who are selling it to the Saudis or something. All they care about is opening the ten thousandth nail salon. They really understand my needs!"

"I see what you mean."

"And it's only the beginning. This has the potential to become a bottomless pit. So I ask you, why are you still here?"

Why was Reg connecting these dots to me?

"People are unhappy," he continued, "I can see it in their faces. You didn't live here then, but believe me, back in the seventies, while the city was going broke, when it was dangerous, it was so exciting in a crazy way, everybody had a sense of community and a *joie de vivre*. So I ask again, why not be living out in Stone Canyon if you could and not in this cold cage?"

By the time he'd ended this rant my hot chocolate was well finished. It had been interesting, especially hearing about a time and place I was too young to have known. But wasn't it all relative? Didn't each age and decade develop its own cultural identity? Yet I suppose each city does have a Golden Age and the seventies Reg mentioned were evidently the bare-assed end of New York City's. But was it really true what he implied—that we were now little more than worms, bottom feeders crawling blindly in some corporate tomb, with no sense of the heart or community Reg fondly remembered?

Really, for one of his rants, this one, though mesmerizing, had been a little over the top and a bit too frenzied. That's because, as I walked back home, I realized this whole death of New York thing had more to do with me than with his own outrage; he was suggesting I move away. Everything he'd said had everything to do with my relocating to Stone Canyon, though of course I had benefited from his sociology lesson along the way. It was bizarre. I didn't want to move to Stone Canyon.

My phone was ringing as I walked into my apartment. I picked it up and said "hello" in a way that sounded both hollow and desolate because I expected the person on the other end to be exactly who he was— Crewe—and since before the first ray of light yesterday morning when he had slipped silently out of my apartment wearing his funereal parson's frock, I had no idea what to say to him, after having listened carefully to his precise, despairing story, yet not having allowed myself to feel emotionally connected to it.

"Well, I've tried you for the last few hours. Where have you been?"

"Out with an old friend having a cup of hot chocolate."

"Oh, not as exciting a day as you're used to having," he said unexpressively this time instead of salaciously.

"No." I was cringing though, waiting to hear him insist on us getting together right away. For the usual. But he had something else on his mind.

I heard him take a deep breath, then, "Listen, I have an idea. About us. I know you weren't happy with the way things were going that night between us, the night of the blizzard up here. Our relationship…you're in a netherworld. It's neither here nor there. I understand your feelings about it. That's why I'm open to changing things around. Listen to me carefully. I'm willing to leave my wife, leave Clemma. It would have to be a process, I'll have to do it in its proper time and place, figure it all out—from scratch—but," he added, and the first sign of annoyance I'd heard since that night in his penthouse crept into his voice, "I'm willing to do it." He paused, letting the annoyance abate in silence, then he continued with some feeling, "I want to be the major person in your life. I want to spend all of my time with you. Or as much as is humanly possible. And until I could separate from Clemma I'd come down and be with you every day. I'd take care of you, you could totally rely on me. I'd be a father to you, you could be my son. You wouldn't have to worry about anything, I'd do all the decision making for you, all the thinking for you. Any of life's perplexing questions you're afraid you might not have answers for wouldn't matter anymore…because they'd be answered by me. I'd take full responsibility for you. You could put yourself completely in my hands…like a boy."

He stopped, waiting.

I stared out the window. Snow was coming down heavily outside now and there was a slow wind which blew it upwards against the bricks of the Seminary wall until the white flakes disappeared into the early evening gloom. I was dumbstruck. I didn't know how to begin to respond, his words had rushed at me all at once like the blowing flakes outside, only they hadn't lost their way upwards and vanished into thin air—they were a part of me and they were so curious and strange. And hypnotic. I couldn't find any words for a reply.

"You'll seriously consider my proposal," he stated.

Finally I was able to get out a yes.

"But don't keep me waiting."

"No…I won't…good-bye for now."

In shock I went to the window. I saw the moment the street lights came on, I'd never seen that before, not the exact moment. A young woman with a cane was the lone person on the street below, making her way carefully on the slippery sidewalk, sometimes pausing to steady herself by putting a bare hand against the bricks, then once she had regained her equilibrium, slowly continuing on her journey, her long dark hair blowing behind her.

I knew I had to go to the Seminary, the place I'd always gone for comfort. The gatekeeper was closing up when I got there shivering in my long navy blue winter coat and pale blue scarf, but without gloves or a hat. The gatekeeper knew me and when I put my hand on the gate to stop him closing it he reluctantly pulled it back and let me into the grounds, telling me to come get him when I was ready to leave and he'd let me back out. I thanked him. He mumbled something and turned away.

Inside the chapel I was alone. I knelt at one of the pews, sparkling snow melting in my hair. I clasped my hands and bowed my head and prayed for God's wisdom to find a place inside me too, like Crewe's words. I prayed to know God's will for me, as I lifted my head to stare at the stained glass, now only panes of blackness against the dark. I waited for a sign. Maybe God's will did enter me, or maybe it was inside me all the time and I didn't know it. But the only thing I felt was an emptiness and the only thing I heard was a silence that shattered the night.

Afterwards I stood outside the chapel in the cold letting the wet snow cover me and stared at an elm that was turning as white as I was. I gazed at it vacantly for a long time.

I envisioned Crewe standing to the side of that elm,

near his bench, anxious for my answer, my compliance. He was covered by blowing snow, which formed a whirlwind around him. He had a winter arm made of dead branches and ice. He tried to conceal it as he fingered a skull creamed in gold. He made me an offering of the resplendent skull, his thumbs massaging the eye sockets. I imagined I held a white spear in my hand, and, deep in thinking, thrust it towards him, but he stepped aside and it struck the elm, the tree doors spread, and an ice pageant of elaborately-carved young men, disentangling themselves from the twisted tendrils and tree guts crawling with ants, stepped down onto the Seminary grounds. They gazed at each other in a moment of shared recognition, shyly acknowledging a common bond, before gradually starting to melt and drift upwards, wraithlike, to become spirits in the night.

The gatekeeper had sidled up next to me, eyeing me tentatively. "Are you feeling all right? No use standing in the snow and cold, and the chapel's closing now."

I looked at him blankly, then turned back towards the elm. Crewe had disappeared. And there was no sign of the ghostly ice men I had inadvertently released from the elm. The lights inside the chapel went out. In the darkness a whipping wind rose up and looking up into the dark sky I watched frenzied clouds blowing across a wan moon. I could barely make out the gatekeeper's face in the darkness, but I grabbed onto his shoulder and told him I was ready to leave with him.

\*

"I think you should feel some compassion for him," Reg suggested, uncharacteristically. "Think of what he's been through. He's a suffering human being like you or me."

"But I don't, I don't feel any compassion for him."

I'd had to let it out. To Reg, someone who really wanted to look out for me. After I'd returned from the Seminary I'd called him and asked him to come over right away saying I had something important to tell him. I hadn't wanted to, I hadn't wanted to reveal anything to him about my hidden life with Crewe, the married man he'd warned me about, or admit to any crazed indulgence of orgiastic sex and drugs, this coming from the most unlikely person, his friend —deep in recovery for God's sake—but all the time nurturing a destructive secret. Wasn't letting him in on things an admission of failure, a well of shame? He'd been told all the sordid details, all right, even about Teresa. And, of course, about what Crewe had told me about his past and of his sudden proposition to me. But exposing myself to Reg's probable anger and disappointment paled in comparison with my keeping it all inside and not reaching out for his help, because, well, I needed help. Right now I was an agitated, pacing basket-case who couldn't extricate myself from what I awkwardly admitted to Reg had been—at least up to now—a fixation on this man.

Reg was good-natured and empathetic. No lofty pronouncements. No I-told-you so's. No speeches this time. He was calm and serious and the first thing he said after hearing me out was, "Allison mentioned something to me about this brunch you went to. She didn't say anything more than that she thought it was a strange scene. But that coupled with you dropping out of meetings did make me realize that something was going wrong in your life, that there was something to be concerned about." I nodded. The second thing he said was, "Look, we all go through a period in our lives when we let ourselves sink. I guess this was your moment. Call it whatever you want, *nostalgie de la boue* if you like."

"Meaning?"

"The nostalgia for mud, literally, but what the French really mean is the love of the gutter."

"I don't think that's what I'd like to call it. And I'm surprised you would know anything about it."

He chuckled knowingly. "The first thing you've got to do is to give yourself a break. Treat yourself gently. Have compassion for this…situation—and for yourself."

That sounded good to me. But his next suggestion, that I feel compassion for Crewe. That didn't sit right.

I continued to pace as Reg sat back calmly on my couch, hands folded on his lap, listening keenly.

"You don't know this man," I tried to explain. "Everything he says is to manipulate a situation for his own gain. I don't mean anything to him. He's just using me for his own selfish reasons."

"Well, then, it seems you've answered your own questions. He doesn't seem to have any redeeming qualities and he's beyond your compassion."

"Not just to me! To anybody!"

"All right. To anybody then."

"You make me sound stingy not to feel compassion for him. But believe me, if I did, I'd be finished."

"Then it's obvious what your next step is," Reg said evenly.

"It's not obvious. The thought of telling him I never want to see him again makes me afraid because I'm afraid of him. He's a narcissist, calculating as hell, used to getting his way and is cruel and punishing when he doesn't. If I told him no, I doubt that would be the end of it. He'd figure another way to get at me."

Reg coughed politely. "Are you sure that's what this

whole thing's about here? Are you sure a little bit of you doesn't like the attention, the drama of it? Doesn't part of you like the feeling of being wanted by a successful man like that?"

"You're missing the point. He's a monster. I don't care how successful he is. We all like to feel needed, I'll admit to that, but didn't you hear me tell you what he's asking me to do. To turn myself over to his care, to let him make all my decisions for me, to think for me..." As I blurted out that last sentence I asked myself could there be some kind of allure, if only a fantasy, to losing myself so completely to someone else? Maybe. Yet it could never be to him. Because Crewe had said I would be like a boy...his son. I remembered how Crewe's own father had treated his son.

"You're beside yourself tonight, John. Of course I understand why, but it's not doing you any good. Why not try to help yourself calm down? Why don't you try to clear your mind of all this anxiety?"

I took his advice and made an attempt. I sat on the living room rug in an almost yoga-like position and took deep breaths. Maybe I should have showered the wet snow off me and taken a warm bath instead, because my attempt at meditation was a wash out. To meditate you have to clear or cleanse your mind. But I couldn't empty mine of my obsessive thinking about Crewe James, no matter how many deep breaths I took. From time to time I closed my eyes but instead of letting everything go and relaxing, I cursed my fate instead. I wanted someone else—Reg, maybe—to resolve this situation for me, as if I had little responsibility in the matter. But how would that work? He couldn't clear my mind of the anxiety. I would have to try to battle myself into a meditative state where some revelation might appear. I doubted I could do it. But I pretended to give it a go. I shut my eyes and took more deep breaths. Whenever my eyes would open I saw Reg smiling towards me, and I smiled back in a resigned way.

"You know," Reg's voice floated towards me, "we all have a gatekeeper at our door. A gatekeeper of the spirit, if you will, who protects us, who won't let those who would work against us inside our own space, in your case, intruders bringing you drugs and insane sex and apparently even worse...Always know that you're protected by this gatekeeper if you want to be."

I nodded, taking his words in.

Reg suddenly stood up. "Are you feeling any better now?"

I got up too, stretching. "I think so."

I glanced towards my door but saw no stalwart gatekeeper there to help me screen visitors. Not a real gatekeeper like the one at the Seminary, a flesh and blood man, who had allowed me to cling to his shoulder as he led me through the icy Seminary grounds and let me pass outside. But of course Reg was talking about a spiritual gatekeeper, yet with spirit there's only faith. Again that thing man lives by.

"Now, you know what you have to do the moment I leave, don't you?"

I looked into his eyes. It was all up to me then.

"Well, my friend, good night. Leave a message on my voicemail letting me know you did it."

"Thanks, Reg. For the whole day, not only this part of it."

In the hallway I could hear Reg making small talk with Bob McBride who was coming in from taking Big Deal on a walk.

"I've had enough of this weather," I heard

McBride's voice as I walked to the phone. The fear of relinquishing what I realized had been my escape, sex with Crewe, was with me every step of the way. But if I paused now to think about what I was going to give up I might never go through with it.

I prayed he wouldn't answer his cell phone. And he didn't. No doubt he was having sex with somebody else right now. That thought disturbed and annoyed me and made it easier to leave the message: "Crewe, it's John calling. This is important to me. I can't see you again…" I paused, feeling a joy swelling in me that I hadn't felt for a long time. I savored that feeling before continuing with relief, "It's not about you, this is about me. This relationship with you just isn't good for me. It's come to an end, it's over. Please don't call me back. There's nothing to discuss. And please don't stop by. I don't want to see you again. Good-bye, good luck. But please honor my request."

# PART TWO

I didn't see the need to stir up memories this year by returning to Stone Canyon for Christmas. Sometimes the good memories were as painful as the bad ones. But not always, at least the good ones had the potential to wrap you in a warm glow. It was hard to reconcile them though with that ending point in New York which had interrupted what had promised to be a vital life for the two of us together, lost forever in Frank's final breath.

Remembering Christmas time in our little rented bungalow tucked away in the brush of the canyon, hidden by spreading vines of jasmine and fulsome willows, reigned over by dry spindly pines, was always bittersweet because there had been plenty of love and plans for the future bubbling inside that cozy space that had remained unrealized. Still, the happiness of that time was in my blood and sustained me.

We lived there in that bungalow all the time we went through college, driving down the breezy canyon roads toward campus, carefree and in love with every day. And after we graduated we still lived there, basking in mornings full of birdsong, in deep red sunsets and in silent, scented evenings.

Christmas time always brought us new ideas, some scatterbrained, some grandiose, and a few that had an organic fit. Our talk of packing up and moving to New York was a combination of the three. As we strung Christmas lights all around the bungalow, in the trees, on the roof, on the frosted windows, we weighed the pros and cons.

Frank wanted to teach film theory but had no prospects in L.A. at the moment, but he had a friend at NYU who was an associate professor of Cinema and he invited Frank to take over a few of his classes while he took a year off to travel through Europe. That would not only help pay the bills but give Frank a break in tuition for the courses he'd need toward getting his teaching certificate. The pros won over the cons even though I didn't have a career set in mind, only a Liberal Arts degree from UCLA, my diploma looking a little forlorn on the mantelpiece. I loved films too, that was the major thing that had brought us together, and I thought I'd like to put my enthusiasm for them to some use, but I didn't see myself as a film producer, director, or writer. The idea eventually struck me to try my hand at writing film criticism, not realizing then how esoteric an undertaking that was or how difficult my pieces would be to place, being an unproven writer who had just graduated from college.

During our last Christmas Day in Stone Canyon, I gave Frank a gift of my first critiques, evaluations of some of my all time favorite films gathered in an expensive loose-leaf notebook, and much of our afternoon was spent, the two of us curled up on the sofa, reading them aloud to each other, reveling in my astute observations, Frank always commenting positively, my biggest supporter. Though later, in New York, when Frank was teaching at NYU, I lost interest in films and became more interested in literature and at trying my hand this time at writing literary criticism, an even more esoteric undertaking and, I realized, a dying art. Soon I put the pencil down and just read.

But what made those days in L.A. special is that we didn't have the pressures of the real world on our shoulders yet. There was very little stress in preparing Christmas dinner, in laughing, dreaming, planning, listening to music, and then exhausted by it all, snuggling together on the floor next to our Christmas tree propped up in the corner. On Christmas night we held each other around the waists, kissed, and stared down into the vast L.A. basin, mesmerized by the millions of blinking lights that were magical and seemed to be never ending.

When our holiday celebration was over and all the lights on our Christmas tree had been taken down, we were still excited. Because we were heading east.

I remember the day we left as if it were today. We'd stuffed our car to the brim, the back seat so full we could barely see out the rear window. The rack on top of the car held suitcases, boxes full of books and CDs, and crates of cooking utensils. Fortunately it looked as if there was just enough room left for us to be able to squeeze ourselves into the front seat.

It was sunset and the warm light of early evening made the canyon glow. The jasmine that stung the air seemed especially redolent.

We tightened the ropes over the suitcases and boxes on the overhead rack.

"Well," I said excitedly. "This is it. Here we go, off on our new adventure."

Frank smiled quietly at me. The sunlit breeze that played around the canyon ruffled his hair and lit his handsome face with warmth. He paused, staring down at

the dusty red clay at his feet then back up at me. Silently
he gazed behind us at our bungalow where we'd shared
so many pleasurable moments together. Then, it having
been decided he would drive the first leg, Frank walked
very slowly around the car and opened the door.

Was there a moment when his eyes, taking in our
canyon bungalow for the last time, saw the past and the
future at once? I think so. Part of him resisted moving
away from what we had there. And leaving the contented
ghosts of ourselves behind those familiar walls to
become two new flesh and blood people somewhere else.

*

I never returned to L.A. until the week following
Frank's death. And after that, I'd been back to L.A. only
one other time, last Christmas.

That first time I'd returned there had been in early
May following Frank's death. Frank's friends and I had
had a service for him and a gathering afterwards at our
former Stone Canyon bungalow where Dan Poet, a
college roommate of Frank's, had taken over paying the
rent. He was a nice, unassuming guy who'd just landed a
job as a story-liner on some sitcom at Universal. I was
glad somebody Frank had liked was starting to make
some kind of mark there and Dan was good to me,
insisting I stay with him on both my trips.

That night during the little gathering he had for
Frank's college buddies, Dan was a great host. I didn't
have to do anything but slump by an open window and
breathe in the competing scents of jasmine and
honeysuckle, hidden in the dark, and think, with gallows
humor, about my plane ride there. I had left at night and
arrived in the morning, traveling across a continent in

220

less time than it takes to get a good night's sleep. I had given my body up to a noisy jet barreling through the night sky, holding Frank's ashes on my lap in a green faux jade urn, sitting next to a man who spent his time flipping through an investment magazine and picking his teeth and sometimes eyeing with alarm the urn that sat squarely on my lap, realizing it could be nothing other than what it was. I had closed my eyes, picturing myself drifting along on starry waves until the last wave washed me right into LAX, to the familiar edge of a shell pink world where all the dreamers with stalled wanna-be ambitions along with tougher, hard nose realists were lost together in endless morning.

At dawn I slipped out of the bungalow and drove along the Pacific Coast Highway to Zuma Beach, north of Malibu, a beach Frank and I had always loved. I parked in the nearly empty lot and, carrying the urn with an almost disturbing carefulness and precision, negotiated both the concrete and sand to find myself at the water's edge where I was relieved to feel my muscles begin to relax and my breaths come out steady and calm.

The morning was gray and wet with fog but there was a wind that helped carry Frank's ashes out to sea. I remember making small fistfuls of his dust and it felt a little like the sand he and I used to run our fingers through as we made thoughtful conversation, but unlike the sand I didn't let any of Frank's dust, all that was left of him, slip through my fingers. I clenched my fists over and over, making the moment last, before scattering him into the silver-headed waves from the sands of Zuma Beach.

Some of his dust had settled under my fingernails. When I got back to the bungalow I took a red-handled knife that had belonged to me and was still in the kitchen drawer, in fact it was the knife I used to peel peaches with, and made a cut on my thumb and pulled back the skin like a layer of fruit and let my blood suck in Frank's particles that were now just as much a part of me as of the vast, rolling sea.

It seems you can never really go back to the spot where you've scattered your loved one's ashes to the four winds and expect to recapture that moment. Though I made an attempt.

When I went back to L.A. last year, Dan drove me to Zuma Beach on Christmas morning. Fortunately I'd packed some khaki shorts because Dan was as thin as a rail and I'd never get a pair of his up past my thighs. We lay on the sand together, sort of sunbathing in eighty-four degree weather, baking in the heat, no ashes this time of course being carried through the air, only sun motes shimmering before a blue sky and green waves, and ships far out on the coastline that were still, seeming to have put up anchor for awhile. I lounged back on my elbows staring at the scenery but also trying to feel the enormity of a past moment. But it didn't really happen. Then I concluded it didn't have to. Because I just felt really happy that this beach we'd loved and these restless sun-filled waves were where Frank had been put to rest. Dan was lying on his stomach. We didn't talk to each other, we didn't need to.

My chest was starting to get that pink blush before a real burn sets in so I had the sense to first put on a T-shirt and drape a towel over my legs, and when the noonday sun was at its zenith and sweat was running down my forehead and the crowds had started coming, I told Dan I was ready to leave. Kids were running and tossing Frisbees in front of me, surfers were hoping to catch a wave, young lovers walked hand in hand; they'd already opened their Christmas presents, I guessed, and dispensed with them, and now, as on any other day, had succumbed to the lure of the surf. I'd had a Christmas present too, just like them.

So why go back again this year when a part of me was always there anyway? Besides, I was feeling a bright energy about myself right here in my own Chelsea apartment. I'd had the courage to make an important phone call, hadn't I? I was already feeling positive repercussions. I rejoiced for Frank's sake as well as my own. He would have wanted me to make that call, and though I hadn't been thinking of it at the time he was probably right here with me when I made it.

*

How wonderful to be named for the clear-singing rooster in Chaucer's *Canterbury Tales*. To me, an initial tactile inspiration had joined forces with some kind of intellectual manifesto. These twelve men collectively named Chanticleer singing *a capella* around the twenty-foot shining blue spruce in the Metropolitan Museum's Medieval Sculpture Hall, in voices ranging from the loftiest countertenor to the most earthbound bass, and amplified by the high, hollow spaces of the hall, were so joyful to hear. The precision with which the group sang ecclesiastical music, scared songs from the canons of Byrd and Di Lasso, the baroque Portuguese carol *Sa aqui turo zente pleta*, Holst's *In the Bleak Mid-Winter*, English pastoral hymns, and medleys of both Christmas spirituals and traditional carols kept me unexpectedly entranced. These guys knew what they were doing, what effect they were having. And hearing *a capella* singing made me realize that the human voice is the most expressive instrument in the world. Only occasionally did my eyes wander to the cherubs and angels shyly peeking through the boughs of the tree or to the 18th century Spanish choir screen from the Cathedral of Valladolid that served as a backdrop to the singers and, even when my eyes did wander, not for a minute did I lose my concentration on the beauty of their sound.

This group was unknown to me but Reg had seen them before at the Met and had raved about them. He'd informed me that they were a San Francisco-based group, quite well known, and toured all over the world. I just kept thinking of the one song I knew about San Francisco—the one imploring everybody to open the Golden Gate Bridge—and like some rube expected that's what I'd be hearing.

I appreciated Reg's gesture of taking me to this Christmas Eve performance—it sounds dumb but it was great to get out of the house.

We, the audience, sat in three groups, one that faced directly in front of the singers and two off to their left and right sides. Reg and I were in the third row of the group that faced them head on.

The audience was as enthusiastic as I was, and we all rose and applauded after each encore, giving Chanticleer the standing ovation they deserved. As the twelve men joined arms and bowed and smiled at each other for a job well done, they suddenly became real human beings to me, like the rest of us in the audience, not just celestial artists.

I imagined if some of them were gay, like myself and Reg and other members of the audience. And wondered if any of them were fighting depression or living with HIV or had nursed a sick loved one through a battle with AIDS. Could any of them be trying to desperately make ends meet or been disowned by his family for being "a queer"? How many of them were battling with addiction? This choral ensemble hadn't given us a hint of their earthly struggles, had only passed along to us heavenly, ethereal music. Could it be there was some kind of pain behind every beautiful endeavor—in fact, is that what made it work?

The applause died down, echoing around the tall chamber, and Reg and I filed outside with the rest of the audience, into the oddly warm night, it must have been in the 60s. We walked down the long steps of the Met to the sidewalk where a fog had come up. It was sticky. But we decided to stroll for awhile anyway, down 5th Avenue, discussing the concert, talking about Christmas tomorrow, how one of our program friends, Linda Kroll, who had a loft in Tribeca, was having us over as part of our recovery group for a late afternoon brunch. As usual we had all agreed on no presents, but Reg fretted that he felt he should get everyone a little something. I didn't feel the need to do that, that was the way Linda had set it up, and besides, until I got a job I realized I should be a little careful about money. But I had a feeling Reg had some kind of present for everybody already.

We hadn't planned to, but we kept strolling along in the fog. Christmas came in at 12 a.m., just around the time we said good-bye to each other on 23rd Street; Reg kept on walking down to where he lived on 13th Street off 2nd Avenue and, suddenly tired, I decided I'd had enough of walking and waited forty minutes for a bus to take me to the West side.

I'd been right—Reg had bought, oh, I'd estimate,

twenty-five guests a CD of *Chanticleer's Sing We Christmas.* I chided him at the expense. Reg was an accountant, he earned a good-enough living I suppose, but enough to comfortably buy twenty-five CDs? I asked him if he'd bought them at the Met gift shop before I met him at the concert, and he reassured me with, "Heavens no, that would have been highway robbery. I've been shopping for the best bargains for that particular CD over the Internet for the last twelve months. I bought half of them the week after Christmas last year when they all went on sale." I wondered if Reg didn't secretly enjoy this Internet shopping about as much as he enjoyed trying to find recordings in the old days in those specialty shops he'd told me about where he had a rapport with the owners and that he now bemoaned the loss of.

I knew most of the program people at the party. Everybody took a hand in hanging ornaments and lights and stringing colored beads and ropes of popcorn on the tree. In recovery it was important to try to do things collectively. Everybody was made to feel important, a part of the whole.

Each guest had contributed twenty bucks toward the food that Linda, who lived in a large, homey loft, had catered. Linda had lost her fourteen-year old son to a Prozac suicide and considered herself an SSRI survivor. Jack, her second husband, lived with her and had a successful mail-order business for alternative medicines and vitamins. There was plenty of food —turkey, ham, roast beef, Yorkshire pudding, Gruyère mashed potatoes, acorn squash with maple syrup, and tons of thickly iced cookies cut into shapes of reindeers, Santas, sleighs, and Christmas trees.

"I'm eating for two now," Allison said as she sidled up to me with Logan, the nice guy who had come over to my apartment on Thanksgiving, "so I have the right to pig out. And this isn't exactly low-caloried fare here."

"When's the baby due?" I asked.

"In May."

"That soon? You hardly have a belly," I mused gracelessly.

"It's because of what I'm wearing. If I took my clothes off, you'd see." Logan laughed. Apparently he'd seen her without her clothes on, no doubt quite recently. Yet when I cornered Allison alone later in the evening she told me she didn't know if Logan was the father, or if the father was this electrician from Long Island she'd had a one-night stand with. She wasn't going to order a DNA test to find out because Logan had agreed to raise the baby as if he were the father, no matter what. She didn't want to know the sex of the child either.

"Wow, you don't want to know much of anything," I said as I bit into a cookie. "Why not? I suppose the more you know—"

"The less you know," she finished. "Right."

Only I was going to say the more you know the more you want to know—and sometimes there aren't any answers. Then I realized we'd meant the same thing, only finished it off with a different phrase. Party banter. It's what I needed and I also needed to scatter myself around the room from friend to friend, from acquaintance to acquaintance. Most of us stayed until well after midnight when we broke into four groups and played charades. I wasn't much good at acting out the clues but I was good at guessing them and my team won. It was five in the morning when I stepped out into the still unseasonably warm weather tinged with fog. And grabbed a cab home to sleep the day away.

The next day I received a piece of mail I hadn't anticipated getting so soon. It was from the Unified Court System of the State of New York. And it held my test score. An 83. I don't know if everybody who takes a test thinks they'll get a higher score than they end up with. I'd expected something in the high 80s. This score seemed dodgy at best. When Bob McBride wished me happy holidays later in the day I stayed mum about the fact I'd gotten my score. I could be called for an interview, I suppose, at some point. But there weren't that many slots to fill, not in New York City. I could be waiting quite awhile, I figured, one year, two years— God, there was the chance I might never be called.

I walked down to the Chelsea piers, carrying the letter, and out onto one of the piers that was nearly deserted where a tugboat was tied to one of the docks. I meandered to the end of the pier, thinking about what my score meant on the most practical level. Uncomfortably, I realized that it meant I had little chance of getting a position with the Unified Court System. I had been a make-believe writer of film criticism but hadn't gone to a movie for months. And didn't want to. I didn't have any real goals. I would take a State job based on a test score, just to have one, so down the line I wouldn't go broke. So I could go on living my life. But what life? Depressed, I tore the letter into shreds and dropped it into the murky still water softly splashing against the wooden pier. But the pieces just floated in front of me, they didn't sink or swiftly move downstream. If I got called for an interview, fine, I'd go, and I might get a job out of it yet. I didn't want to be negative. That's why I didn't want the notice lying around the apartment, reminding me I could have done better.

The week between Christmas and New Year's was

very warm. I think that was one of the things that got me out of the mood to go to the upcoming New Year's Eve party a rich member of our bereavement group was hosting at the country club he belonged to on the Jersey shore. He was picking up all the expenses for the party, including the limousine service he'd arranged to transport Reg, Allison, Logan, and me to the country club and bring us back home after the party was over. It was going to be a mix of us in recovery alongside a bunch of his Jersey friends I'd never met. The best thing about the week had already happened. There had been no phone call from Crewe. He'd evidently taken me at my word and knew I wasn't playing games. Hopefully he'd moved on. After all, there were plenty more where I came from.

I didn't want to offend anyone but when New Year's Eve came I did beg off going to the party with sincere apologies. Maybe Christmas and New Year's were a little too close together. I didn't want a country club bash. I needed a quiet time to reflect on the year on my own and to see if I could envision a better way for myself in the coming one.

"But you'll be all alone," Allison protested over the phone.

"No, I won't," I said. "Because of you."

"But I won't be with you."

"You will be with me in a sense. I was thinking back to that day when you, Reg and I went to the exhibit of Blake watercolors at the Met. I'm in the mood to revisit them online. Try to reawaken my intuition, my inner being so to speak, by meditating on them while ringing in the New Year."

"Well, good luck. Sounds a bit heady."

"Happy New Year."

"Ditto."

I spent a few hours at the computer with Blake's imagination, indeed revisiting some of the imagery in his *Paradise Lost* illustrations, which I found that I remembered well. The soft blue light from the computer cast a compelling spell of its own, drawing me in. It was easy to align myself with the longings of Blake's creations of Adam and Eve who wanted to break free from their bonds of love and hate, good and evil, and roam outside the garden, but who were trapped inside the faint watercolors they inhabited. The way I, a Pisces, occasionally felt trapped. But Blake had rendered the personages he'd drawn forever immobile. Allowed them only to stand poised on the brink of some spiritual discovery but unable to move towards it. Surely I, who was not a beautiful, lifeless figure drawn by an artist, but a human being made by God, was free to journey toward metaphysical wisdom. I let my arms swing to the side of the chair. With my head at a downward incline, I slept wide awake.

Until through my open window came the noise of the celebrants twenty blocks away at Times Square. The roar of the crowd. Was that big ball dropping now? I shook myself awake, went to the window and listened to the horns honking, whistles blowing, screams of celebration. My reverie broken, I shut the window, though it was still muggy, and reduced the human din to a distant droning. I turned off the computer, wholly myself again, standing in the New Year. I wondered how my friends were doing at the country club on the Jersey shore and now I wished I was there among them, throwing confetti and blowing a tin horn. I laughed. How odd life is, how fickle.

Well, what to do instead? I thought of making myself some hot chocolate, turning on the TV and watching humanity baying at a fallen ball, or maybe seeing if there was a good movie, some old gem, on Turner Classics. I rejected all of them and decided that tonight was the perfect occasion to curl up in bed with Robbie Burns, found a red velvet bound volume of his poetry from the top shelf of the bookcase in my living room, got into bed, puffed up the pillow and pulled up the covers, making myself comfortable, opened the book to the place where it was already bookmarked and read:

*Should auld acquaintance be forgot,*
*and never brought to mind?*
*Should auld acquaintance be forgot,*
*and auld lang syne?*

*For auld lang syne, my jo,*
*for auld lang syne,*
*we'll tak a cup o' kindness yet,*
*for auld lang syne.*

*We twa hae run about the braes,*
*and pu'd the gowans fine;*
*But we've wander'd mony a weary fit,*
*sin auld lang syne.*

*For auld lang syne, my jo,*
*for auld lang syne,*
*we'll tak a cup o' kindness yet,*
*for auld lang syne*

*We twa hae paidl'd i' the burn,*
*frae morning sun till dine;*
*But seas between us braid hae roar'd*

*sin auld lang syne.*
*For auld lang syne, my jo,*
  *for auld lang syne,*
*we'll tak a cup o' kindness yet,*
  *for auld lang syne.*

•

The day broke dark and cold. Winter was back, bringing along a fine sleet that tapped on the window pane. I woke, groggy, pulled the covers over my head but couldn't fall back asleep. My mind was racing along a road to nowhere, and like a car with someone's foot on the accelerator, it just wouldn't stop. This unwelcome stimulation told me this would be a day I couldn't sit very well with my feelings. And this coming after a night where I'd done some meditating. I shivered under the covers for awhile then decided to make a cup of coffee, which I supposed would make me even more jittery. When I opened my closet to pull out my robe, my eyes fell on the red shoes. I picked them up and took them to the window and stared at them in the dark winter light where they gave off that familiar scarlet sparkle. I thought now with excitement of how I'd worn them for Silvio, how he'd been turned on by them, what hedonistic desires they had unleashed in both of us. I'd kind of brushed Silvio off these last couple of months, but maybe he wasn't the kind to take offense. Maybe he'd like to come over tonight. Maybe I'd have to eat a little humble crow first, but so what? It would be worth it.

I raced to the phone and dialed his number only to hear his message that he was in Florida for the holidays and wouldn't be back till January 6. Of course, now I remembered his dad lived down there and no doubt Silvio was lying on the beach at this very moment, maybe sipping on a "brew," his mind on anything but me, while I was with him in fantasy land, holding a pair of red shoes in my hand and thinking of the G-string in my drawer going to waste. Disappointedly I hung up.

For the first time I was at a total loss to come up with something to do. Probably Reg and Allison were sleeping late, not having gotten back to the city till after daybreak, or the dawning gloom that passed for it. I didn't want to go to a meeting. I didn't want to go to for a walk, to a movie, a café, or a museum or read a book. I took a shower and found myself preening in front of the bathroom mirror, my blond hair having grown out of that spiked style, falling onto my forehead and heading straight down the back of my neck towards my shoulders. Like a peacock, I liked my plumage, but there was no one to admire myself but me.

I was anxious all day and into the evening. I needed something. But what? I couldn't think of anything to calm me down until I thought of Teresa. I wasn't proud to admit it but I'd liked sniffing a little coke; well, I'd sniffed more than a little with Crewe, but I didn't have to overdo it. I could go easy on the stuff without him around constantly pushing a plate in front of my face. What was so wrong with the idea? Actually, plenty, to be honest. I didn't want to lean on that stuff as an escape valve. Yet I was in the mood for some now. With a few sniffs, I could relax. I'd even endure the pain of a short conversation with the neighborhood phantasm. I checked my watch. It was going on ten at night. Would she be sleeping off some New Year's Eve crack extravaganza or would she have some rock to sell me?

Hurriedly I removed a couple of hundred dollar bills from my sock in the drawer, put on some black slacks and a gray sweatshirt, threw on an old charcoal colored London Fog raincoat that had actually been my dad's, slipped on the red shoes, and walked briskly to her 16th Street apartment.

But when I got to her building I was startled to find someone else standing in the entryway ringing her bell. A cute, slim kid in his twenties with curly brown hair sticking out from underneath a Yankees baseball cap, dressed in jeans and a yellow jersey. He pressed her bell insistently over and over as I stood back watching cautiously. Totally devoid of patience, he kept cursing, "Goddamnit!" Once he looked at me over his shoulder and asked if I lived here. When I bit my lip and looked down he said, "Oh, I get it. You're here to cop some too. Well, fucking hell, she's not answering, the silly drugged cow."

A young couple who either lived in the building or were visiting somebody there were just leaving. They opened the lobby door and the kid yelled over his shoulder at me, "Well, come on, let's go," and we bolted inside as they went out. They turned around in amazement to see our disappearing figures make a hurried left turn down the hallway. The kid ran up the stairs to the fourth floor while I followed him slowly in confusion only to hear his voice cry out when he reached the top, "Holy shit!"

When I caught up with him I saw Teresa's door was open and she was lying in the hall on a stainless-steel gurney, two EMS workers putting an IV in her arm. She was moaning, her eyes closed, bruises covering her face, blood dripping slowly out of her quivering, parted lips onto the white sheet that was pulled up to her neck, her blonde wig having slipped off the back of her head to reveal some kind of laceration on her bald spot on top. The EMS workers were discussing the laceration, which looked like a cut made with some object, maybe a knife or a screwdriver. The wound didn't look deep. It just looked like a long piece of flesh that had been ripped and was now parted in two and puffed up like the mouth of a fish. They were debating whether or not to apply some treatment to the wound but decided against it. One of them tried to ease her wig back over her bald head, carelessly, embarrassedly, not finishing the job, so that it ended up hanging, in a cruelly comical way, halfway on her head and halfway down her face. I felt like throwing up but didn't have time. The kid was urging me again, "Well, come on, let's go for it," as he slithered past the EMS workers into her apartment, clomping down the hallway full of twisted junk as I followed behind. When he reached her squalid parlor, he repeated himself, blurting out, "Holy shit!" His limited vocabulary said it all however. There was blood splatter covering the walls, dripping down the frilly costume drawings dangling precariously from their carefully mounted spots, and coagulating on the dirty yellowed sheets. A lamp, the one with the pink shade, had fallen from her table. It lay at my feet broken into pieces.

One of the EMS workers shouted out to us, "What the hell are you two doing in there. Come out."

The kid called out, "I'm her brother, goddamnit!"

Then he turned to me, "Well don't just stand there, we don't have much time, the cops will be here any minute." He was rummaging, expertly, through her kitchen cabinet, knowing exactly where her rock was kept and he swooped some packets into a handkerchief that he pulled out of his back pocket. "Are you going to help or what?" he demanded as I watched one of Teresa's frilly drawings give up the ghost and waft onto the bed with the carelessness of a dead leaf.

"No," I said.

"The hell you aren't," he said, rustling through her kitchen drawers and finding six or seven crack pipes. "You have deep pockets." He thrust them into the so-called "deep pockets" of my London Fog raincoat while he stuffed the handkerchief with the packets of rock into his back pocket. "Now let's get the fuck out of here," he muttered and we dashed back down the cluttered hallway outside to the landing where the kid asked the EMS workers, cool as day, "When are the cops going to be here? I want a full report on what happened to my sister."

They ignored him but an older woman in a pink bathrobe standing in her doorway across the hall said, "The police were here already. I'm the one who called 911. But I couldn't give them a good description of the man. Through my peephole his face was just a blur as he made a run for the stairs. Though it looked like he was in a heavy black jacket of some kind. They gave chase anyway. Maybe the camera in the vestibule was able to capture him—if it's working that is." She pulled the edges of her bathrobe protectively around her neck and added, shivering, "The noises coming from her apartment, all the screaming and cursing, were enough to scare the dead. I'd say your poor sister's in an awful way." The kid motioned for me to follow him down the stairs, which I did, but not before hearing the last salvo from the 911 savior, "Not that I'm surprised."

We got outside and rushed, nonchalantly of course, to the corner where the kid hailed a cab, jumped in the back, and pulled me in next to him. He instructed the driver to go to Cornelia and Bleecker and to step on it. I still felt like throwing up but held it down.

"I'm Baily," the kid said with a relaxed, disarming smile.

"Oh...hello, I'm..." I debated whether to lie or reveal my real name. "I'm...never mind...it doesn't matter..."

He laughed at my reluctance to tell him my name. "Mr. Mysterious, that's what I'll call you. How's that?"

Smart ass. "That's just fine."

"Well, Mr. Mysterious," he pulled the handkerchief from his back pocket and showed me four or five full packets of rock, "we've hit the jackpot tonight."

The cab blasted forward at a dizzying speed, narrowly missing sideswiping the car next to us.

"But Teresa, what happened?" I asked.

"Bad karma, that's what happened."

Baily had the cab stop on the corner of Cornelia and Bleecker, and we walked halfway down Cornelia where he stopped at a rustic tenement in the middle of the block and ushered me down the steps into a tiny vestibule. He put his key in the lobby door then paused as if he had all the time in the world and tapped his finger on his mailbox where his name was prominently displayed. He pointedly announced, "My name is Baily Cantevelter. See it. 'Cant-te-velter,' Mr. Shy and Secretive. Just emphasizing I have nothing to hide."

"That's a relief," I murmured.

He led me down a flight of stairs into his basement flat, a studio, very well-kept up, sparsely furnished with a chintz sofa, a small round dining room table and chairs, and a double bed with mosquito netting tied onto a makeshift rod like a curtain which you could pull around the bed and enclose it completely, like a bed in the tropics. There was an open window facing up against a brick wall. The kitchen was compactly built into a corner recess. There was a small fridge, a smaller stove and a sink with an adjoining spotless shelf that might provide the space you would need to make a modest meal for one. The bathroom door was open and I saw it was the size of a postage stamp with just enough floor space to turn uncomfortably from the toilet towards the sink and with one more step find yourself in the shower. The studio was painted a sweet powder blue.

"Make yourself right at home while I cook." He emptied the contents of his handkerchief onto the counter. "Help yourself to juice or water. It's in the fridge."

"I'll pass for now," I said, slipping off my coat and sitting at the table. "You're not Teresa's brother, are you, not really?"

"What do you think, knuckle-head, did you notice a family resemblance? Jesus Christ, the brother of that schizoid. No way."

I couldn't quite let it go. "But what do you think happened?"

Baily was hunched over the stove, engaged in all kinds of convoluted machinations, heating water, wrapping ice in a towel and smashing it into chips with a hammer, breaking off a clump of rock, giving it a taste test with his finger, evidently passing muster, then putting some rock in a spoon with some crushed ice and making circles with the spoon held just so over the boiling water. It reminded me of how I used to move Jiffy Pop popcorn around and around a flame waiting for the sound of that first kernel to pop.

"You know how to cook, right?" he asked me.

"Not at all."

"Then you better watch me so you can do this."

Unknown to Baily, I had zero interest in learning the fine art of cooking crack and never could have managed it anyway. Baily worked quickly and deftly with the concentration, knowledge and delicate touch of a brain surgeon. "I hope this cooks up OK," he said gravely.

"Are you cooking all of it?"

"Not right now, I just want to cook enough so we can each get a couple of hits."

"If you don't mind, could you set some aside for me so I can cut up a couple of lines that I can just snort instead."

"Oh, sure," he said a little disappointedly. "You don't smoke?"

"No," I said, in horror at the thought. Sniffing coke was one thing but smoking crack like Teresa had done was obviously dangerous. It had melted her brain. I didn't know what crack was. Was it rock cocaine or did it turn into something else when it was all cooked up? I didn't even want to know the answer. Baily put some doughy white liquid on a plate and watched the gel like an entomologist studying an insect under a microscope. "Yeah, it's hardening up nice," he announced with relief. "Hand me the pipes."

I fished the pipes out of my raincoat pocket and like a surgical assistant put them into his hands. He evaluated them with professional expertise before taking some chopsticks from a drawer. "Ripped off from Sammy's Noodles," he announced, smiling with pride before using them to clean the pipes. Though I'd grown tired of watching what seemed to be such impossibly elaborate preparations, I decided nonetheless to see this production through to the very end. Baily opened his kitchen drawer and pulled out little screens or wire netting and fitted them into the head of the pipes, massaging them down with his fingers like a sculptor until they fit tightly. What a shit load of trouble, I thought, while noticing the raw excitement in Baily's eyes as he performed this ritual. A surgeon, an entomologist, a sculptor, and a crack aficionado all in one. He lay out a selection of acetate torch lighters. "Almost ready," he announced with an air of success. "Here, I'll chop up some powder on a plate and here's a straw. So you can do your lines. Just relax. Enjoy."

When he had my plate prepared I sat at the table and snorted a line. If I'd known what I'd had to go through tonight for one little sniff, I would have stayed home. But I hadn't known and I did get off on the shivering glow slithering through my body.

"She had the wrong guy over, picked up a bad trick, she wasn't real careful who she let in, seeing she was always strung out." Now that the important stuff was finished he could go back to my question.

"You mean it could have been a stranger."

"Yeah, one who might not have known she had a dick instead of a cunt. Getting himself all worked up about her missing slit, you know the drill. Hey, do you mind giving me a feel while I take a hit?"

I walked over to the stove, while he put a piece of rock in the pipe and fired it up. Not sure I had understood what he wanted I just stood there until he grabbed my hand and put it on his cock through his jeans as he sucked in on the pipe, held the smoke in a minute, then blew it all out. It was about as foul a smell as I'd ever encountered, a cross between a belch from an iron foundry and a dead skunk. "Harder," he urged and I increased the pressure on his cock as his eyes went all glassy and he sighed in ecstasy. "Excellent shit," was his happy assessment. Then, "Poor bitch, she may not be having the greatest of nights right now, but I've always agreed it's better to give than to receive and she gave like a patron saint!"

Not very nice. But who could say it wasn't the truth. Baily had benefited from her misfortune and come to think of it so had I. But I'd relinquish my line of coke in an instant if Teresa could start her night over and keep her door locked this time. I wondered if Baily would have though. He was busy putting another rock in his pipe, firing it up, and asking me this time to unzip his fly and go down on him while he sucked in the smoke. Shyly but eagerly, still glowing from the line I'd snorted, I dropped to my knees and I sucked on his juicy, perfectly-shaped American cock. He blew out the smoke and groaned with pleasure. "This combo's great shit! Your wet mouth on my cock at the same time I suck in a hit of crack. Oh, boy. This is better than I expected. Happy New Year."

I laughed, I don't know why. It was ridiculous. And I thought his mind must be going through all sorts of hallucinations as he sucked that crack smoke down. But he was so cute, like a boy, with wide brown eyes and a cherubic face and pretty curls underneath his Yankees cap. Yow, though I was only going to be thirty-six in February I had a momentary flash that I could be robbing the cradle. Was this kid of age?

"Baily," I massaged the cock that was sticking straight out of his blue jean fly. "How old are you?"

"Sixteen," he said. "Why? That's old enough to get hard, isn't it?"

I looked up at him in panic. He was sixteen. I got up, ready to leave.

"No, you cocksucker, I'm twenty-four. Now does that make you feel any better?"

That made more sense. He had his own apartment after all.

"Oh, I see, I have to reassure the gentleman that he's not a pedophile." He pulled out his wallet and showed me his driver's license, albeit one from Tennessee, but it did prove he was twenty-four. "And you, Mr. Mysterious, is your age as secretive as your name?"

"I'm thirty-five," I said, wondering if he'd freak out to find out I was eleven years older than he was. I knew how kids that age were, they saw everybody over thirty as way over the hill.

"No big deal. I dig older men."

"Well, we're quite a match then," I said drolly. I took my London Fog coat off the chair.

"Stop!" he howled, elongating the word so it sounded as if it was coming from an angry little boy who'd just had his toy taken from him. "You're not going?"

"I am. Just put some blow in some aluminum foil for me if you don't mind."

I couldn't believe it. He literally stamped his foot, pouted, and whined, "How is it when we were just getting into it you want to leave?"

"If I had a reason I'd give you one. I just want to, that's all. Maybe thinking about Teresa lying on that gurney is putting a damper on me getting into it with you, as you put it. Who knows?"

"You're not taking into account she was a no good cheat and ripped me off like crazy."

"You said 'was' like she's dead already."

"No way, baby, she's too mean to die." He turned back to the counter and put a generous amount of the crushed coke plus a whole new rock in a piece of foil. I was so used to Crewe's parsing every little line so I wouldn't come out with a bit more than he had, I was surprised at Baily's generosity. He read my thoughts. "It's to be shared, you know. God forbid the day comes when you have to crawl on the floor to search for a spilled crumb and hide it from the…the guy you're with…" His voice drifted off, sadly I guess, because he wouldn't be with this guy tonight. Or sadly because he couldn't think of anything more unfortunate than running out of crack and crawling around on his hands and knees to find that last particle. He was a crazy brat, a crack head I guess, but there was something disingenuous about him, or so I thought, still ready to give the kid the benefit of the doubt, at least after Crewe. Hell, they were probably all rotten. Anybody hooked on drugs. He handed me the foil. "Don't go. It's New Year's Day."

"Baily, for God's sake. What are we going to do? Where is there for us to go from here? You smoke crack and I don't. You know?" Then I added melodramatically, "There's a huge gulf between us."

"Just stay awhile. Please." No response. "Pretty please." I crossed my arms. "I'm sorry about what I said about Teresa. Of course I hated seeing her like that. I wouldn't wish that on my own worst enemy and sometimes when she fucked me over I thought she was. But nobody deserves that. And since we can't change it, well…why don't we forget all about that now?… Stay with me, don't make me beg you for God's sake."

I put the coat down, laid the foil on the table, opened it, picked up the straw off the plate and took another sniff.

"Yay! Let's party, dude!"

The party consisted of me blowing him as he sat back on the couch, legs spread wide, in a pair of boots he put on, baseball cap flipped around backwards as he smoked crack and turned on the flat screen TV to watch porn. Some party. The smell of the smoke was awful, like a sweet breeze from a grave where a corpse had been newly buried. Wouldn't the smoke drift out into the hall? Couldn't his neighbors smell it? Maybe not, we were in the basement after all.

We ended up in his double bed where he oiled me up with scents and lotions and gave me a pleasurable massage, working his fingers deep into my back and shoulders, finding those tension points, and lingering on my butt crack from time to time where I felt his finger once pause on my ass lips.

"You can forget that, Baily. It's off limits."

"Oh, well, next time."

Like fucking hell. I'd let Silvio and Crewe fuck me—with condoms—but Baily was younger, wilder, and thus, in my mind, less cautious and trustworthy.

"No, not next time," I said emphatically. "I don't know you from Adam."

"Oh, so you don't know Adam well either. But from the drawings I've seen of him, I bet he could change your mind, and so will I."

Cheeky bastard, I thought, but I didn't want to argue.

Suddenly I found we had begun to make out passionately, probing each other's mouths with our tongues. Of course I stopped him when I could finally catch my breath and made him rinse his mouth out with cherry flavored mouthwash—twice—so I wouldn't taste that nasty chemical odor. He wasn't a bad kisser. In fact he was quite adept at it. We held each other all night in a half-sleep, Baily whispering to me as dawn broke, "Thanks for staying."

*

I didn't think Baily Cantevelter had even noticed my red shoes. Of course he'd been preoccupied with number one—his addiction—which always steals the front row center seat during any drama. You always come second. And from where I sat in the balcony, my face was fuzzy, out of focus, my purpose unclear. I hardly remembered slipping on the red shoes when I hurried out to Teresa's; I recalled having taking them out of the closet in the morning and that they were lying on the floor all day so I just put them on without thinking. But at Baily's I'd been aware they were on my feet, especially when we were snuggling in bed, naked except for Baily's leather boots and my red shoes, while we crisscrossed each other's legs all night long, tossing and turning.

We'd exchanged phone numbers—on reflection I decided Baily was more than cute, his face was handsome with classic features, he had a well-proportioned body covered by just the right amount of milky flesh, and dark nipples, and a butt straight from the gods. That night I never got tired of watching him strut around naked, except of course for his leather boots and baseball cap. He was a hunk, period. And he was funny in a wicked but not cruel way. I was somebody who let him do his thing. My easy tolerance I could take to the bank since apparently it was a real asset with drug addicts. Though I was eleven years older than Baily, I was still as supple as a plum and ripe as a new moon and young in the swift scheme of things, and mellow with beauty, the mirror had told me that, the motiveless piece of glass that never lies.

"Red lipstick. Like fire engine red. That's what you need to match your red shoes," were Baily's first words the next afternoon when I picked up the phone. "If you come over with that lipstick and those red shoes, I'll let you be my ho."

"You're full of it," I laughed, picturing myself as this white boy's ho and failing in my role.

"Come on, you're underplaying your potential. You know you want to be my ho—it's written all over you."

"I don't want to be anybody's ho, much less yours, and sorry to disappoint you, but I'm not into drag. Never have been. I've never 'dressed up.' I don't want to be a female."

"Just the lips. Not a dress, ditzoid. You can be as masculine as you want. Who's trying to turn you into a woman, anyway, I like men myself. I just want you to accentuate your lips while I watch you bobbing up and down on my cock. You know, leaving red traces of your undying love on my white shaft. It'd be a cool contrast."

"Hmm… Undying love."

"Besides it keeps the whole red thing going…continues the motif…"

"Our motif has yet to be established."

"Well, get your butt over here and we'll establish one."

Timidly I scanned the red lipsticks and glosses at an upscale boutique on Greenwich Avenue. I seemed to be the sole customer in the store and the salesgirl behind the counter was only paying cursory attention to my browsing, figuring, I hoped, that I was there to pick up some essential cosmetic for my wife, girlfriend, sister, or mother.

I hadn't been able to help making my way there via Teresa's block, curious to see what? In a fine mist all that caught my eye was a tape marked CRIME SCENE—DO NOT ENTER that had originally been stretched across the lobby door but that someone had ripped in two so the residents could have access to their apartments—all that was left were two torn fluttering pieces. Could there still be an investigation going on inside there this late into the next afternoon? I passed by, putting it out of my mind.

The lipsticks I perused all had amazingly sexy names from Fire Down Below to Red Lizard to Stiletto and ranged from semi matte true reds, to Kryptonite orange-scarlets, and rich blue-cherries, to even a mellow wine-colored shade called Bitten. I figured Baily would want me to get the reddest one of all, which finally jumped out at me—Shanghai Red, a flame at its zenith— and when I bought it the salesgirl nodded in approval. I must be on the right track.

I walked the rest of the way to Baily's. The rain came down in gentle fits and starts, enough to create small puddles, which didn't help my red shoes much. When I got closer to his apartment I saw Baily tinkering with a motorcycle parked in front. The machine looked like a monster to me.

"Yep, it's mine," he said, confirming my worst fears, "and I'm gonna take you for a spin."

On that? "Go to hell," I said cheerfully.

"Sometimes it feels that way, like a trip to hell—and back. But we'll take it nice and easy the first time."

"It looks downright evil."

"I hope so. It's a Harley Night Train. It's supposed

to look evil. It's supposed to scare the living bejesus out of everybody. It defies time, space, even gravity. Why shouldn't that make you scared? Every firecracker fuse you've ever lit is child's play when you decide you're ready to take back the road with this motherfucker."

"You do have a charming way with words, a unique descriptive gift."

"You're such a faggot."

"And what is it you're trying to prove with this macho crap? That you're the baddest dude on the block?"

"It's my transportation to work, that's what it is. My boss got it for me."

"Your boss? It looks expensive."

"Starts at seventeen grand. This model does. Only he got a deal on it. Bought it used. Wasn't even half that." We each paused at a standoff until he added smugly, "Do you mind or what?"

I shrugged. "It's your life."

"Thank you. Here." He handed me a helmet as he put his own on. I'd never gotten on the back of a chopper in my life. In fact, it had never ever crossed my mind. But suddenly I felt like proving to him I wasn't such a wilting gardenia after all.

"I'm all yours," I said with the falsest bravado anybody had ever mustered. "For one ride, just one, and only once around the block."

"Here, Clarabelle." He had to fasten and tighten the helmet on me. "I don't have time to take you out on the highway anyway, I have to get to work." Oh, nice, what was I doing here in my red shoes with my newly purchased Shanghai Red lipstick in my pocket then? He settled himself on the seat and told me to sidle on behind him and hold on tight. I did as he instructed, wrapping my arms around his skinny frame as he revved up the motor and kicked the clutch with his boot. As he pulled away from the curb he gunned the damn thing and the whole front end roared up in the air like an angry horse. It was a horror show from the start. The few people on the street did a double take with either shock or anger as he took off. It quickly hit me that he'd removed the muffler so he could purposely try and set off every car alarm on the block and at that he was very successful—the alarms all started whining in rapid succession while he chortled like a maniac. "That's what crack does to you!" he shouted back to me as I closed my eyes, keeping my head low to keep the rushing wind from decapitating me.

One corner down, three to go. I kept my eyes shut tight while I silently cursed the hell out of him, car horns blaring at us from every direction. The next corner couldn't come soon enough. I just held on to the fact that there would be an end to this as he rounded the next bend, leaning with the curve of the cycle, sideways, and angrily clawing my nails into his belly to make it known that I didn't like my head at a ninety degree angle to my body. There was nothing else I could do to make my point. He seemed nonplussed by my nail digging and at the next intersection we skidded through a puddle, Baily weaving wildly, almost losing control of the bike before finally bringing us to a stop. I opened my eyes and stared up through the handlebars at a red light dangling in the air above us.

"Slow down, for Christ's sake!" I finally got the chance to shout. "You're skidding…"

"Yeah, this street's as slick as a wet pussy." The light turned green, I closed my eyes and clenched my jaw as he let out a whoop and jumped the damn bike again so the front of the beast lurched straight up, then, his skills challenged, Baily managed to maneuver unsteadily around the final corner back onto Cornelia. I'd lived to make it back to where we started but as he pulled in to park and then shut off the motor, the Night Train gently wobbled, and it was then I lost my balance and fell onto the sidewalk. To the sounds of the car alarms still going strong and neighbors hurling curses at us through their open windows.

My jeans were torn all the way down my right leg and I could see my skin was scraped.

Baily calmly stood by his Harley, slowly removing his helmet, taking his handkerchief out of his pocket and fastidiously dusting it off, oblivious to the blasphemous cries directed at him and also at me who was down for the count.

"This is one time I can truly say there's a first and last time for everything," I said as evenly as I could, looking straight up into his face though I was shaking and my guts felt stuck to my brain. I finally stood up, wobbly, glaring at him, removing my helmet and shoving it in his hands. "Get me inside before I'm put to death by your neighbors."

He laughed happily and put his arm around my shoulder and guided me into the vestibule. "I'm proud of you," he praised me. "You never said 'die.' Wow. Did you see how many alarms I got to go off, though it's more of a kick to ride down Fourteenth or Twenty-Third Street about three in the morning and set them all off. You wouldn't believe the noise."

I hobbled inside his studio and asked him, "Did you ever think that a more pleasant or even thrilling thing to do at three in the morning might be to put your feet up on the table, lean back, close your eyes and take a deep breath and listen to some Erik Satie piano music, say the *Trois Gymnopédies*?"

He just looked at me like I was crazy. I must have been, actually, after accepting a ride on a sudden dare from a daredevil. He was the sane one, I guess.

"Go in the bathroom and see to your wounds," Baily commanded me, sounding like a sergeant ordering one of his troops to clean up after some avoidable accident. I didn't like hearing the word "wounds," it conjured up Teresa's laceration, not that I could draw any comparisons between her two pieces of flapping skin and my minor cuts and scratches. It's just they'd both been unexpected, that's all. But enough already, it was time to banish Teresa from my mind once and for all.

I located a small bottle of Mercurochrome, or "red medicine" as I'd called it as a boy, in Baily's bathroom cabinet. I carefully washed the dirt off my scrapes, soaped them pink and clean, before applying the stinging purifier. There. All better.

"Well, Sergeant, I'm battle-ready now," I joked, coming out of the bathroom to find Baily in his little kitchen alcove torching up his pipe and melting a big piece of rock.

"Good," he answered, sucking in and blowing out a cloud of smoke, then leaning against the stove for a moment, overcome, but managing to get out, "Goddamn, that's fucking amazing." Then, recovering he said, "We have to hustle up something for you to wear. You're going to accompany me to work tonight."

"Sounds like fun. Sitting next to you at some desk keeping you awake on the graveyard shift."

"Hardly."

Hardly. What did he mean?

"Oh, no, Mr. Mysterious, I think you'll have a lot more fun than that."

I eyed him warily.

He started to walk across the studio then suddenly turned towards me and said, "Stand back, I'm not going to hurt you, just demonstrate something. Trust me, I'm not even going to come close to making contact with you." Then he executed a kick toward my groin with lightning speed. Then a second kick thrusting towards my stomach with his full body weight behind it to give it extra power. Though he'd had one foot firmly planted on the floor during both kicks, he still gave the illusion that he had flown right through the air at me. He'd stood far enough back from me that I hadn't been afraid, but it did give me pause to think of some poor somebody on the receiving end that he was actually going for. He'd screwed up his face, too, so that his expression had been merciless and full of hate. I guess that was part and parcel of it.

"OK," I acknowledged, putting on a game face. "Thanks for giving me fair warning that I was only watching a dispassionate exhibition."

"No problem. I didn't want to scare you."

Scared wasn't the right word, intimidated was. Even though I knew he didn't want to harm me, his sudden ferocity reminded me that men actually went after each other like that if they had to, sometimes with lethal intent.

"You know some convincing karate moves," I said. "But I'm not putting the bigger picture together."

He picked up a broom that was propped up against the kitchen cabinet and tossed it to me. Somehow I caught it.

"Let me show you another move," he said. "You

never know when it could stand you in good stead."

Now what?

"Come on. Attack me," he continued, waving me towards him with his hand. Tauntingly.

"What do you mean? Hold the broom crosswise like a bar and rush forward?"

"No. Like it was a baseball bat. Swing it at me."

"Baily," I said nervously, "I don't want to hit you accidentally."

"If you only could."

"You know something. This isn't a lot of fun. I'm not a violent person by nature."

"But others are. You've got to be able to protect yourself. It's a fucked up world out there. Come on, come at me, you won't get hurt, I promise. I like you for God's sake."

I thought it over. "I'll do it," I finally said, "but only in slow motion."

I stepped forward, swinging the handle of the broom towards his face while he brought his right arm out in an upward crossing movement, his left arm across his face. He twisted his right arm, bringing his palm forward, rolling my attack over his head and with his left arm at about a forty-five degree angle deflected it. The broom slid off to his side and went past him. I had the feeling I was falling into outer space, everything had happened so quickly, he had disappeared from my sight, and I was losing my balance fast; he grabbed me from behind to steady me, pressing his crotch up against my buns, and whispered lasciviously in my ear, "I should never give a witch a broom now, should I?"

"Let go of me," I protested unconvincingly.

He kept his arms locked around my chest,

continuing to rub his crotch up and down my ass, then finally released me.

"That move I did, in Japan it's called a 'uke,'" he announced with the comfortable air of an expert, "or an upper block to you."

"Like I'm going to learn this shit?"

"Obviously not, but that's cool. I'll be around to protect you."

"Thanks."

"So now, what does all this signal to you about my job?"

Though I was out of breath he was breathing serenely. I noticed when I rushed towards him, pathetically, that he inhaled when he brought his right arm down and exhaled when he locked his block in position. I think this whole thing had a lot to do with breathing.

"It's obvious. You're a karate instructor with a black belt."

He grinned. "Oh, I've got plenty of black belts. The kind with big silver buckles. I've never taken karate classes, not one, much less given any instruction. What I learned I learned the hard way—from my mean-ass brother and dad and from some hillbilly bullies in my own back yard...Got it?"

For my money he was probably a better fighter than a biker but that still gave me no clue where I was headed tonight. I sank down at the kitchen table toying with the stupid broom and presto, Baily placed a plate of coke in front of me, all nicely chopped up into long lines with a straw at the ready.

"Something to amuse yourself with while I jump in the shower."

Amusing, no. Apropos, absolutely. I listened to him

running the water while I snorted a nice long line then heard him cursing, "Goddamnit to hell, I can never get this temperature right!"

"So, Baily, you're a real redneck from Tennessee," I mused.

"Yep."

So he could hear me as he showered.

"You don't sound Southern."

"What's Southern?"

"I don't know but not you."

"Do you think you're right about everything? Just listen to this," he sang, "*I'm on a Smoky Mountain high...*" He stretched out the word "high" so it slid up the scale from a mellifluous baritone to a sweet tenor and he held the note; it had a nice ring but he still managed to make it sound silly. He continued singing snippets of real songs now, tried and true country songs, some of which I recognized, from Hank Williams, Johnny Cash, and Patsy Cline.

When he came out of the bathroom nonchalantly toweling his balls dry in front of me, I could see he was still intent on me figuring out his life. "If you guess my line of work I'll give you a hit of crack."

"Thank you, no. I don't want a hit of crack."

"Not even a teensy-tiny one?" He had the pipe in his mouth torching up the rock.

"No."

He sucked in a hit then blew the stinking smoke out murmuring, "Not even an infinitesimal one that you couldn't even see under the strongest microscope in the entire world?"

"I know," I said emphatically. "You're somebody's bodyguard."

"Not even close." He came up to the table, still toweling his balls, and leaned over, locking eyes with me, and finally revealed, "I'm a bouncer. In a club." Then, beyond his control, he added deadpan, "A bouncer of zombies," unquestionably demonstrating to me for the first time the effect crack had on somebody. He shook his head to clear it out, like he hadn't just blurted out that crack-inspired mumbo-jumbo line, "a bouncer of zombies," and became Mr. Cool again real quick and said eagerly, "It's a great club. You're going to dig it. It has everything going for it. Great DJs, you know, spinmeisters, atmosphere, a fast crowd and I've got the best boss in the world. You've got to love him."

At first I couldn't picture Baily as a bouncer, he was too skinny, though his arms were politely muscular and his karate skills undeniable. Maybe somebody had actually matched this young man to his acquired talents.

The deal was this. Baily was going to take the monster, his Harley, to park in an overnight garage as he didn't want to ride it back and forth to work. Then he'd come back and we'd cab it to the club. During his absence, I was supposed to forage in the closet for something "hot" to wear. He told me that his old boyfriend had been about the same size as me. Baily said this boyfriend had walked out on him in a hurry, though he didn't say why, leaving most of his possessions behind. I could help myself to whatever duds remained.

"By the way, the old boyfriend didn't just leave his clothes behind. He left the ring I gave him too, you could even put that on if you want, it's real gold with a little sapphire in the center, it's around here somewhere—"

"No, that's OK…"

"Oh yes, he left the ring behind all right, indeed he did, along with his undying love."

"You're still on that 'undying love' thing you mentioned before, though in a slightly different context."

"That's because love never dies, now, does it?"

"No, Baily, it never does."

\*

It was just before midnight. Drifting couples and lone wolves, mostly straight, but with a good mix of gays too, losing themselves in the slow, druggy techno beat of the demimonde. Dancing. Wandering from room to room with different spatial points of view, spotlighted in ever-changing colors of rose, red, purple, blue, lingering at long white neon-lit bars or moseying up a winding staircase, the banisters holding silver pots of lilies, to an upper level, a horseshoe balcony with seats arranged like in a movie theater, where there was plenty of socializing going on, or making out or making do with a drink or a vial of coke. This was Tenebrae. Baily told me it was the trendiest new club in Chelsea, meticulously designed for maximum beauty and set seamlessly inside a red-brick warehouse on 11th Avenue and 27th Street. It was obvious I didn't get out much. I just took it all in, having no other scene to compare it to. For all I knew there could have been a club just like this one down the street but Baily admonished my query with, "No way. Are you fucking kidding? This is state of the art. Do you know how much this place cost to build much less run?"

"I couldn't hazard a guess."

"Well, then." I realized he had no idea himself but of course when he saw me waiting for a more complete answer he assured me with a knowing whisper, "Big bucks."

"Well, I figured that," I said nicely not wanting to dampen his enthusiasm. "And lucky for you to have a job here."

"That's an understatement."

We were standing stiffly in the middle of the biggest of the rooms that seemed to have a curved glass ceiling, one that didn't look onto the night sky, however, but onto black plaster. To my untrained eye that seemed to be a big error in design but God forbid I should say anything. Two slinky women with their boobs hanging free from care outside flimsy spangled silver or glowing gold material bumped into us, spilling their drinks, laughing and moving on, chatting excitedly in a foreign language.

"Of course there's a lot of Eurotrash hanging around," Baily advised me. "What Americans could afford to come here? It's a three hundred buck cover just to get in."

"Luckily, I have an 'in.' With the bouncer no less. I get in free and I don't have to worry if somebody throws a punch at me."

"Are you being sarcastic?"

"No. I'm just stating a fact."

"Well, loosen up a little, you're like a fish out of water. Why don't you get a drink?"

I might as well tell him now. "I don't drink."

"I don't either," he admitted. "But I do other things to have a good time, to party, and so do you."

"Aren't you on the job, Baily? Shouldn't you be standing at the door or something if you're a bouncer?"

"That's so yesterday," he said dismissively. "My boss doesn't want the bouncers to look obvious, that annoys the crowd, we're supposed to fit in and have a good time. So do a line of coke."

"I didn't bring any."

His mouth fell open. Then he frowned.

"Sorry."

People were starting to dance more all around us and they looked at us like "dance too or get the hell out of our way."

"Let me show you something crazy." Baily moved me away from the crowd and down a little staircase near the bar. Into a hallway plunged in semi-darkness with only one naked blue bulb hanging overhead to show the way. He pushed open a swinging door at the end of the hall and ushered me into a big well-lit bathroom with twenty sinks in a row, a line of marble urinals, green Plexiglas toilet stalls and a group of bidets lined up in the open. Some chick was giving a guy a blow job at one of the urinals, two cute men were making out against the wall, cool customers were smoking cigarettes and shooting the shit, some were even lighting up crack or meth pipes, and perched on one of the bidets was a beautiful woman with black hair to her waist, legs spread, giving the world a bird's eye view not only of her crotchless panties but of her shell-like pink pussy lips that lay dramatically uncovered, tilting her head back and taking a good long sniff from a spoon attached to an opaque golden vial. Talk about a scene stealer. All this under the watchful eye of a blank-faced attendant who stood in a tuxedo, wet towels, Japanese style, draped over his arm.

"It's strictly co-ed," Baily said proudly, as if I couldn't tell, while he fished his crack pipe out of his yellow satin jacket, put in a rock and lit up. Behind him through the green Plexiglas door of a toilet stall was the shadow of a girl bent over the toilet, her breasts swinging, getting rear ended by some sleazehead. Baily did an extra hit for good measure as my eyes wandered to a neighboring Plexiglas stall where the shadow of some guy was crouched in front of the toilet obviously giving some freak a blow job who was kicking back on the throne.

The only thing I could think to say was, "I didn't think they allowed people to smoke in these clubs nowadays."

"Nitwit. They smoke in the head. Nobody gives a crap. The cops get paid off, don't they? In fact…I've been the one to hand them the cash once or twice."

It's funny but seeing other people act out sexually in a group does absolutely nothing for me. It's a major limp-on. I don't feel a thing, probably because I'm not caught up in the heart of something with someone myself, in the privacy of my own home. I didn't want to judge anybody, I'd come here, hadn't I, but it wasn't for me. I pushed open the door and went back into the hall, Baily following, evidently feeling a good rush now.

"Well, thanks for the trip down Decadence Lane," I said. "I hope everybody was really having a good time."

"Are you kidding or what? I'm sure they were. We'll check it out a little later again. It gets steamier as the night wears on."

"You're the boss."

"Oh, that's right, I forgot, I want to introduce you to my boss." He stopped me before we went back up the stairs, making way for two druggy men to stumble past us down the stairs into the hallway, feeling their way towards Nirvana. The naked blue bulb played on Baily's face, softening him, making me appreciate his handsome looks anew. I could tell he saw something going on in me he wanted to respond to. "I just want to say I didn't take you in there to do anything. That's not where I'm coming from. I'm a bit modest for that. My Tennessee upbringing you know. I just thought..."

"That I'd like to see for myself something that if you swore to me was going on down there I wouldn't have believed."

He paused, trying to be as sober as possible after two hits of crack. "Something like that." He looked down with embarrassment. "You know, you're pretty OK."

I was saddened by his words. I'd rather have heard him make light of everything and blow me off as a bluenose. Some people don't take compliments well, however awkwardly or beautifully they're expressed, and I was one of them. I cringe inside. Why? Because I feel I'm undeserving of them? Or is it that I don't want to think there could be something good about anybody, much less me, in this tenuous, rotten life?

Maxo Gauchette was playing bartender behind one of the blinding white neon-lit glam bars even though he owned the place. He liked it hands on. Baily had told me he was a quarter Spanish, a quarter French, an eighth Portuguese and half Italian, but Baily's math was a little off, that would have made Maxo more than one man. He could have been from the looks of him, tall with long dark hair slicked back, unshaven, filling out a T-shirt that showed tattoos cascading up and down his developed biceps, and with white teeth that gleamed like diamonds when he let loose with a more than affable grin. He shook my hand heartily and asked Baily if I was his latest. To my amazement Baily said I was. I didn't contradict him, not wanting to turn him into a laughing stock in front of his boss, but I definitely was not.

"Then let me give you a hug." Maxo leaned over the bar, putting his arms around me, pulling me close and kissing me on both cheeks. I thought his accent was more French than anything but I was no expert.

"Have you shown…I'm sorry, I didn't get your name," he said, fixing his eyes on me.

"Mr. Mysterious," Baily said with some disgust. But Maxo only laughed, saying, "*Il uomo mysterioso.*"

"No," I was mortified. "John, that's my name," letting the cat out of the bag.

"Gianni," Maxo confirmed, while Baily stared daggers at me. "Well, did you show Gianni around the place?"

Unfortunately, I thought, but when Maxo asked me what I thought of it I waxed poetic. At least that pleased Baily. "You have a good guy here," Maxo indicated Baily, "very nice, very trustworthy. I'm lucky to be his employer." That made Baily even more pleased.

A woman whom I'd hardly noticed had been standing next to Maxo behind the bar and had apparently been taking everything in, because she extended her hand to me as well and said, "Nice to meet you, John. I'm Patrizia." She then threw her arms around Maxo and clung to him, giving him kisses and whispering sweet nothings in his ear.

"She's my lady," he laughed. "Sometimes she gets a little carried away."

A little? She was drunk but very pretty, in a star sapphire dress, with long wavy light brown hair and just the right make-up to accentuate her sultry lips and limpid eyes. She picked up a thin fluted glass with a slimy green liquid in it and took a sip. "Absinthe," she said. "It's legal in New York now. Would you like a glass? It's on the house, of course."

"Oh, thank you very much, no," I said, disappointing her.

"What's going on these days? Your boyfriend doesn't drink either."

Baily shrugged.

"I do drink however," I said. "If you'd be so kind, I'll take a glass of water."

"Well, you're certainly not breaking the house with that request. Baily?"

"Naw."

Maxo moved down the bar to greet some other customers while Patrizia, tipsily, filled a glass with water and came around the side of the bar to join us on the floor. She handed it to me and I gulped it down greedily. She stared at me, sweetly but with curiosity. I became a little uncomfortable under her steady gaze. I could see she was relieved when Maxo motioned Baily over to him to point out a few drunks who were getting a little rowdy and hitting on some chicks who were pretending to be offended. I could see they were discussing whether or not Baily should intervene. Meanwhile Patrizia stared at me in puzzlement. I noticed she had a shimmering beauty to her, like some far off pristine lake hidden in the woods, inaccessible somehow, and known to only the few men who'd been determined to discover her.

"It's quite a place here," I stammered witlessly.

"You know, I noticed you earlier tonight. I've been keeping my eye on you."

"Oh, yes?"

"It's those red shoes. They caught my attention right away. I've watched them every time you've passed by. They're beautiful. Very unusual. They sparkle in the dark, that's what I love about them. You know the name of this club is Tenebrae. That means darkness in Italian. And those shoes, they have a life of their own in the dark, in the night."

I looked away, knowing too well their upsetting history, ostensibly to see if "my boyfriend" was going to have to take on a group of drunks. Apparently not. Maxo was giving him the sign to leave well enough alone.

The techno beat got slower, more sensual.

"There's something so haunting about them." Patrizia was staring down at my shoes. I looked too. Then she suddenly laughed and threw back her hair and held onto my hand and said, "May God go with you."

I guess Maxo and Patrizia must be mostly Italian as Maxo had used Italian phrases, and the club had an Italian name, as I'd just been informed, still Maxo looked Gaelic to me. As Baily returned to my side I realized this was useless, abstract musing. Who cared?

There was a lot of dancing going on now, women and men, men and men, a few women and women, coupling, slow dancing, moving a little lewdly, feeling no pain. Baily was staring at the crowd, I guess on the lookout for troublemakers, yet his fox eyes told me he was getting horny and his facial ticks told me that crack was the major instigator.

"I have to take a leak," he suddenly announced.

So?

"Come with me."

"Back down there?"

"Yeah, I feel a little wobbly on my feet." Maybe he did but I felt skeptical.

"I'd do the same for you," he said sweetly. He was up to something.

"I'll come with you but you better hurry it up—and let me tell you, Baily Cantevelter, I'm not going to look at one jackass in there but keep my eyes glued to the floor. You understand?"

"I have to piss!"

But apparently not that badly as he had time to lean over the bar to discuss something with Maxo and Patrizia and he kept his voice low. Patrizia indicated a door over her shoulder behind the bar. Then Baily made his way through the crowd with me following behind as down we went, down that dark staircase where the light from the blue bulb cast its glow.

"Remember not to look at anything but me pissing, of course," Baily warned as he pushed open the bathroom door, the room filled with smoke and the sounds of nonsensical conversations mixed with some moaning from God knows what area of the zoo. Baily ushered me quickly into one of the Plexiglas stalls and unzipped his fly and took out his cock.

"Myswell do myself a hit while I'm here," he said. He took out his pipe, inspected it, arranged the mesh just so with his fingers, and worked in a big rock.

"Can't you leave that stuff alone even for a minute?" I said impatiently, waiting for the piss to flow. But it didn't. He torched it up and took in the smoke and held it there for eternity. Meanwhile I smelled sex all around me, the pungent odor of sweating flesh. It sickened me.

Suddenly, Baily spun me around and got me in a headlock, his mouth full of smoke.

"Stop it, you fucking bastard," I yelled as he twisted my head back, prying open my mouth with his fingers and blowing in a cloud of smoke before he covered my mouth with his hand. I struggled with his arm tight around my throat, but there was no way to slip out of his vise. That is until I exhaled the smoke. Then he let go. I sank listlessly against the stall wall. Silently. He put his cock back in his pants and zipped up. I felt like I'd been turned loose in Eden, my purpose to gambol among all the wonderful things in the garden, not trapped in some toilet stall in a Eurotrash club basement.

"Yeah, that's how it felt my first time too. Sorry it had to be this way. But I want you. On my terms."

\*

We danced slowly, sensually and alone, arms around each other, in the little back room behind the bar, the one he'd arranged to take me to with Maxo and Patrizia before we'd gone downstairs. The beat of the music kept jump starting us to more and more caresses, more and more kisses. Baily's mouth didn't stink anymore, it tasted like mine, delicious and fragrant.

I'd worn a zigzag black and gray striped spangled shirt, one of his old boyfriend's leftovers, and a pair of his boyfriend's black tights I'd found on the top of the closet shelf. Baily wore his yellow satin jacket and jeans and his Yankees cap. And his boots.

In the back room was a small mirror on the wall that Patrizia had pointed out to me before she left Baily and me alone, which I could use to apply my Shanghai Red lipstick. She watched in pleasure as I applied a liberal coating to my lips. Then she said, "Well, I'll leave you two boys to it. This is a special place, you know. Only Maxo and I have done it in here."

"We're not going 'to do it' in here," Baily said. "We're going to 'do it' at home. We're just going to have a little foreplay now, John and me."

Maxo popped his head in the door and told Baily he was letting him off early but just this once as he realized Baily had a new boyfriend now and knew we wanted to celebrate and who could blame us, he added.

Alone, holding each other.

"You have such beautiful red lips," Baily said and kissed them tenderly. "And such sexy red shoes."

"And you have such a handsome face. I want to wake up in the morning and just gaze at it all day long."

"You have such luxuriant blond hair," Baily said, slowly running his fingers through it. "I'm the luckiest man in the world."

I threw my arms around his neck and kissed him. "And you have such a sexy cock. And a butt to die for."

"And you are so sweet and tender. Kiss me again with your beautiful red mouth."

I brushed my lips along his neck, softly, then found his mouth and kissed him deeply, closing my eyes.

"And you are mine."

"And you are mine."

"Forever."

"Forever."

\*

"Maxo really seems to like you," I said, resting my head on Baily's shoulder in the back of the cab.

"He gave me another chance," he whispered, nibbling my ear lobe with increasing intensity until I had to pull away. At that moment I didn't want to know anything about this other chance, I just wanted to watch the pink and blue sunrise coming up between the brownstones, a low band of soft light matching my sexy mood. Mellow. Just beginning.

"What did you think of the club?"

"It was almost as hot as I feel about you right now."

"You changed your mind about it then?"

"Maybe. It's all a blur to me now."

"Well," he laughed. "I'm glad you feel hot for me, that at least you're sure about that. For my part, I can't wait for you to jump my bone."

One image that hadn't blurred was Patrizia in her star sapphire dress, weaving her way around the brilliant white neon-lit bar, bringing me a glass of water. "Man," I said. "Does Maxo have a pretty girlfriend. Very classy too. If I was straight, she's the kind of girlfriend I'd like to have."

"But you're not straight. By an act of magic. I've just decreed it!"

"That's a big word." I almost added—for you—then wondered what was up with me, I normally wouldn't say something biting like that for no real reason. Yet I almost had.

I opened my eyes and saw the early risers and revved-up all-nighters trying to mark their respective territories as they passed each other on the street. The way Baily and I were trying to mark ours. It was that strange changeover time when the dawn was rising very quickly now, a few pastel rays penetrating a street corner here and there, forcing the revved-up all-nighters to pick up the pace, anxious to get back to their apartments before the full light of morning hit. I took Baily's hand in mine and squeezed it.

He squeezed back then took my chin in his hand and turned my face towards him. "Since you're a faggot," he reasoned, "why not let me be the boyfriend you'd like to have?"

There, let him make the cutting remarks. They came more naturally to him.

"*Capisci*, Mr. Mysterious?"

*"Capisci?* You've been hanging around Maxo too long. Soon you'll be moving me to Rome."

Baily sat bolt upright. "Are you my boyfriend or what?" he demanded impatiently.

He didn't like to be teased, no matter how playfully, or sidetracked, at least when he had something important on his mind.

"Yes. Yes, yes." I answered. "Only you can call me by my name now. Not that there's anything special about it, I'll admit. But...it's me."

"John," he mulled it over. Then, "It is dull. How about Gianni? Now that's hotter. That's what Maxo called you, wasn't it?"

"Yes and so can you," I laughed. "Gianni. It's not so bad actually. It's a step up from your other pet names for me, like 'faggot,' 'ditzoid,' 'nitwit,' 'Clarabelle,' and...well, 'cocksucker,' though that one suggests something a bit more pleasant, I suppose."

Baily drove in the stake. "And it's spot on."

I yawned, feeling the tiredness of a day and night crammed with unanticipated events.

"Don't worry, soon you won't be sleepy anymore."

Sleep. Though the thought of getting some appealed to me, it was out of the question, I was too turned on by Baily who, as soon as we got back to his studio, stripped to his boots, leaving his baseball cap on, which he flipped around backwards. Cool and confident, he rubbed up against me, then held me tight and kissed me passionately until I was breathless and said, "Welcome to the world of love, baby."

I sat down at the little dining table slowly removing my clothes.

He put on a CD, more of that techno music with

deep chords and pungent, repetitive riffs.

Inspired by the pulsating sounds, Baily suddenly started to dance in front of me, intimately and sensually. Closing his eyes, he put his arms behind his head and did a bump and grind, his cock semi-hard, swinging back and forth between his legs. Eventually he turned around and bent over, putting one hand on the floor, keeping the other hand behind his head while he rotated his bubble ass in time to the beat. Eventually he righted himself and faced me again, spreading his legs wide, bending at the knees, and slowly leaned his torso back with his crotch extended towards me so that his milky body looked like a loosely constructed, limber and inviting hot white human plane. He tweaked his nipples with his fingers, groaning, until they were hard, then moved his fingers lightly up and down his muscular thighs.

To be that young and supple...He had it all and knew how to display it.

He switched off the light but the early sunlight glowing on the brick wall outside his window kept his body moving within its exquisite white radiance, though he disappeared now and then into an occasional shadow. He moved deftly, without inhibitions, in a trance, occasionally feeling one of his biceps, or massaging his nipples, or gripping his penis softly and masturbating it for a few easy strokes before letting go of it so he could turn his attention to pleasuring a new part of his body.

As the last track ended he fell out of that muted ecstasy that had affected each of us. The dim roar of the traffic heading up 6th Avenue brought us back to Cornelia Street and far from the lingering influence of the Tenebrae club. He'd been shameless. To his credit. Expressing such pleasure in his own erotic identity. I sighed. "I could watch you do that all day."

"No way, Gianni, my love. We have better things to do. Go put on your lipstick while I cook up some crack."

Looking in his bathroom mirror in the telling light of morning, I looked a little haggard. I applied some Shanghai Red magic to my lips which brightened me up.

"Perfect," Baily said as I came out of the bathroom, but I couldn't decide if he was talking about my lips or the way the crack was cooking up. "Spread a towel across the sofa, will you, while I finish up. There's a clean one in the bureau drawer." I pulled out a thick big soft blue towel, realizing that Baily was quite the amateur interior decorator as it complimented the powder blue walls of his studio. On one of the bureau shelves was something I hadn't noticed before, a cuddly stuffed koala bear, with thick white fur and a black nose and droopy eyes that called out for love and attention. "What a cute bear!" I exclaimed, surprised at myself, as I'd never found stuffed animals much to coo over.

"It's Victor's. The old boyfriend. He left it here."

"And you decided to keep it."

When he made no comment I spread the towel out on the sofa.

"And put some pillows down in front of it to make yourself comfortable," Baily added. "This is going to be good shit. It cooked up better than Betty Crocker's wildest fantasy." He was cleaning out a pipe with the end of a wire hanger. I sat down on the pillows and waited while he fussed.

"I've got to put this screen in just right," he explained.

A lot of me was apprehensive about how this stuff would affect me, but seeing Baily naked and ready for sex tipped the scales so that just a little bit more of me was ready to let loose and go with it. Finally he seemed ready to roll. He carried over a plate of crack, his pipe, and several acetate lighters and the control to the DVD player and eased back on the sofa, carefully placing the plate next to him, staring lingeringly at it with the wonderment of a child. Then he hit the play button and I heard the sounds of sexual grunts from a porn DVD. I felt like some addendum or asterisk.

"I'll give you the first hit, OK, then you can go down on me while I do mine. Now do you want a little, medium, or big hit?"

"A little one." I erred on the side of caution.

"Open your mouth and I'll put the pipe in. You just hold it there and I'll do everything else." He slid the pipe into my mouth, telling me to close my lips around it and keep it upright, which wasn't easy, while he dropped what looked like anything but a little piece of rock onto the screen. He torched it up until the piece of rock melted all the way down while I sucked on the pipe, Baily insisting I hold in the smoke while he hurriedly put another rock in for himself, the only time I'd seen him move with any real urgency. Meanwhile the smoke was gagging me.

"Don't swallow it. That's not necessary. Just keep it in your mouth," he advised as he sucked in his hit. Then he grabbed the back of my head and moved my mouth down onto his cock where I felt it stiffen in my mouth. Through clenched teeth and with a throat full of smoke, he mumbled, "OK, let it go." We blew out the smoke at the same time and I felt myself groaning with pleasure as the smoke easing out of my mouth curled around the base of his cock and the smoke that he blew out drifted across my face like a silky mist. Immediately I was picking up the pace and deep throating him eagerly.

Anything else but my going nuts on his cock had gone from my mind. No one could have pried me off such a succulent piece of flesh that was bringing me such pleasure with each deep suck I gave it until I'd made it fully engorged.

And so it went.

Baily kept asking each time did I want a little, medium, or big hit. The higher I got, and the more intense desire I felt, I timidly admitted to him that I was ready to try a medium one, though the rocks he melted for me always seemed the same size—large. Sometimes, for prudence's sake, he shotgunned a blast directly into my mouth "not to waste any since you'll get just as much benefit this way." Every time he shotgunned the smoke into my mouth, I held it as long as I could before passing it back to him, kissing him longingly, mingling the smoke, until I couldn't stand it any longer and was back down on him.

"Great breath control," he complimented me.

The hours passed in this way, though I thought they were only minutes ticking by. Looking up at him, legs spread, his handsome cock at full throttle, he seemed like such a stud. And I some crazed worshiper of his manhood. Yet at some point the bottom dropped out. You had to keep taking so many hits just to sustain the sexual level you were aspiring to that the whole routine became more of a chore than anything else. I realized if you paused too long between hits you felt lower, emptier than if you hadn't had one at all. The dream was dissipating.

"What's going on?" Baily asked.

"I'm tired. I need a break."

"Not right now," he complained.

I felt wobbly. "Yeah, right now."

"Just while I was getting off on how beautiful you look, naked in front of me, in just your red shoes and red lipstick. By the way, you might want to put a refresher on your lips."

"Later. Let me rest." He pulled me up on the sofa while he went into his kitchen alcove, mentioning he might as well take advantage of my "rest period" to cook up some more crack, leaving me to gaze down at my red shoes in confusion. The shoes looked anything but sexy now and felt like dead weight. I saw what was playing on his flat screen—some naked kid getting gang-banged in a sling by a bunch of men in leather chaps.

Baily was going through that tiresome ritual of moving a spoon with ice and rock over a flame.

"When did you first turn on to this stuff?" I asked.

"Well, at Tenebrae to be honest, in the same place you did. The head. Some guy was in there smoking and offered me a hit so I thought, why not? It was one of those times where I knew after my first hit that something had changed forever. That I was hooked. No question about it. Nothing else really mattered much anymore. Except crack."

"You were still with Victor?" I must have been really high, though I didn't feel it, or I wouldn't have asked, since it was none of my business and might have been a sore point. Though Baily didn't admit it, I saw that it was, as his muscles tightened in an uncontrollable reflex. I reached down to take off one of my shoes. Don't ask me how he knew what I was doing, but he spun around and said, "Don't you dare."

"They're hurting me. They're tight. I've had them on too long."

"Just a little longer. Please. Gianni."

"We'll make a deal. I'll leave them on if you answer my question. Was Victor still with you when you turned onto crack?"

"You've got yourself a deal, love, because Victor's gone but you're still here. Yes, he was living with me at the time. And, yes, you could say my smoking crack ended our relationship. He didn't dig the shit. Said it turned me into somebody else than I really was. Now how could that be? How could someone so sweet like Victor be so entirely wrong?"

I didn't know. Besides that, I didn't know what to say.

Baily had put some of the doughy gel on a plate to firm up. As he watched it anxiously, he suddenly exclaimed, "You just made me remember where I put it. The ring I gave him." He opened a kitchen cabinet door and pulled out a box of Cracker Jacks and dumped the whole contents into a bowl and fished around in it until he pulled out a ring. "Now, isn't that the perfect place? I removed the fucking little toy that was in there and slipped the ring in instead. Because if a thief broke in it would be the last place he'd look for it."

"Why would a thief be looking for that ring?" I asked innocently.

He turned to me in amazement and brought it over and held it in front of my face. "Look at it, then ask me that. It's beautiful. I never saw anything as beautiful as this in my life. Never."

It was pretty, a sapphire set in diamonds. But isn't a ring like that always pretty? It was hardly Elizabeth Taylor's Krupp Diamond.

"It cost me so much money. Not that that mattered. You know what mattered?"

"No, what?"

His lips trembled and I could see he was hurt. "The fact that I'd never given anything to anyone in my life until I bought this ring. And he didn't want it."

He returned the ring to the Cracker Jack box and dumped the contents from the bowl back into the box then placed it carefully on the shelf and shut the cabinet door to hide it, I guess, from a thief. Before he did that though, he had held it for an instant in front of my face with a quizzical expression on his own; my gut feeling was that he was offering it to me to put on, at least for the night, but I'd cast my eyes down.

The kid getting gang-banged in the porn DVD cried out, "Stop, no more, please, I can't stand it!" Baily came over and switched it off, grimly.

"You keep your part of the deal now and keep those shoes on," he said. His face had darkened. I wondered if that was because of the crack. "And, goddamnit, put some more lipstick on."

I was surprised to notice that there wasn't any light shining against his brick wall. Could it be nighttime already?

I walked mechanically into the bathroom and turned on the light and reached for the lipstick. As I looked up into the mirror, I noticed Baily was behind me. I jumped.

"I'm just here to help you." He smiled and took the lipstick from my hands and began to paint my mouth, so I'd "look more like a ho," then broke jauntily into a song, *"Born on a mountain top in Tennessee, kilt me a b'ar when I was only three, Davy, Davy Crockett, king of the wild frontier."* He turned the word "frontier" into a ridiculous sound that lasted forever and somehow morphed into what seemed like a different word entirely, completely unrecognizable to anyone who knew English, as he went overboard and smeared my mouth with lipstick.

"Happy now?" I asked.

"More than. Ecstatic!" He started laughing like a jerk. "And ready to fuck!"

"What do you mean?"

He suppressed a weird giggle and drawled slowly, "I mean that I'm ready to insert my penis inside your asshole."

"I don't get fucked. By anybody," I lied. "And not by anybody as crude as you."

He bowed at the waist. "I beg your pardon, madam. Have I said something to offend you?"

He must have sucked down bigger hits than I had. Or the cumulative effect of all the crack he'd smoked beforehand had turned some new tide. He was now a nutcase.

Horrified, I felt myself laughing with him and not at him.

He stood up straight and extended his hand to me. "Please take it," he intoned in what he imagined to be a courtly drawl. But he was a hick. It didn't gibe. But that made it all the funnier to me. There was something bizarre about this drug, it wasn't a smooth, quick rush like cocaine that mellowed you out for a moment, there was something delusional about it that lasted long after you thought the whole trip was over.

I extended my hand and let him lead me back to the couch where he placed me in an upright position like some mannequin and brought over the plate of crack, lit a candle on the little table, and sidled down next to me.

"So, madam does not enjoy the finer pleasures of life." He lit up, the flame of the acetate lighter turning the pupils of his eyes black. "What services can I offer?" He shotgunned me. "After all, I expected to be lying between your legs with your beautiful red shoes up around my shoulders.... However, I'm available for anything and everything."

"And so am I," I answered, putting my arms around his neck and kissing him, then whispering in his ear, "except for the one thing we've agreed to exclude."

We didn't need it since we did everything else. After we made out for who knows how long, he shocked me by kicking off his boots and carrying me over to the bed, drawing back the mosquito net curtain and placing me down on my back. Of course before he got in bed with me he ran back for his plate of crack, pipe and lighters and gingerly laid them by my side imploring me in exaggerated tones of earnest supplication to be oh, so very careful that I didn't knock everything onto the floor. No chance of that. And face his wrath?

Between hits, we nibbled on each others toes, nipples, butt cheeks, fingers, armpits, thighs, until there was nothing left to lick. Except the plate of crack. I laughed out loud at the thought.

"What?" he piped up like an unruly boy.

"There's nothing left to lick."

"I believe I'm lying next to you, aren't I, my dear, in case you're a bit forgetful."

"I'm tired, Baily. I need a rest period."

"No, no, no. Just suck my big toe again."

"I can't."

"Of course you can. Just close your eyes and think of England."

I laughed at that while he shotgunned me at the same time. I almost choked but managed to get his toe in my mouth before blowing out the smoke. I guess, as he'd made a point of letting me know, I did have an awesome pair of lungs.

We devoured each other's bodies again, wandered all over them at quite a leisurely pace, as if we were following a map to a buried treasure which was the ultimate indulgence of the psyche, concealed somewhere around here, and luck being with us, we had all the time in the world to discover where it was hidden, and we did search diligently until, surprisingly finding myself once more back at the point of embarkation, sucking on his big toe, I noticed daylight on his brick wall. "My God," was all I could think to say.

That broke his high—to an extent.

"Shit, I need to piss," he said, stumbling out of bed and weaving unsteadily towards the bathroom like a drunken sailor, but with the crack pipe still in his mouth, trying to light up a rock. But the pipe fell out of his mouth and he promptly stepped on it, crushing it. Blood gushed from the bottom of his foot. "Fuck it to goddamn hell, hand me another pipe."

I sat up. "Let me see your foot. It's bleeding like crazy."

Resigned, he returned to the bed and lifted his foot. Luckily there was only a thin shard of glass sticking out of it. I found myself wavering towards the kitchen where I found some paper towels, hobbled with him into the bathroom, had him put his foot on the rim of the toilet and got down and pulled out the shard with the paper towels. I found the "red medicine" I'd used on my scrapes after falling off his bike and washed his foot off with soap and water and applied the ointment to his wound while he howled and bitched. In his medicine cabinet were some gauze bandages which I wrapped around his foot to the best of my fucked up abilities.

"What did you just do, inject crack into my foot?" he inquired in all seriousness.

"No. Don't be stupid. I just doctored you up so you wouldn't bleed to death."

"Well, why don't you be a nurse instead and nurse on my prick?"

"Would you please behave?"

"Whatever you're saying there. Hand me another pipe."

"There is no other pipe to hand you."

"But I put a bunch of them in your raincoat."

"That was days ago. My raincoat's hanging in my closet."

"Then give me your fucking keys."

"And I threw the pipes away."

"Liar."

I didn't respond.

"Fuck," he said, holding his head in his hands.

The fun had come to a screeching standstill.

But Baily wasn't one to throw in the towel that easily. He got dressed, pulled on his boots and began lacing them up.

"You're going out?"

"You bet your sweet ass I'm going out."

"Where are you going?"

"To a smoke shop to buy a couple of pipes. There's one place where they know me. They won't sell them to just anybody, like to a collegiate type or somebody they figure could be an undercover cop. But they'll sell a couple pipes to somebody who has the look, you know."

And he had it.

His eyes were wandering to the broken pipe. "Maybe…there's a way to scrape some resin out of those pieces," he said.

That's what Teresa had mentioned to me once. Resin. I never forgot the word. I assumed it was like the butt end of a cigarette or something, the addict's last hope.

"Are you crazy? You'd be sucking down broken glass!"

"Yeah, you're right," he admitted, calmly finishing dressing and putting his boots back on and lacing them up.

"Baily. We've had enough. And I'm tired. I don't want anymore. Let's go to sleep. You can't go out like you are, anyway. You might walk in front of a car."

"Are we talking about something important here?" he asked as he opened the door to leave. "Try to sleep then if you want to, but be here when I get back. I'll hurry." And he slammed the door and locked it.

I lay there in the bed in slow motion where time disappeared. The mosquito netting made me think I was lying in the tropics, prey to flying, malaria-carrying insects. Alice had never gone down a rabbit hole like this one. The last thing I saw before passing into a half sleep of fear and loathing were my red shoes sticking up from my feet at the bottom of the bed.

When I heard the key turn the lock in the door and I opened my eyes, I saw darkening shadows playing with the light on the brick wall.

As Baily walked in, I heard his voice inform me, "You know, it's the goddamnedest thing, when you do crack you speak in different voices, in different tongues. I chatted up a few people on the street, and in the bakery where I bought you some apple turnovers. Sometimes I was my hillbilly self, other times quite the high class gent, you know, and other times a little kid. Wow. Bizarro."

I turned my head to see him in the alcove, several new pipes on the counter. He was fixing one up. Pushing in a screen and putting in a rock. "But before we eat, let's do a hit."

I was speechless and depressed. He brought the plate of crack over to the bed, took a hit, then gave me one.

"Thanks," I mumbled. I hadn't turned it down. That made me more depressed. I knew now the longer you went without, the more you wanted one.

"Oh, shit," Baily said. "Your apple turnovers. I must have left them at the bakery."

"Well, why don't you go back and get them then?"

He laughed uneasily. "I know, we'll call in for a pizza and some chicken wings. Would you like that? Oh, and I'll get you a big glass of water. Cleanses the system you know."

He brought me a big glass of water and I drank it. Then he said, "Let's get back to business. I have a horny cock."

We returned to the sofa where he stripped, put his boots back on and sat back on the towel. I grabbed the pillows and put them on the floor and knelt between his legs as he flipped his cap around backwards and switched on the porn. We'd been here before. Long ago it seemed. I was a zombie now, one of the ones Baily had mentioned when he'd referred to working in a "club for zombies" or something like that. But I didn't have to be in a club and he didn't have to be working for both of us to join the living dead. Hello? "Somebody give me a star, please, for that revelation."

"What are you going on about now, Clarabelle?"

Oh, so it was back to Clarabelle. Yeah.

"Suck," he begged me.

The only way to do what he wanted was to keep doing hits, because I had no interest in having sex. Hitting the pipe was the only way I could be jolted into performing. And it was pleasurable for just a few minutes between hits before the bottom—unkindly—dropped out. Then you'd left. And you knew you'd left, only you didn't know where you'd gone—you only knew that time was deceiving you again, and there was no more light on the brick wall when you gathered the courage to turn around and take a look.

Like robots we performed our appointed sexual tasks, and I could sense each of us was deriving less and less enjoyment from it, even though we pointedly increased our efforts to make it work. We were engaged in a frenzy of emptiness. I was considering this, while blowing him of course, when his downstairs buzzer rang and we stopped immediately, looking at each other in shock, not daring to move or make the least bit of noise. What the hell? Who was it?

Baily silently got up and stood at the door, listening. Maybe he could hear something. After all, the front door to the building's entrance wasn't far from his basement flat's door.

"For God's sake, don't let anybody in," I whispered.

He put his finger to his lips to shush me up. Then took control and answered the intercom, "Yes," he said sternly. "You just woke me up. Who are you and what do you want?"

I waited breathlessly until I heard a voice come back at him, "Pizza delivery."

I sighed with relief as Baily wrapped a towel around

his waist. "Hold on a minute," he spoke into the intercom. Then he turned to me and whispered, unnecessarily now, "Do you have any money?"

Uncomfortably, I stood up and wobbled on my red shoes over to my pants, pulled out my wallet and gave him a twenty.

"That might not be enough," he whispered. "There's chicken wings too and a tip."

I fished him out another ten. It was worth it if he'd be the one to answer the door and let me disappear. I hid in the bathroom. I heard Baily buzz the guy in. And open the door. There was a quick, indecipherable exchange muttered between Baily and the Pizza Man, then I heard the door shut and Baily shout out, "The coast's clear!"

When I came back into the room Baily had eagerly begun to set the table—with nice linen from his bureau drawer. He got some china plates and cutlery from the kitchen and found some orange juice in the fridge and poured us each a glass and tore open the pizza box, pulling the slices apart and dropping them onto our plates, then he ripped open the box of chicken wings and loaded up our plates with them, adding celery and blue cheese to the mix. But before we dug in, starving, he insisted we toast each other with our orange juice glasses and said, "To us." We ate like pigs on a desert island who'd been the happy recipients of an airlifted package a plane had dropped for us as it buzzed by overhead.

"I didn't hear you phone for a pizza," I said.

"I don't remember either, but I must have."

"Yes," I agreed with him. "You must have."

"And thank God I had the wherewithal to do it as I'm hungry as a motherfucker," he said, wolfing down the goods.

I didn't wolf anything down as I didn't want to

choke and didn't know if Baily knew how to give CPR or even if he did if he'd be able to do it. But I slowly ate every scrap on my plate. When we finished, I saw that the brick wall was pitch black so it was the dead of night. But what night?

"Well," Baily said as he cleared the plates away and quickly washed them up. "Back to the main event."

I sat frozen. I could see the food had done Baily some good, or so I thought, as he seemed more "with it." It must have had a beneficial effect on me as well because I knew I couldn't take anymore of this, even though my body wasn't exactly saying no. But what was left of my spirit was preparing to resist. Yet it was saved the trouble.

"Oh no," Baily said softly.

"What's wrong? Is it your foot?"

He turned to me, white as a ghost and crestfallen.

"Oh, no," he repeated, sinking down at the table next to me. "It couldn't be."

I stared at him.

"It's gone. We've finished it."

I smiled inwardly with relief.

"All of Teresa's stuff. And it was a fucking goddamn shitload," he shouted, pounding his fist on the table.

"And that fucking goddamn shitload is in our bodies," I added. Then I couldn't help it, "When it belonged in hers and not in mine."

He ignored me. "There must be a way. But I've burned so many bridges…"

Thank God.

"I can't go to Maxo anymore…" Suddenly he looked at me gratefully as if I'd just saved him from drowning. "But you could." Then he quickly changed his mind and added bitterly, "No, you couldn't, he'd know it was for me."

"You might as well come clean and tell me what this is all about."

"Maxo paid for my rehab." It wasn't easy for him to admit it, but out it came. "He told me if I didn't clean up my act it was over. I couldn't work for him anymore. What choice did I have? If I didn't go, I didn't have a job, and if I didn't have a job, I didn't have any money, and if I didn't have any money, no more candy. Get it?"

"Yeah. Go on."

"The day the little rehab trolley came I was sucking down crack right at this table while the driver waited outside honking the horn. I made him wait fifteen minutes while I smoked so much I thought I'd pass out. It was hilarious, a little trolley full of addicts just waiting for me so they could get started on their way down recovery road! Eventually the driver had to get off his ass and come press my buzzer. Even then I was sucking down hits. Finally I got on the damn trolley. Two weeks. Getting clean. I was only allowed one phone call the whole time I was there. Maxo thought I'd call him to let him know how I was doing. But I called Teresa instead, just to shoot the shit."

"And keep up your connection."

"Maxo thought the whole thing had worked for me like a charm. He welcomed me back with open arms and I was real careful in the club, only doing hits in the toilet stalls."

"But it didn't work like a charm…" My words were slurring. I was drifting in and out, totally exhausted. A numbness had stolen me away, like the thief Baily swore was going to steal the ring in the Cracker Jack box.

"And when I came back, I couldn't believe it, I'd forgotten all about it, I opened my kitchen cabinet and…" He paused, then said, "That's it! Why didn't I think of them? We may get a lucky break after all!"

He jumped up as I rose to my feet unsteadily, having to hold onto the back of my chair for support. We moved in different directions. Full of energy, he went rummaging through his bureau drawer while I pulled aside the mosquito netting and fell back onto my bed of tropical diseases. He made so much noise that I craned my neck around to see what he was up to. He'd spilled the contents of the drawer onto the floor and was hurriedly flipping through the pages of a little book.

He glanced up at me. "You can take one of your little rest periods now. I'll wake you up in awhile."

As my eyes closed I saw the brick wall. Unexpectedly, the bricks weren't black as night or shining gold anymore, but seemed a ghastly red.

I had no idea how long I slept in my netherworld, but I woke up to the unpleasant sound of Baily's buzzer ringing incessantly.

"Quick." He shook my shoulders as he pulled a pair of cotton briefs up over his boots. "Go hide yourself in the bathtub. They're here."

The ring of the buzzer again.

"Who's here?" I asked groggily.

"Shauna 'Fe, she's a pro, and she's with Oliver and Prince Rockefeller."

"A pro?"

"A prostitute. A hooker. They'd freak if they saw you here. Just stand in the tub and be real quiet until they leave and be sure you pull the shower curtain closed in case somebody has to go in there to piss."

My dear Jesus, had things come to this? Somehow I made my way into his bathroom and held onto the shower rod for support as I lifted one red shoe up over the other to climb into the tub while I heard Baily buzz "them" in. I didn't know much, but one thing was clear. I was delusional. I thought I was traveling down some mindless road, seeing eye pyres in the middle of it, socket-like craters, dead, jellied, staring up, and I was playing on their edges. I grabbed onto the shower curtain for support, trying to reclaim some semblance of sobriety. I shook my head, trying to clear this crazy stuff out of my brain, and thankfully, I heard voices in the other room, real voices, Baily's, a woman's, two other males. Then I lost them again. And fell back into those disturbing high-flown will-o-the wisp phantasmagorical deceptions. Now I was standing on a sunny skeleton of land, and some kind of tragic eyelids were trying to pull me into what a high-pitched crackling voice was telling me was called the red dimension.

Finally, and suddenly, and by the grace of God, my mind returned to me, completely, the hallucinations stopped, and I was John Laith again, clearly understanding the words of a four-way conversation in Baily Cantevelter's studio apartment on Cornelia Street in the heart of Greenwich Village.

Never again would I take a hit of crack. My sanity meant a lot more than that. It meant everything. If only God would allow my mind to stay clear and focused, I would keep that promise to my grave.

Meanwhile with a return to sanity came a fury, at Baily, at myself, and at the situation I'd put myself in.

I heard Baily pleading his case to these lowlifes. "But Oliver, you've always given me credit before."

The voice of a young man answered, "Look, I've

got someone to answer to myself at the end of the day. Know what I mean? If I don't bring back cash, it's not good for me."

I heard an older man's voice speaking with a Spanish accent, "We've been good to you, Baily. I spent time cooking this up myself to save you the trouble."

Baily was contrite. "I know. I appreciate that. But can't you give me credit, just this once? Oliver, you know I'm good for it."

The young man called Oliver thought it over. "I don't know. What do you think, Shauna?"

"I don't know," Shauna replied casually. "I don't have a dick in this race."

My blood boiled. Who were these creeps and why was I cowering naked in a bathtub? As quietly as I could I stepped out of the tub. The bathroom was dark and there was only one candle lit in the studio. I had to peer around the door, even if somebody saw me. I had to take my chances just to see this shit for myself. I moved where I could stand behind the crack in the door and looked out.

It was pretty ugly. Baily, looking like the stoned wrath of God in his cotton briefs, boots, and baseball cap, trying to sweet talk a young blond man in jeans and a denim jacket with a pleasant but extremely fake smile pasted on his face, who was no doubt Oliver; an old man with a scraggly beard and a few crooked, rotting teeth protruding from his lips, and with eyes that easily conveyed they'd seen the worst of life, must be the one answering to the name of Prince Rockefeller; and maybe the best for last, Shauna 'Fe, a prostitute with dyed red hair in a short black leather skirt and bra, standing taller than everyone else in her hot pink high heels, who had a face carved in ice that even the equator couldn't melt. This was no gross triumvirate. This was scum.

"Baily," Prince Rockefeller cajoled, "don't make trouble for Oliver. He's done you so many favors in the past. His boss won't appreciate him coming up short."

Oliver came up with a wise solution. "Just go to the ATM machine and withdraw some cash."

"I can't," Baily stammered. "I can't."

"And why not, Baily?" Prince Rockefeller asked with sympathy.

Baily's voice choked. "I'm too fucking high to even make it there, that's why! And you know it."

"Then it'll have to be like last time," Shauna 'Fe snapped. "Give us your card and we'll do the transaction for you…and return your card tomorrow."

Oliver pressed a packet into Baily's hand. Baily closed his fist over it.

"Do what Shauna asks, Baily," Prince Rockefeller advised. "You have what you want and we're saving you all of the trouble of going to get the cash yourself."

"Why waste time going to the ATM anyway," Oliver reasoned, "when you could be happy doing your thing right away?"

"So you won't give me credit?" Baily asked coldly, seeing the jig was up.

Oliver shook his head no, but very nicely.

Baily went to his closet, fished his wallet out of his pair of jeans, and took out his ATM card. He went back and held it out in front of them, like a card in a playing deck, forcing one of them to take it out of his hands. It was Shauna 'Fe who relieved him of the card, but it wasn't the Queen of Spades, it was the trump card and she coveted it. "It'll be back to you tomorrow, Baily, as always. Maybe sometime in the late afternoon," she said.

They left in a hurry. Only Prince Rockefeller showed enough courtesy to thank Baily and wish him a friendly good-bye.

I stepped out of my hidey-hole. To find Baily just like some kid on Christmas morning, already in the kitchen, turning on one of the gas jets.

"You gave them your ATM card," I said in disbelief.

"Oh, I've done it before," Baily said without regret. "It's no big deal. They always bring it back the next day."

"But how much do you have in your account? More than the stuff they gave you is worth?"

"Yeah. There's probably about eight hundred bucks in there right now."

"But there won't be anything in it tomorrow."

"All right, you've made your point. But what choice did I have? Sure, they're the bottom of the barrel, the last of the lot to be called, the final resort. But I figure I'm just about even with them. When Oliver heard I was going to rehab, he came over early that morning just before I left and put a big clump of rock in my kitchen cabinet—at no charge—so's I'd have some when I got back. So they didn't necessarily make out like bandits."

"How thoughtful and forward thinking of Oliver," I said. I wondered how many times Baily had made the same kind of transactions with these characters. He may have been bullshitting himself, but not me. Of course they'd come out ahead of the game, or why would they still bother with him?

I looked at the brick wall. The bricks were black again. It was night. And long past time to go. I put on my underpants and opened Baily's closet, pulling out my torn jeans, sweatshirt, and jacket. Baily had thought my London fog raincoat had been in his closet. And for a split second when I'd opened the closet to pull out my things, I expected to see it hanging there too. Quite a *folie à deux*. And a sad one.

I put on my clothes as Baily put a piece of the rock that Prince Rockefeller had cooked up for him in his pipe and bent sideways over the stove, his head an inch away from the flame, yet he could still talk for all that.

"Come on over," he called to me, not even realizing I was fully dressed and ready to leave. "We're gonna do a stove hit, it gives you a much stronger high. It's gonna blow your head off. I'll do one first to show you how it's done."

Dangerously, pipe in mouth, he melted the rock, his head hanging over the hot blue naked flame, his eyes almost scorched by it. He sucked in a deep hit, stood up, blew it out, muttered, "Christ almighty," and leaned recklessly against the stove like someone in a submarine that had just been torpedoed and who was now trying to steady himself to see if he could stay alive.

"Oh, God, it's your turn now," he got out the words, breathing deeply.

I was at the door. "I'm leaving now, Baily."

He whirled around in surprise. Before I could turn the handle, he was in front of the door blocking my way. How he had got there so quickly I had no clue. He had that screwed up expression of hate on his face that he had displayed to me when he was showing me his karate stances, when we were playing. Only this time it was for real.

"Victor," he said calmly. "The only way you're going to leave here is in a box. And that box is going into the East River."

I tried to diffuse this with a fake chuckle. "I'd rather go into the Hudson."

"Oh, no. I'm going to chop you up in pieces and stuff you in a box and drop you into the East River."

"I don't think that's a very good idea, Baily," I said evenly.

Something passed over his face, a black cloud that ever so slowly was turning white, and he finally shook his head. "Victor...no, you're not Victor...you're...who are you, anyway?"

"I'm John Laith, your friend."

"Oh." Tears welled in his eyes. "Gianni, yes. Gianni, my dear." He dropped to his knees and grabbed my legs. "Forgive me."

I stood there, pained, and let him clutch onto my legs. Finally, I said, "Baily, lie down. On the sofa. Just put your head back and relax." I helped him to his feet and he lay down as I crossed to the alcove and turned off the gas flame.

"Gianni," he said softly. "What time is it? What day is it?"

I sat on the sofa next to him. "It's not daytime anymore, Baily. It's night. But to be honest I have no idea what night it is or how many of them I've spent here."

I could see his face working into a kind of panic. "Gianni, you have to help me, please."

"How can I help you?"

"You've got to call Maxo. He'll think I've slipped if you don't. I must have missed a couple of nights of work. Don't you think?"

"I don't know."

"I have," he said. "Damn."

"It can't be helped now."

Baily was starting to shiver a bit. I went to his bed and brought back a blanket and covered him with it.

"Thanks," he said. "I'll give you his number. It's his private phone at the bar. He'll pick up. You have to tell him I'm sick."

"What if he doesn't believe me? What if he thinks I'm covering for you, which, of course, I am."

"He'll believe you. You've got to try. It's winter. Tell him some guy at the bar kept coughing in my face the night we were there. That you saw it all yourself. And now I've got the flu."

"Oh, God," I sighed. "All right."

His phone was a wall phone in his kitchen alcove. Baily gave me the number and I dialed it. Somebody picked it up. I could hear music and raucous laughter in the background. The voice on the other end said, "Gauchette."

"Maxo?"

"Yes."

Baily was nodding encouragement to me, mouthing what words to say, trying to coach me. I turned my back on him, as I didn't want that kind of distraction.

"It's John Laith here, Maxo. Baily Cantevelter's friend. I met you at the club the other night. You nicknamed me Gianni."

"Oh yes, I remember you. That was some time ago, though, wasn't it?"

Was it?

He continued, "My lady took quite a liking to you, I remember, thought you'd be good for Baily. Who by the way I haven't seen for awhile. Have you?"

"Why, yes. He wanted me to ring you up and let you know he's come down with flu. Actually he caught it the night I was there. Some guy at the bar kept hacking in his face."

"Oh? Lucky you and I didn't get it too."

"Well, yes."

"How is Baily? It's not like him not to call in sick."

"Oh, he's recovering. He didn't really feel well enough to even pick up the phone. He had quite a fever, you know, for awhile."

"But he could pick up the phone to call you."

"No, not really. I just happened to drop by in the daytime and saw how sick he was and brought him in chicken soup and heated it up for him, that kind of thing."

"Good, you're a real pal to him."

"I'd like to think so."

"Well, do you know when he'll feel well enough to make it back here?"

"Oh, he's much better now. I would think maybe even tomorrow night."

"Give me your phone number, if you don't mind, in case he doesn't. I wouldn't want to disturb him. I could ask you for a progress report."

Hesitantly, I gave him my phone number.

"By the way," Maxo continued. "He's not doing anything he shouldn't be doing, is he?"

"I'm not sure what you mean. He shouldn't be suffering in bed with the flu, if that's what you mean."

"Give him my regards, will you, and tell him I hope he's back to his old self. Tell him there are always enough troublemakers around here to keep him busy and that we need his muscle."

"Will do. I'll tell him. He's anxious to get back on the job. So, thanks, Maxo, for being so decent about it."

"No problem. Just tell him to feel better."

"I will. Good-bye."

"Good-bye."

I hung up the phone.

"Did you fix it for me?" Baily asked breathlessly.

"I think so. He said everything was cool."

"Good old Maxo," Baily said, relieved.

"And now, young man, I'm going to take my leave and let you recover from your flu. You need plenty of rest. And I mean that."

"God, you're right. I'm too tired to even get up and let you out."

I could see he was half asleep already.

"Gianni," he murmured, "you could take my spare key with you. That way you can lock the door on your way out. It's under the gold china tea cup on the bureau shelf. You can give it back to me when I see you next. Which will be soon, of course, as you have to bring me over that chicken soup you mentioned."

"If you're sure," I said, drawing a key ring out from underneath the cup. If Baily could trust those fuck faces with his ATM card, he sure as hell could trust me with his keys.

"One opens the lobby door, the other my door. You'll figure it out."

I looked at Baily lying there under the blanket, his eyes closed already. On an impulse I grabbed the koala bear off the shelf and put it down into the crook of his arm.

He opened one eye. He smiled. "Thanks. But what I'd really like is my plate of crack and pipe and a lighter."

I couldn't say it went against my better judgment. It was what it was. I found his plate on the bed, the pipe and the cooked crack next to the stove, arranged them all neatly on the plate and laid it down gently on his chest. Asleep now, instinctively, his hand curled around the plate. I let myself out and locked his door.

\*

The walk home was all in darkness, so said the color of the sky. I followed my footsteps solely by an osmosis that had gone into operation full force, my mind not in sync with my feet, my mental acuity operating under a new kind of radar that pinpointed an unknown passerby's face here, the unremarkable door to an apartment there, a taxi's wheel spinning like a turning clock, or more practically, like the round face of my watch that I could have checked to see what time it was, that is, if I'd remembered I even had a watch around my wrist.

I recalled passing many dark alleyways that seemed to hold an unanticipated fascination for me. The sight of dark alleys had never quickened my heartbeat before. They were symbolic of something dangerous, perhaps the ideal location for a mugging or rape, or a spot that rats delighted in, when they had the run of the place, crawling or even leaping with eagerness into garbage bins to get their fill of refuse. Or a place of unquiet rest for the homeless. Both sad and sinister, they were finite spaces of ugliness in an urban sprawl that considered them a necessary addition to an otherwise cheerful enough neighborhood. But at night they were also caves of uncertainty.

That's why I was surprised when I finally turned down one, not just any one, but an alley I'd chosen for a particular purpose, because it was wedged between an empty building marked for demolition that had once housed several bodegas, and a semi-vacant lot with a broken chain fence, where spindly dark tree branches protruded through the links.

A big garbage bin stood at the alley's end, couched in semi-darkness. I approached it cautiously. I heard some furtive noises from inside the bin, probably rats. Otherwise I was alone.

My hand felt inside the pocket of my jacket and I pulled out one of Baily's acetate lighters. Why it was inside my own jacket that had been hanging in his closet was a mystery—yet I'd somehow known it was there. Pieces of newspaper had blown up against the fence, their edges wavering in a light wind. I broke off one of the branches that was sticking through the link fence, picked up a piece of the newspaper, lit it, and when it started to burn, used it to fire up the branch. I lifted the top off the garbage bin. A few rats scurried up out of the bin and slithered down its sides as the piece of wood in my hand burned more brightly. I dropped the burning branch into the bin and immediately the refuse went up in flames, throwing a frightening orange glow onto the building and the silver links of the fence and down onto my red shoes, which I slowly and methodically removed from my feet. As recklessly as Baily's face had hovered over his gas flame, now mine hovered inches from the flames into which I dropped, without ceremony, the red shoes I held in my hand. Then, emotionlessly, I turned and walked back down the alley onto the street and my feet turned me in the direction of my apartment, while I heard a voice cry out with fervor, "Fire!"

It seemed hours before I reached my lobby door. Tony, who was up at this hour for some reason, opened the lobby door and let me in, smirking as he stared with suspicion at my bare feet. In the elevator I wondered how

I'd managed to make it back home without cutting or scraping them or having them turn numb from the cold. But God had more wisdom than I did, only He knew the answer...

One of my eyes opened onto the light of day. I was surprised to find myself in my own bed. The curtains were drawn back so I could see the garden and the backs of the brownstones across the way. I didn't remember walking or taking a cab back home. It was as though I'd been transported from Baily's netted bed to mine on a magic carpet which, as it carried me along, had been busy removing memories and experiences from me along the way. Except for the red dimension. I remembered that.

With a head that felt full of gibberish, I got out of bed and walked to the window and stared out into my garden where I was relieved to see familiar winter roots of dark red and purple intertwining and lavishing in a light glow, as dappled sunlight between quick passing clouds shone down on them. I longed to take hold of the earth again like those roots.

I was naked. At my feet were the clothes I'd discarded before getting into bed—my torn jeans, which restored some memories, my sweatshirt and jacket, and my red shoes.

To ground myself, I tried to reconnect with lost time by listening to messages on my phone machine. But there weren't any. Not even from Crewe. At my firm request, he'd never called back. I was quite surprised. Of course I hadn't wanted him to call, but I figured a little thing like that wouldn't stop him. Maybe I should phone Reg or Allison. But what would I have to say to them? Catch them up on my last few days?

Exhausted I fell back into bed and slept.

When I woke it was evening. Lights were coming on in the brownstones across the court. I pulled the curtains closed and decided to try to act instead of just react, maybe start by cleaning up the place a bit. I put on a bathrobe, hung up my discarded clothes, and put the red shoes back in the closet.

Suddenly I sat squarely down on my bed and thought hard. I recalled throwing those shoes into a fire I'd set in a garbage bin in an alley on my way home from Baily's. Obviously that hadn't happened, as I'd just placed them safely back in my closet. It had been a waking dream, a crack-inspired one of the druggiest kind, so that it didn't hold the reassurances of a normal dream, the kind you woke from knowing it hadn't been real, but one that left you feeling it had been a cold stone reality. It's then I knew I had smoked so much crack that the effects would probably last for days.

Proof of that came as I found myself not focusing normally, doing tasks twice, putting away linen in the wrong drawers, forgetting where I'd placed my keys, leaving the refrigerator door wide open after I'd gotten out some cold water in a jug, accidentally placing my toothbrush on the kitchen shelf and spending ten minutes searching for it in the bathroom cabinet. And thinking I'd burned my own shoes to cinders. These were the rewards of a crack binge, I couldn't soften it, or call it other than what it was.

Somehow the dream of the shoes was the worst of it. To me it endowed a simple inanimate object with dangerous powers, like some wicked talisman. A rational person, I didn't care to imbue them with that kind of black magic, an evil object forcing me to act in a certain way. They were just a pair of shoes, for God's sake. It was easier not to take responsibility for my own actions but blame a pair of fucking shoes instead. I'd continue to wear them whenever I felt like it. If there was anything I wanted to do differently, it was myself I would change, not a pair of shoes.

My phone rang. I answered, as usual these days, with trepidation. I heard loud pulsating music, laughter, and then Baily.

"Gianni, love, it's me. I can't thank you enough for clearing things with Maxo. As you can probably hear, I'm back at my old post, keeping my eye out for possible trouble, thanks to your smooth, silvered devil's tongue!"

"Oh, I'm happy for you. But where in the world did you get your energy to spring back like that?"

Before he answered, I already knew the answer. "You know how," he said. "Only it's not cool to talk about it. I'm using Maxo's line."

"Well, congratulations. They're in order, I guess."

"Are you kidding me? They're more than in order. Why not pop over for some fun? I'll leave your name at the door so you can get in for free. We can kick around together and just hang. Come on, slide on those red shoes and hop a cab. I'll pay you back for your car fare."

"Rain check," I mumbled. "I'll take a rain check."

I realized he was so ebullient about not being canned that he wasn't all that crushed by my response. "Yeah, all right, a rain check then. I told Maxo that you just kept feeding me that chicken soup, that you were a regular Florence Nightingale, wasn't that the name of that famous nurse from World War II?"

"I think."

"Oh, and Patrizia wanted me to send her best to you."

"That's nice, thank her for me, will you?"

"You bet. She said she'd like to see more of you too."

"That's sweet of her," I noted, surprised. "Well, I liked her too. Definitely."

He lowered his voice, conspiratorially. "And thanks again for squaring things for me. Who knows," he giggled softly, "otherwise tonight I might be grabbing cash out of little old ladies' hands at ATM machines."

"Baily…"

"Just kidding, Gianni, come on, can't you take a joke? I'd never do that."

Wouldn't he? Who could say for sure?

"Gotta go, Maxo's signaling me."

"Thanks for calling and letting me know you're OK."

"No problemo. Later." He hung up.

Still exhausted and not exactly thinking straight, I sunk back on my sofa and brooded. My room rang with an emptiness. And a loneliness. I was someone called Gianni. I wasn't even me anymore.

Why hadn't Crewe called me, I wondered. I'd never go back to Baily because I'd never take a hit of crack again, ever. And Silvio was too rough. He manhandled me in a way that was good for only one or two rounds. But Crewe, we'd had the most glorious, smoothest, fantastic sex possible. The best two people could ever have. Had I really ended it? Why had I been so afraid of him? I couldn't remember. Wasn't it because he'd held all the power? But that didn't have to be. Really, in a relationship like we'd had, I'd held the power. If I'd only realized that. I'd been the one to blow up his ego like a balloon but I also held the pin to be able to prick that balloon and deflate it whenever I wanted to. He was only a man, nothing more. The great and powerful Wizard of Oz had been revealed as only a man as well, when he'd had the curtain pulled back on him. I could pull the curtain back on Crewe too if I had to. To think of all the incredible sex we'd had—and then to have just let it go, without trying to right whatever had been wrong. Yet there was a strong reason I didn't like him though, why I'd broken things off, but right now I couldn't remember what it was and why it was so important at the time. All I thought was that I'd acted in a precipitous—and rude— way. And now I regretted it.

The least I could do was ring him up. On his cell phone. And tell him I'd meant to wish him a happy holiday. And hadn't gotten around to it. That should be a believable enough reason to phone, without seeming like I was begging to get back into his good graces. I wouldn't leave a message. I'd need to speak with him directly. That way I could see what his reaction would be. I wouldn't ask to get together, of course, just feel out how things stood.

He answered my call after a few rings.

"Crewe?"

"Yes?"

"This is John calling."

"Oh, hello. This is quite unexpected. I believe you'd ask me not to have any further contact with you. Or did I mishear that?"

"No, you didn't mishear it. I'm just phoning to send you good wishes for the coming year, that's all. I felt I was remiss in not calling you during the holidays to wish you a good season. So I'm doing it now. I thought the last message I left you may have sounded too abrupt and given you the impression I felt you'd done something wrong."

"I didn't take it that way. Not exactly." He paused. "I have to speak quietly, you understand, because Clemma's sleeping and I had to take the cell phone into the study."

"That's quite all right. I hadn't meant to disturb you. In fact, is it late? I'm not quite sure."

"It's just after midnight. But luckily, I was in bed reading, so your call didn't disturb me."

"That's good," I said, depressed by my lingering disorientation of the passage of time.

There was a silence on both ends, but nobody hung up.

Finally, humiliated, I decided to ring off. "Well, there was no other reason for my call but to wish you, and Clemma and Sidonie, of course, a wonderful New Year."

"Yes, well, the same to you. By the way, it's Clemma's birthday in two weeks time, January 24. I'm having a little cocktail party up here at the penthouse for a few close acquaintances of ours. Of course, we don't have much room, it's not as if we live in a palace after all, but I'm sure we could fit you in. If you'd like to come, please do, and feel free to bring someone if you like, perhaps that girl, the one you brought to brunch, or perhaps someone you're seeing. It starts at six o'clock. Just for cocktails. No dinner. Would you like me to add you to the list?"

"Well, yes, I'd like to greet you for the New Year. And wish Clemma well on her birthday."

"Let's see, I have the list here in front of me on my desk. Let me add your name. John...now let's see, dear me, I'm having a momentary lapse...what is your last name again?"

I blanched. The man had an encyclopedic memory.

"Laith," I said.

"Of course," he said. "I'm so sorry. And shall I put down just one guest or two?"

"Two."

"Very well. It's done then. I'll look forward to seeing you. And your guest as well. I'm sure Clemma will be delighted. Oh, by the way, you do remember how to get here?"

"Let me think," I returned tit for tat. "Not really.... How ridiculous!... Oh, yes, of course I remember now."

"Oh, good. Saves me the trouble of giving you directions! Well then, thank you for phoning, and we'll see you on the twenty-fourth at six for cocktails."

"That will be a very nice start to the New Year," I said, insincerely.

"Yes," he agreed, insincerely. "Have a nice sleep now."

"You too, of course, after you finish enjoying your book."

"Good-night now."

"Good-night."

I put down the receiver. My hand was cold as ice. What had I just done? Why, why, why?

*

I had a phone call the next night from an unexpected caller. Maxo. I'd remembered giving him my number at Baily's, but that was ostensibly for the purpose of checking up on Baily's condition. But now that Baily was back on the job he had no reason to phone me that I knew of.

"I'd like you to come down to the club tonight, Gianni," Maxo said. "If it fits into your schedule."

"Oh. Any particular reason?" I asked.

"I'll let you know when you get here."

It was almost eleven. I wondered if Baily was there yet. Probably not. "I'll ring Baily and see if I can catch a ride over with him."

"It's Baily's night off," he said. "Just come on your own. I've left word with Piers, he's on the door tonight. He'll let you in."

"All right," I said. "I'll drop by hopefully within an hour or so."

"Just take a cab over now. It'll be easier. Piers will pay the fare."

"If you say so."

"Ciao."

"Yeah."

I couldn't figure out what this was all about. But I put on some teak colored slacks, a long-sleeved white Polo shirt, a black jacket, and my red shoes, for Patrizia, as I knew she liked them, hopped in a cab, and was there in no time. Piers, "the man on the door tonight," was six-foot-four, had a blond Mohawk, gold earrings, a scruffy beard, was handsome overall, and on the lookout for me. When I got out of the cab, Piers paid the fare as I'd expected and hustled me inside the club where it seemed to be business as usual, wall-to-wall clientele, sinuous music, multi-colored lights, the main room pulsing with a kind of low-key amorality. Or gentle moral turpitude. As befitted Maxo's magnificent creation.

"Where's Maxo?" I asked Piers, who was guiding me slowly through the crowd.

"Monsieur Gauchette is waiting for you in his office," he informed me.

Which happened to be the little room that was nothing special behind the white neon-lit bar where Baily and I had danced together and traded words of everlasting love. When Piers ushered me in and closed the door behind us, Maxo was sitting alone at a table playing solitaire.

"Gianni," he rose and greeted me warmly, kissing both cheeks. For some reason I didn't buy the studied tableau of Maxo calmly playing solitaire when he had dozens of customers clamoring around the bar to attend to.

"Nice to see you again," I said. "Where's Patrizia?"

"Oh, somewhere around the bar. She's looking forward to seeing you a bit later. But this business is between us, it's not for her. Sit down."

Piers pulled back a chair for me and I joined Maxo at the table. Maxo gave a nod to Piers who removed a shining silver plate from a safe in the wall that Maxo had already opened, probably with a combination only he knew. I began to get nervous. But when Piers put the plate in front of me I was relieved to find it only contained a big rock of cocaine, with several lines already cut up from the mother lode and a straw at the ready.

"Baily told me, and forgive me if I'm mistaken, that you liked this kind of thing. Was he telling me the truth?"

"Yes. He was."

"Well, I didn't really doubt that he wasn't…That being the case, I'd like you to sample what I have to offer, *ami à l'ami.*"

"Friend to friend," Piers quickly translated unnecessarily.

"I think you'll find it's the best you've ever tried." Maxo shrugged lightly. "I could be mistaken of course. But help yourself. And see if you don't agree."

I didn't care for this set-up; but there was something about the position from where I was sitting that would have seemed disrespectful not to comply with his offer. I felt I had no choice, not that it was the worst dilemma I'd ever faced. I picked up the straw and snorted a nice-sized line. It was gold, Maxo was right. I sat stunned by its sublime taste and slowly increasing intensity.

"It's as pure as it gets, not dangerously pure of course. But it's not cut with the usual shit you'll find here in New York. No Draino or soap powder additives," he laughed, flashing that brilliant smile that sparkled with a purity equal to the powder he'd let me sample.

He was right but I didn't want to comment, figuring it was better to let him do the talking.

But it was Piers who chimed in. "Do you agree with Monsieur Gauchette?"

Maxo made a point of coolly studying his fingernails, not wanting to appear to be rushing me into stating the obvious.

"I agree, of course," I said, still basking in the glow. But what the hell, had Baily told him I was made of money and could afford this?

"For you, my friend, I have a special price. A full eight-ball for five hundred. Guaranteed to be the same quality every time—or your money returned, no questions asked."

Eight-balls ran around two-hundred. Though I'd had a fairly limited experience of using, as these things go, I felt what I had normally ended up with had been something decent, or even better. But not Cuervo Gold like this.

"Of course anyone seriously in the game knows it's wiser to buy in bulk," Maxo advised me. "Sometimes I'm in the position of waiting for a new supply and customers don't like to be without. For those special occasions."

I didn't have any special occasions. And just as well. I couldn't afford the price. But I kept quiet about that. I sat there as Piers returned the tray of goodies to the safe while Maxo disingenuously picked up his pack of cards and shuffled, his tattoo-covered biceps rippling subtly.

"Well, thank you for including me in your trusted circle," was the smartest thing I could think to say. "I'll certainly mull this over."

A special occasion did come to mind, but one that might never happen. What if in my wildest imaginings I ever had sex with Crewe again? It would be perfect for us. But, after speaking with Crewe on the phone, I felt the odds were against it.

"It's a generous offer, Gianni."

"Yes, I recognize that, thanks, Maxo."

"And now I'm sure Patrizia would love to see you." Maxo nodded his head at Piers who pulled my chair back for me. I stood up.

Maxo handed me a slip of paper. "My private number in case you're ever in a mood for a little chat. Just say you'd like to have a drink with me."

I made quite a show in front of Maxo of carefully putting the paper with his coveted number in a secure section of my wallet.

"Ciao for now, Gianni. And thanks for stopping by."

"The pleasure was all mine."

Piers led me to Patrizia who was handling the

customers at the bar. When she saw me she seemed delighted, suddenly full of sunshine, I didn't quite know why, and was quick to cover my face with kisses. She looked more ravishing than ever, in a gold lamé dress, her hair done up in a twist, with a little gold tiara holding everything together.

"Piers," she said. "Take over for me please. I'd like to dance with John."

Refreshing, she didn't go in for this Gianni pablum. She put down her glass that held her favorite drink, that fairy green absinthe, slithered around the bar towards me, and put her arms around my waist.

"There," she smiled, "I knew you'd wear those red shoes just for me." She quickly backtracked. "Or did you wear them for Baily?"

"It's his night off."

She didn't blink. "Then you did wear them for me."

I laughed. "In a weird way, yes. I did think of you, I have to admit, when I decided to put them on, as you'd told me how much you liked seeing them sparkle in the dark."

She gazed thoughtfully into my eyes and mused, "You're a kind person. I can tell. I have the gift to know these things, I was born with it, this gift. The way you helped Baily through his illness…" She paused, thinking. Then, "In fact, you're a very blessed person, as well."

I wasn't sure what she meant by that but I wasn't unhappy to hear it.

She leaned against me and suddenly we were holding each other closely; she felt so small and soft against me, her head resting on my shoulder, pressing her body fully against mine. Her hair smelled like the air that passes over tropical islands, sea-fresh and sunny.

"When I say blessed," she continued, "I mean that

you're blessed with an understanding of the world as it really is and of the people, good and bad, who live in it. And to have an understanding of the world in that way means everything in this life."

As we danced the music became slower and slower until we were practically just standing still against each other. And continuing to hold each other close. Thank God Maxo knew I was gay or if he saw us it might give him pause. Problem was, though I was definitely gay all right, I was attracted to Patrizia and popped a boner, which she didn't seem to mind, as she purposely rubbed up against it as we swayed in place to the music, even holding it to her by ever so lightly squeezing her thighs together. Maybe she was having these revelations—and even letting herself get a little loose—because of the absinthe. "Don't you think?" she asked.

I'd been very distracted. "Think about what?"

"That to understand things as they are means everything."

I didn't understand this boner, that was for sure. But I managed to get out, "Yeah, I see what you mean."

"To just accept and not to question. Because the only answer to any question lies within yourself. No one else has it or can give it to you."

Yeah, it was the absinthe talking. But it didn't make her any less captivating.

Suddenly an idea came to me and I wondered if she'd go for it. Or if Maxo would let her go for it. I'd informed Crewe I would be bringing a guest to Clemma's party. But I wanted to hit on somebody just right. Allison, as much as I loved her sweetness and caring, had been ruled a bore, a non-entity, by Clemma at least, and probably by Crewe too. Reg, well, he might prove to be a little hostile to a family that lived in a silver tower and become provocative. And Baily would be my ticket to oblivion. But Patrizia would be perfect. She was lovely, sensitive, spellbinding. At least to me. She was my best bet. But would she agree to go?

I pulled away from her and asked her point blank if she'd consider accompanying me, as a great favor, to a party in honor of someone's birthday, a rather arch rich woman, I couldn't lie, who lived in a penthouse on Central Park West with her husband and daughter. To my surprise she agreed immediately and said she wouldn't think of turning down my offer. When I asked her if Maxo might object, she laughed off the thought, telling me that not only would he not object, he'd be pleased, and would even let us use his limousine so we could arrive at the party in style, he loved her that much.

*

In the days before Clemma's birthday I began to obsess about her husband again, even before laying eyes on him. When Baily called I could hardly be bothered listening to his prattle and declined, much to his astonishment, all of his invitations for a return visit to his apartment for a little party. The truth is my mind had finally cleared from all the effects of that terrible mind-destroying substance that had him by the throat. But I liked Baily and told him to get some time under his belt at work and to go easy with that shit so Maxo wouldn't get suspicious.

"He thinks I'm clean as a whistle," Baily said, trying to put my mind at ease. "No problem there. I know what to do. I wasn't born yesterday."

Also I hadn't told him that Patrizia was going with

me to the birthday party, not that he would have wanted to go anyway. I was just trying to gently pry him away from my life, giving him as few details as possible about my business.

When the night finally came, I was ready. I'd decided not to go the shirt and tie route, trying to look my best in a simple white poplin shirt, black pleated dress slacks and dark shoes and a charcoal gray overcoat, strands of my blond hair falling down around the collar. I felt comfortable with my appearance, but inside I was as nervous as hell.

Patrizia phoned me from Maxo's limo and said it was waiting outside my door. This was a first. To the titters of Tony and a few lingering residents gathered in the lobby, I marched straight from the elevator into the back of the creamy stretch limo where Patrizia waited, wearing a floor length emerald green silk dress, a thin ivory belt with a mother-of-pearl clasp around the waist, her long wavy light brown hair glistening, having applied little or no make-up to her beautiful sculptured face. An opera cape, cut from the same emerald silk, lay at her feet. Without saying a word she lifted up a bottle gift-wrapped in emerald green, which slyly matched her ensemble, the already agreed upon birthday gift for Clemma, absinthe. It beat the Blake tarot card deck she'd unceremoniously discarded as my last, or rather Allison's last, offering.

This time Crewe's concierge, the one who had sized me up as a faggot whore not too long ago, waved us toward the penthouse elevator with a relaxed smile that spoke volumes about heterosexual entitlement. How differently the world seemed to judge you when a beautiful woman was attached to your arm!

We were admitted by that man in waiting whom I'd forgotten all about and didn't remember his name but when I saw him, I had my own Proustian moment, and like Proust's madeleine that had jogged that particular author's memory, I recalled my own remembrances of things past, a bowl halfway filled with lukewarm melon soup and a couple of stale rolls. And then it came back to me that the manservant's name was Douglas. I'm not sure how much else I really wanted to remember.

It didn't seem particularly eerie to be back, because standing in the entryway I saw a dozen or more guests milling around, people I'd never seen before, in the kitchen, in the living room, interacting quietly, outdoing each other with studied airs of privilege. Quite a different scene than when I'd last graced this aerie. As Douglas relieved Patrizia of her opera cape and me of my overcoat, I thought, oh my, I'm not going to enjoy this one bit. I was a nobody and Patrizia an exotic European. How could we fit in? My eyes instinctively sought out Crewe, even Clemma, but didn't find them.

I ushered Patrizia into the kitchen where a few guests were pouring themselves drinks. I guess Douglas didn't have to do double duty as the bartender. And from what I knew of Crewe, I figured he'd been too cheap to hire one.

An elderly lady I'd estimate to be around eighty extended her hand to us, one covered with age spots but enlivened by a diamond bracelet. "I'm Clemma's aunt, Beth Sager," she said, smiling sweetly, hoping we were somebodies. I trembled, but Patrizia took the old woman's hand to hers, brought it to her lips and lightly kissed it.

"I'm Patrizia Gauchette," she said. "The art dealer."

Charmed by Patrizia's gesture, she said, "Oh, yes?"

with interest.

"And this is my assistant, John Laith," Patrizia added casually.

Bless her heart. She'd picked up that I didn't know anyone here and was willing to cover for me. Of course she wasn't an art dealer, was she? And she wasn't married to Maxo, was she?

As Patrizia poured herself a bourbon on the rocks and I held a glass under the kitchen tap filling it with water, Beth Sager engaged Patrizia in a rather deft discussion about art, even describing specific paintings she owned and asking, in Patrizia's opinion, how much they might be worth. Astonishingly, Patrizia knew the paintings Beth Sager was referring to, could describe them in detail, and named a price she felt they might fetch at different worldwide auction houses.

Clemma stiffly entered the kitchen. I extended my hand and realized she had no idea who I was or that she'd met me before. And I didn't feel like reintroducing myself to her as her former brunch guest who dabbled in book discussion groups and had never purchased an apartment from her husband after all. But I was saved the embarrassment. Beth Sager made the introductions. Clemma eyed us both with suspicion even as Beth sang Patrizia's praises. I could see Clemma had hoped to quickly size Patrizia up as some kind of common Eurotrash imposter who had no place at her party, but auntie wasn't having any of it, so she sighed and said with great ennui, "Perhaps Crewe is going to be purchasing a painting for my birthday, could that be it, Mrs. Gauchette?" I could see Clemma's mind hard at work, taking note of Patrizia's name so that later she could do a little investigating to find out if she was a fraud. Meanwhile they made quite a contrast, Clemma in her workmanlike tweed suit and Patrizia draped in languorous green silk. Of course there was an instant dislike between them. It went with the territory.

"Birthday presents are surprises, aren't they now?" Patrizia got away with waving a finger at Clemma because she did it with some jocularity.

"Many things are surprises," Clemma replied tartly, "birthday presents being the least of them."

"Clemma," Beth said. "What on earth do you mean?"

"I hardly think it's necessary to repeat what I just said."

Happy Birthday, Clemma, I thought to myself, and then, where the hell is Crewe? Wouldn't it be just like him somehow to have disappeared for her party?

"Let's mingle," Patrizia suggested, taking my arm in hers and leading me into the hallway. "Mrs. Sager," she called back over her shoulder, "if you think of any more questions you'd like to ask me, please feel free. I'll be easy to locate in one room or another."

"Why thank you, I will," she said, moving her hand with satisfaction along her wrist that held the diamond bracelet.

In the hallway were consummately dressed bankers or upper echelon real estate types standing alongside their sedate wives. They at least nodded to us as we "mingled," but didn't ask us to join in their conversations. They didn't know us, and that being the case, we weren't entitled to be included, unless we could convince them otherwise. I didn't care enough to try and Patrizia didn't find it necessary to convince them either because she'd already found one ally and for her that one was enough. Nonetheless, these successful businessmen, deep in their private conversations, kept casting furtive glances her way, probably sizing her up as a potential mistress or perhaps even wondering if she could actually be someone of importance that it would behoove them to introduce themselves to. But in the end they didn't. It was a small enough world. They already knew all the players. So they stayed true to form and let their own egos rule the day.

Someone was pulling on my shirt sleeve. It was Beth Sager. "There's a draft in this hallway. There's a nice fire in the living room."

It was an order issued with the utmost kindness, to join the rest of the group in the most intimate spot in the penthouse.

"I didn't realize, Mrs. Sager, that you had a fire going in there. What a wonderful idea," Patrizia thanked her. But before following Mrs. Sager's advice, she returned to the kitchen, herding me with her, where Clemma was talking to several of her girlfriends. Patrizia picked up the elegantly wrapped bottle of absinthe and interrupted them by handing it to Clemma, "Here, Happy Birthday. I don't know if your husband is getting you that painting for your birthday or not, so to tide you over, John and I brought you this, for those long winter nights to come, or if you wanted, you could break it open now and you and your friends would find yourselves having a most delightful experience."

Clemma put it down, unwrapped, on the kitchen table, without thanking her, or missing a beat in the conversation she was having with her friends who, picking up the vibe from Clemma, totally ignored her. Patrizia gave them a sprightly laugh, which did unnerve them because they fell out of their solidarity for a moment and became silent. But then they picked right back up again where they'd left off. At Clemma's cue.

"This isn't a real birthday party, you know," Patrizia took my arm, guiding me into the living room. "There's no cake, no frivolity, nothing to enliven anybody. Or give them a good time."

"No, it's just a cocktail party," I said, shrinking, sorry I'd put her through this because of my ulterior motive she knew nothing about. She hadn't deserved it. I felt like a rat.

Into the living room, where a few slightly younger couples were gathered who did take notice of us and smile our way before moving into a new cluster of guests, like stars in the universe, seemingly without any rhyme nor reason. The warmth of the fire felt good. A young man and his wife, or girlfriend, were lying back in front of it on their elbows, speaking to each other in a candid way, laughing at times, even giddily, as if one of them had just cracked a joke.

Where I grew up in a poor household, when neighbors stopped by along with their friends that you didn't know, you extended your hand in a polite gesture and made them feel welcome, asking them something about themselves. Apparently that wasn't cool among snobs.

I turned around to see Crewe, in a sweater and slacks, less dressed up than most of his other male guests, sitting on the sofa, Sidonie on his lap, going through a book of pictures with her in front of some interested onlookers. It seemed like the same picture book that had been on the bureau in her room, the one she'd pasted the word ST. BARTS on its cover with gilt letters. The one I'd had no interest in looking through. But others seemed to be quite interested, or were pretending to be. With this group, nothing was certain. Crewe looked up and saw me standing with Patrizia, but didn't bother to nod to me or get up and introduce himself as host of his wife's party, which galled me, not for my sake but for Patrizia's.

"And there, the last picture." He sounded relieved. "Of the finished pier. That took some real doing and some real leg work for Clemma, given how lazy the workers were."

Everyone congratulated Crewe on what a lovely villa it was, on such a profitable piece of land no less, and yes, what a relief to have that pier finished off at last. That led to a general discussion of the special getaways some of the guests were either building or anticipating building for their own family's enjoyment, and how much they envied Crewe's and Clemma's ability to see the St. Barts project through, how it gave them all hope, and that they were determined now to try and emulate Crewe's hard work. That's when Sidonie looked up at me and said, "Look, Dad, there's that man."

A pin could have dropped. Everybody finally gave their attention to someone other than themselves or their close band of associates. They gave it directly to me. Not that it was wanted attention in this case, but at least I got some.

Crewe was forced to respond and end his little game sooner than he would have liked. "Yes, my dear, there's that man." He lifted Sidonie off his lap and came to shake my hand as everybody watched with a kind of bizarre fascination. Patrizia clung instinctively to my arm.

"This is Mr. Laith," Crewe announced. "He's going to be buying one of my buildings."

"Oh, which one?" I heard a voice from somewhere in the room inquire.

"That's top secret—for now," Patrizia saved me.

A low murmur went around the room.

"I'd like to introduce everyone to Patrizia Gauchette, the art dealer." I'd found my voice.

Crewe smirked openly. But Mrs. Sager had entered the room and went to warm her hands by the fire. "That's correct," she confirmed. "She's been giving me advice on some of my paintings, which she was quite familiar with, fortunately. I may put some up on auction. And she was quite helpful there too, suggesting which European auction houses might be interested."

Crewe's smirk slowly disappeared and he turned away, back to his daughter, and told her in an annoyed tone to go put her book away, that everyone had had their fill of seeing those pictures. Sidonie threw him a perturbed look and walked out of the room as everyone called out after her to thank her for showing them. I noticed as she left the living room that one of the pictures slipped from her book onto the floor. When everyone went back to chatting, I moved to retrieve the picture, to go and return it to her. No one noticed me picking it up, not even Patrizia, as she was busy talking to Mrs. Sager in front of the fire. I started down the hall with it, glancing at it cursorily, then stopped. It wasn't a picture of the St. Barts villa or the pier. It was a picture of one of the white balloons Sidonie let fly up into the sky, heavenwards, each Sunday, but scrawled underneath the rather unremarkable photo in what I assumed was Sidonie's handwriting was a remarkable line: *Sending up my father's soul to God.*

What could she mean by that? I suppose what I knew already: that her father's soul was bereft, or at least sometimes bereft, of kindness, and it was up to God to help it along. If He could. So this revealed the secret of her white balloons. She knew her father as well as I did. And like me, hadn't been quite able to let him go. Hesitantly, I slipped it under her closed bedroom door.

But she wasn't to remain in her bedroom for long. As I returned to the living room, the young man who'd been lying in front of the fire was still showing some life in him yet and was telling the others, "Don't you remember, there's an eclipse of the moon tonight?" He checked his watch. "And it should be happening right now. Let's all go out on the terrace to watch."

"Hurry, Douglas," Mrs. Sager called out to the manservant hovering by the entryway. "Go get Sidonie so she can see it too."

Douglas did as he was bid and returned with Sidonie who was excited at the prospect.

"This is a treat, I must say," the young man remarked enthusiastically. I heard his wife, or girlfriend, agree, then impossibly call him Dickie. Well, why not, that suited him. His name and mannerisms seemed to come straight out of some early thirties movie, where rich young things holed up at somebody's country house on a lark for the weekend and couldn't repress the urge to wring fun out of anything that strayed from some ordinary event.

There was a general flurry while the door to the terrace was opened and about half of the guests went out to enjoy the spectacle. Crewe and Clemma weren't among them. As Patrizia went to ask Douglas for her opera cape, I turned and heard Clemma say to her husband, "What a ludicrous idea. To stand on the terrace on a cold January night and wait for a cloud to pass over the moon. Please don't ask that young man who suggested it back here again."

"That's not exactly what happens during an eclipse," he advised her, but not educating her further.

"It's close enough."

Crewe brought up some bread and butter issues. "And never mind that that young man just married the daughter of one of the most influential waterfront developers in Boston."

But Clemma wasn't taking the bait. "That's right, never mind."

"Well, it's your birthday after all. I wouldn't want you to come down with a cold tonight, of all nights."

"Thanks for your concern."

While Crewe and his wife sensibly stayed indoors and made small talk with the other half of the guests, Patrizia, donned in her opera cape, led me outside to join the brave ones. It was chilly, but hardly unbearable. Patrizia put her arm around my waist and led me to the edge of the terrace where Dickie was kneeling down next to Sidonie and pointing upwards towards a dim object surrounded by a red rim hanging in the sky directly over Central Park.

"That's it?" Sidonie asked. "That's the moon?"

"Of course it is." Mrs. Sager joined them. "What else could it be?"

"But I thought we'd all be plunged into darkness," Sidonie complained. "At least for a few seconds."

"Hardly," Beth Sager corrected her. "At least not in New York City. Why, all the bright lights of Manhattan would still be glowing, as people have to go about their normal business, don't they?… Maybe if you were out on the beach…"

Dickie cleared his throat. Now it was his turn to

correct Mrs. Sager. He did so with impeccable manners. "Mrs. Sager has a point, you'd be better able to see it more clearly from a dark beach. However, even during a total lunar eclipse like this one, when the earth intrudes itself between the sun and the moon, the moon never goes black completely. And plunges us all into darkness," he laughed, then continued, "because sunlight's still reflected through the earth's atmosphere. So you'd always see that thin red rim circling around it. See that, Sidonie, that faint illumination around the moon's edges?"

"Of course I see it. I'm not blind," she answered imperiously.

Mrs. Sager commented, "Why, Sidonie, you're so know-it-allish sometimes."

Patrizia and I were just listening, enjoying the exchange. The light wind blew around the edges of Patrizia's cape. For a moment she reminded me of some penitent making her way on a long journey back to her cloister in inclement weather, until I noticed her radiant smile, which transported me back to reality, and then I saw her clearly standing behind the white neon-lit bar at Tenebrae, her natural habitat, calmly sipping absinthe.

Dickie tried to keep things spirited, as most of the others who'd come out onto the terrace by this time had had their fill and were filing back into the living room. "Now here's the fun part," he said to Sidonie. "What if you were standing on the moon during an eclipse, and looked back down at the earth? What do you think you would see?"

Sidonie was silent. Maybe she wasn't interested. But I was.

"Something amazing and beautiful," Dickie told her.

"You'd see the earth surrounded by a slim ring of gorgeous sunset colors."

"How would you know?" Sidonie challenged him. "You've never stood on the moon, I wouldn't think, to know what anything looks like."

At this Dickie gave it up. Sidonie whirled around and went back inside. Patrizia took Dickie by the hand and helped him up from his crouching position. "Bravo," she said. "I thoroughly enjoyed your description."

Mrs. Sager remained quiet, a bit embarrassed, choosing not to comment further on Sidonie's behavior. After all she wasn't a disinterested observer, but family. I took her arm to walk her back inside. She was right about one thing. New York never stopped. Nothing turned out its lights.

Once inside, Dickie asked Crewe for permission to put more logs on the fire as a slight draft from the terrace had seeped into the room. Permission was granted. The fire began to crackle and gave off a deliciously warm orange glow. Guests settled themselves on the sofa, or pulled chairs together in little groups, and someone had the presence of mind to wish Clemma a happy birthday. She was standing back against the wall, next to Crewe, and acknowledged the salutation with a polite smile while Crewe put his arm around her waist. Mrs. Sager had Douglas fetch her a chair from the kitchen and put pillows down on it as a cushion, as she "wanted something strong to support her back." Sidonie settled down on the floor in front of her and timidly stroked her hand, the one with the diamond bracelet, perhaps in some attempt to make up for her snippy behavior. At least to Auntie Sager. That simple unguarded gesture, however, showed me where the real money sat in this room.

Patrizia, rather shamelessly, pulled a rocking chair

up next to the fireplace, and stretched out, one could almost say intemperately. I sat down next to her on the floor as every other seat was taken. Patrizia had made herself the center of attention. And the group was somehow buying it.

"Tell me, Mrs. Gauchette," one man inquired, "how you advise your clients about which international auction houses might be interested in certain pieces of art and why. The kinds of pieces we all might have up in our attics, ready to be dusted off." He chuckled knowingly, looking around at the others for encouragement and pleased to see they were in agreement. This man had obviously made it a point to make a note of Patrizia's name and he introduced himself to her as Neil Birnbaum, a vice-president of Chase Bank.

"Oh, yes, tell us something that would help us all," Mrs. Sager pleaded with her.

Patrizia laughed easily. "Perhaps I will tell you something that might be of interest to you. But really, I only dabble in that world now, advising a few friends I've known for years. You see, I wasn't always Mrs. Gauchette, but Mrs. Stewart. I was married previously to George Camber Stewart, quite a famous art dealer who was very active in the business about ten years ago. I'm afraid whatever expertise I have I stole from him. He was a Scotsman from Edinburgh. But very well known on the international circuit."

"Oh, yes, I've certainly heard of him," someone said.

"But is he still in the business?" someone else asked.

I looked at Clemma. I could see from her expression she hated being upstaged, but what could she do, her own guests were interested in the subject.

"In a nominal way, but he's developed other interests as well. For instance he's quite taken with the art of alchemy now."

"Well, that's certainly strange," Mrs. Sager commented.

"And quite a leap of faith," Clemma spoke up for the first time.

"Not really, not after the experience he had," Patrizia refuted her.

Dickie was in his element. "Do tell us. I'd like to hear a good story, sitting around the fireplace on a cold winter's night." He put his arm around the woman I now knew was his wife. I thought, you'd best enjoy the fun while you can, you're not being asked back.

Patrizia continued, "My husband told me there's a place in Scotland unlike any other. It's called Findhorn. Supposedly people live there because they're in touch with the nature spirits. Findhorn has a cold, inhospitable environment, yet with no effort the people who live there don't have to eke out a living—it seems lush, large, luxuriant vegetables and flowers grow there at will."

"How could they?" Dickie asked. "If the place is so inhospitable…"

Patrizia shrugged. "Scientists looked into the matter, of course, but couldn't come up with any scientific explanation for this phenomenon."

There came a soft snort of disbelief from Clemma.

"Anyway," Patrizia continued, stretching her legs out further and basking in the glow from the fire, "George told me that when he was a young man he'd been fascinated by the legend of Findhorn and had gone there to see for himself if what he'd heard about the place was true, and he told me that it was. He lived in Edinburgh then and would often take walks in the evening along a manicured park at the city's edge. At twilight. He told me he sometimes had the feeling he was being watched and he peered between the trees more than once to see if some stranger was hiding himself in the woods. But George never saw anyone. Finally, though, after a number of walks, he did see something. A pair of eyes staring at him from between the branches."

"My dear!" exclaimed Mrs. Sager, while Sidonie put her chin in her hands and listened raptly.

"George would return to the same spot every night at twilight and on one of his walks, at last he saw who was looking at him. It was a faun."

Another snort from Clemma. Otherwise the room was silent.

"Every twilight my husband couldn't help returning to the same spot to see if the faun was there and he always was. And during each of George's visits, the faun lost some of his timidity and came closer until one twilight the faun came up right next to George, who saw it had hairy legs, hooves, and horns, and said to my husband, 'don't you know that I'm the Devil?' My husband answered, 'I know some people think you are the Devil but I think you're part of nature, of human nature,' and with that the faun came right into my husband's body. George wandered a long time through the woods until he came to a precipice that looked down onto a valley, one very much like Findhorn, and he saw all the nature spirits gathered together, other fauns, satyrs, dryads, nymphs, spirits of the plants, of the earth, cavorting over the landscape and reveling in magic…"

With this Patrizia ended her tale and looked up, her eyes meeting Crewe's, who quickly turned his gaze to the floor impassively, but kept his arm more tightly than ever around his wife's waist.

Patrizia told the assembled guests, "This is the truth, I swear it. The faun came into my husband's body and they became one. And that's the man I was married to. The famous art dealer you asked after."

There was suddenly a flurry to leave on everybody's part. No one came up to Patrizia to ask any questions, in fact she was studiously ignored as the guests fell back into their appointed clusters and hurriedly dispensed with the requisite good-byes. Douglas was busy sorting out the coats. Even Mrs. Sager seemed flustered and told Sidonie she'd see her to her room and tuck her in. Clemma was chatting up her girlfriends with a barely suppressed glare on her face. Patrizia was in the hall, once again sliding into her opera cape. I was thirsty so I ducked into the kitchen for a glass of water. As I filled a glass at the tap, I noticed Crewe was standing next to me. We were alone at least momentarily. My heart beat fast.

"You didn't think I wasn't going to call you back, did you?" he asked.

"To be honest, I didn't think you would because I asked you not to."

"You're quite wrong. I planned to call you back all the time. I thought I'd just give you a little time to cool down, that's all, and let you start seeing things with a clear head. I was going to give you say another month, maybe even two, to be sure you had your head screwed back on right. I'm certainly glad to find now that it is."

Standing in the kitchen I remembered the argument between Crewe and Clemma the day of the brunch that had taken place here in this room—when she'd mentioned something about the police—and later Crewe's admission that some kid had made a complaint against him for continuing to try to contact him when he'd expressly asked him not to. I realized that's what had played the biggest part in this waiting period. Crewe was a little afraid I might be the type to get him in trouble again by my reporting him if I felt harassed and he couldn't take that chance. That was the real reason he hadn't called me back right away. He'd needed to utilize the passage of time as his ally.

Clemma came into the kitchen so I left quickly to join Patrizia in the hallway. From the kitchen I could hear Clemma say in a ringing voice, "Crewe, I had no idea you had ordered up a Rent-a-Clown for my birthday party."

In the lobby, the concierge almost tripped over himself to open the door for Patrizia and me, nearly knocking the doorman aside. We slid into the back of the limo, helped by her driver, who handed her a fluted glass before he shut the door.

On the ride back to my apartment, we were silent, though Patrizia did open her bag and bring out a bottle of absinthe. She rubbed her fingers along the fluted glass the driver had given her, then lifted up the empty glass and considered it for a moment, before pouring just a little of the green liquid into it and taking the tiniest of sips.

\*

"Well, bugger me gently…" Those were the first words I was to hear from Baily when I answered the phone. "I never thought this could happen."

"What?" I asked, afraid of the answer. Had he run out of crack again?

"I've been let go," he said softly, bewildered.

"Fired."

That was worse, I guess. "But why?"

He struggled for some kind of explanation but didn't have one. "For no reason."

"There must be a reason. Maxo likes you. Did he catch you—"

"No," he interrupted me. "Not at all. I never even did a hit in the stall. Well, maybe just one that I can remember. And I showed up on time every night, or even showed up early—and worked my ass off. And for all that, Maxo just phoned me and said my services would no longer be required, effective immediately."

"Oh, Baily, that's tough luck," I sympathized. But I wondered if Baily wasn't holding something back. There had to be a better reason for firing Baily than just a sudden whim on Maxo's part. Yet Baily seemed genuinely confused. And bereft. "Didn't you ask him why he was letting you go?"

"Of course. After he told me my services would no longer be needed, I asked him 'Why not?' But he just answered me with, 'Effective immediately, Baily, effective immediately.' That's all he would say. Then he hung up."

"That's odd," I agreed, but tried to look on the bright side. "Look, there are plenty of other clubs around town. I'm sure you could get another gig easily enough with your skills."

"I suppose…"

"Why not brush it off, Baily? You aren't alone. After all, people lose their jobs every day." I didn't mean that line to sound cavalier but there was no other way it could sound. "Just get back up on the horse right away. Don't give yourself time to brood or slip into a funk. Make some rounds today. Once you've landed something else, it'll make all the difference, you'll forget about this…unfairness."

"Yeah, you're right…But I thought maybe I'd take a day off first, before I make the rounds…and that you might like to come over for awhile and hang…"

"I'd like to," I said, trying to soften the blow, "but I have an engagement with someone today that I can't break off." Crewe was dropping by within the hour.

"Is it so important that you couldn't put it off to be with me? Just for today?"

Is it so important?… I quivered inside at his question. I thought long and hard before answering, "Yes, it is."

Anyway, how could I see Baily? It wasn't just the fact Crewe was coming over. What if Baily went on a crack binge, which was likely, and I was there with him? He might shotgun me again from out of the blue.

"Gianni…I've never asked you for much, not really…well, maybe some money for that pizza…"

I was firm. "It's impossible. Make me proud of you, Baily. Go out now and check out some clubs. You might find something right away. Then call me back tonight."

There was a silence, then, "Thanks for your support," he said sadly, and without irony, and hurriedly hung up.

What could I do, go plead his case to Maxo…or try and enlist Patrizia's help in the matter? Baily was a big boy—though I have to admit he really did look about sixteen. Still, I needed to steer clear of this.

"My goodness," Crewe said as he swept into my apartment shortly after I hung up with Baily. "You've gotten a bit thinner since I saw you last. Did you know that?"

"That was only about a month ago. I doubt I've shrunk all that much."

"Let me correct you. It's been a month and a half at least. And you *have* shrunk all that much. What's going on with you? You need to fortify yourself. And drink plenty of tea. It's a real restorative, I've been reading very informative articles about its benefits. Clemma's gotten me into green tea, especially. Says it cures just about everything." He took a jar from his knapsack and placed it on my counter top. "Here, I brought some for you. As a token for the New Year. I'll admit the taste takes some getting used to at first. But now I wouldn't think of drinking anything else."

The image came into my mind of him constantly fixing us tea during the night of the blizzard up in his penthouse—and me being afraid he'd spill it all over himself. Which in the end, to his credit, he'd managed not to do.

After I'd let him into my apartment, I'd just sat back on the sofa and watched him strolling about, reinspecting my volumes of literature, reacquainting himself with the view of the Seminary, which he pronounced as "jaw-dropping really, just as magnificent as the view of Manhattan from my terrace, but in a completely different way." The Seminary tower did stand out clearly today, almost in bas-relief against a light blue sky.

There was something reassuring about him being back, his fussing, constantly plying me with questions, making himself at home. I wasn't even in the mood for sex, but was just enjoying this kind of back and forth with him, surprised at how emotionless I felt at this highly anticipated reunion.

"Mind if I boil up some water for a spot of tea? I'll make you a cup as well, if you'd like."

"I don't mind, but I'm surprised you didn't bring along your usual beer."

"Oh, didn't you know? No, of course, how would you? We haven't been in touch, after all, have we? I've given up alcohol. It eats your system up alive."

So he was on a health kick now. "Strange, then, to have just given a cocktail party where your kitchen table was full of every kind of liquor imaginable."

He brushed my observation aside with a knowing smile. "You have to think of other people besides yourself, don't you? It's only good manners. For instance, my bringing you a present of this tea. Some might think that a thoughtful gesture."

"It is...I don't believe you've ever given me a gift before."

"I'm sure you're right. But come to think of it, I don't quite remember receiving anything from you either."

True enough. But that was because I'd been too shy and insecure to give a married man a present. What was his reason?

"What you must think of me, deep down," he ruminated. "That I'm selfish and aloof. And only care about what can benefit me. Is that it, is that why you phoned and said you didn't care to be involved with me anymore?"

"Why, no."

"It may interest you to know I do empathize with other people. That I do care. Just because a man doesn't lay his whole hand out on the table doesn't mean he's not holding a worthwhile card."

Suddenly I sighed. Now he was back to purposely obfuscating. But I felt the need to respond and reassure

him otherwise, so we could try to take a step forward.
"I'm sure you've held many worthwhile cards in your
hand over the period of your lifetime. Any man has."

"Oh, good, for a moment I thought you might not
include me. It just so happens I have many philanthropic
projects on my desk at the moment taking up a lot of my
time." I wondered. "But not all of these projects are so
far removed from myself that I just instinctively write out
a check for some worthy cause and then forget about it."
He shook his head. "No, that would be too easy.
Sometimes you have to get your hands a little dirty—as
if you were pulling up weeds in a garden."

I waited, not anxiously, for some further explanation.

"Have you ever heard of the organization God's
Love We Deliver?"

"Of course I have, and a worthwhile one it is, too," I
replied enthusiastically, having a vision of Crewe
donating money for such a commendable cause, to a
group that fixed meals for people homebound with AIDS
and then delivered them at appointed hours.

"I don't know if you've ever volunteered your
services there…" he said diplomatically.

"No," I answered with sudden embarrassment and
shame. I guess I'd been too busy fucking. Wait, that
wasn't exactly fair. I'd given service elsewhere.

"Can you imagine me, a successful real estate…?"
He paused at length, searching for the right word.

"Magnate? Tycoon?" I prompted him, not in jest, I
just wanted to finish his damn sentence for him.

"I'd prefer to say developer," he stated. Then
continued, "…going for an interview in front of a board
of this non-profit organization to see if they felt that
someone like myself might be qualified to spend one day
a week delivering meals to those in need. And to be able

to spend some time with those young men who are homebound and perhaps even be capable of cheering them up...I imagine a few of them have nobody to open up to, maybe no family here in the city...or perhaps they had former friends who deserted them in their hour of need...That's what I'm talking about. Giving them real service. To the ones that probably need it the most."

I fell silent for a moment.

Eventually I managed to get out, "That's thoughtful of you. Tell me, what did the interviewers say?"

"Can you believe it, they said they'd have to let me know. After more careful consideration...They advised me they have so many volunteers already. I wouldn't think an organization like that would believe there could be such a thing as too many volunteers, would you?"

"No, not at all," I mumbled slowly. "But at least you made the effort and offered your services."

"I certainly did."

The water in the tea kettle had come to a boil.

"Let's not bother with the tea, after all, unless you'd really like some," Crewe said, pulling his little silver pipe and clump of grass out of his jacket pocket.

"No," I said. "I guess I don't feel like any either." I hated green tea anyway.

He went to the kitchen and turned off the flame, asking, "By the way, did you have a good time at Clemma's birthday celebration?"

"Yes, I did."

"I thought you would. That's why I invited you. Oh, and I must ask who that charming woman was you brought along with you. Many of my male guests phoned me up the next day asking what I knew about her. I'm afraid I had to tell them 'Nothing.'"

"I believe she explained herself in some detail," I said.

He chuckled. "My wife seemed a bit jealous of the attention she received, no—let me rephrase that—the attention she demanded. Just by being so alluring, I suppose." He was working the clump of grass into the pipe.

After all the trouble I'd taken to swallow my pride and phone Crewe to get him back, the idea that we were about to have sex now was a definite downer.

"I don't suppose you have any of the white stuff, do you?" he inquired. "To mix with the green? I'm afraid I didn't bring any, but I can't help thinking what a delicious combination that would be."

"No, I don't have any," I answered.

"I heard through the grapevine that the woman you used to score it from is dead."

I looked up shocked. I hadn't known. But, of course, her obituary would hardly have been featured in the *New York Times*. "The Sam Martinson grapevine?" I ventured.

"Well," he said, with perfectly controlled anger. "You weren't available, were you, or believe me, I'd never have seen him."

I believed him. Which didn't help. It made me bitter, like he was, and that bitterness made us both forget about Teresa real quick so we could wallow in our own resentments. God, this could never work. I was back with that sick feeling in the pit of my stomach. Yet, if there was a way, I wanted so badly that sexual oblivion I'd experienced with him on such a visceral level…It had been the only ticket I'd had…and was still the only ticket I knew of that could get me out of the fun house politely called the world, that for me was filled with the terror of always being alone, and like a carnival mirror, threw back a mocking glee at all of my unhappiness.

"So, what are we going to do about it?" he asked, folding his arms across his chest.

"What?"

"The white stuff?"

"Just hope that it snows."

"You're very witty, but not very helpful."

"Another backhanded compliment from you," I said softly. "It's worse than not getting any."

His mind went to work. "Look," he said suddenly, heaving a sigh himself, "I'm sorry."

He settled down on the couch next to me while I stared down at the floor.

He continued, "It's too soon, isn't it? We still have feelings to work through, don't we?"

"I suppose."

"You don't want to have sex with me now, do you?"

"You mean right now?"

"Uh-huh."

It was the startling admission of some truth that had seemed well hidden, but out it clearly came, "No."

"You don't trust me, do you?"

"No, Crewe," I looked into his face. "And I don't think I ever will."

"I see. And where does that leave me?"

"On the same road you were on before you met me."

We sat silently for what must have been about five minutes. Then he said, "I know what it is. If you were high, really high, you could forget. Or maybe even..."

"What?"

"Forget who I am."

I frowned uneasily.

"And just go with it. So you could still get those perfectly normal feelings that you need satisfied. The ones I can satisfy better than anyone else—and you know that's the truth."

Sighing, I stood up and asked him to leave.

Always the gentleman, he complied gracefully. But not before insisting I answer him, "You do want them, don't you? The incredible sex, those feelings we shared together. You do want them back again?"

I didn't answer. But we both knew that I did. Yet how to retrieve them…or begin again…

At the door, Crewe said, "You know, Clemma and Sidonie are going to St. Barts in a few weeks' time. I'll be perfectly free then. Why don't you give yourself some space to think things over, I won't pressure you, and see if you want to give it another try then? Don't worry, I won't put you through the anguish of having to call me to say 'Yes, Crewe, let's do it,' or 'No, Crewe, I've decided against it.'—I'll phone you and you can just tell me what you want. In one word. And I'll leave it at that. Of course, you know how much I want it again. Or I wouldn't have come back after you brushed me off. I have an ego too."

Oh, really? That must have managed to slip my mind.

I had to stop with these cunning silent replies. As if he could hear them. They weren't doing me a bit of good. Because as long as I kept throwing these off-the-cuff ironic rejoinders around in my mind, they just kept spinning me into a wind of obsession, straight back to him.

I decided to just come clean and cut the bullshit and said, "Fine, call me in a few weeks time. I may be farther away from you or closer to you. But just let me say one thing, and it's not meant to hurt you, I hope it's farther away from you. But I don't imagine I'll have any control over it one way or the other."

He left. We'd made our pact.

\*

I didn't hear from Baily that night and wondered first if he'd gone out and looked for work, and then how he was feeling. I called him but his voicemail came on so I left a message casually asking him how things were going. I didn't want to play the role of big brother, but some encouragement on my part couldn't hurt. As I hung up the phone, I had the sinking feeling he might be alone in his apartment on a crack binge, refusing to take any calls.

I was on my own slippery path, after Crewe's visit, feeling untethered and vaguely upset, about to turn to drugs myself for relief. Subconsciously, deep down, I must have known this was yet another dismaying turn of events for me, with unforeseen risks, but on a fully conscious level I felt it was a great idea and made perfect sense.

"Maxo, it's Gianni," I said when he picked up the bar phone. It was only ten o'clock, but he was there.

"Gianni, how are you?" he said.

I had no intention of questioning him about Baily. It was none of my business, and besides, it might interfere with my own mission.

"Oh, fine, fine," I answered. "I thought you might like to get together for a drink."

"Sure. I'd be up for that. We could have a drink together, catch up. Patrizia was telling me a little bit about your party the other night."

My party? "Well," I said, "she certainly was its highpoint. And she was a good sport to go."

"She said I might have been a bit bored, though," he laughed. "Why don't you stop by around midnight, then? Piers will let you in."

No offer of paying my car fare now. It was down to business. I would have preferred to go for that drink immediately rather than wait till midnight, then crawl home in the dead of night. Since I'd drifted back to my apartment from Baily's, before dawn, when the late night had played tricks on my mind, the thought of being out during those hours held some kind of new dread for me. Whether that was rational or not, it was real. But I had no choice if I wanted to follow this clarion call.

"Fine, I'll look forward to our drink and catching up. Ciao."

"Ciao."

My idea was to buy a lot of Maxo's Cuervo Gold coke. All at once. As he'd suggested. And then hide it somewhere around my apartment, so I would always know there was some around, to help me through any difficult or confusing moments, or bad feelings. Which seemed to be cropping up more and more. And, of course, for the sheer pleasure of a snort now and then. I'd just squirrel away the goods for the right moment.

Sometimes we look at ourselves in the best light, sometimes in the worst. When it came to this scheme, I looked at myself in the best. I wasn't a desperate drug addict like Baily, or a regular user like Crewe. I was an occasional dabbler, like Sherlock Holmes, the man who'd had untold energy, a keen mind, and sharp wit, and had been able to solve the greatest crimes in London when everybody else was clueless. This with a snort or two of cocaine!

I walked to Tenebrae along towards midnight with five thousand bucks in my trouser pockets. I'd made the withdrawal that afternoon from my gradually but ever decreasing bank account. I just hoped I wouldn't be held up and robbed before I reached the club. But this was the only way. I'd hated copping drugs, ever since that first afternoon I'd gone to Teresa's, and had only done it once afterwards, when I'd visited her again, the day of the blizzard. There was something demeaning about the whole process. But this would be the finale. I'd buy ten eight-balls that would probably last me the rest of my life. I disliked the thought of constantly being put in the position of ringing Maxo up and asking if he'd "like to have a drink." And then running back and forth to Tenebrae. I had no other contacts and I didn't want any. Teresa was dead and I cringed to think of having to deal with refuse like Oliver, Prince Rockefeller, and Shauna 'Fe. This seemed the perfect solution. Just get it over with and then retreat. Ignominiously.

When I got to the club, plenty of patrons were already queued up, but Piers recognized me right away and took my arm and moved me ahead of everybody else, ushering me inside. Of course I'd worn my red shoes, for Patrizia, whom I saw immediately as I made my way through the euphoric crowd already treading on air with a transporting indulgence, in rhythm to the techno-beat and magic colored lights. She was behind the bar staring into space, lost in her own thoughts, lit by an overhead white spotlight, one of many that dotted the ceiling that ran the length of the bar. I paused for a minute just to revel in her beauty. She was dressed in a violet crinoline dress that bunched out as it reached her knees, and throughout her wavy hair were dozens of violets strung together by nearly invisible pieces of string. I watched as she calmly lifted a fluted glass from the bar and took a sip. Afterwards she seemed a bit more distant, even alone.

Someone tapped my shoulder. It was Maxo. "Gianni, come along, let's have that drink." Had he been standing next to me in the crowd? Or had he seen me standing still from his vantage point behind the bar as I studied Patrizia, and strolled over to escort me back into his office? "You can talk to Patrizia after we settle things."

Patrizia was still in her own world and didn't even notice me as Maxo led me inside and closed the door and offered me a seat at his table. He sat down across from me. I was surprised to see his wall safe had been ingeniously covered over by a piece of paneling that seamlessly matched the rest of the wall, so seamlessly I couldn't have said where the safe was located. He had a pad of paper in front of him and wrote a question for me, "How many?" He passed the pad over to me along with a pencil. Anxious, but determined to see it all through, I wrote down the figure "10."

Was the place bugged? I doubted it since we'd had a rather frank discussion in here before. I guess he was just taking the proper precautions, which actually put me more at ease. When a real deal was going down I guess you couldn't be too careful.

He turned his back and placed a call on his cell phone, mumbling something quietly. A wave of nausea quickly ended any ease I'd just felt. Could this be some set-up with the cops? Why the hell couldn't you just go buy this stuff at the corner pharmacy like customers did a hundred years ago in a more enlightened era and earmark the money for the school system or something? I started sweating, thinking paranoiacally about the Rockefeller laws, where for some minor infraction, a victimless crime, like I was guilty of, they threw you into someplace no better than Devil's Island for the rest of your life. Didn't they?

Maxo seemed aware of my discomfort and handed me a handkerchief. "It's hot back here," he said. "Overheated."

I wiped my brow. I couldn't even reply and Maxo wasn't saying anything, just taking his lighter and burning the page with his question and my answer on it until it morphed into a charred remnant that he dropped into a waste can next to his desk. There was a quick tap on the door and trusty Piers came in, closing the door behind him, and Maxo thanked him for bringing us a round of drinks.

Silently, Piers handed me a small manila envelope. Inside it I could feel clumps of something hard. Quickly, to show I was keeping my side of the bargain, I fished in my pants pocket and pulled out a wad of cash, but what was the protocol here, did I hand it to Piers?

Maxo came to my aid. "Thank you, Piers," he said and the big blond Mohawked employee quickly left.

I gave the cash to Maxo, who didn't bother to count it but, taking his time, took out a key ring from his vest pocket, located a small key and opened a drawer in his desk, laid the bills inside and locked it. Then gave the handle a pull to make sure it was locked. He'd trusted me to deliver the correct amount agreed upon, so I decided it wasn't cool to open the envelope I'd been given and look inside to check the goods. Instead I stuffed it into my pants with an unconcerned air, hoping for the best.

Maxo was already getting up. "Well, back to work, no rest for the boss. I appreciate your stopping by for that drink. And more importantly, it's good to acknowledge we've taken our relationship to a new level, one that will continue, I have no doubt. We have a closeness now, *ami à l'ami.*" He smiled. I was just relieved the exchange had gone off according to plan. "By the way I hope you weren't disappointed by the quality of that drink. It's the same as you had before."

I got up too and together we went back out behind the bar where we both noticed a commotion going on in the crowd. It didn't take long to see a whirlwind sweeping through the room, parting the crowd like the Red Sea, a whirlwind named Baily Cantevelter in his baseball cap, yellow satin jacket, and boots, followed at a discreet distance by a limping Piers who was clutching a sore arm, his face in pain. Baily was headed right to the bar. Patrizia, alarmed, moved closer to Maxo and me, all three of us taken by surprise and unprepared for a scene.

Baily rudely pushed his way between two patrons sitting on bar stools and took in all three of us in turn. Me first. "You?" he said in disbelief. "What are you doing here? Come to dance on my grave?"

"Of course not, Baily. I'm here for a reason that has absolutely nothing to do with you. I'm your friend and you know it."

Patrizia was next. He sized her up. "You could do better than what you've got—with him." He nodded his head towards Maxo, without looking at him. "A woman with your class working in a shithole like this." He managed to shrug and sneer at the same time. "Go figure." Patrizia looked down sadly, not, I thought because she was with Maxo, but because of Baily's distraught state.

Then he turned his guns on his former boss. "Tell your girlfriend to leave."

"You seem to have things all turned around, Baily," Maxo said, calmly but firmly. "I give the orders here, not you. And she's staying right here."

Baily pounded his fist on the bar. "Give me my pay for the last few weeks I worked here. You fucking figured you could cheat me out of it. Blow me off before you paid me. No way, big man."

"You'd better leave now, Baily, and I'll forget about this."

"Pay me what you owe me, you fucking asshole. Then I'll be happy to be on my way."

Piers huddled in the background, afraid of Baily.

I felt frozen next to Maxo and Patrizia, somehow feeling it was my place to be in on this unpleasantness too, as I was now involved one way or another with all three of them.

Maxo picked up an empty glass from behind him on the shelf, held it up to the light, and with a cloth studiously cleaned it. Finally, he said, "No," continuing to wipe the already spotless glass clean.

"No?" Baily was outraged. "Tell me I didn't hear that right."

"You did hear it right."

"You mean," Baily raised his voice so the customers close by could clearly hear, "that you admit to pulling a dirty trick like this and not paying a guy fairly who finished a job for you." If he'd hoped to get an anonymous group of club-goers behind him, he failed, as no one here was going to take the side of some loser against the man with all the money and power. In fact, they stared open-mouthed at Baily like he was some poor deluded soul.

Maxo hoped to bring the matter to a close. "You've been more than fairly compensated by me."

"Oh, I get it. The time I was out sick. You figured I was on a binge when Gianni called and told you I had flu."

"I didn't have to figure. It was as clear as your brain is muddled. You don't have somebody call for you unless you're too wiped out to call yourself."

He turned his attention to me in a rage. "You told him!"

Maxo stood up for his new customer. "Gianni never told me anything except the lie you had him tell me. And I don't hold that against him, but against you."

"You paid for my Harley. And you paid for my rehab. Then you figured that wasn't money well spent. Since I slipped. So you decided to take what you could out of my pay before you fired me. To punish me."

Maxo's eyes carefully checked the glass for spots. He found it to his liking and replaced it on the shelf. "Something like that."

"And you won't even give me a second chance? As hard as I've worked for you."

"There are no second chances in life, Baily. Not with you. Your second chance would turn into a third, then a fourth." That wouldn't have been everyone's assessment, some would have agreed to give Baily a break, that second chance, young as he was, but Maxo had a definite point of view.

Baily didn't give up, only tried a softer touch. "But Maxo, if I don't have this job, I'm in deep shit. I have bills to pay, I have to eat like everybody else."

Maxo was silent. Patrizia came up next to me and took my hand in hers and squeezed it.

"And the rent on my apartment is overdue. I could be evicted in a month or so if I don't come up with it somehow. And end up on the streets. It's tough out there, trying to land a new job. Especially in a hurry. I went to a few places. They either told me they weren't hiring or gave me a line to come back another day when the boss was around. It was embarrassing, making the rounds, cup in hand."

"Get off the cross, Baily, we need the wood," Maxo said.

Livid, Baily picked up a customer's drink and hurled it straight at Maxo who ducked. The glass hit the mirror on the wall, shattering both a section of the mirror as well as destroying the glass, sending tiny shards flying towards Patrizia, speckling her violet-strewn hair, while the liquid from the drink spilled down the front of her violet crinoline.

"Are you all right?" I asked her.

She nodded she was, but of course she was shaken. I was more so, because I realized, right at that moment, how much I cared about her.

"Come outside, you weak motherfucker," Baily challenged Maxo who had uprighted himself, "and fight me like a man. For all your big biceps, I could beat the living crap out of you."

But Maxo had already gone into action by giving a secretive signal with a simple nod of the head and before Baily knew it, four bruisers I presumed to be other bouncers had him in the air. To subdue a kid who was now like a wild animal took all four of them, each of them grabbing one of his legs and arms and then carrying a kicking and cursing Baily towards the door and hoisting him back outside. Maxo hustled Patrizia and me into his back office as the clientele began to dance and party again, excited to have witnessed some drama which let them feel that being in a club like this one kept them on the cutting edge of something.

Maxo eased Patrizia down into a chair in front of his desk and softly rubbed the cheeks of her beautiful face, which, thank God, didn't show any signs of having been cut. He said to her gently, *"Il mio tesoro, siete ferite?"*

"No," she shook her head, *"ma soddisfa, lascia da solo ora. E molto turbata."*

"What's she saying?"

He gazed at me perplexed, "That she isn't hurt, and to leave Baily alone, he's upset."

He found a cloth and began to dry the front of her dress while I picked the pinpricks of broken glass from her hair, trying not to crush the violets, though that turned out to be impossible as I wanted to get every last piece of glass out. I remembered as a boy being afraid to reach out to touch the roses growing in my mother's dirt-filled box because I was afraid I'd prick my fingers. I had none of that same fear now. So what if I pricked them?

Patrizia was still in a bit of a daze. She turned to Maxo and said, *"Ringrazi Gianni per l'uso dei suoi pattini rossi."*

Again I had to ask for a translation.

"She told me to thank you for wearing those red shoes."

I knelt down beside her. "You're welcome. But let's all speak English, since we can. So nobody has to act as a translator."

She smiled. "Of course. I'm so used to talking to Maxo in my first language, especially when I'm upset. I forget I'm fluent in several. When I was married to George, he'd sometimes catch me muttering in Italian and ask me the same thing. To please speak English."

Maxo picked up a call on his cell phone. He listened, then, "Why am I not surprised?" he answered, then shut off the phone. "I've just had a report Baily's hanging around outside the club, just sitting quietly now on some trash can."

"Let him sit there, Maxo," Patrizia pleaded. "He's not doing any harm."

"You're so trusting," Maxo answered her. "Believing the best about everyone."

"No," she responded thoughtfully, as if she were remembering something. "Not everyone." I wondered what she meant. For some reason I thought she might be referring to Crewe, why I don't know, it was just a hunch coming out of nowhere, but it was a strong one.

Maxo didn't exactly share her same level of trust. He said he wasn't worried about himself and Patrizia who would be escorted by bodyguards into a limo after the club closed, but he was concerned about me. "Baily sees you as some kind of Judas now."

"I'm sure he doesn't. He knows me better than that."

"Best to wait a bit until he leaves before you go back out," he advised.

"And do what? Now that I've gotten all the glass out of Patrizia's hair, I might as well go."

Neither of them spoke and I took that to mean they didn't agree. Shit.

Maxo left Patrizia and me alone to go back out and work the bar. There were a couple of couches set against the back wall.

"Let's get some rest," she said. We each picked one to curl up on, both exhausted by the turmoil, I guess, and the late hour. She fell asleep first. With one hand I reached out and very gently, so she wouldn't wake up, touched her hair, while with the other I reached into my pocket and twirled my fingers around the packets of rock in the envelope. I drifted off.

When Maxo shook me awake, he whispered to me to be quiet and not disturb Patrizia who was still asleep. He said it was four-thirty, that the club was closed, the doors bolted, and that the crowd had dispersed. However he advised me Baily was still outside sitting on the trash can. I was alarmed not so much by that, but by the fact that when Maxo had woken me, he'd found my fingers entwined in Patrizia's hair. I expertly extricated them so she wouldn't wake up, figuring I didn't have to worry about Maxo's reaction as he didn't appear to have one; he must just think that's the kind of stuff gay guys do.

He took me out by the bar, softly closing the door behind him. It was startling seeing that big empty room, all shadowy, smelling of sweat, with no music and no people. "Patrizia and I won't leave till seven or so, not until I'm finished going over the night's take with a couple of the guys. You'd better leave through the back door. It'll take you to 28th Street. Through an alley. So you won't have to run into Baily."

He let me out the back way, then closed and bolted the door behind me.

It was cold. I pulled the collar of my jacket up and headed down a dark thread of a passageway wedged between two buildings that quickly brought me into the alley Maxo had mentioned. A big trash bin waited, nearly concealed in shadows, at the end of it. I could hear the frenzied scampering of rats inside it all the way from where I stood. Nonetheless, I walked towards it, I'd have to pass it to get to the entrance of what I'd been promised was 28th Street. Then suddenly I stopped. I couldn't continue. Not down this alley. Not towards that trash bin. Not after the hallucination of burning my red shoes in one very much like it.

I was full of fear, not of a bin where rats rustled in an otherwise deeply silent gloom, but because I felt I'd ignored some omen that last time, insisting it wasn't one, and now I thought I was being forced to relive that same moment again, this time to accept the omen or forewarning for what it was. That somehow my red shoes held the essence of something evil.

I turned around and made my way back down the narrow passageway, coming out onto 27th Street where I saw Baily sitting despondently on a trash can. Of course he saw me too, but only looked down. I went up to him. "Baily, for God's sake, go home. You'll catch pneumonia sitting here all night long."

"Then you could call up Maxo and tell him I've got the real deal this time. Or maybe I could make a crawl for the phone and somehow manage to dial the number myself."

"Why are you acting this way? It's no good. Face up to it. You got a raw deal, you did. But you can't do anything about it now."

He looked up at me suspiciously. "And just what were you doing in there?"

"Patrizia went with me to a party, a horribly stuffy one, as a favor. I went to thank her."

"And pigs can fly."

"Come on, I'll drop you off at your apartment in a cab."

"They're still in there?" he asked, eyeing a waiting limo he knew was Maxo's parked discreetly down the block.

It was useless to lie. "Yes."

He suddenly got up, picked up the trash can and hurled it against the door of the club, yelling, "Come out of there, you no good cock sucking, ass licking, cunt slurping lowlife thief. Come out of there, I know you're in there. I'm just waiting to bust your fucking jaw in two!"

The crash of the bin had made a loud ricocheting sound when it hit its mark and was now barreling noisily down the block. Unfortunately, there was another can close by, which Baily hurled ferociously against the door and screamed with even more invective, "Did you hear me, Gauchette, you shit eating son of the town whore, get your tired, worthless ass out here and give me what you owe me—or show me your fists!"

Again the can bounced off the door and hurtled down the block.

"What's wrong, Gauchette, afraid of a little pansy, is that it?"

Baily's voice echoed into the night, which only threw him back his own question and nothing more. He was so enraged he didn't notice a car slowly moving up the street, headlights off. God, was it some undercover cops, ready to arrest Baily and frisk me with ten eightballs of blow in my pants? The car stopped silently while Baily's back was turned.

Before he could say "Jack shit," Baily was backed up against the wall by two heavies, the barrel of a gun ground hard into the center of his temple. A couple of Maxo's goons, I guessed, that must have received a little cell phone call.

These guys wouldn't have stood out in a crowd. They wore dark knit caps and sweaters and jeans, were thin, and though I couldn't see their faces clearly, their tense, purposeful body language suggested they weren't playing games. And with a gun pushed so deeply into Baily's temple, he didn't dare make any karate moves. Especially after hearing the trigger of the gun click into place.

One of them said, "Out of New York City by morning."

They weren't playing good cop, bad cop here. They were both bad news, because the other goon chimed in with, "Never come back. Not within five miles of this city. Or you can kiss your ass-fucking mess of a life good-bye."

Then they pistol whipped him enough to keep him dazed and in no shape to retaliate while they made their getaway, jumping back into the car and gunning it, spinning the tires, making them squeal, putting an exclamation mark at the end of their threats.

I walked up to Baily who was now slumped down against the wall of the club that he'd "worked his ass off in," to quote him. His face had already begun to bruise up.

"You can't say I didn't try," he said.

"Baily, let me hail a cab. We'll get you to some emergency room."

"Fuck off."

"Baily, please let me help you, you're hurt."

"Listen...I have an idea...why don't you knock politely on the club door and see if Gauchette lets you, his new buddy, back inside...and ask him nicely if you can suck his dick?"

That was that. I didn't hold it against him. If I'd had a gun in my face, the trigger pulled back, and been pistol whipped like he had, who knows what would have come out of my mouth. Still, I saw no way that he was going to accept help. Not from me, not from anybody. I rummaged through my wallet and found a hundred bucks. Too bad I still didn't have any of the five thousand left, but I did have the envelope full of what I'd spent it on. I pulled it out of my pants pocket, tore it open, saw that Maxo was good with his word, as I quickly counted ten packets of rock inside. Not thinking too clearly, I stuffed both the hundred bucks and two of the packets into Baily's shirt pocket. He didn't say no. Then I moved away and started walking down the block, leaving him slumped there, after having done a terrible thing, given him cocaine. But God help me, I wanted to give him something besides a hundred bucks and that was all I had. I kept on walking, shivering from the bitterness in the air. When at last I reached the end of the block, I found I was unable to turn around and look back before I crossed the street to head towards home.

*

But when I woke up I was worried. They'd given Baily till the morning to get out of town —forever. And they were serious. Groggily, I got out of bed and saw it was almost noon already. I called Baily but he didn't pick up, I only got his voicemail. All kinds of thoughts went through my mind, the worst being that he'd shacked up with Oliver or one of his ilk and was hiding out. Or a worse one yet, that he was sitting alone in his apartment, having ignored their warnings, still smarting from that pistol whipping, and having no money to leave town with. I couldn't let him stay with me and bring all his insanity and the shroud of danger he'd been wrapped in like some strait-jacket along with him, but I could give him money so he could get out of here, withdraw say a thousand bucks from my bank account, and take it over to him. So he could at least make it home to Tennessee. But for me to get the money to him, he had to be at home. Well, if he was there and afraid to answer his intercom, I had his spare set of keys.

I threw on some clothes, hopped a cab, had the driver wait outside my bank while I withdrew the thousand, then had him drive me to Baily's Cornelia Street apartment. I fingered his spare set of keys during the whole ride. Though, as it turned out, I only had to use one of them when I got there, to get into his lobby. When I got to his studio door, I saw it had been jimmied open, though it was shut now. All I had to do was give it a light push to get inside.

It was dark in there, blinds drawn. I didn't like the feel of it. My hand felt around for the light switch on the wall, found it, and flipped it on.

The place had been trashed. The couch overturned, table and chairs on their sides, broken, dishes tossed around the room lying everywhere in jagged pieces, the mattress on the bed ripped apart, springs protruding and the stuffing pulled out in big clumps, the tropical netting that had surrounded it tied in the shape of a noose to the top of the blinds. Clothes scattered haphazardly, his flat screen shattered, the bureau tipped over on its front, all that had been on it obviously crushed beneath its weight. Except for the koala bear, which was lying face up at my feet, smelling unmistakably of urine. And no sign of Baily. Dismayed, I wanted to sit down and put my face in my hands, but there was nowhere to sit, so I just stood there and put my face in my hands.

The bathroom door was closed. My God. It suddenly dawned on me. What if he was in there, dead? I couldn't bear to look. Yet, what if he was in there injured and needed help? I had to look whether I liked it or not. Gingerly making my way through the minefield that only a few hours ago had been a normal studio apartment, I reached the bathroom door. And bravely opened it.

It was empty. Thank God the shower curtain was pulled back and I could quickly take note that Baily's body wasn't lying it. No one had bothered with emptying out the medicine cabinet and strewing the contents around. However, a parting gesture had been too good to pass up. The word "FAG" had been scrawled in my red lipstick on the bathroom mirror.

I went back out into the studio. Drained. And frightened. Yet not without some hope. Who would have kidnapped Baily, to go dump him somewhere, leaving all these clues behind with obvious DNA and other forensic evidence? Not two goons with their heads on straight. No, I didn't think that scenario was the likely one; they'd have jumped him somehow, made him disappear into thin air, and left the apartment alone. Another of my hunches was at work. Somehow I figured Baily had left already before this happened or maybe had never even come home.

I felt I could bolster my hunch by checking his kitchen cabinet. Weaving my way through any path I could find through all the breakage, I got to his kitchen alcove where the cabinet door was standing wide open, from which, of course, the kitchenware had been pulled out and smashed on the floor. However, the Cracker Jack box was still on the shelf, overlooked during the rampage. I had to laugh to myself. Baily had been right when he'd advised me that that box was the safest place to hide his ring. If Baily had come back here, wouldn't he have taken that goddamn ring with him, if nothing else? I shook the contents out and there it was. The prize ring Victor, and I, in turn, had rejected. But I didn't reject it now. For all my denials of the power of talismans, I felt this was one. A good luck charm. I put it in my pocket and left, turning out the light and shutting the door behind me.

Like some rookie detective on a routine job, I made my rounds. To all the parking garages in the area. I'd seen this scene dozens of times in movies, usually a filler between the dramatic bits, with voice-over, as some cop flipped a badge, gave a parking attendant a brief description of a suspect, asked if he'd seen him around, got a hurried, uncooperative shake of the head "no," then moved on for his next try. Though I was doing the same thing, this was no movie, I was no detective and I wasn't hunting down a suspect, but trying to find out information about a friend. Which proved to be more difficult as I didn't have a badge, only a ring in my pocket, yet that alone kept me optimistic.

The afternoon dragged and my feet got sore. But I didn't let that bother me. Doggedly I went from the 12th Street Garage between University and 5th, the Barrow Street Garage between 4th Street and 7th Avenue, Central Kinney between 5th and 6th, giving whatever attendant was on the job a description of both Baily and his Harley Night Rider. Usually I got disinterested grunts back for my pains. In fact, at Central Parking between Mercer and LaGuardia, some gruff old geezer even told me to buzz off, couldn't I see he was busy collecting fees, before I could even finish my spiel.

But finally as the sun was starting to set, a kid about

Baily's age, though with a dark crew cut and a more hardened look to him, smoking a cigarette outside the Minetta Lane Garage on MacDougal, the garage that was actually closest to Baily's apartment, admitted he knew that Harley well, because he'd always envied it, and that being the case, had taken note of the kid who owned it.

"Yeah, he came for it this morning, just as I was coming onto the job. At the crack of dawn. I couldn't help but wish it was mine when he took off on it. "Some kids have all the luck," he complained, taking a deep drag. "Having enough bread for a bike like that one. I always wondered who he was and what he did for a living. Never asked him though."

"You're sure he was dressed in a yellow satin jacket and wore a baseball cap? And had wavy brown hair?"

"And a pair of black boots. Sure. He was here all the time. I hate rich twits."

"Well, listen, thanks for helping me out. It means a lot."

He ground his cigarette under his boot. "I'm off the clock now. Going home. Need to pick up a few things along the way…" He was waiting. For a tip. I reached in my pants pocket and pulled out a fifty and handed it to him. "Thanks," he said.

At home I sat on my couch and quietly studied the ring. In the light of a candle I'd lit. Then I wrapped it in a handkerchief and placed it in the top bureau drawer of my bedroom dresser and threw myself down on the bed. Baily was on the road. With a hundred bucks and two packets of rock cocaine. And the clothes on his back. Speeding down some unimaginable highway on his way to some mysterious future. But for tonight at least he was still alive to begin that journey.

I hated Maxo. I really did. Of course he hadn't enjoyed being insulted in front of Patrizia and the patrons of his own club. But he'd overreacted. Or maybe this was just the way of that world and Baily had gotten what was coming to him. But it was a world I'd decided to leave quickly, as I wanted no part of it. But you leave one world to go to another. That new world was spiraling, unseeable, off somewhere out in the universe.

Over the next few days I lay around reading. Light sophisticated comedies, of all things, from past eras, Waugh and E.F. Benson, even the early Agatha Christie Tommy and Tuppence series, real PBS material. I guess I needed to lighten up and forget a few unsavory recollections of my own. Through it all I did manage to open that small manila envelope and hide the packets of rock in different locations around my apartment, minus much enthusiasm. In a book, in the can of green tea Crewe had brought me that I'd never brew, in a pair of socks, in an envelope in my desk. But who was I hiding them from? I was the only occupant of this apartment.

Most of the time that is. Once when I was hiding a clump of rock in one of my old sneakers in the bedroom I happened to glance up to see the angel in the mirror behind me. Studying me. I whirled around to face him and saw his expression was one of dashed hopes and disillusionment. Angry at being spied on and furious at being caught, I tossed the sneaker into the drawer and slammed it shut then decided to tell him to leave me alone from now on, but before I could get the words out he'd retreated, stepped backwards into the fog of the mirror leaving no trace of himself in the glass.

The days passed. When Bob McBride bumped into me in the hallway, letting me know he was up for a chat, I told him almost imperiously that I wasn't in the mood, which left him with a bewildered look on his puss. For the first time since Frank's death, I felt like snapping at just about everyone who crossed my path. This tenseness I couldn't seem to shake, though for the most part I did manage to repress it, yet sometimes it showed some teeth anyway, like with poor Bob.

One afternoon the buzzer rang. I answered and someone shouted, "Delivery!"

When I opened my door, I found two men, huffing and puffing, struggling with a huge, heavy silver vase that stood four feet tall at least, and held gigantic lilies, not real ones, but meticulously crafted silk fakes. Momentarily confused, I waited a moment before inviting them inside and had them put the vase down, which they did with a thud and a few curses, next to the window that looked out onto the Seminary. After they gave me the card that went with it, I handed them a tip and they were on their way.

I shut the door and opened the card. It was a handwritten note from Patrizia. "John," she had written, "Forgive Maxo for what happened. Deep inside he was upset himself. But Baily wasn't harmed. Maxo promised me he wouldn't be. This little present I've sent you is to remember me by. So you'll know I'll be thinking of you sometimes. You know I have the gift. And because of that, think about what I've said to you before, that you're a kind person who has the ability to see both the good and the bad in people, which is a most profound gift of your own. But what you do with that knowledge rests with you alone and no one else. Love, and good-bye, from Patrizia."

I'd seen that vase before. Or one like it. Of course, it was one of the ones that decorated the staircase that wound up to the balcony at Tenebrae. It was a nice gesture, but it was so big, it overwhelmed my living room. Yet I couldn't think of throwing it out or giving it away. It was a good-bye, an unexpected one, though I'd said good-bye to both her and Maxo in my mind already and somehow she knew that. I would keep it, and when I gazed at it, remember her body full of milk and honey, her rhapsodic face, her visionary mind.

It was Logan who came up with the idea of giving me a round table burnished with a golden sheen he didn't want to take along with him to Vermont. He said it was just the item that would hold something heavy like the vase I'd described.

It was news to me, but evidently he and Allison were moving to Burlington where he was originally from and where the rest of his family still lived. It would be a good change for Allison and a splendid place to raise the baby.

When they brought the table to the apartment, he carried it in, Allison tagging along behind him, very pregnant now. I told him where I thought it should go, in front of the window, where it would provide a very dramatic foreground to my view of the Seminary. Together we lifted the heavy vase up onto the table.

"Now, that's a beautiful place for it!" Allison exclaimed, coming over to kiss me on the cheek. I hugged her.

"Thanks, guys," I said. "The least I could do is take you both to dinner. It's something I'd enjoy doing very much—and it's way overdue."

"Sorry, we've got the U-Haul parked down in

front," Logan said. "We just stopped by on our way out of town. It's going to be a long trip for us and we've got to get moving."

I looked at Allison in surprise. "You mean you're going just like that, moving to Vermont today?"

"It really isn't 'just like that,'" she responded, a little disappointment in her voice. "We've been around quite awhile."

It was the gentlest of reminders I'd been out of touch. It was true, I had been, because I'd been callously self-absorbed. They'd called and e-mailed me a few times asking to get together and I'd put them off, promising to see them in the near future. But I'd never made it happen. How could I make up for it now? I couldn't, of course. I could only go downstairs with them to see them into their U-Haul, promise them I'd come visit them in Vermont when the baby was born, e-mail and call them in the meantime, of course, then stand there and wave good-bye as their U-Haul disappeared down the street and turned the corner.

When I got back inside my apartment I had the feeling everybody was leaving me or had already left. God, how I missed Frank!

Yet I didn't want to think about him at all, it was too painful.

The days passed some more. And I lay around, depressed. I recalled chiding Baily for not going out and looking for a job when he needed one. Well, I needed one too. I hadn't heard a word from the courts about an interview. If I didn't get my ass up off the couch and do the same thing, look for something myself, my funds could really dwindle to an alarming low. Though, I reassured myself, I had plenty for now and for the fairly foreseeable future.

Reg called from time to time and we had pleasant conversations. He had to remind me my birthday was coming up at the end of February, and he and a few group friends wanted to fete me, at Linda Kroll's Tribeca loft. Everyone was wondering what I'd gotten up to, just dropping from view like the sun in the evening. I thanked Reg, begging off any birthday celebration, telling him I wasn't feeling all that well. We'd celebrate it next year.

"Don't be ridiculous. Linda's already making plans for it. And so am I."

"Really, Reg, I don't feel up to it. I could have mono or something."

He didn't give up. He called again on the day of my birthday telling me it wasn't too late. I told him I still didn't have any energy but thanked him and asked him to give Linda a special thanks for me too. Then after I hung up, I picked up the plate in front of me and did a nice line of coke. What more pleasant way to spend your birthday, anyway? And it kept me from thinking about Frank.

I drifted like a cloud. As March blew in. Sometimes I stood at the Seminary window and stared at the building for hours, blankly.

I soon came to realize that I couldn't take a little sniff and feel good and let that be the end of it. I had to pay later. The next day. When I'd told Reg I had no energy, that was the truth. When you go up you do have to come down. Down like the sun in the evening Reg had mentioned. And I was spending more hours on the down curve, recovering from the night before, than on the up, when I'd just taken a few sniffs.

Nothing much alarmed me as I was existing pretty much in a daze. Not even the fact that when I went to look for my second eight-ball in the envelope where I'd hidden it in my desk drawer, it wasn't there. The envelope I mean. In a momentary panic, I realized I'd put my rent check in that envelope and mailed it to the landlord, along with an eight-ball included free of charge. I thought quickly about asking Bob across the way, since he worked for the Post Office, to see if he had or could get access to the key to the corner mailbox and could somehow retrieve the rent check. But it wasn't worth the effort. The envelope was obviously further along than the corner mailbox by now. And so what if the landlord got it? He'd either evict me or keep it for himself and say nothing. And it would probably be the latter.

It was only when days later I found that packet in the drawer, hidden inside an envelope under several others, having been there all along, that I knew trouble lurked in a deep way in my life. Even so, when Reg called next, I had already delved into that packet, was high and effervescent and couldn't help but mention Crewe's party, even admitting to Reg I'd been the one to phone Crewe back, not the other way around, although he'd been planning to get back to me himself in time, and that we might see each other again. Though he hadn't called me yet, I should be hearing from him any day now, as his wife and daughter were going down to St. Barts.

That's when Reg said angrily, "Put down the drink."

What drink? I didn't drink. Oh, he meant Crewe, my drink.

"Your life has gone to hell," he said. "And that's not where it belongs. Do you know you're not a worthless piece of shit?"

I was dumbstruck by his words. But I listened.

"Don't you know how many people, you, John Laith, have helped. Through the worst moments that human beings can go through. Helped them, through your own generosity and unflagging determination, to find their way to the other side. Do you know how many people in those cold, desolate meeting rooms have started new productive lives because of you? They've told me so themselves. Yet instead of building on your good works, you've chosen to sit in a haze of self-pity and a world of addiction, waiting for something transforming I can promise will never come your way. You don't stand a chance. Not unless you give up your quest for empty thrills and your contentment with isolation and return to service."

"But how?" I asked him softly.

"By coming and speaking to the group on Friday night. I'm chairing the meeting. Some new people are coming, people who've lost loved ones, the same as you or me. They could use some of your help."

"All right, I'll be there. What time?"

"Seven-thirty. At St. Veronica's."

*

St. Veronica's was an oversized red brick edifice set right up against the sidewalk on Christopher Street, down close to the Hudson, a Roman Catholic church built in the Czech style, in need of some repair, glum with the passage of time and the loss of parishioners. Its attributes seemed few; cheerless and graceless on the outside, damp and dingy, with the biggest cobwebs I'd ever seen dangling from the rafters in its basement where our meetings took place. But it was a haven for our bereavement group, where any member could just drop in when they needed a meeting. You shared your story and listened to everybody else's. And usually heard something useful from someone that you could integrate into your own healing process. Grief has a ruthless commonality.

Reg had been so right. I needed to do this, to reestablish my connection with the group. But I was nervous, I'd lost my bearings by being away for six months.

I got there early, making sure everything was still familiar, and hung around the empty basement auditorium that seemed less like a part of a church than a theater, since a large stage had been built at one end that was occasionally rented out to theater groups. Some members liked to speak from that stage, standing behind a lectern. As I set up folding chairs to form a circle, I decided I'd sit with everybody else. I needed to look into their faces and I wanted them to look into mine. So they could see I was here again, the same old me.

As people filed in, I recognized some old friends and engaged them in conversation, remembering their stories and asking how they were progressing. When they asked after me in return, I told them I'd been fine. Linda Kroll, and her husband, Jack, were there and we all hugged each other and I apologized to them about my birthday. I told them I hadn't wanted them to go to any trouble for me. I left out the fact that I'd preferred sitting at home alone snorting cocaine.

I introduced myself to some new members, welcoming them, and letting them know I'd be speaking tonight. Several of them said they'd heard of me and were happy I'd be personally sharing my story with them.

I helped an old friend, Kevin S., who was doing service at the literature table, set up the books, pamphlets and meeting schedules. He told me he was writing letters to his fiancée who'd been killed in a sudden car crash, the midnight victim of a DUI trucker. He was compiling a loss history, one of the elective tools in our recovery. He was doing this grief work with his sponsor, Bertha C., whom I knew as a helpful, experienced member. I noticed her now as she sat down on one of the folding chairs. Kevin told me how important writing these letters on a regular basis were as they were helping him work through his grief to the point where he felt some kind of resolution was forthcoming. I'd never built a shrine to Frank or written him letters. That remained a concept filled with an infuriating finality.

"Sorry, I'm a bit late," Reg apologized as he swept up to me breathlessly. "Don't judge me too harshly, but I was having dinner with someone I met on the Internet, our second date, so we just have a third to go. A very nice, stable man who's a computer analyst on Wall Street. Age appropriate too. So far, so good."

"Then you have every reason to be late," I laughed.

When it was time to begin, Reg and I sat down in the circle side by side. Since he was the meeting chair, he led the opening prayer. Everyone joined hands, bowed heads, and murmured back in unison. Afterwards Reg asked the group members to introduce themselves by first name, last initial. I looked into each person's face as he or she said their name, smiling towards them in turn, suddenly missing Allison.

Then Reg made some introductory remarks, "which I'll keep to a minimum, so you can hear our guest speaker and then share. I just want to remind the group, especially our newcomers, to stick with it. There's no timetable for making peace with grief. We're not competitive here, there's no moment when the clock runs out. The Kubler-Ross stages, the five stages of grief—denial, anger, bargaining, depression and acceptance—are only blueprints, and she was the first to admit it. Just as there's no typical loss, our responses to loss are as different as our own lives. Keep that in mind and always bring along the willingness to help and be helped."

Reg cleared his throat. I took that as a sign I was about to speak. There was a respectful silence in this dark, ample space.

"Oh," Reg added. "Do excuse me. I forgot to mention. There is something called pathological grief. An extended period of depression where, despite the passage of time, a person is unable to make progress. Often this is caused by a combination of trauma as well as grief, after an unexpected death, a suicide, say, where the grieving person had no time to prepare for the event. Trauma affects you in a different way than grief. We're all grieving, but with trauma, you, yourself, change. You may feel a new helplessness, self-blame, concealed anger, so that you own self-image is undermined. Or sometimes the loss of the capacity to enjoy your own life as you used to can leave you psychologically vulnerable. Grief and trauma together become a two-headed Hydra. And need two separate solutions. If your symptoms aren't lessening over time, I encourage you to seek professional help as well as attending these meetings, no judgment intended…And with that, I'd like to introduce you to our speaker." He turned towards me, quickly touching my shoulder.

"Hello, everybody, I'm John L."

"Hello, John L.," they called back warmly. And I was immediately at ease.

"I'm grateful to be able to share my experience with

you tonight," I said. "You know, the word 'grief' comes from the old French '*grève*,' which means to carry a heavy burden. It's what I carried with me when I walked in here. But this group gave me such strength, hope and support during such an impossible period in my life, that burden has lessened now. I can't say I'm where I'd like to be yet, but as Reg said, there's no scheduled arrival time for my destination. But I'll get there—and you will too.

"I'll dispense with my upbringing, quickly, as that's not what I'm here to focus on. I come from a family of meager means from a city in the Midwest. My dad died of a heart attack in his sixties, he worked in construction, his life wasn't easy. My mother died in her late fifties of diabetes. I have a brother, ten years older than me, who lives in Brazil with his wife and two sons, working on some kind of ecological project. I can't tell you what it's all about because we aren't in touch anymore, not only because of our age differences, which kept us from ever being close, but because he married a woman with a homophobic family, who talked him into having as little to do with me as possible. I never read him as prejudiced when we were growing up, but then maybe I didn't really know him, he was just my older brother. My mom and dad, who never finished high school, surprisingly were never that way, in fact, they accepted my partner, Frank, as one of their own. Frank's family accepted me as well. Naturally. They were all from California."

Reg laughed at my line and a few others followed suit.

"Frank's dad was a part-time history prof at Pepperdine, his mom a state social worker, and his sister a journalist who married some English book publicist and moved to London. Coming from a more liberal environment, I suppose it was less unusual they accepted my relationship with their son.

"Frank and I met at university in L.A., eventually moved to New York and set up our home. With the blessings of both our families.

"Let me tell you one thing right off. No two people were ever more in love. They couldn't be. As much maybe—but not more—since there wasn't any wiggle room at the top. We were taking up too much space up there. And I was as fulfilled as I could have hoped for.

"Though today our relationship would have been labeled 'codependent,' that concept was unknown to us at the time. We just felt we were like most other couples with intertwining lives. The same as our parents and I suppose their parents before them. Frank was more naturally a caretaker, the one who assumed a more protective role and actually took on most responsibilities in our relationship, probably more than he should have. Honestly speaking, I had the abilities of a child in an adult world and the impatience of one, too, when I was forced to take care of practical day to day matters. That was Frank's domain. I say 'was' because he's no longer here. I lost him. I don't quite know why to this day and I don't think I ever will. But this group has taught me I never have to find that answer. All I have to do is remember him as the kind and gentle person I was blessed to be with. And most of our friends liked being with Frank as much as I did, for his irreverent humor and nurturing spirit. They would have traded places with me in a minute.

"Frank was my rock but even the strongest rock breaks. He had a drinking problem that had built up over time, so slowly I hardly noticed. I'd discovered empty bottles tucked away in odd places around our studio and confronted him. Asked him what was going on. He told me. He drank every day. Even at work. At first that didn't mean much to me. I thought drinking was a kind of frat house lark, something you just stopped when common sense kicked in as you saw the world start to crumble around you. I didn't know alcoholism was a disease from which few people ever recover. When Frank's world continued to fall apart and he didn't stop, I was still naive enough to think there'd come a moment when he saw the meter was in the red and give it up.

"I remember that first night…" I looked up shyly for the first time into the faces of the group. Seeing they were silently expressing kindness and empathy allowed me to continue to open up. "Like most couples, we kept each other informed about our whereabouts, whether we were going to be late coming home, or going to be missing dinner, so neither of us would worry. But one night Frank didn't come home for dinner. And he didn't call. That had never happened before in all our years together. I just knew he'd been in an accident. There was no other explanation.

"The hours ticked by and I didn't hear any word. I became more and more worried, then frantic. I called friends. No, they hadn't heard from him either. At midnight, the city hospitals. No, they hadn't admitted him. At two, the morgues. No John Doe's in the last few hours. At three, I was at the police station, demanding the sergeant at the front desk log in a missing person report and get the precinct searching for him immediately. I explained Frank was always so responsible, he'd always called me, you see, to let me know if he'd be even a few minutes late…I tried to convince the sergeant that something terrible had happened to Frank and that this was a real emergency…

"The sergeant finally looked up at me and said one sentence: 'The bars close at four o'clock.'

"It was then I knew I was in terrible trouble. Sure enough, around seven or eight in the morning Frank came home rip-roaring drunk, puking, without a care in the world. Or an apology. The desk sergeant knew his stuff. And I knew nothing.

"Frank's drinking progressed. To protect his reputation, I felt I couldn't share this with anyone. It was our dirty little secret. One I held inside through what were now alarming dire daily episodes. He wouldn't face the fact he was self-destructing in front of us. Though he went to some A.A. meetings, they hadn't helped. They needed time to sink in and he didn't have any left. He turned away from all my pleas. Just to drink. Morning, noon, and night. And he became a haunted man. There were terrible fights between us and threats and I knew he was becoming delusional. One night he just disappeared. Where was he? Nobody knew and nobody could help me find him.

"A few days later, the cops called. With bad news. They'd found my phone number in his wallet. They told me Frank had died. And asked me to come down to the morgue and identify him. It seems he'd checked himself into the Chelsea Hotel where it took only a few days for him to drink himself to death. He'd died in a hotel room not too many blocks from our home.

"Shortly afterwards I joined this bereavement group. And it saved my life. When I timidly came to my first meeting, I was too ashamed to speak because I was afraid of being labeled a loser and a failure. I was full of self-pity and despair. Then I heard other people speak about making a recovery, from the bottom of hell, describing specific events and timetables as proof of how and when things had gotten better for them. As time passed I took advantage of their support, learned what had worked for them, tried some of what they'd tried for myself and decided whether it would work for me. It almost always did. I came to realize I wasn't a loser or a failure, but a strong person who was surviving adversity and at last had something worthwhile to give other people. Besides my own ego."

I heard some laughter travel around the circle and I laughed myself.

"I made friends in this group who never neglected me, who were always here for me. They didn't ever 'not have time.' I gave back what I'd received, gratefully, and made a gratitude list of all the good things I had in my life. And I had plenty. It helped keep my problems in perspective.

"My first sign of progress came when instead of continuing to lament that I had no one to turn off the light anymore, I told the group I'd gotten out of bed and turned it off myself and that it wasn't so bad! Light switches work no matter who turns them on and off."

There was more laughter from the group and at first I felt an exhilaration.

Yet for some reason I pulled back, becoming cautious and less confident. "Of course, I still have days that don't work for me…When I dwell on a question like 'how can I replace something that can't be replaced?'" Suddenly I trembled, and my voice cracked, and I choked out the words, "My loss has been real and has impoverished my life…"

There was a silence from the group in the circle, I

noticed some members looking down at the floor or away from me. Had I said something wrong or offensive?

I tried to get back on track. "Of course, this group convinced me I'd be all right if I took care of myself. They assured me I wasn't responsible for Frank's death. What a relief. He died from a disease, plain and simple. Just as…just as…"

My voice drifted. I stopped thinking clearly, forgetting what I was going to say.

"You know," I finally continued. "I passed an apartment house on the way here. Everybody's curtains were drawn back and sunlight streamed in through the windows where the residents stood gazing out at a clear blue sky, savoring signs of the coming spring. But I noticed one apartment that had its blinds drawn tight. It stood out from all the others. And I knew that an addict lived in that apartment…Don't ask me how, I just knew it.

"We all have to take responsibility for our own lives, our own addictions. You know, they're never anyone else's fault. If the person you're with is bugging you, go seek help. Don't blame them. Don't blame your parents or your lot in life. Or if you're sitting alone in your apartment…doing drugs…or trying to numb your feelings by constantly engaging in sex as an escape…that's your own loneliness, that comes from inside you…no one can do anything about it except you…you and God."

The silence in the room was even heavier.

Reg asked for shares from the group. I could hardly concentrate, but pretended to listen, nodding my head at the speakers in encouragement, but shocked at what had come out of my mouth. It seemed an eternity until a half hour had passed and the shares were finished. The group stood up, I took Reg's hand and squeezed it tightly and grabbed the hand of the stranger on the other side of me and squeezed it too and joined with everyone in the Serenity Prayer. Afterwards I hung around a few minutes, as was customary, and was thanked by other members for sharing.

Reg said good-night without much comment. But he told me he welcomed my return to the group. I wished him good luck on his third date. He shrugged. "We'll see," he said, a little disappointment in his voice. Because of my share? He didn't say. Jack and Linda waved good-bye without a word.

I was the last to leave, after I'd set all the folding chairs back against the wall.

Inside the church it had gotten cold. I could hear the March wind howling outside the doors. I put on my cap and coat.

How weird. I'd brought up sex and drugs at this bereavement group meeting and I guess it had been obvious who I was referring to. Why had I blurted that stuff out?

I had my own feelings of inadequacy. And fear, I guess. My own addiction problems. My own stressors. Had it been the same for Frank?

Tonight what I'd said to the group had been the truth, yet there's always another truth behind the truth.

Man is not a monogamous creature by nature. I truly believe that and I'm not alone. Most couples have slept around or had affairs, but usually on the sly, keeping them hidden from their partner, living a lie. I couldn't do that to Frank. I'd always told him the truth.

One day I met a man and began to have a purely sexual relationship with him. I don't know why. I'm sure there's no simple answer, especially since I didn't even like him. But I continued it, explaining to Frank that since I felt nothing for this man, it didn't have anything to do with the two of us, and when it ended, we'd continue our happy lives forever without him. In my willful mind, it all made perfect sense. I didn't take the time to look and see that it was full of holes. I had inadvertently hurt Frank, badly. It was a humiliating thing to do. No one you love deserves to be treated like that.

I didn't know if I could ever forgive myself, but that was less important than seeking Frank's forgiveness. Or telling him how deeply sorry I was that I had hurt him. We had each caused so much pain for each other—yet the love I felt for him was stronger than ever. It was unconditional. I imagined his love for me would be unconditional as well, and maybe, instead of screaming or talking through the terrible mistakes we'd made, all we'd have to do would be to look in each other's eyes and say nothing, just touch each other's cheeks, and love each other. That might be enough. But it was too late now. He was dead.

I stepped outside. Directly across the street from me was an amazing building, built of red brick three inches thick, the largest building I'd ever seen in the Village, filling an entire block, rising at least eleven floors, with cathedral windows that provided the occupants with spectacular views of New Jersey's Watchung Mountains and the Palisades. The apartments themselves looked like huge lofts, and the wind whipping the sepia clouds over the building made it seem like it was floating along with them, as if it were untethered to the earth.

Suddenly the clouds flew past a full moon that shone directly down on the building, illuminating it so it looked like a sharp razor blade sticking straight up into the sky. It was then I realized this was the Archive Building. One of the evil houses I'd read about—one of the houses of the damned.

I leaned back against the doors of St. Veronica's for support as the wind had picked up and was howling around me. I pulled my coat collar up around my neck. From inside that building I thought I could hear cries, sobbing that seemed to be unrelenting, and desolate sighing, coming from who knew what tormented souls, and for an instant I thought I recognized Frank and my sighs intermingled with them.

\*

This was my fourth visit to Crewe's penthouse. I'd had a different welcome from the concierge each time. The first when I went up with Allison on the elevator that took us straight to the terrace, it was with a polite smile. The second with a sneer as he'd distastefully admitted a trick sneaking up on the sly to see the man of the house while his wife was out of town. The third with noblesse oblige and an ingratiating manner when I had Patrizia on my arm. This afternoon with a businesslike nod that spoke of indifference. Somehow it made me feel I was four strangers boxed into one and that the real me had never set foot in his penthouse.

Clemma and Sidonie hadn't "gotten it together" to go back to St. Barts till now, the end of April. Or that was what Crewe had told me after I'd given him my perfunctory "yes," when he phoned, as he'd promised he would, to ask the question whether or not I'd like to see him again. Not showing surprise or relief at my response, he'd only complained it was high time they'd left him in peace so he could attend to some business matters. He hadn't mentioned he was particularly horny, just invited me up, adding it was warm enough to have a salad on the terrace if I'd like.

However, I'd spent more than one night, after coming back home from being out socializing with Reg or the Krolls, or after finishing a phone conversation with a new member of our bereavement group, or after putting down some novel, feeling horny for him. I hadn't gotten high since I'd spoken at St. Veronica's. But after Crewe's phone call inviting me up, I'd eagerly stuffed a packet of Maxo's Cuervo Gold into my jeans while throwing my navy blue windbreaker over my T-shirt and putting on a pair of tennis shoes. Now as I stood in his vestibule, ringing his buzzer, I wondered if he would even be in the mood for sex.

My fears were allayed when he opened the door, his silver pipe in hand, sucking down smoke before he even closed the door behind me. Then he worked a new clump of grass in the pipe and gave me a hit before saying his first words to me, "Oh, I forgot to ask, did you…"

"Yes," I felt that relaxing warmth slither through my body while I brought the packet of rock out of my jeans and handed it to him.

"Good! The same old John Laith. Some things never change." He finally added, "Thankfully." I followed him into the kitchen where he took the rock from me and did his thing, pulverizing it and evenly distributing it onto two plates, using a razor blade to fine chop the lines before handing me a straw, saying, "Visitor's first."

I did a line and it hit me pretty intensely. I guess because I'd been away from the stuff for awhile. When Crewe did his, a line twice the size of mine, it seemed to have no effect on him whatsoever. Unimpaired, he busied himself pouring each of us a cup of tea. "Don't have green tea this time, only black. Still, it's good for you." I was happy at the news since green tea tasted like liquid chalk to me. "Did you finish what I brought you?"

"I'm still working on it," I lied. He handed me my cup and we stood there sipping the tea. I noticed two plates of radicchio sprinkled with balsamic, which smelled wonderful, a few finely chopped vegetables hidden amongst the dark leaves, and a basket of wheat rolls to the side.

"I thought you might like a bite. Douglas prepared it just before he left. You may have passed him as you came into the building."

"I didn't notice…"

"He's perfect to have around. When the wife and daughter are away. You can't believe what a big help he is to me."

"How fortunate."

"Isn't it?"

Crewe helped himself to another line, this time sighing with pleasure and complimenting its quality.

"I'm glad you've found a good source. That's sure to come in handy." He returned to the subject of Douglas. "He's a gem. He set up a table for us out on the terrace. The weather's temperate enough to allow us to eat outside. For the first time this year. Spring is here. Always means a new beginning, it seems to me."

Crewe was dressed in tan khaki slacks, a white shirt, a rusty hued cashmere sweater and a pair of ash colored sandals. Neither of us would freeze to death on the terrace, obviously, though it was hardly midsummer.

"Oh, go on, do another line," he encouraged me.

"We haven't done this together for ages. Let's take the opportunity to celebrate."

I snorted another line. Which made me want him right now. After my crack binge with Baily and my subsequent search for him, Allison's leaving and my enduring a general bout with depression, and then my return to the group, I suddenly realized how on edge I'd been from it all, and how much I could use an afternoon of forgetfulness.

Crewe read what was on my mind. "But let's not be in a hurry to go outside. The time that's passed between our being together has been way too long. For me at least."

He led me into the living room where he sat down on the couch. The light streamed in from the glass doors to the terrace, casting a sweet white glow everywhere.

Crewe leaned back and unzipped his fly, pulling out his cock, lazily putting his hands behind his head, closing his eyes and sighing, waiting for me to go down on him. I grabbed one of the Persian pillows and knelt down on it in front of him and took his cock fervidly into my mouth, wanting to show him how excited I was to be back. He moaned uncontrollably. Both of us seemed shot through with a radiating desire. The beauty of the mottled sunlight flickered across us, an outside accomplice to our own fulfillment.

Crewe kept tapping his finger on his khaki slacks. Which was impossible not to see out of the corner of my eye as I knelt in front of him. It was the finger with his wedding ring on it, a ring he'd never put on after the first time I'd been with him. He was sending an obvious signal to me.

I pulled off him. "I'm hungry now," I said.

"That's quite obvious," he agreed.

"For a few pieces of greens," I insisted and stood up. "By the way, was any decision made about your volunteering to do service for God's Love We Deliver?"

He stood up as well, trying to stuff his stiff cock back in his pants.

"Be careful you don't get it caught in the zipper," I cautioned.

He ignored me, doing his best. "Yes, and can you believe it? They turned me down. They have enough volunteers at the moment."

"How disappointing for you, after you wanted so badly to help."

"Not at all. I've just gone on to the next good deed." He didn't elaborate.

Fortunately it was about one in the afternoon and the sun was at its zenith, as strong as it was going to get. If we'd gone out any later it would have been chilly and unpleasant. Crewe carried out the salads, the basket of bread, more tea, and we settled down. He put on his glasses and opened the *Wall Street Journal* and began to read while I stared at Central Park, just beginning its process of greening up. We ate silently while Manhattan buzzed spiritedly in a semi-circle around us.

"Did you read about the newly-found fossil of this Ventastega creature?" Crewe asked with a sharp interest.

"Can't say I have."

"It seems the scientists have just made an important discovery. They found the fossil of a four-legged fish that had the head of an animal. A creature that began the evolutionary journey from sea to land. The missing link between fish and mammals." He turned the paper towards me and showed me something that looked a little like an alligator with fins. "Evidently these creatures preferred the land to the sea. You have to understand this was eons before the dinosaurs. In fact," he edged his glasses down his nose, "it's said they were crawling about here four hundred million years ago." He put down the paper which rippled in the breeze and stared at me. "Doesn't that put a lot of things in perspective?"

"What things?"

"Just time. The passage of it. What it means. For instance, all of those books you read by all those wise and wonderful authors, chronicling the saga of the human condition, are just going to be turned into a swirl of cosmic dust someday. They're really just empty baubles, totally meaningless, to be frank, providing the authors' egos with the illusion of a false posterity. In the end they won't even exist. Of course, neither will the buildings I own. They'll become infinitesimal particles of dust too. Buildings built...or books written...they're all constructed or created with the frenzy and purposelessness of ants running circles around themselves in their own anthills. Wouldn't you say?"

"I don't think I've ever heard you be this philosophical before."

"I'm not being philosophical. I'm stating a simple truth."

I put my fork on my plate and stared off at the sky.

"So you see, we only have these few seconds in time to engage in what's really important." Crewe stood up and started clearing the plates off the table. "By the way, I'm not going to leave my wife, that's out of the question."

As he disappeared into the living room I thought, good, she can have you, with my blessings, I wouldn't want you. I was thrilled the offer had been withdrawn. He suddenly stepped back outside, plates still in hand,

"Oh, and you'd be proud of me. I've stopped inviting those strange men up here into my own home, you know, the ones you said might try and steal my silver. You'll be happy to know I totally agree. I took your advice and that kind of thing is all in the past. Except for having you up, of course." Then he went back indoors.

What had happened? Had the concierge shared a few words of concern to Clemma and she'd put an end to his practice? I believed what Crewe had just told me, though not from his own words, but by the concierge's nonchalant attitude towards me today, as if I were a normal visitor, not one in a long line of sexual trysts making their way upstairs.

In the kitchen he was boiling more tea. And smoking dope and snorting lines. I joined him. I'd come to a bizarre and disquieting revelation. I hated this man, yet still wanted to have sex with him. But could that work? And if so, how? I sat down at the kitchen table. And considered it. Hadn't he said, the last time he was at my apartment, if I got really high, I might be able to forget who he was. Well, maybe I could—and forget who I was too.

I could become anyone, a whore, down on my luck, whom he was paying to have sex with, a young hitchhiker forced against his will into granting sexual favors to a surly truck driver, even a mentally disturbed patient from a loony bin who didn't know what I was doing. Or conversely, he could be a kind man I'd totally misread, one who was terribly shy and had an awkward time demonstrating any sensitivity or consideration behind his brusque exterior, or a rapist who'd drugged me and made me his powerless victim, or my real lover.

He'd just said authors cling to their illusions. Real

estate developers as well, no doubt. So must the simplest human being.

I got as high as possible, higher than I'd ever imagined possible, totally coked-up, and we had delirious, intense sex in his and Clemma's big brass bed, sometimes floating dreamily on the oversized down pillows in brief moments of respite, or clinging to them tightly when the sex became exquisite. Hating him was no impediment, because neither of us were who we were.

For hours, we let ourselves stay very lost.

Until suddenly I found myself alone in the bed, wondering where Crewe had gone off to. Suddenly I noticed him standing still at the foot of the bed, in his bathrobe, looking blankly down at me. Disoriented, I turned myself around onto my stomach and crawled along the mattress to the foot of the bed, grabbing onto the brass bars with my hands.

"You're in a prison," he said quietly, "one of your own making."

Then he tossed one of his bathrobes to me, advising me he was going back to the kitchen to boil us some more tea.

I stumbled out of bed and put on the bathrobe. But instead of going to the kitchen, I wandered into his study. His blinds were open. It was evening now or even night as the room was dark, yet there was an eerie glow coming from the center of it. Shaking myself, trying to clear my head, I noticed the glow was coming from his computer. While I was lying in bed, had he put his bathrobe on and come in here and turned it on?

I crossed in front of it and peered down at the screen. There was a picture of a beautiful plant with purple bell-shaped flowers hanging from spiraling green leaves. In the center of the bell-shaped flowers were clusters of shiny black-colored berries.

Above the picture was the name of the species, *Atropa belladonna*. And below it a brief description. This attractive perennial herbaceous plant was not only commonly known as belladonna but also as deadly nightshade, a plant whose leaves and berries were extremely toxic. In fact, it stated, this was one of the most toxic plants in the Western hemisphere. The seeds of the berries were poisonous and, if ingested, could make one's breathing and heartbeat extremely irregular, causing the pulse to beat rapidly—at first—and then stop.

I heard Crewe's voice call out. "Where are you? Come to the kitchen. I've got your tea ready."

I took a slow walk down the long shadowy hallway into the light of the cozy kitchen where Crewe thrust a cup of tea into my hands. "Have some. It'll do you a world of good. You do look a little peaked, if I say so myself." Something in my expression made him add lightly, "From all our extracurricular activity!"

I sat down silently at the table as he fixed a plate of crackers and cut some blocks of cheese. When he looked towards me now and then, jabbering away about how happy he was I'd decided to start seeing him again, as he couldn't find sex like we had anywhere else, I pretended to take a sip. Finally when his back was completely turned and he'd begun a search in the fridge for his favorite black bread, or so he informed me, I quickly stood up and poured the tea down the sink. In my drugged state, I peered over his shoulder as he rummaged through the fridge, seeing if there was a bowl of black shiny berries on any of the shelves, or a vial of crushed seeds from the berries that could easily be slipped into a cup of black tea, but all I saw was a swirl of color, and, dizzily, I sank back down at the table.

"My goodness, I guess we've overdone things," he said, aware of my faltering state.

I was faltering, but somehow my gut feeling told me it was from the grass and cocaine. I didn't feel symptoms different from the ones associated with, as Crewe had laid out in his fussy style, "overdoing things." I wasn't nauseous, I wasn't sweating, my pulse wasn't beating rapidly, my tongue wasn't hanging out of my mouth and I hadn't gone into convulsions.

Crewe looked at me with concern. "I think you need a little help getting home. I'll take you back in a taxi. I'll pay for it. Don't worry, I won't come upstairs. I'll let you rest."

"No, I'm fine…" I said without conviction.

"I didn't come down out of the last shower," he said. "You're not capable of getting home on your own. And I'm going to see to it that you get back safely."

He had to dress me, or help me get dressed, making sure I had my keys and wallet. Afterwards when he went to get dressed, I sat on the couch in the living room, staring at the empty fireplace and my own blurry reflection in the glass doors to the terrace. On an impulse, I got up and swung open the doors and stared at the lights of Manhattan to try and put myself back in my real environment. The lights were there, blinking back at me. I felt like one of them, one that could be turned off at any minute and hardly be missed.

I didn't remember walking past the concierge, whether Crewe had to keep me steady on my feet in front of him or not, and I hardly remembered the doorman flagging us a cab and helping us into the back seat. But we were off. I didn't feel any motion sickness, or any kind of unusual symptoms, I just didn't feel capable of carrying on a conversation. I realized the driver had made it to Lincoln Center, I recognized the Metropolitan Opera House, and the fountain, people mulling around it, and then we were speeding down 9th Avenue in the dark.

*Clemma...my wife...she's trying to poison me...*Crewe had said that once to me in my apartment when I'd been high, not as high as this, but too high to take it in. Whether he had good reason to feel threatened by her or not, what did that say?...If he'd felt threatened by her...and then in turn by me...or furious by my rejection of his request to become his boy...the boy he could completely control...he being someone who kept up such an elaborate facade and was never vulnerable to anybody—except that one time with me—with that one request...what if somehow he thought my refusal had turned me into his enemy...that, by my refusal, I wished him ill...or worse...and now since I'd been the one he'd seen as rejecting his grand, ultimate gesture, he'd decided to poison me because of it. All bets were off, after all. He was no longer offering to leave his wife, I was never going to be his boy. And there was a beautiful plant named belladonna with black shiny berries whose seeds were toxic.

But it was ridiculous. It couldn't be possible. It was the overload of drugs doing the talking, the reason for the pure paranoia I was in the grip of. I was overreacting. There had to be a simpler, less ominous explanation. Even now as we were only blocks from my building Crewe was rubbing the back of my neck, thoughtfully and with care. He eased my head gently down until my mouth was over his stiff cock sticking out of his fly. Dazed, I gave it a few sucks, mortified at what the taxi driver would think if he could see any of it. Or even if he couldn't, whether he'd be able to intuit what was going on. And mortified at how Crewe had me doing something he'd suggested the night of the blizzard that I'd told myself I would never let happen, not in my wildest dreams.

The cab pulled up in front of my building and I got out and slammed the door shut without looking back. Luckily Tony was sweeping up the entryway so I didn't have to fumble for my keys to get into the lobby. I just had to make it to the elevator and wait for the doors to open.

Inside my living room I sat on my couch, took long, deep breaths, and did a visualization.

I was sitting in a garden, in a rocking chair, on the day of the summer solstice, cherries weighing heavy on the boughs of the trees. The wind had been blowing but had stopped and I could hear a lullaby far off. I was holding a child on my knees. We had come to this garden together in the past to pick wild fruit. I remembered him, knee high in the brambles, reaching up into the thickets and grabbing fistfuls of berries and putting them into his basket. I loved this child. I rocked us together, back and forth, in the chair. At some point I looked down into the child's face and realized the child I was holding on my knees was myself, that little boy from long ago, whom the adult me was now nurturing. I hugged him to me and kissed his little brow, assuring him everything would be all right. I could feel his love intensely on this longest day in summer and could hear the lullaby far off ending...

Though it took some doing, I found all of the packets of cocaine in my apartment, the ones hidden in my books, in my socks, in Crewe's box of green tea, and with an unbridled enthusiasm, emptied them into the toilet bowl until all the powder disappeared, mixing with the water into a silvery mist, then dropped the empty packets in after them and flushed them down.

But that was only part of what I had to rid myself of.

I brought the red shoes out of my closet and inspected them. It was true, they were cursed. They had brought a curse down on my head, as they'd brought one down on Jared's. A curse that had brought evil. Their bright sparkle had blinded me into coupling willingly in the depths of darkness with a cruel and fearful man.

I carried them to the window that looked out onto the Seminary and laid them on the floor. The moonlight passed over them, giving them a fluorescent beauty. They had to be destroyed, crushed forever. And what better way than with the silver vase of lilies born of decadence from the Tenebrae club. I would pulverize them to smithereens with that vase.

They lay before me ready to disappear. And end the curse that was on me and prevent it from being passed on to someone else. I lifted the silver vase, but it was too heavy to hold. It slipped from my grasp and crashed down onto my right foot. I screamed in excruciating pain while I heard my bones crush. I screamed out again, one more time, before passing out.

\*

I don't know how long I was out cold. It seemed forever. But Bob McBride told me later it was less than ten minutes. He'd heard my screams, pounded on my door, and when I hadn't answered, had gotten Tony who'd opened up my door with the spare key to my apartment his dad kept in the basement.

I woke up to find both McBride and Tony leaning over me, my foot having been wrapped in a towel. Bob and Tony were each rubbing an ice pack over the towel, ice packs Bob had brought over from his apartment, I heard him tell me, as everything started coming back into focus. But rubbing gently, even ever so gently, wasn't going to cut it. "Stop," I managed to get out. "I can't take the pressure there. Please, that hurts."

"Don't wimp out on us," Tony said, a cigarette dangling from his mouth. "Your foot's as swollen as a fucking beach ball. It needs ice to reduce the swelling." He glared down at me to let me know I'd better hold up like a man.

Bob was less sure. "Maybe we'd better stop. We could be making it worse."

"Don't be stupid," Tony said, flicking a few of the fake lilies lying between my legs out of the way with disdain. "My cousin had a broken foot and the only thing to do was wrap it in ice and keep it from moving. That's all you can do."

I winced. "But I can't move." I admitted in despair, "I couldn't even get up if I tried, it hurts so bad." My eyes wandered to the pair of red shoes in perfect condition lying beneath the window. Tony followed my gaze.

"What the hell were you up to?" he demanded. I could tell he didn't care for the rather high-flown remnants surrounding the scene of this accident. "Flowers, red shoes, and a silver vase so heavy it could have gone all the way through to the apartment below when it fell. Or when you knocked it over. You're a menace to this place."

"Oh, shut up," Bob said. "He's nothing of the sort. Can't you see he's hurt? I'd like to see what you've got in your room."

Tony backed off and asked if I had an ashtray.

"Of course he does. It's right there on the kitchen counter," Bob said.

Tony got up and stubbed out the butt, then casually removed his pack from his shirt pocket, pulled out another cigarette and coolly lit up. "If you're just going to lie there like a big baby, go ahead. But I have better things to do with my time."

"Such as?" Bob asked.

Tony blew some smoke rings our way.

"Help me get him to St. Vincent's emergency room," Bob said. "We're no doctors. He needs looking at."

Tony shrugged and came over and knelt down, telling Bob, "You grab one arm, I'll grab the other, and we'll get him up on his feet and downstairs into a cab."

"No way," I pleaded. "That's impossible. Don't even try it yourselves. Call an ambulance."

Big Deal started up a howl in Bob's apartment. He wanted in on the action too. But of course Big Deal didn't get to accompany me to the emergency room in the back of the ambulance like his master did. And Tony. For all his pointed disinterest, Tony wouldn't have missed it for the world. In fact, he spent the whole ride there calling his buddies on his cell phone and telling them what had happened and giving them a detailed blow by blow description of the ambulance ride and what kind of equipment they had inside it and about how much of a jerk I was that it made me laugh, a little at least, and kept my mind, a little at least, off the pain.

Turns out my foot was in a pretty bad way. The emergency room doctor who evaluated it exuded a serious, professional air, though he looked all of twenty-five. He found multiple fractures, one of them displaced, so he had to manipulate pieces back into their right positions before immobilizing my foot with a splint. The muscle relaxants and sedative he gave me helped ease the pain. Then he wrapped it in a cast. I was ordered to keep the foot elevated at all times. Even though the cast came up over my ankle, I was told I could still wrap a towel over it and apply ice packs regularly, to relieve the swelling. How I'd feel the benefit of any ice through a cast that felt like undiluted dead weight I had no idea. Maybe that was just what the doctor was supposed to say. I could be wearing this cast for weeks or months. It all depended on me. How I behaved as a patient. Immobilization was the key to healing. When the cast came off the proof of how immobilized I had been would be in the pudding, the doctor added, before moving on to his next emergency.

"You're just like a mummy now," Tony said as he and Bob helped me into the cab for the ride back home, making sure I wasn't putting any weight on the broken foot. "Shouldn't be able to get up to any more tricks in your condition. And I was dead right about the ice."

"Yeah, you were. Thanks, guys."

Bob made sure I was settled as comfortably as possible in the back before he slid in next to me. "Feeling better now?"

"Feel like a million. The sedative hasn't worn off yet."

"What time is it?" Tony asked.

Bob checked his watch. "Six a.m."

Tony said, "I'm not gonna ride back with you guys. I'm gonna walk home and stop at the diner and get some bacon and eggs on the way. I'm starving."

I had plenty of help from friends. They each quickly assumed specific roles and saw to different tasks I wasn't able to perform. Linda Kroll stopped by each day and brought in groceries and pre-cooked some meals for me and did a general dust up and sometimes even a full cleaning. When I protested and told her she wasn't my hired maid, she told me to go ahead and think of her that way.

"Why the hell not?" she asked. "Then you won't feel guilty about it."

She'd been the one to put my red shoes back in my closet and gotten Tony and one of his buddies to throw out the big silver vase and lilies. "That's a pretty ugly piece of work, anyway," she said. "Wherever did you find something like that?"

"It's a long story." And one I didn't want to tell. As for the shoes, I almost asked her to throw them out, but I didn't because I pictured her dropping them into some trash bin where a stranger might discover them and, liking the looks of them, take them home to try on.

As for Tony and his buddy, they refused a tip for carting the vase away, Tony telling me he was doing the building a favor by getting rid of a hazard like that. I figured they'd try to sell it off and make a few bucks, and more power to them.

Linda's husband, Jack, came up and played Scrabble with me nearly every night, whether I wanted to or not. And chewed the fat. And iced my foot. And gave me aspirin. He told me that he secretly thought Linda loved coming over and taking care of me because it reminded her of being with her son who'd been a Prozac suicide. I didn't know how I felt about that, if it was healthy or not, but what could I do about it anyway, I was immobilized.

Until it dawned on me I didn't have to be quite that immobilized. The doctor had mentioned after a week or so I could try some crutches. That's where Reg came in. He and Bob took me to an orthopedist who fitted me for a pair, adjusting them for my height and weight, and showing me how to use them in a "non-weight bearing" way, telling me never to balance myself with my broken foot, but bend the knee and let that leg swing a bit, keeping the weight on my arms and hands and not on my armpits. And if I found myself putting weight on my broken foot when I was on the crutches to stop using them. It seemed a tall order.

Reg was into regimentation and took me for walks each day, increasing the length of the walks gradually, always starting with me managing to get down the four steps of my apartment building on my own, then to the end of the block, then halfway around the next one, and finally circling the Seminary all the way back around the block. After making it around the Seminary for the first time, it seemed like I'd just finished a victory lap, so Reg and I sat on the steps outside my building to relax, no pressure on my foot of course, and soak in the May sunshine for a bit.

"I'm going to have to start working out to build up the muscles in my arms," I told Reg.

"I guess I should find you one of those arm pulleys, you know, the ones on springs."

"That's OK. I was kind of kidding. I'm building up my muscles just by using these damn crutches, which have sure made my arms sore."

"Well, that's all part of the deal."

Funny, Reg had never asked about how the vase had happened to topple over on my foot. I had a lie waiting, that I'd simply bumped into the table Allison and Logan had brought me and the rest was history. But I never had to use it. At this point I was tired of always having some kind of lie at the ready, even a little white one, to cover my behavior. To me that was a sign of a fracture in my life separate from the ones in my broken foot.

"By the way, how did that third date go?" I asked Reg, remembering he'd told me he'd thought he'd found a prospective mate the night I spoke at our group. He looked a bit perturbed by my question.

"We're on our sixth now—and counting."

"Oh-oh."

"And you shouldn't worry about that, but concentrate on the way you're walking. Sometimes I've noticed you let your bad foot touch the cement. You need some kind of DVD that shows somebody demonstrating how to walk correctly."

"Are you kidding? That would bore me to tears."

That afternoon I got an e-mail from Allison. She'd had a little girl whom she'd named Anne. The baby was healthy and she and Logan had acclimated well to Burlington. I quickly e-mailed her back and said how happy I was for her. I told Allison to kiss the baby for me and say hello to Logan and that I'd had an accident and broken my foot, but when I was fully healed that Burlington would be my first destination, to see all of them.

She must have been right at her computer because I got an immediate e-mail in return asking, "Oh, my God, how did something like that happen? Did you get run over by a delivery boy on his bike or something?"

I e-mailed her back. "No, Allison, I was lifting that vase Logan helped me put up on the table to try and crush a pair of shoes and it slipped out of my hands, landed on my foot, and broke it."

She e-mailed me back. "Very funny, I'll take the delivery boy version. Love and xxx's from Logan, Anne, and Allison."

That night my door buzzer rang unexpectedly. I hoped it wasn't Crewe, who'd left a message on my voicemail I'd erased without listening to. I wasn't ready to deal with him—yet. But he had shown up unannounced at my door one night before and if this was him again I wouldn't let him in. That's what peepholes were for.

As I was sitting back on my sofa, my leg elevated, I had to reach for my crutches on a nearby chair and hobble over to the door. The distorted face on the other side of the peephole belonged to Reg. I opened the door and he hurried in excitedly. "I found just the thing," he announced.

"Hold on," I said, easing myself back onto the couch and elevating my leg. "Did you know Allison just had a baby? I thought we could send her some flowers."

"I already took care of that. Sent her a bouquet of white roses in both our names."

"Oh, you're so good. Let me pay you for my share. My wallet's on the bureau in the bedroom."

"Skip it. You can take me out to a swank dinner when your cast comes off. To thank me for nursing you back to health."

"It would be my privilege."

He was turning on my DVD player and putting in a disc. He used the control to fast forward it to some scene he'd already scoped out.

"You didn't get me some instructional thing," I groaned.

"Yes, I did. Watch."

It was the movie *Double Indemnity*. The scene where Fred MacMurray walks down the length of the train corridor, on crutches, after he and Barbara Stanwyck just finished off her husband in her car. His plan is to be noticed, but not identified, by all the passengers, since he's impersonating her husband who happened to be on crutches with a broken leg, jump off the back end of the slow moving train, then place Barbara's dead husband on the tracks to make it look like he'd had an unexpected fall from the train, and of course, collect the insurance with the double indemnity clause for accidental death.

Reg played the scene in slow motion and showed me the dexterity with which Fred walked a straight line down the train corridor, how he turned to maneuver himself in tight quarters, how he opened the door to the observation deck, and, how, once on the deck, he unexpectedly ran into a good old boy and had to twist and turn to avoid his scrutiny. Reg pointed out the way Fred either stood still or swiveled around, using just his arms and hands, always keeping his foot inches off the ground.

And something clicked.

I understood the way Fred was utilizing his crutches as an extra set of limbs.

The next day even in a light rain, even though the sidewalk was slippery, I made my way around the Seminary block with a newfound ease and confidence, taking my cue from Fred. Then tried it again. Before, my mind had been over-engaged in each little movement I'd been making. But now the crutches were a part of me, not something alien, and I'd finally gotten the hang of using them instinctively. I was no longer immobile.

\*

The trip to Binghamton was supposed to be four hours in duration, according to Greyhound information. As a handicapped person I was able to reserve the seat across from the driver, right by the door, so I could keep my leg stretched out, which was a necessity. I mean, I couldn't have it sticking out in the aisle or cramped up against the back of some seat.

My departure time from Port Authority was seven a.m., my booked return time four-thirty five p.m. I'd planned the trip for a Saturday, and had arranged for car service to take me to Port Authority and to be waiting for me there when I got back, hopefully in one piece. I was relieved I wasn't going to have to fight rush hour traffic, though come to think of it, any hour in the vicinity of 42nd Street and 8th Avenue was rush hour. But that wasn't the reason I was going up on a Saturday. That was the only day Philip Deerman had advised me that Jared would be available to see me.

I'd never spoken with Philip Deerman before. I found his name and phone number in my address book, the librarian friend whom Jared had consulted before coming down to New York, and the contact whom I'd asked Jared for the morning I'd packed him off to Port Authority, in case I felt I needed to check up on him later and be sure he was doing OK. I never had.

But I'd had a lot of time on my hands, being laid up, time for thoughts to rumble around in my head, some of them new and unexpected, and I'd come to the realization that I had some unfinished business with Jared.

When I'd phoned Philip Deerman and told him who I was, a friend of Jared's from New York, he'd sounded wary. No, alarmed.

"What's your name?" he'd demanded.

"John Laith from Chelsea. He'll remember me, I'm sure."

"I don't know that," he said. "Give me your number and I'll consult with Jared and phone you back and let you know one way or another if it would be all right for you to visit." Then he'd hung up abruptly.

What an asshole, I thought. If I'd only known Jared's last name, I'd have looked him up and phoned him myself.

I'd gotten a call back an hour later though. Not from Jared, but from this Deerman character. "You can come this Saturday. Take the seven a.m. Greyhound from Port Authority and we'll pick you up at the depot on Chenango Street at eleven. You can have four hours with Jared. That's all." Then another hang up.

What the fuck? Was Jared in the slave trade now and was this guy his pimp? I could have four hours. What the hell did he think he was arranging? Well, Jared could have been in the slave trade, I suppose, as handsome as he was, with his long black hair and dark-blue doe eyes and finely shaped porcelain face and milky chiseled chest, the one he'd proudly displayed when I'd first seen him in the gay parade, weaving his way dizzily down my block in his red shoes.

From my handicapped perch in the front row of the bus, I looked out at the scenery, at farms dotting newly verdant fields, small towns clustered here and there in low valleys, sometimes the trickle of a stream or two surrounded by tall oaks and sycamores with new full leaves. Clouds passed overhead, sometimes dark gray, sometimes white, the sun piercing through to light the landscape now and then, but sheets of rain obscuring it just as often. It was off and on weather.

When I heard the bus driver blurt out "Binghamton," through a scratchy mike, I'd almost fallen asleep, was ready for a nap. Four hours had gone by quickly. We turned abruptly off the highway and made our way through the suburban streets. Or, God, what passed for suburban streets. The area was urban blight unexpurgated, shops and buildings sloping in disrepair, lots of seedy laundromats stuck between fast food joints, and dozens of sorry little houses with "Rooms to Let" signs in the windows, the sidewalks occasionally occupied by a few dreary souls who looked like life had bled them dry. No wonder Jared had tried to make an escape.

As the bus approached the depot I could see the streets of the downtown area, which were much more seemly, with old historic red-bricked loft type buildings which appeared to have a few businesses in them on the ground floors. Yet there was something that even seemed forlorn about them. As if they existed for no good reason.

I waited outside the depot on the sidewalk. I'd told Deerman I would be hard to miss, on crutches with a broken foot. But I waited there a good ten minutes. Was I being stood up or what? Finally a man in a shiny blue Ford Taurus that had been parked in a metered space across the street the whole time I'd been standing there, and who had glanced at me a few times as I waited, finally moved the car out of its spot, did a U-turn and pulled up right in front of me and opened the passenger door.

"Get inside," he said.

I lay my crutches on the front seat between him and me, eased myself down in the passenger seat and shut the door. The man extended his hand, "Philip Deerman."

I shook it. "Where's Jared?"

"Waiting." He pulled away and started driving. I looked him over. From his voice I'd expected somebody more rough hewn. But this man who seemed to be in his mid-thirties looked like the stereotype of the placid, erudite librarian, bespectacled and rather mild-mannered, that you'd find in Any Town, U.S.A. Though I'd long ago come to stop stereotyping anybody. It was always a mistake.

Deerman looked me over like I was the new animal just brought to the zoo—and on exhibit. He was the keeper who was going to decide whether or not he would keep me caged or let me have a little space to roam. And he was going to feel his way first before making any final decision.

"Nice, quiet town," I made conversation. "Are you from here?"

"Born and bred a few streets from here, and I'll never leave Binghamton. The lights of the big city hold no fascination for me." Then he sneered.

"Good for you. A man who knows what he wants."

"That's right…"

The place was a dead end. It was crumbling in front of him. Didn't he know it?

"And what happened to you, Mr. Laith? You look like Fred MacMurray from that movie *Double Indemnity*."

I laughed, naturally. For some reason that put him at ease. And he laughed too.

"Only I didn't kill anybody, Mr. Deerman. And arrange their body under the wheels of the bus so I could collect the insurance."

I guess this humor was a little too black for him since his laughter died pretty quickly. He frowned. "Look, Mr. Laith," he started, but I interrupted him with, "Call me John, you don't have to be so formal."

"All right, John, you see—"

"Excuse me, can I call you Philip?"

He thought awhile. "I'd almost rather you didn't. That presumes a familiarity I'm not sure I want to have with you."

You rude fuck, I thought.

"Then you can return to calling me Mr. Laith, as well."

"Thank you. I'd prefer to anyway."

We were crossing a bridge over a big river. Deerman could see my interest and surprise. "The Susquehanna," he announced with a keen pleasure, as if he'd just mentioned the Seine or the Thames.

"Very lovely river."

"You see, Mr. Laith, as I was starting to explain, Jared and I are an 'item.' We have been ever since he returned from New York."

I should have expected it, but hadn't. I mean it had been staring me in the face, yet I couldn't see that wild boy settled down with this…well, sort of drip.

"I see. I hadn't known. That's wonderful."

We'd crossed the river and he pulled into a space in a parking lot adjacent to it then turned and looked at me sharply. "Yes, it is. And it's been a godsend—for Jared."

And for you, you horny piece of work, I thought.

"Just keep it in mind," he said.

He led me along the river walkway, boats streaming

down the rough-crested waves. The sunlight was still playing games, like Deerman, I thought, peeking through now and then and sometimes disappearing altogether as drops of rain blew into your face. People were sitting on benches watching the river or the tired buildings that made up the downtown area across from it. Deerman stopped in front of one of the benches. There was a boy sitting on it staring into space. He looked up at me, then stood and put out his hand to clasp mine, but saw that would be difficult to do with me on crutches and withdrew it.

"That's OK, Jared. Don't worry about it." It was Jared, but not the Jared I'd known.

"Hello, there," he said and gave a shy smile. "It's been a long time."

"Almost a year now," I agreed.

His long black locks that had hung alluringly over his forehead were gone in favor of a standard crew cut. He wore a conservative Ivy League white sweater with blue and red bands around the collar and cuffs, a white shirt collar sticking out, navy blue slacks and dark dress shoes. He stood formally and stiffly.

"Are you all right?" he asked me.

"The crutches? Yeah, don't worry about it."

"Well, let's all sit down, why don't we?" Philip Deerman said. We did, on the bench, the three of us, but with Deerman sitting between Jared and me. That was an awkward arrangement to say the least as I'd come to see Jared. But Deerman wasn't having any part of it. He started off, "You see, Mr. Laith, across the river, that's Court Street, the nicest street in town, it's where we live, you see over there, that loft with the gabled roof, the whole top floor is ours. We own it," he stressed. "I dearly love this city but it's best to have a government job here, I'll admit it. We have a slight unemployment problem. But I'm so proud of Jared. When we became partners…when he got back from Manhattan," he added distastefully, then quickly cheered up as he continued, "I coached him for the civil service Librarian Assistant test and he passed it. In fact, we work in that building directly behind us, together, in the Broome County Library. And Jared's busy taking classes at the Broome County campus to get a degree in Library Science."

I leaned forward and looked over Deerman at Jared. "Is that right?"

Jared smiled. Genuinely. And nodded yes.

Philip Deerman continued to talk and I leaned back on the bench and stared across at the loft where they lived. "Jared's family is so proud of him. His dad's bursting his buttons. No one in his family has ever graduated college before. Sometimes his younger sisters come down here to the river walk and we all have a picnic during our lunch break. You see, Mr. Laith, Jared and I are involved in building up our community here. Well, I am, and Jared will be too some day. I was recently named to the River Trails Commission by the Waterfront Advisory Council. I work on the Arts and Entertainment Board and review and make recommendations for what kind of events to plan along the river trails. During the summer and autumn months especially. It's all part of the Local Waterfront Revitalization plan and I've recently booked—"

"I'm really happy for both of you," I interrupted him. "It sounds like you've made a wonderful life here together," I added, obvious impatience showing in my tone, even though I was happy for them. And maybe I'd misread Deerman. He did seem to have Jared's interests at heart in the purest sense, to want to help him develop and see him prosper. But I hadn't come here to have a conversation with a stranger about the city of Binghamton and its revitalization plans.

Philip Deerman got the picture. But didn't change it. He just suggested we all go find a nice place for lunch as we had more than enough time before my bus was scheduled to leave for New York.

I was silent. So was Jared.

"Well," Philip Deerman laughed uneasily, having to admit the truth. "I suppose you didn't just come up here for an old-fashioned chin wag, did you?"

"No, I didn't, Mr. Deerman. In fact I'd like some time alone with Jared."

"That's not going to be possible," he answered.

"Philip, please," Jared finally spoke up. "Give us a minute to ourselves, will you? My…friend…has come up all this way to see me."

Deerman grimaced. "Each new rich day," he sighed. "You never know what's coming down the pike at you."

"You don't have to leave us. Just let us have a conversation by ourselves. Go stand for awhile by the railing over there and give us a moment's privacy," Jared urged.

Philip Deerman turned to Jared, unhappily, and I saw him vacillating. Finally he relented, "Yes, all right then, I don't suppose I could deny you anything." He moved off at a discreet distance and stood at the railing as instructed, looking out at the waves—for now—but biding his time I suppose until he was back with the two of us.

Again and suddenly, a new swath of rain started coming down, spring rain, light, but blowing every which way. Jared seemed to ignore it, while I loved it, finding it refreshing. Suddenly it brought back the night of the storm with both of us huddled together under the awning in the Meatpacking District. But had that ever happened? This wasn't the same person.

I turned to him. "Jared, do you like your life here? With Philip? Are you happy?"

"Yes. I am. And you?"

"That's not important right now. I came up to ask you a question, if you don't mind my asking. It seems you've made such a transition to a new way of living, I almost hate to bring it up, in case it makes you uncomfortable, but I have to know. And I won't say anything to Philip."

"What is it?" he asked with the same nervousness I remembered he'd exhibited in my apartment when he'd told me his story, after the storm. There. I'd finally found the boy again that I was looking for, the one I needed answers from.

"Jared, those red shoes you gave me, did you ever feel they brought you bad luck?"

He thought for a minute. "I couldn't really say."

"But didn't you tell me, that after you'd seen them in that window, and knew you just had to have them, that after you'd bought them, your gift for dancing disappeared…and that you gave up…you told me your career as a dancer was over…"

I could see his lip trembling ever so slightly but he remained quiet.

"And you turned your attention to other things…"

"You mean sleeping around with a lot of different men."

"That's right…and when you lived at that hotel…well, you told me about a fantastic man you called the Electric Man...the Electric Man, who would come after you, bothering you...who wouldn't leave you alone...who you were afraid of..."

His mouth opened and through the misty rain I could see fear in his eyes. The same fear I'd seen before when he'd described him to me almost a year ago.

"Jared, did you ever know a man named Crewe James?"

He was silent. And seemed stunned.

"Answer me, Jared, please," I said.

"Yes, I knew him," he said slowly and dejectedly.

"Did he come to see you at the hotel?"

"Yes."

"A lot?"

"I don't remember."

I looked into his eyes. "Were Crewe James and the Electric Man one and the same to you?"

I could see he didn't want to answer me, that it was hard for him, but he did. "Yes."

"They were? When you told me the story of the Electric Man, you were really talking about a man named Crewe James who came into your hotel room and had sex with you? Only you were afraid of him and didn't like to think about him, so that in your mind you turned him into someone that you called the Electric Man."

In the distance I could see Philip Deerman had tired of staring at the river and was now watching us, and I knew my time was quickly running out.

"Please, Jared, let me know if what I'm saying is right."

"I told you 'yes.'"

"And at some point you were so afraid of him, you called the police and asked them to contact Crewe James and tell him to leave you alone."

Jared stood up, covering his face with his hands. Deerman was sprinting our way.

"Did he ask you to be his boy…did he say he'd take care of you…did he ask you to put yourself in his hands…was he the person you meant when we were standing under the awning in the storm and you cried out the words to me, 'that man!'"

"Yes, yes!" Jared yelled, his hands still covering his face.

"That's enough of this!" Philip Deerman, the meek librarian, had me by the collar.

Jared brought his hands down from his face, which was pale.

"Get up, Mr. Laith. You've upset Jared. Happy now, are you? I knew what a mistake this was from the minute you phoned. I'll leave you off at the bus depot—and you can feel lucky I'll provide you with even that courtesy."

I pulled myself up, with great dexterity, I must add.

Deerman grabbed my shoulder and moved me along the river walk. I turned to shout good-bye to Jared but he'd gotten off his bench and was at the railing staring down at the river. As Deerman was ducking my head in the car, like I was some suspect who'd just been arrested, I looked back towards the railing and saw Jared, now turned towards us, and he was waving good-bye to me. As Deerman tore out of the parking lot, Jared continued to wave good-bye slowly, like someone beckoning to a ship to come in from the ocean out of a fog, letting the captain and crew know they'd found safe harbor.

Meanwhile Philip Deerman bristled and brooded all the way to the bus depot, which wasn't that far away. As he purposely jerked the car to an abrupt halt in front of the entrance, he said, "Don't call here again, Mr. Laith.

Jared has left your kind of life behind for good. The sad life of a drifter in a world of other sad drifters. He doesn't need to have anything to do with you people."

I hobbled out of the car and let him shut the door behind me himself.

Inside the terminal I sat down on a plastic orange chair and stretched out my leg. Unfortunately there were a few hours left to wait until departure time. But I'd gotten answers to my questions though. And finally understood perhaps the most fearful of the curses the red shoes had passed along from Jared to me, the same sociopath.

But I'd also been put in my place. It's too bad Philip Deerman didn't realize I'd found Jared with a champagne bottle up his ass, had taken him in when he was wet and naked and didn't have a dime, had made sure he was all right, and then given him some money so he could get back home, the only reason he was with Deerman now, yet I was one of "you people," that's who I was.

\*

I'd never had a voice with Crewe, had never allowed myself to have one, not like I had with my friends, or even with strangers. It had always been different with him. I'd never been able to speak to him in a way that stood up to him or that let him know I knew who he was. In a way, I'd always been that boy he was looking for and hadn't even realized it. But today would be different. I'd invited him to my apartment not just to let him see I wasn't that boy that drove our dreams, his consciously, and mine, perhaps, subconsciously, but to have a discussion with him about the red shoes.

He came in unaware of my purpose, expecting, I suppose, things to be business as usual, whether that meant he hoped to have breathtaking sex with me or try and find a way to poison me or both. His agenda wasn't clear. Mine was.

When he arrived and saw me standing on crutches with my foot in a cast, his mouth fell open in genuine amazement, one of the first reactions I'd seen from him that hadn't had some calculation behind it. "What in the world happened to you?" he asked in bewilderment.

"I had an unexpected accident," I replied.

"Well, yes, I can certainly see that. But how did this accident come about?"

"It's a private matter," I answered.

The hint of a frown creased his forehead. It wasn't a response he liked. "You know me, I like to have specifics," he said, anticipating them, then realizing when he wasn't going to get them, continuing lightly, "I brought you a second gift." He pulled out a tin of tea from his knapsack. "Black, this time, hope you don't mind, but I got the distinct feeling you didn't really care for the green."

"I thought I'd mentioned I'm not much of a tea drinker, period. Just put it on the counter for me…If you don't mind."

"Oh, of course…it's going to take me some time to get used to you like this, but in the meantime, just let me know how I can help you along," he said, passing in front of me to lay the tin down on the kitchen counter. "In fact, I should offer to brew some up for us, I suppose. It would be just the thing for you in the state you're in and it's so much more beneficial than coffee. And seeing that you're going to have plenty of time on your hands while you mend, I could show you the best way to brew it."

"I'm not interested. But brew some for yourself, if you like."

"No," he answered slowly, mulling it over, "let's not bother. I'll just pour myself a glass of water, if that's all right. You have some that's cold in the fridge, as usual?"

"Yes, help yourself."

"Would you like a glass?"

"No, thanks."

He washed his hands at the sink before pouring himself a glass of water. Then he returned with it to the couch where he sat down. He was wearing a starched white cotton shirt with gray stripes, a gray blazer with silver buttons, dark slacks, and a pair of gray suede shoes, while I'd made myself as comfortable as possible in a loose pair of beige pants, a navy blue T-shirt, one foot in a sandal, the other in a cast. He pulled his little silver pipe out of his blazer pocket and a Ziploc bag of grass from his knapsack. As he unzipped it, I could smell its fragrance. "Oh my," he said. "This is very fresh. That only means good things for the two of us. And with a mixture of the white..." He looked up at me. I didn't tell him I didn't have any of the white stuff anymore. And because I didn't comment, I could read in his expression that he knew something in the air was different, but it wasn't his way to confront any situation directly.

"I can see it won't be easy having sex with you in your condition," he observed. "Or will it?"

I left him to ponder that and propelled myself over to the window where I stood staring out at the Seminary.

It was a brilliant May afternoon, breezy, with billowing white clouds slowly moving overhead beneath a light azure sky, the kind of sky you only see in the spring. The planters on the streets below were full of blue irises with yellow centers and clusters of grape hyacinths. A few people moved leisurely along the sidewalk. It was quiet for this hour.

I heard him sucking in on his pipe then smelled the aromatic smoke wafting my way.

"Want your hit?" he asked.

"No," I said, staring at the red rust bricks of the Seminary, bright in the mid-day, flushed with sunshine. A vine of wisteria full of rich clumps of violet blossoms cascaded down over the Seminary wall and their scent drifted in through my window on a pleasant breeze.

"You know," I said, "today reminds me of the first time you came up here to my apartment. That was a beautiful day too, like this one. We stood together in front of this same window, only it was a little later in the afternoon then. The bricks of the Seminary were a deeper gold as evening was coming on." I paused. "We rubbed up against each other, held each other, and kissed...remember?"

"Yes," he said, taking another hit and blowing out some more smoke.

I studied the high clouds moving across the light blue sky that stretched beyond the roof of the Seminary before I turned around, hanging on my crutches like a marionette, but one without strings, and faced him. "You know, there was something I always wanted to ask you about that night but never had the courage. After we'd been so intimate with each other, and had such amazing sex, you said to me, 'I feel dead inside.' Why?"

"It's just the kind of thing you can say to a stranger."

What an unsatisfactory explanation. But, I guess, when it came right down to it, the expected dodge. There was no use pushing it further.

I made my way into the bedroom, tooling rather expertly on my crutches, a little bit of the showoff in me, and returned with the pair of red shoes and, bending carefully at the knee, set them down in the middle of the floor.

"Have you ever seen these shoes before?" I asked, straightening up, and leaning forward expectantly on my crutches.

Crewe glanced at them disinterestedly, his eyes glazed over from the grass.

"Well?" I asked, waiting for a reply.

"No," he answered. "I've never seen them before."

"I think you have. You used to know a kid named Jared. They were his."

His lips tightened, almost imperceptibly. "Jared?"

"Yes, Jared. You used to go to his hotel room to have sex with him. On a regular basis. On one of those visits you must have noticed these shoes. They're too unusual to miss."

He decided not to deny it. Or ask me how I knew about it. With him being so clever and superior, it would have been a sign of weakness if he had. Because, like Houdini, I knew he prided himself on being able to extricate himself from the most elaborate confinements, the most cumbersome shackles.

"Maybe I saw them before," he admitted. "I'd hardly remember, would I? That was some time past."

"What ever happened to Jared, I wonder."

"I wouldn't have the slightest idea and I don't care either, to be frank. But I have to ask why all of this has any importance for you?"

"Because I was thirty-five. Old enough to know

better. Only I didn't. But Jared, an eighteen-year-old. Isn't that stooping a bit low, even for you?"

He calmly considered for a moment before answering in an even tone, "If you're asking me if an eighteen-year-old is more supple, more beautiful, and more innocent than a thirty-five-year-old, my answer would have to be 'yes.'"

"I can only imagine what you did to his innocence."

"Yes," he said, unperturbed, "you can only imagine."

I swiveled around on my crutches and returned to the window where I stared back outside, this time seeing nothing, as, after that little exchange, my own unhappy thoughts kept me from appreciating any of the beauty that lay before me.

Crewe asked suddenly, "Are we going to have sex here today—or not?"

I stood still, shoulders slumped. Yeah, it was all about getting back to the nuts and bolts. Nothing else mattered. Nothing else existed.

When no answer was forthcoming he said with annoyance, "For some reason I have a feeling you could have slipped into one of your 'I'm not in the mood' moments."

The Seminary came back sharply into focus and with it, the resplendent sky full of white clouds blowing by overhead. I sighed with relief.

"You know, I had a dream once that took place over there," I said. "In the Seminary. But in my dream it was nighttime. It began in the garden, close to the Chapel of the Good Shepherd, near your bench. I was making my way past all the flowers, as it was summer, anxious to get inside the Seminary itself and up the stairs to where the students were sleeping to warn them about something, some imminent danger. On my way through the garden I'd noticed a menacing figure in a black robe with a hood like a monk's, leaning silently back against the garden wall, hiding. I couldn't see his face. Yet I knew he had a key in his robe pocket, to the students' rooms, and I felt he was a stalker who planned to harm them. So I realized I had to reach them quickly, before this hooded figure did, who was following behind me, who was right at my heels on the stairs. And I did. I got to their rooms first and tried desperately to wake them up, shaking them, begging them, 'Please, please wake up…wake up…I'll tell you everything I know…'

"For the longest time, when that dream would come back to me, I figured the whole thing was about me trying to warn the students about this shadowy figure. But I was wrong. Now I know what it was that I'd wanted to warn them about…to never move far from their own hearts or from their own well-being. That had been the 'everything I know,' but I'd only known it in a dream, in the shadowy depths of sleep, not in my own waking life."

I heard Crewe stand up. He said with a stifled fury, just on the edge of being kept in check, "The answer about whether we're going to have sex today or not is apparently 'no.'" He continued, "It seems I was invited down here to witness a theatrical performance of some kind, to sit passively in the audience and watch an actor without any talent try and deliver an irrefutably mediocre soliloquy. I really must thank you for your consideration."

I felt I was standing on a wavering plank, first tilting towards my own revelation, then to the reality of Crewe standing in my apartment and what he'd just said. The plank finally settled with a thud on Crewe's side. But his black mood had changed. Gone were the anger and the biting words. He was cheerily packing up, putting his pipe into the Ziploc alongside the clumps of grass and stuffing them back into his knapsack. He caught my eye. "There's no use in my getting so wrought up, I suppose," he said. "Certainly not with you being hurt and in the circumstances you're in."

My performance, he had said. If so, this must be the finale. But it wasn't the big curtain closer I might have expected. In fact, I could only hear the curtains hanging above the stage barely drawing shut.

"I'll let you get on with what you were doing," he said gently, coming up to me. "Enjoying the nice view from your window. I've always said how much I admire that view as well...I hope it continues to be pleasant for you to gaze out onto the world. I surely wouldn't want to interrupt your contemplation of it."

He opened the door to leave then paused. "You see, you really don't have to worry about my welfare."

"Your welfare?" I stammered.

"It was bound to happen. With my profile on the Internet. That eventually I would end up meeting someone in the area equal to you...just as talented sexually...just as sweet...only perhaps...a bit fresher... My needs are being well attended to... Anyway I couldn't forgive myself if I were a trouble to you now when you have this injury. Best to let you heal up and not be such a pest." He smiled at me, then said, "Good afternoon," and left, closing the door behind him.

Dazed, I returned to the window. Everything was as beautiful as before...with the Seminary bathed in light and the blossoms on the wisteria vacillating airily back and forth in the soft breeze coming up from the river...But this wasn't the way things were supposed to have gone. When I'd been lost in a moment of revelation, he'd attacked, just like the first time when he'd been waiting on the bench outside the chapel, when I'd been lost in contemplation and in prayer. But this time around it was meant to have ended differently. I was to have had the last word. I was supposed to have asked Crewe to leave, after revealing I knew all about him and Jared and the red shoes and how I thought that made him one sick fuck. But he'd left on his own with a smile and an air of unconcern. Letting me know there was someone else waiting for him in the wings, someone he preferred over me.

Suddenly furious, I wanted to scream at him, tell him to fuck off for good, to drop off the face of the earth and take his shadow with him. How dare he give me a parting kiss-off like that.

I threw open my door and hobbled to the elevator, angrily pressing the button. I could hear the car practically stopping on every floor. I'd take the fucking stairs if I had to, on crutches, if it didn't come soon, because I wanted to be sure to see the back end of him. With my own two eyes. And to shout out to him to stay well away from me.

I was seething when the elevator doors finally opened and I wiggled inside with a bunch of other residents, ticked off at having to make room for me.

The elevator began its descent. I'm sure everybody looked at me like I was crazy or a volcano ready to erupt. Well, they had it right, I was.

When the doors opened onto the lobby, I pushed my way out of the car in front of everybody else, the handicapped first, and swung my body on the end of my crutches towards the lobby door and then, once outside, leaning against the side railing, down the four steps and onto the sidewalk.

I could see him in the distance nearing the corner of 9th Avenue. I'd gotten to see the back end of him after all. But that wasn't enough. I started chasing along after him, as I still wanted to give him a piece of my mind. But I'd never be able to catch up with him and I knew it, though I was giving it a hell of a try, moving so fast I was letting my broken foot drag on the cement until it was starting to hurt.

When Crewe turned the corner, heading north and disappearing from sight, I ground to a halt, giving up, now really aware of the sharp pain in my foot.

My sprint had exhausted me, left me bereft of energy. I turned around and limped slowly back to the apartment, trying not to drag my broken foot which felt just like a pincushion for thousands of tiny sharp invisible pins. But I had managed to see the back end of him…I'd accomplished that much at least.

Getting up the four steps that led to the building entrance was a chore. I had to secure each step with my crutches first, then lift my whole weight with my arms to move up step by step. It was slow going. But I'd seen the last of him…

No more phone calls, no more mind games, no more sex. He had somebody else now, didn't he, to mind and body fuck.

I pulled myself up the last step and dragged myself inside the lobby, using my crutches like the oar of a boat, trying to bring a tired drifter back to shore.

Someone "a bit fresher," hadn't he said?

I waited at the elevator.

I doubted that. How could he have possibly found someone to rival me in any way—or to put up with him.

The elevator doors opened and I moved inside and leaned back against the wall and wiped my sweating brow with my hands.

What was going on? Was part of me jealous now?

The elevator door opened onto my floor and I could hear Big Deal barking away like on any other day. Bob would probably look in after me sometime later on. Maybe Linda would bring over some supper.

I opened my apartment door, crying out in pain, as I'd just managed to turn my foot in such an awkward way that it felt like the blade of a knife was cutting into it.

Jealous? I closed my door and slumped back against it. Maybe, but it went deeper than that.

The red shoes were lying in the middle of the room, a sunbeam dancing around them.

It went way deeper. He was leaving. It was almost worse than him staying. In fact, it was worse.

I was always going to be left behind. By somebody. I was always going to be lonely and adrift. If I could honestly tell myself that Crewe's leaving me was worse than his staying, I was in trouble beyond any hope. That meant at some point there was the possibility of him drifting back into my life, a phone call to him, a phone call to me, a reunion, and if I could accept him, take him back, I'd take anybody…it wouldn't matter who he was. Any stranger, who'd just be an escape. A prop. Like I'd be to him.

There would always be a new Crewe, a new Silvio, a new Baily, and always plenty of drugs to go with them, if we wanted, and no doubt we would. They were out of eyesight now, but just around the corner, waiting to take away the pain.

I heard movement nearby, the sound of something faintly rustling, and I realized I wasn't alone. I turned my head to see the angel standing by the window.

His long white robe was crisp and filled with sunshine, his strong muscles rippling beneath it, his two long wings sweeping down, their tips touching the floor and curling a bit, the colored lights that lined their edges dimmed by the daylight, but still twinkling. The angel's broad and shining sword was tucked securely in his belt. His beard was even longer, more luxuriant than I'd remembered, as was his thick hair that hung down to his shoulders. And the expression on his face was very solemn, even gloomy, his eyes sad and disappointed.

I hobbled over to the red shoes and stared down at them, unable to face the angel or look into his eyes.

"I tried, I really did," I said aloud. "But somehow I just couldn't make it happen—" My words broke off with an involuntary sob, and I brought up the back of my hand to cover my mouth and stifle it. Then, embarrassed, I took some time to compose myself.

Finally I turned around and approached the angel on my crutches until I was directly in front of him and boldly looking him in the eyes.

"I can't do this anymore," I said. "I just can't." I slowly reached out and touched his shining sword.

He recoiled, stepping back from me in reproach, understanding what I was asking him to do.

"Can't you take me on that journey now? Why make me wait?" I implored him.

I saw myself standing at one of the French windows, leaning forward, seeing the Seminary tower starting to spin, and the sidewalk laid out before me. But then I saw there was no need for that. The angel, who was real, was with me. I only had to convince him that I wanted his intervention and mercy. To transport me where I longed to go.

I threw my crutches on the floor and dropped down on my knees in front of him. There was a long silence between us.

Finally I tugged on his robe and he looked down at me. His muscles tensed and his expression became even bleaker. I could see he was frightened.

I stared up into his face with a reassuring smile. "It's all right… Please… It's so easy… and it will all be over with so quickly…"

Suddenly he began to waver, I could tell.

Taking advantage of his indecision, I shrugged my shoulders and said simply, "You die because you're born…"

With that he withdrew his sword, held it high above me for an instant, then with one swift movement, he plunged it straight down through my breast. I saw its fiery silver blade coming at me and heard the tip of the blade penetrate the floorboard underneath me. My mouth opened wide, I rocked back and forth unsteadily on my knees, grabbing for the sword that had impaled my body, my eyes staring into space. I let out one gasp before falling backwards into a pool of my own blood, dead.

# EPILOGUE

He was incredibly strong. The angel.

That was my first conscious thought...afterwards. And because of his tremendous strength, I felt safe.

He'd encircled my waist with one of his muscular arms, until he had me in a firm grasp, and was carrying me upwards until we were drifting in the sky above Manhattan. I could feel the adrenalin rushing through his body. With his free hand, the angel held his shining sword aloft, pointing towards the sky like a magnet. I felt no pain in my breast and when I looked down, I was amazed to find there was no sign of any wound there.

Down below me, past my feet, one in a sandal, the other in a cast, I watched as Manhattan slowly receded from view...the Chrysler Building, its ornate silver-crested columns awash in the light of the late afternoon, the Empire State Building, whose spire was now only the thinnest of needles, Central Park in full bloom and crowded with bicyclists, silver glinting off the spokes of their bicycle wheels, and the blue East River, winding its way in the distance.

It was dizzying. I closed my eyes.

As the angel ascended higher, with me tucked close to him, I dared to open my eyes again and, taking a deep breath, gazed down. Now everything was turned over on its sides, the buildings sticking out horizontally like bridges you could walk across to reach the bicycle riders who'd folded their bodies onto the sides of their instruments as if they were taking a nap, and the East River…just a hardened curvy blue line that ran along the rim of the earth.

Then the angel pulled my body up inside a large swiftly floating cumulus cloud. It swallowed us whole. I might as well have been blind as all I could see was pure white. Everything else was gone from sight. But sensations were still there. I could feel the bristles of the angel's long beard running up and down the back of my neck and his warm breath against my face. His powerful arm gripped me even more tightly. It was comforting. I snuggled up against him and dug my fingers deep into the bunches of his robe.

There came a sudden moment when the thick white cloud parted slightly and, peering down through its opening, I saw my French windows thrown open onto the Seminary. I could see inside into my living room, filled with sunshine, empty except for the red shoes lying in the middle of the floor with my pair of crutches thrown carelessly down beside them. A breeze blew in through the French windows and the panes rattled and I could smell the scent of the wisteria and hear its vines rustling against the Seminary wall. Then, as I felt myself being lifted higher, I watched my room full of light shrinking slowly in the distance, until the white cloud enveloped us once again, completely obscuring my view below.

I must have slept. At least my eyes were closed. When I opened them I found we were no longer trapped inside the white cloud, but floating on a wraithlike smoky web of sky fog. I parted the damp wisps of fog with my hand and through the holes found myself looking down onto Zuma Beach on a gray day with heavy clouds blowing low over the ocean. A small group of people were gathered together on the sand. Whenever they tried to approach the water's edge, they were driven back by the swirling, incoming tide. I recognized Reg in a windbreaker shouting out orders to the others, and Allison, her hair whipping in the wind, clutching onto Logan's arm and now and then patting the baby strapped onto his back, making sure she was tucked in snugly with the corners of a blanket. And Jack and Linda Kroll…they were there too. When the tide ebbed, they grabbed their opportunity and quickly formed a small protective circle. They took turns dipping their hands into a blue urn that Reg held and flinging handfuls of my dust out onto the choppy waves. Eventually Reg turned the urn upside down and shook it. None of my dust remained. Then they hugged each other for a long time, spent. I lost sight of them as the web of mist I'd been parting blew directly into my eyes. Don't go…I still want to see you…but we're all scattered somewhere along the edges of the wind…and I have fog in my eyes…

But when it dissolved, I found the angel and I had been plunged into a gathering storm in the black of night. Threatening clouds and the sound of thunder rumbled and sometimes even a bolt of lightning struck nearby. But I wasn't afraid. Because the multi-colored lights always blinked along the fluffy edges of the angel's wings, assuaging the darkness around us.

Other lights were blinking in the dark. The lights from airplanes. Sometimes they blinked quite close by, as the planes flew near us. If the passengers looked out their windows, would they see us? And would they be dreaming if they did? The airplanes were flying towards their destinations with the confidence and arrogance of human stars come to challenge the heavens, like the angel and me, unexpected explorers as well.

Two dark funnel clouds wrapped themselves around us, spinning us in a circle, yet through the vortex they formed I could make out the river walk in Binghamton far below. Blasts of snow were shooting up off the icy Susquehanna, nearly concealing the walk. The dim morning sunlight could hardly light a path for anyone. Yet I spotted a figure steadily moving down the walk against the glaring whirlwind, like someone trapped inside a snow globe that had been carelessly shaken by a child, but determined to make his way...As the figure came closer I saw it was Jared, wrapped tightly in a long dark coat and scarf, a knit cap pulled down on his forehead. Philip Deerman, impatiently waiting on the steps of the library, was waving him forward. As Jared made his way up the library steps, Philip put his arm around the boy's shoulder, smiling with relief, and hurried him inside. I heard the sound of a foghorn from a boat stalled on the river. The vortex closed.

Shutting my eyes again, I drifted in a half-sleep.

I woke to the sound of what I thought was an ecstatic cry coming from the angel. Startled, I looked up into his face and saw that his expression was full of triumph. We'd been cast above the clouds into a night of spiraling darkness across which thousands of stars were scattered, a vast universe, punctuated by other worlds, spinning far away, light glancing off them from the sparkle of many suns. Yet even though I was in a navy blue T-shirt and beige pants, I wasn't cold but warm. I saw that the sharp sword in the angel's hand had changed into a bright flame. I could feel the excitement pulsing through the angel's body as our speed accelerated sharply and we rose forever through the blank terminus of space until we found ourselves in front of one of the stained glass panes from the interior of the Chapel of the Good Shepherd, one of the panes I'd meditated on during my prayers, seeking some mystical sign, some answer, and I could see shadows of the leaves from the trees moving across the pane, exactly as I'd seen them during my prayers. The angel put his hand against the pane and indicated I should follow his example. Together we put our palms onto the stained glass and passed through it like shadows to the other side.

A long road of shining gold stretched into the distance as far as the eye could see. The angel set me firmly down on my feet. I hesitated, unsure, clutching onto his robe with my fingers but he carefully extricated them. I sighed. The pain in my broken foot had lessened but it was still sore. But as the angel nudged me forward I found at least I could walk without crutches and I threw them aside.

The angel and I moved forward, side by side, down the broad swath of gold. His sword of flame had now become a tall lily. We journeyed down the golden path for a very long time. The Northern Lights lit the air on both sides of this path, their brilliant colors hanging in the ether and constantly changing. The angel seemed transfixed by these magical lights, as if they were calling him. The blinking lights on the edges of his wings pulsated more strongly, the colors became more radiant, and I noticed they were the same colors as the Northern Lights. Without a warning or good-bye, he suddenly took flight, his wings spreading and flapping wildly, and headed directly into the lights, disappearing into their streams. Only the beauty of their incandescent colors was left.

"Wait for me!" I cried to no avail.

I was alone now but no longer on the golden road.

I found myself in a garden. There were tall willows everywhere and perfumed flowers of all kinds. The air, deliciously soft, was scented with spices, figs, and pomegranates. The iridescent sky was almost transparent. A dove flew past me, shining like a pearl. The surrounding trees had fulsome branches which sagged under the weight of golden fruit. Preening peacocks strolled contentedly among the lilac bushes.

I began to walk through this shimmering landscape. Moving between the trees were clusters of people engaged in tranquil conversations, delighting, almost secretively, in each other's company.

I looked up into the gauzy sky and saw the morning star.

Then I heard birdsong, the splash of water, and laughter without care…the same mysterious sounds I'd heard many times before during my meditations in the chapel.

I realized the laughter without care was coming from those clusters of people slowly wandering among the trees and bushes.

I came upon a winding stream clear as the air itself. Flowers drooped languidly down into the water from the stream's edges as black swans floated silently by on its surface.

A fresh breeze enlivened everything around me.

I meandered along the banks of the stream until I noticed the figure of a man stretched out on the bank near the water's edge, in repose, taking in the landscape. Instinctively I felt drawn to that spot. When I came up close to the man I saw it was Frank.

My heart beat quickly. I approached him slowly and with great care, savoring, with each step, the great joy that had suddenly come into my heart. He'd been here all along. By this stream. Waiting for me. Only I'd never known the way to find it.

Silently I sat down next to him on the bank of the stream, on the soft grass, and we shyly gazed into each other's eyes. I reached out and touched his cheek. Then he touched mine.

After awhile, Frank moved his hand down to my cast and began to unwrap the bandages, taking his time, making sure not to cause me any discomfort, until my foot was bare. Then Frank gently lifted my foot and laid it down into the cool stream. Right away I could feel the healing and regenerative spirits coming from the water. I looked at Frank in surprise, wondering how he'd known to do that, to take that step to make me whole again. But he only smiled at me. Apparently, here in this garden there were many new things we both would come to learn, no, that we already knew, and would only learn to accept.

We leaned back on the knoll on our elbows, hands clasped together, our fingers entwined, watching other couples strolling across from us on the opposite side of the bank, talking with each other in knowing whispers. Sometimes they looked at us with a quiet interest and raised their hands in a way that conveyed a shy welcome.

No one in Paradise ever asked about the red shoes.

# ACKNOWLEDGMENTS

I would like to thank my agent Harold Schmidt, my editor Donald Weise, and my Writers Group for their help and support.

# ABOUT THE AUTHOR

John Stewart Wynne (aka John Wynne) is the author of the novel *Crime Wave*, the short story collection *The Other World*, and the chapbook *The Sighting*.

Wynne's poetry has been featured in *The American Poetry Review* and numerous other poetry journals. His controversial long narrative poem *Two Struggling Actresses*, about an actor consumed by the personality of Jayne Mansfield, appeared in *The Paris Review*.

Wynne is also the producer of over one hundred audio books. They range from William Styron reading his *Darkness Visible: A Memoir of Madness* to John Waters reading his *Shock Value*, and from James Patterson's *Kiss the Girls* to *The Great Gatsby* read by Christopher Reeve.

He is the author of the first popular guide to spoken word recordings, *The Listener's Guide to Audio Books*. The author lives in New York City. Visit him online at www.johnstewartwynne.com.